FORCE OF EVIL

Charles Holborne Legal Thrillers
Book Six

Simon Michael

SAPERE
BOOKS

FORCE OF EVIL

Published by Sapere Books.

20 Windermere Drive, Leeds, England, LS17 7UZ,
United Kingdom

saperebooks.com

ISBN: 978-1-80055-109-1

In memory of Tony Michael, the real Harry Horowitz, and a mensch of the first order.

ACKNOWLEDGEMENTS

Firstly, my thanks go to Mr Robin Chandler, ex-RAF Police Sergeant, and the "Snowdrop" who provided the intriguing true story behind this book. He also read an early draft to ensure I included no incongruous or erroneous fictionalised elements.

I am also deeply indebted to former Metropolitan Police Sergeant (and now accomplished author) David Lister. His fact-checking was, as ever, invaluable, but it was the minor details, for example the layout of the police stations and his wonderful anecdotes of life in the Metropolitan Police in the 1960s, which so delighted me. His details provide the authentic policing flavours to much of this book which no mere barrister could manage unaided.

My thanks also go to Sir Ivan Lawrence QC, whose book *"My Life of Crime, Cases and Causes"* is well worth a read. In particular one of his retorts to a judge so impressed me that I had to include it, and place it in Charles's mouth. I hope he will forgive me.

Thanks are also due to Carly Jordan whose eye for detail and chronological inexactitude is simply astonishing, and to my patient friends and beta readers who read and contributed to *Force of Evil*, in particular Neil Cameron, Debbie Jacobs and Elaine Ibbotson.

I remain very grateful to Amy Durant, Caoimhe O'Brien, Richard Simpson and the rest of the Sapere Books team for their support.

Last, and never least, my thanks go to Elaine, for everything else.

CHAPTER 1

Charles Holborne, barrister, but presently dressed as a decorator in paint-spattered overalls, flat cap and a patched tweed jacket, jogs across Cricklewood Broadway and heads for the door of *The Crown* on the opposite pavement. He's a big man, not particularly tall but immensely broad with a bull neck and heavily muscled limbs, courtesy of a lifetime's training in a boxing gym and teenage years spent working as a lighterman on the Thames. He's never been to the famous Irish pub before, but he knows its reputation; to wear barrister's attire would likely attract comment, maybe even confrontation, so his present garb is fortuitous.

He finds his way across the forecourt of the pub blocked by two flatbed lorries disgorging their contents. Labourers in rolled-up shirtsleeves, flat caps and dirty trousers scramble over the sides and off the back, laughing, talking and jostling, most hastening towards the same pub door as Charles. These men are being dropped off where they were collected that morning to start their day's work. These are casual labourers, not even working the lump, taken on for a day here or half a day there; Charles spots pound notes clutched in more than one muddy fist.

He waits for them to precede him. These are also large men, some as large as Charles himself, and they smell of hard work and impatient thirst; it'd be impolitic to impede their progress.

He follows the last of them through the door to find his senses assaulted by a riot of Irish accents and the mixed odours of beer and meat stew. The place is heaving. Charles apologises his way through the men laughing, drinking and clamouring for attention at the bar and scans the room with a frown. He turns on his heels a full 360 degrees but is unsuccessful in locating his quarry. He stands on tiptoes with his hands on his hips, trying to look over the heads of the customers.

'Charles! Charles! Over here!'

He turns to see a hand waving briefly above the boisterous drinkers and pushes his way through to the estimated location of the hand. 'There you are, Sean,' he says, arriving at a wooden trestle table almost full of men engaged in the serious business of eating.

Detective Sergeant Sean Sloane is a handsome man in his mid-thirties with a wide brow, tousled light hair, and blue eyes set in a triangular, impish face. The two men have been friends since Sloane investigated Charles for the murder of Henrietta, his late wife, some years before. Sloane has been reading from a beer-stained newspaper folded into quarters and has a half-eaten plate of steak and boiled potatoes before him. There are two pints of beer to his side, one almost empty.

'I see you started without me,' comments Charles with a smile.

'Sorry, mate, but I was starving and —'

'— I'm half an hour late. I needed to finish undercoating a door so I can gloss it tomorrow. Apologies.'

Sloane points to the full pint, indicating that it's Charles's. Charles squeezes into half a space at the end of the bench opposite, apologising to the men who have to shuffle up, and takes a long draught of ale. 'Thanks,' he says, wiping his mouth with the back of his hand and looking up at his friend. 'That's better.'

'Seen this?' shouts Sloane over the din, pointing with his fork to the newspaper article.

Charles cranes his neck to look. The newspaper shows two black and white photographs side-by-side: a curly-haired young man with blank fisheyes and a downturned mouth, and a young woman with a masculine jaw and a thick mop of blonde hair. Underneath are two names: Ian Brady and Myra Hindley, soon to become notorious around the world as the "Moors Murderers".

'No. Have they been charged?'

The other nods. 'Two murders so far,' says Sloane in his soft Irish accent, 'but from what I hear, they're still finding bodies.'

'Interesting venue,' says Charles, pushing the newspaper back and looking about him. 'Home from home?'

'Not really. I slept on a floor near here when I first came over, but not after that. Then, you know, Buckinghamshire Constabulary followed by Vice. But seeing's I'm now local, I thought "Why not?" It is an Irish institution, and I've been a regular ever since. And I'm careful not to advertise…' Sloane says, dropping his voice and opening his coat enough for Charles to see that he too has abandoned his daywear. 'I want no trouble from Fenians while I'm off-duty.'

'How're you enjoying S Division?' asks Charles.

Sloane shrugs. 'It wouldn't have been my choice, but to be honest I'm just bloody glad to have a job. And to be out of Vice.'

'You were lucky.'

Sloane nods his agreement, mouth full. Framed by members of his own team for taking bribes, the charge hadn't stuck and he'd been reinstated, but the writing was on the wall. He'd never progress in Soho and as the junior member — and apparently the only honest copper — in his team, he'd never be safe. His application for a different posting went through on skates.

A young woman arrives at the table to clear some glasses.

'You couldn't get my friend a plate, could you?' asks Sloane, indicating his own meal with his knife.

She hesitates. 'I'm not supposed to...'

'Ah, come on Kathleen,' he wheedles, 'do an old friend a favour.'

Charles holds out a ten-shilling note. The girl looks down at it, and then up at the man offering it. Her expression softens and she takes the money.

'Give me a minute,' she says, and carries the used glasses away.

'You're a shameless flirt,' comments Sloane.

'Me?' asks Charles, all innocence. 'A mere novice at the seat of the master,' he says, nodding across the table at Sloane.

Sloane shakes his head. 'All that twinkling? It was positively blinding. And she's too young for you.'

Charles smiles. He is just shy of forty but looks younger.

'Anyway, aren't you and Sally...?' asks Sloane.

'Nothing definite. She's agreed to a drink next week.'

'That's a start, then.'

Charles's meal and his change arrive and the two men eat.

'How's the building work going?' asks Sloane, between mouthfuls.

Charles has recently acquired a near-derelict three-storey Georgian townhouse in Wren Street, just off Gray's Inn Road. It's a rough area, the houses dilapidated and, when vacant, used by drug users and toms undertaking quick knee-tremblers, but over the last couple of years Charles has noticed early signs of gentrification. In Wren Street alone three or four properties besides his own are being done up by new owners, and at least one houses a young family.

Charles is not entirely sure why he bought the property. His tiny apartment on Fetter Lane, less than a hundred yards from the Temple, is incredibly convenient, but it's been his only proper home since Henrietta died and he feels he's outgrown it. He made an impulsive offer to buy the house on Wren Street, an offer which was accepted with worrying haste. Charles is now the possessor of a mostly uninhabitable building that still requires new floorboards, wiring and plumbing, some form of central heating and complete redecoration. He reassures himself that in years to come, when the area has moved sufficiently upmarket, it might be worth a fortune.

'It's going well,' he replies, having to shout over the noise of the drinkers around them. 'The roof's been replaced and most of the old lead pipes have been stripped out. The kitchen's now functioning — sort of — but no bathroom yet. My DIY skills are a bit rudimentary, but I'm getting there.'

'Sally was your go-to interior designer, I recall?'

'Yes. She was brilliant at it.' Charles shrugs. 'I'm not naturally skilled like she was, but I think the results are okay.'

'When are you planning to move in?' asks Sloane.

'I don't know. But definitely not till it's got central heating. Maybe around Christmas if I'm lucky.'

Meals completed, Charles buys them another round, but after a few further minutes of shouting to be heard they decide to leave.

Charles follows Sloane out of the pub. He notes, in passing, money and goods changing hands, and knows that Sloane must have seen it too. He says nothing; his friend is off-duty.

They fall into step together. It's now gone eleven but the pavements are still crowded, light spills from the windows of shops and Irish accents can be heard everywhere. The two men chat as they stroll away from the crowds.

'So,' asks Charles. 'West Hendon?'

'Still finding my feet, but first impressions are okay. Most of my colleagues spend half the day in the pub and only start working when overtime clocks in, which I find frustrating, but as far as I can tell there's no wholesale corruption like in Soho.'

'Colleagues?'

'Friendly enough. A couple were suspicious of me at the start 'cos I was in Vice, but they're coming round. I'm pretty much left to me own devices. How's work for you?'

'Busy, as always. I've either been at my desk or at Wren Street till midnight every night for weeks.'

'Got anything interesting on?'

Charles smiles. He has to answer carefully. He is much in demand, particularly with the East End criminals with whom he grew up. Although over the last couple of years he's started to develop a more "establishment" prosecution practice, many of his friends, acquaintances and clients are people with whom Detective Sergeant Sloane would have a competing professional interest.

'Just finished an armed robbery. My guy claimed he was a passer-by.'

'And was he?'

'Of course. A passer-by acting as lookout.'

Sloane laughs. 'I thought you'd risen above common or garden blaggers.'

Charles shrugs. 'So did everyone. I was supposedly a shoo-in for silk in April.'

The previous year Charles prosecuted one of the country's top judges for murder, about as high-profile a case as you can get, and his imminent promotion to Queen's Counsel on the back of it was widely predicted. But word had been received by Charles's head of Chambers that Charles's name would *not* feature on the April list of new appointments, and discreet enquiries as to why he would fail to secure the coveted initials had received no response.

'There are numerous theories why it didn't happen. In summary, I'm too Jewish, too working-class and still too closely associated with the East End.'

'You mean the Krays.'

'Probably.'

'Sorry, Charles. That must be hard. Will you apply again?'

'I don't know. My face is never going to fit. But it's hard watching younger and, dare I say it, less able barristers get it.'

Their idle strolling has brought them over the railway tracks at Cricklewood Station and along Brent Terrace, parallel to the sidings. They lean on the parapet wall, looking down at the sleeping trains. Cricklewood Depot is situated beside the Midland Main Line and houses the largest servicing depot for trains terminating in London. Its marshalling yard is huge, full of dark lines of goods wagons awaiting departure to destinations all over London and the south-east.

They watch a man walking along the side of one long goods train, testing each door. He's in almost complete darkness and can be identified only by the faint orange light cast by the paraffin lamp swinging from one hand. He reaches the end of a long line of wagons and pulls at the final door. Something about the stance of the watchman suggests that he wasn't expecting it to open, but open it does, sliding a foot or two on its runners, and faint moving light spills out of the interior.

'What do you think you're doing?' comes the watchman's voice from down on the tracks. 'You're trespassing. Get out of there!'

Charles and Sloane hear the watchman utter a sharp cry which is cut short abruptly. Sloane stands upright, immediately alert. The watchman's lamp drops to the ground, the glass smashes and its light is extinguished. The watchman can no longer be seen. The brighter light from inside the wagon also goes out, only to reappear a second later a yard lower, near the tracks. Its loom moves about, as if whoever is holding it is casting about underneath the goods wagons looking for something.

Charles turns to Sloane to find the policeman already sprinting to his right.

'Stay there!' calls Sloane behind him.

Sloane vaults a gate in the parapet wall and disappears from Charles's view as he scrambles down a flight of concrete steps towards the train tracks. Charles runs after him to the gate but pauses there, watching as Sloane reaches the bottom of the steps and runs diagonally across the rows of multiple train tracks, lifting his knees oddly high to avoid tripping over the rails. Sloane reaches the point where the watchman disappeared. Charles sees the torch illuminated again. It swings in an arc and his friend's face is suddenly illuminated.

'Police!' shouts Sloane. 'Stay where you are!'

There is indistinct movement and Sloane drops to the ground, also disappearing into the shadows. The torch is again extinguished.

Charles jumps over the gate and runs towards the goods wagon and a jumble of silent shadows and movement. Charles can't work out who is doing what to whom but as he closes in on the tableau, he sees that someone is on the ground taking a kicking.

He reaches the kicker, grabs him by the shoulder and hauls him round. He has just enough time to see something glinting in the other man's hand as it flashes towards his head, and he ducks. The fist just misses Charles, skimming the top of his hair. Charles straightens up and delivers a left-handed uppercut to the underside of the man's chin and follows up with a right to the gut. The man expels air in an audible *whoosh!* and he drops to his knees, doubled up, fighting to re-inflate his lungs.

Charles swing round at the shrill blast of a police whistle. Running footsteps approach.

'Police! Everyone stay put!'

Charles does as he's told but holds himself ready to land more blows. Sloane is now sitting up groggily, holding his face.

'Right! I'm Sergeant Hawkins, British Transport Police,' says the newcomer. 'What's going on here?'

The man Charles downed begins to scramble away and Charles lunges after him, grabbing him by the scruff of the neck, and throwing him back onto the railway tracks. He stands with his foot compressing the man's lower back into the ground.

'The man nursing a painful head,' says Charles, pointing and breathing heavily, 'is Detective Sergeant Sloane, stationed at West Hendon. We saw this one —' he indicates the man underneath him — 'attack this watchman —' he gestures at a stationary mound of dark clothes curled between the rails — 'who was checking the goods wagons. Sergeant Sloane intervened and was also attacked. I went to help out.'

Hawkins looks down at Sloane. He's still sitting on the track but is holding something out to be inspected. Hawkins inclines his head to inspect Sloane's warrant card.

'You all right, sergeant?' asks Hawkins, offering a hand to haul Sloane up.

Sloane nods, struggling to his feet. 'I'm not sure. I think he hit me with something. I've got a lump on my face the size of a duck's egg.' He speaks indistinctly, through clamped jaws.

'Yes; a knuckleduster,' says Charles, pointing at his prisoner's right hand. The heavy brass weapon glints in the dim light.

'Take your foot away, sir,' orders Hawkins.

Charles hesitates but complies. A low moan escapes from the watchman. Charles turns to the sound and crouches. He helps the bundle of clothes turn over. The watchman's not a young man and he looks dreadful. His breathing is ragged and blood pours from a hinged flap of flesh hanging from his temple.

'I think this man needs an ambulance,' says Charles, looking up at Hawkins.

'Your name, sir?' asks Hawkins of Charles.

'Charles Holborne. I'm Sergeant Sloane's friend.'

'Well, I'll take it from here, sir, if you don't mind.'

'Call an ambulance, sergeant,' grimaces Sloane through clenched teeth. 'Do you have a personal radio?'

'Don't make me laugh. I'll have to go back to the office.'

Hawkins pulls the attacker to his feet, and Charles gets to see him properly for the first time. He appears an unlikely candidate for violence. Shortish, chubby and balding, he wears a heavy overcoat and thick-rimmed spectacles. He looks like a bookkeeper. 'I'm arresting you on suspicion... Oh!' Hawkins pauses for a very long five seconds. Then he turns to Sloane. 'I know this man, Sloane.'

'Good. Then you can fuckin' nick him for trespassing on the railway, assaulting a watchman, and assault with intent to resist arrest.'

There's a further puzzling moment of hesitation from Hawkins.

Hello; what's going on here? wonders Charles.

'Don't tell me my job thank you, sergeant. This is my patch.'

'Well if you won't arrest him, I shall,' says Sloane. He takes a step forward and is so unsteady he almost falls. He lowers himself to the trackside and sits.

Hawkins turns to the man. 'Don't run off. Got it? I mean it.' The man nods briefly. 'And you,' he orders Charles, pointing at the watchman who is now sitting up trying to staunch the flow of blood down his face, 'stay with Herbert.'

Hawkins beckons for Sloane to follow him and without waiting moves back down the line of wagons until he's out of earshot. Sloane stands and staggers after him.

Charles focuses on the injured watchman. 'Lie down, chum,' he says, and he takes a blood-saturated handkerchief from the man's loose grip and applies it to the deep cut on his head. The man is mumbling indistinctly, and Charles lowers his head to hear but still cannot make out what the old boy's saying. A heated whispered conversation starts between the two police officers further up the track.

There is a sudden noise from behind Charles and the bookkeeper takes off, sprinting across the tracks towards the staircase.

'Hey!' Charles shouts at Hawkins. 'He's legging it!'

After what seems to Charles to be a deliberate pause, Hawkins breaks into an unconvincing attempt at chasing. Sloane sinks back to the trackside, holding his face. The bookkeeper has disappeared up the steps before Hawkins is halfway across the tracks. The sergeant slows, stops, and retraces his steps.

'What the hell —?' starts Charles.

'Don't worry. I know where to find him,' says Hawkins.

19

'That was Billy Gervaise. One of the Greene Grasses.'

Charles isn't convinced. 'You could've caught him. He just assaulted two men with a knuckleduster! One of them a policeman! Sean?' he calls, but Sloane is on his hands and knees and looks incapable of standing unaided, let alone supporting Charles.

Hawkins bends to lift Herbert to his feet. 'Come on, chum. Let's get that cut looked at.' He drags the watchman upright, props him under his shoulder and moves off towards the lights of the railway buildings, half-carrying Herbert, whose legs are not working properly. 'I'd get your pal to a doctor, if I was you,' he says to Charles over his shoulder.

CHAPTER 2

The time is 00:43 hours and the base at RAF Cardington, Bedfordshire, has settled for the night.

Sergeant Julian Maynard of the RAF Police steps out of the guardroom for the last routine patrol of his shift, his breath making a sudden billow of condensation. He looks up. It's a cold night but the sky is clear; the stars are bright and, out here, unaffected by light pollution. Behind him, as always, half the sky is obliterated by the two huge hangars. They are impossible, incongruous buildings, giant's bricks dropped straight out of the sky. When he and Jean were first posted here, everyone said they'd soon get used to the massive hangars, constructed to accommodate the largest airship ever conceived by man, the doomed R101. They were wrong: at sixty yards high and almost three football pitches long, Maynard still finds the buildings oppressively omnipresent, dwarfing the entire countryside around, looming silently over parked aircraft, barracks, railway sidings, Shortstown and all.

Tonight, however, Maynard is in good cheer, so much so that he's left Corporal Boyce dozing in the warm guardroom instead of ordering him out into the cold to accompany him. Maynard's good humour lies in the weekend pass sitting on his desk and the two complete days in prospect to be spent with Jean and their baby, Archie, whose first birthday falls on Sunday.

Most of the camp is asleep, but noise still floats across from the sidings where a train is being readied for the transfer of the 800 new recruits to the Training Camp at RAF Wilmslow at

21

daylight. Maynard wanders across to see how they're getting on.

Next to the troop train is a line of goods wagons also soon to depart. Cardington station used to be on the line between Bedford and Hitchin. It is now closed to the public but still services the base, the main store for personnel welfare and the principal gas plant for the entire RAF. It's not uncommon for supplies to arrive and depart at all times of day and night on the forgotten branch line.

Maynard begins walking the length of the goods train.

'What are you up to Sergeant?'

Maynard turns to see a man climbing down from a wagon. He knows many of the railwaymen working the line, most of whom are local men, and he's on first names with several. This one is new to him.

'Just making the rounds,' replies Maynard.

'Why don't you just get on with your own job, and leave us to ours?' says another voice from behind him.

A man appears out of the darkness, a four-foot spanner angled over one shoulder, as he cleans a metal component with a greasy cloth. He wears stained overalls bearing the British Railways logo. Maynard does recognise this man, a truculent diesel driver named Carragher, who's forever moaning about something.

Sergeant Maynard is an easy-going chap. He's good at his job and has been promoted steadily since he joined up. He always prefers a quiet life, if a quiet life is to be had, but he's confident and he knows when he's in the right.

'This is my job,' he replies shortly. 'The sidings are within the camp boundary, and my authority as an RAF police officer runs to everything within that boundary.'

'Yeah, well, we're in a hurry, so you just stroll on and we'll move out.'

For a second, seeing Carragher's oily hands and the tools, Maynard puts down the gratuitous rudeness to a frustrating delay in the train's departure; equipment failure, probably. But then he sees the man's nervous glance towards his companion, and his policeman's instincts suddenly tingle.

'What's in these wagons?' he asks.

'Oh, come on Sergeant,' replies the other man, 'we've really got to get moving. We're over an hour late.'

'What's your name?'

'Bryson.'

'Well, Mr Bryson, you're going to have to wait a few minutes more. I want to see the movement authorities, bills of lading and manifests.'

'Are you trying to lose us our jobs?' complains Carragher.

Maynard holds out his hand, waiting patiently.

Bryson turns and walks down the line to the diesel engine and climbs into the cab, muttering loudly. He reappears after a few moments with a sheaf of papers which he thrusts into Maynard's hand.

Maynard illuminates his torch and flicks through the documents. As he does so, he catches another worried look passing between the men, but the documents look in order. They corroborate the proper movement of a dozen laden wagons, each assigned to a different RAF camp across the UK.

'This looks fine,' says Maynard.

'Of course it's fine…' replies Carragher angrily and he turns away, but Maynard catches the muttered end of the sentence, '…fucking Jobsworth.'

'But I think I should make a quick check of the wagons themselves.'

'What?' says Carragher angrily, spinning back round. 'That'll take ages!'

'Then the sooner you get the doors open, the sooner you'll be away.'

'You've got no right!' says Bryson, but now nothing's going to dissuade Maynard from checking further.

'I have every right,' he says dangerously. 'And unless you assist me, I'll be forced to assume something's up. If you get yourselves arrested, you won't be going anywhere. We'll start at the back.'

With a lot of grumbling and muttered abuse, the two men accompany Maynard to the back of the train. He moves forward methodically. Every wagon door is unlocked in turn and slid open; every wagon is checked against its paperwork. By the time he has reached the fifth or sixth wagon, Maynard notices that Carragher has slipped away somewhere, but he continues with his cross-referencing. Twelve wagons, each supported by the appropriate documentation, each destined to a different RAF camp across England. The problem is that, by the time he's reached the head of the train, Maynard has counted thirteen wagons. The last is supported by a manifest, but there's no movement authority and no destination.

'Where's the movement authority for this one?' he asks Bryson.

The other man shrugs. 'How should I know? It's your paperwork, so there's obviously been a fuck up in your office.'

'Always possible,' concedes Maynard. 'Let's open her up, shall we?'

Bryson unlocks and opens the last wagon and Maynard climbs up. He shines his torch around. This wagon is loaded to the roof with RAF bedding, pillows, sheets, blankets, cutlery, enamel mugs, boots, weatherproof clothing — in short everything used by RAF personnel in their daily duties. He is still poking around when he hears the crunch of footsteps marching up the gravel towards him. He looks out. Carragher is leading another man in British Rail overalls and two senior NCOs from the stores wing, one of them Warrant Officer McKeith. McKeith looks furious.

'What the fuck do you think you're playing at, Sergeant?' he demands.

'I'm checking the cargo on this train, sir.'

'Well, stop it immediately. You've delayed it for over an hour and a half.'

'No, sir, only twenty minutes or so —'

'Don't fucking argue with me, Sergeant, or you'll find yourself on a charge. Get down from there immediately.' Maynard hesitates but eventually complies. He is now surrounded by four angry men. 'Now, give the chits back to this chap, release the train and fuck off.'

Maynard hands the sheaf of papers to Bryson. 'I'm putting it on record, sir, that all future goods trains must be subject to checks both by the MoD and the RAF police. There's thirteen wagons here and full paperwork for only twelve. It may just be a mistake, but it's my arse on the line.'

'I don't give a flying fuck what you put on the record.' McKeith turns to Carragher. 'Well? What are you waiting for?'

Carragher and Bryson scurry off, and Maynard turns and retraces his steps to the guardroom. He hears the train pulling out of the sidings as he opens the door. Only after he's closed the door behind him does he remove from his tunic the single document relating to the thirteenth wagon.

'Wake up, Boycey,' he says to his corporal, shoving the man's feet off the desk and awakening him rudely. 'We've some phone calls to make.'

CHAPTER 3

The *Fountain* pub is situated on a tiny corner plot on St John Street, Bedford, and in earlier days would have been entirely unsuitable for a clandestine meeting. But the coaching inn, popular with farmers and cattle drovers for over two centuries, is scheduled for demolition, and its regulars have long since melted away in search of watering holes that lack the *Fountain's* smell of sad decrepitude and impending execution.

At present, the bar is occupied by only two men. Even the barman finds the place too depressing, and he's abandoned his station to sit in the back room where he can read his newspaper with half an eye on Maigret on the black-and-white television until a customer shouts for his attention.

The two men sit hunched over a corner table, heads close together, deep in discussion.

'Maynard's not the sort of man to let it be,' says one, a young man with a short military haircut. 'If I know him, he'll start digging.'

'Which is why you've got to stop him,' whispers Billy Gervaise hoarsely.

'Me?' asks the other, surprised. 'That's not my game, Mr Gervaise, and you know it. You're the one with … you know … expertise in that area.'

The speaker is a young man wearing a heavy overcoat. When he moves to lift his pint, it's possible to see the blue uniform and brass buttons of an RAF serviceman.

Gervaise shakes his head firmly. 'What do you think I've been paying you for, all this time, Freddie?'

Aircraftman Freddie McParland leans forward. 'You've been paying me to turn a blind eye,' he says firmly, and he sits back in his seat, satisfied that his answer should bring the discussion to an end. Then he leans forward again briefly. 'You've been paying me to fiddle the manifests.'

He sits back again but then repeats the movement a third time to put the point beyond argument. 'What you've not been paying me for, is do someone over!'

Now he sits back in his seat for the final time and crosses his arms in a challenging "That's all I'm going to say on the subject" manner.

'That may all be true. But who are the Snowdrops going to come for first, when Maynard starts digging?'

Gervaise leaves the question hanging in the air. He watches the young man's assurance waver slightly.

'Who's got access to all the manifests and waybills?' Another long pause. 'I can walk away from here, and no one'll ever be the wiser. Unless you tell them of course, which I really wouldn't recommend. But what about you?'

McParland stares at Billy Gervaise. He is not even averagely endowed with intelligence, but the first glimmerings are beginning to form in his potato-shaped head that this isn't quite the money for old rope it was presented. He's the one on the ground, the one taking all the risks, and the one at whom the finger will be pointed. The possibility of defying Gervaise or, worse still, reporting him, doesn't even enter his head. He's known the man sitting opposite him long enough not to be taken in by the thinning hair swept over a domed head, the thick-rimmed spectacles and, always, regardless of weather, the heavy overcoat. Gervaise might look harmless, but looks can be — and in this case are — deceptive.

'But what can I do?' asks McParland plaintively. 'He's a big bloke. And he's really fit. And he outranks me. I can't do nothing.'

Gervaise takes a sip of his pint and leans back on his chair, smiling, now relaxed. 'Well, I've got an idea about that.'

Charles sits by the bed at Finchley Memorial Hospital eating his way idly through the grapes he brought with him, while examining his friend's sleeping face. It's five days since the fracas at Cricklewood and two since Sloane underwent surgery to fix the fractures to his jaw. It took Charles three days to persuade Sloane to go to Casualty and get an x-ray, with Sloane still protesting that he'd just suffered bad bruising.

Charles had been right. The x-rays ray demonstrated a double fracture, one to the cheek and one to the lower jaw. Fortunately, neither was significantly displaced, but even Charles can detect that Sloane's eyes no longer look quite as symmetrically placed as they did before. The surgeons are of the opinion that that might still improve, once the swelling reduces. At present, however, the DS resembles a blue-tinged hamster.

'It's only fair,' Charles had laughed when he visited Sloane the evening after the surgery. 'You were too bloody good-looking by half.'

Sloane stirs and opens his eyes. 'Oh ... hi ... sorry. Been there long?' The fractures have been wired and Sloane speaks through clenched teeth.

Charles evaluates the remaining grapes. 'About half a bunch.'

'Any good?'

'The grapes? Lovely, thanks. How're you feeling?'

'Guess.'

'As bad as that? You feel up to talking?'

'No. But that won't stop you.'

'I'd like to know what that BTP copper was saying to you before that thug did a runner. What's a "Greene Grass"?'

'You've not heard of Detective Inspector Greene of the Flying Squad?' says Sloane, sounding like a ventriloquist.

Charles frowns. 'No, I don't think I've had that pleasure.'

'He makes the rest of the Flying Squad look like choirboys. There isn't a dirty pie in London into which Sidney Greene hasn't inserted a pudgy finger, and he's got narks all over the place. Hence "Greene's Grasses". Most of the Squad are in awe of him, and the rest are frightened.'

'Frightened?'

'He's got no "Off" switch. When he loses it, he really loses it. He's been suspended twice, once for a supposed rape and once for wounding with intent.'

'And?'

'Both complaints withdrawn.'

'Why's he tolerated?'

'He gets improbable, sometimes impossible results, probably 'cos he's plugged into so much of the crime in London. But as long as his clear-up rate continues, he's left alone.' Sloane winces as he tries to lever himself upright.

'Can I help?' asks Charles.

'No, I can manage,' says Sloane, but he's clearly struggling.

Charles stands and goes to the back of the bed. There's a small wheel which seems connected to the bed somehow, and he starts experimenting.

'I think I should do that,' says an accented female voice.

A young woman in a white coat has stopped at the foot of the bed on her way past. She is fair-skinned and her shoulder-length dark hair is curly. She is very pretty.

'Thank you, nurse,' says Charles.

'Doctor. Doctor Alexandrova.'

Charles stands back to allow the doctor access to the head of the bed and she turns the wheel, slowly raising Sloane's upper body until he is comfortable. She takes the clipboard from the foot of the bed and flicks through the medical records.

'How are you feeling, Mr Sloane?' she asks.

'Hungry,' he replies through gritted teeth.

'Have you had anything today?'

'Porridge this morning and jelly and ice cream for lunch. You don't happen to have a steak about your person, do you?' asks Sloane.

Dr Alexandrova smiles and approaches him. She feels his forehead and lifts his wrist. 'How far can you open your mouth?' she asks, timing his pulse.

Sloane opens his mouth gingerly, managing about half an inch.

'I daresay we could get you a sandwich,' she says, satisfied. 'No steak for the present, however.'

Sloane says something unintelligible.

'Pardon?' says the doctor.

'Allow me to translate, doctor,' offers Charles. 'He said "Where're you from?"'

'I'm South African. Are you a member of family?'

'No. I'm a friend.'

'Well in that case, I'll have to ask you to leave now. Visiting times are on the board outside the ward door.'

Sloane gives a thumbs up in approval of the suggestion.

Charles stands. 'That's fine. There're no grapes anyway. By the way, doctor, he's a lousy patient. I spent weeks in a bed next to his a couple of years back. Dreadful. Just dreadful. I'd watch him if I were you.'

Sloane mutters something very rude but barely audible. Dr Alexandrova looks at Charles with her eyebrows raised in inquiry.

'He's wishing me a safe journey,' says Charles.

CHAPTER 4

DI Greene crosses Brewer Street at an angle, heading towards Green's Court. It was the coincidence in name which first led him to explore the Soho walk-up and introduce himself to the girls working there. That was almost a decade ago, when he was an ambitious young detective constable, just out of uniform, working Vice and impatient to establish his reputation. Now he and his partner own the building.

DI Greene is a bland man. Average height and build, unremarkable face and colouring, one could pass him on the street on a dozen occasions and never notice him. He is forgettable, possessed of an absence that allows him to disappear into the background when necessary, a useful skill in his profession.

He passes the record store. The ever-present spivs hanging around the entrance turn their heads away in unison, discovering a sudden interest in a box of second-hand LPs just inside the door. He smiles.

Jazz music and cannabis smoke drift up the steps of the cellar bar next to what's become known by cognoscenti as "Maisie's Staircase". As always at this time of night, the street door is open, indicating that at least one of the girls is working. The illuminated light above the door saying "Models" has another bulb out; the remaining illuminated letters spell "Mode" which somehow pleases him. So that no passing punter might be misled, someone has taped a piece of paper to the door with the words in marker pen "MODELS – COME UP." It half-obscures the older dogeared postcards pinned underneath advertising "French lessons" and "Large chest for sale".

Greene climbs the staircase to the first floor, pausing at a door. He inclines his head to listen. This room, the smallest in the building, suffered from a broken pipe somewhere above it and was empty for weeks, working girl and clients put off by the stink, the mould and the chunks of damp plaster that fell at intervals from the ceiling. Greene had words with his agent, reminding him of the benefit to both of them if the room again had a paying occupant. Within twenty-four hours the pipe was fixed. Greene notes with satisfaction that the room is now occupied again, as low voices emanate from behind the door. He continues climbing. He'll discuss terms with the new tenant in the morning.

A girl sits on the top step of the next flight, smoking, a bottle of beer by her side.

'All right, Gloria?' he says. She shifts to one side to allow him space to pass, but doesn't reply.

He climbs the final flight to the sole door leading off the second-floor landing. He takes the latchkey from his pocket and is about to insert it into the lock when he hears voices beyond the door. They are lowered but strained, as if in suppressed argument. He hears Maisie's voice, not her words but the pleading tone, and then a man's response. Greene listens for a moment, his mouth set in a grim line. His hand reaches into his jacket pocket, his fingertips touching the cold smooth brass of the knuckleduster that always resides there, the sister of the one wielded by Billy Gervaise. He changes his mind and withdraws his hand. Delicately, silently, he inserts the key into the lock. He readies himself, takes half a step backwards and launches himself at the door, turning the key at the same moment. He bursts into the room.

The two people standing in the centre of the large room turn towards him simultaneously, both with identical shocked open mouths. Maisie is fully dressed in ordinary clothes. She's not been working. A young man stands a few feet from her, one hand frozen in an outstretched movement towards her. He too is fully dressed. He wears a slightly old-fashioned but well-cut tweed suit, gleaming brown shoes and a crisp white shirt. Greene's detective's eyes note that his cheeks are flushed and his shirt tails not fully tucked into his trousers, the belt of which has its tongue outside the buckle.

Without speaking, Greene strides across the room towards Maisie. He raises his hand.

'I've warned you about this before,' he says as he approaches her.

'No, Sidney!' she cries, but the blow comes anyway.

It's not the punch he would have delivered to a man, more a backhanded cuff, but it's powered by his anger and Maisie is knocked to the floor. He whirls towards the frightened young man who backs off, hands held up in submission.

'No, Mr Greene, no…'

As he retreats, the man collides with a coffee table and the lamp on it topples over. Greene follows him.

'No, Sidney!' repeats the woman from the floor. 'He's come to say goodbye!'

'And a quick hand job for old time's sake?' bellows Greene, pointing at the other's belt buckle. 'I weren't born yesterday!' The young man's face colours scarlet. 'I told you: if I found you here, there'd be trouble.'

'Honestly, Mr Greene, I only popped in to say goodbye!' he says, the words tumbling out of his mouth. 'It's true! I'm off to Argentina in the morning.'

'Fucking off without paying me, no doubt.'

'No, no, I've got it all here!'

Greene pauses in his advance, watching the young man desperately patting and reaching into trouser pockets, then jacket pockets, then back to trouser pockets.

'Here! See?' He thrusts a roll of notes in Greene's face. 'Count it!'

Greene takes the money, rips off the rubber band holding it, and leafs through, counting. He relaxes a little. 'All right then. Two hundred. All square.'

The young man takes the opportunity to scramble further away, around the periphery of the room towards the door.

'And what about tonight?' calls Greene over his shoulder, but the hapless suitor is through the door and running down the hall.

Greene leaps after him, catching him up as he takes his first step off the landing onto the staircase. Greene lifts his foot and connects with the departing man's backside. It's less a kick than a push, and the young man is propelled off the stair. He stumbles, almost regains his balance, stumbles again, and finally clatters in a windmill of arms and legs to the bottom of the flight. Maisie has followed Greene onto the landing and stands behind him, her hands on his shoulders, trying to peer past him.

'Jesus, Sidney … I think you've killed him.'

For a long moment the young man lies completely still, limbs crumpled underneath him, face pressed at an odd angle into the skirting board, eyes closed. Then he stirs and groans.

'He's fine,' says Greene, and he turns and propels Maisie back into the flat. 'We'll call it quits.' A further thought causes him to pause. He looks over the bannister, down at the young man struggling to his feet. 'But if I see you again, here or anywhere in Soho, you'll get a kicking, and I'll be calling your old man.'

'You don't need to worry —' groans the other, but Greene's not interested. He's already slammed the door behind him.

Back inside, Greene walks to the other side of the room and rights the lamp. He looks around. The flat, the only one in the building with its own bathroom and kitchenette, is large. Built into the roof, its outside walls are less than three feet high, but it spans the full length and breadth of the building. Dormer windows on three sides make the space light and airy, with views over the rooftops to north, west and south, and the main room is large enough for a double bed, a couch, a table and four chairs.

Greene nods with approval. The flat's clean and tidy, and there's a smell of furniture polish. Even with a cleaner coming twice-weekly, Vanessa, his wife and best friend of twenty years, is incapable of keeping their house in Camberwell as tidy as this; he's given up complaining about it.

Greene sniffs again. 'You been cooking?' he asks. 'What can I smell?'

'Just some hotpot,' replies Maisie. 'I turned it off 'cos I thought you weren't coming.'

'Well, I'm here now,' he says, pulling off his tie and dropping his jacket over the back of a chair. 'So serve up, eh? I'm expected home tonight, so I ain't got long.'

Greene collapses in an armchair and kicks off his shoes, watching Maisie's back as she ties on an apron and busies herself at the stove.

It's eight years since he first nicked her, a skinny drug-addled teenager working the streets, but even half-starved, he could see she was special. She was as gorgeous as most of the models he saw on television and in the magazines, and handled right

— and off her habit — she could make him a fortune. So he paid her bail and let her sleep in the small room. Then he got her checked out at the special clinic — all clean — and, when she started work again, managed her money.

He'd intended to take a cut, but he found himself giving her enough to live on and opening a building society account in her name for the rest. In the end, he didn't keep a penny.

As she filled out and settled in, he discovered a girl with a sense of humour and more brains than he'd assumed. He started going round to Green's Court after his shifts ended, sometimes carrying a Chinese meal, sometimes a bottle of wine. A year later, she offered him a freebie by way of thanks. Greene knew he could've taken it before then, whether she was willing or not, but an odd delicacy had prevented him. They became regular lovers.

A year after that, he did up the roof flat and moved her in, rent-free, and thereafter she only worked part-time. She still liked the money, and she didn't actually mind the work as long as she could choose her clients. The arrangement worked for them both.

'Is he really going away?' asks Greene.

'Walter? Yes. His dad threatened to cut him off unless he agreed.'

'Did you?'

She turns to him, saucepan in hand. There's a red mark high on her cheek where his blow landed. 'Oh, Sid, you should've seen him! He was so pathetic.'

'Still in love with you, I 'spect.'

'He wanted me to run off with him. I was trying to let him down gently.'

'I get it. So…?'

'No, of course not. Just a quick hand-job, to send him away happy. I've washed my hands. Actually, do you want to wash yours? I'm ready to serve.'

After Jean and Archie, the love of Sergeant Maynard's life is his motorcycle, an increasingly rare wartime BSA B40 with sidecar attached. He spends long patient off-duty hours maintaining it, servicing, tuning and cleaning. Before Archie was born, and before Jean's increasing girth made it uncomfortable for her to get in and out of the sidecar, they would often use his weekend passes to explore the surrounding countryside on the bike, stopping here and there for a picnic or pub lunch or to walk the footpaths criss-crossing the county.

So it's unusual for Maynard ever to get onto the machine without checking tyres, brakes and lights. But then it's unusual for him to be called out, at night, to ride to RAF Croughton to collect some supposedly urgent dossier from the Yanks.

He slips on his helmet and gauntlets, guns the motor and waves to the guard post as he rolls out onto the main road. As he enters Harrowden Road he opens the throttle. It's a fine night, the road surface is dry, and with a little luck Maynard expects the journey to take only three quarters of an hour.

Harrowden Lane is a quiet meandering country road overhung by trees, fields to each side. Maynard's motorcycle is the only vehicle on the road.

A few hundred yards before the Lane's junction with the A600 it describes a gentle S-bend. Maynard double de-clutches into third gear, keeping the revs of the engine high so he can accelerate out of the second part of the bend, but as he does so the bike is suddenly unstable. His heart leaps with shock and disbelief as the sidecar separates from the bike and continues in a straight line towards the verge while he continues to the left. He and the bike are thrown off balance, tipping vertiginously so far that he fears his elbow will scrape the road surface. He squeezes the brakes gently, knowing that any violent deceleration will lead to a complete loss of control, and drags the heel of his left boot along the tarmac. For a split-second he thinks he's going to make it, but then the bike encounters a slight dip in the road surface.

It's that which does for him. Coming out of the depression the front tyre loses traction altogether and, as if in slow-motion, he's ejected out of the seat. His hands, gripping the handlebars, are the last part of his body to lose contact with the bike and he realises that he is describing a somersault in the air, watching the bike continue on its side underneath him. His last thought before he sails backwards and neck-first into the wall of the barn by the side of the road is that it's going to take months to repair her.

CHAPTER 5

In a well-practised manoeuvre, Charles jumps off the platform of the moving No. 15 bus at the junction of Fetter Lane and Fleet Street and runs to a halt. He waits for a gap in the traffic and jogs across Fleet Street and through the gates arch into Sergeants Inn.

It's a beautiful sunny day with barely a cloud in the sky, more like late summer than early winter. He crosses the cobbles and enters the Temple via the arch under Mitre Court Buildings. Originally the English base of the Knights Templar warrior monks, the Temple has been home to most of the English barristers in practice since the fourteenth century. Every day Charles enters the hushed courtyards, strolls the manicured lawns sloping gently to the river or just sits under the tall plane trees, he gives thanks to whatever god decreed that this is where he'd spend his working life. Only yards from bustling twentieth century Fleet Street, here the invisible threads of English history are rendered corporeal. Charles still dines most days in the Tudor hall where Queen Elizabeth I saw the first ever performance of Twelfth Night; the emblems of the Houses of York and Lancaster were plucked from the rose bushes in Temple Garden; and the heraldic shields on the walls of Hall include five former members who were signatories to the American Declaration of Independence. It's a privilege to be a member of such an institution as the Honourable Society of the Middle Temple; even if many of its members are less than honourable, and their society has never been much available to a working-class East End lapsed Jew.

Charles is nonetheless in high spirits. This morning he won one of his rare cases in the Chancery Division, for which he was paid the very acceptable sum of one hundred guineas for half a day's work, and his diary is full for the next couple of months with good quality trials for both defence and prosecution. Ronnie and Reggie Kray have been uncharacteristically but mercifully quiet since their triumphant acquittal of the protection racket charges earlier that year (Reggie is in any case too busy playing happy couples with his new bride) and the simmering resentment borne by Millie Horowitz for her elder son, his change of name, his lack of religiousness — in short, *all* his life choices — has been notable by its absence since the Jewish High Holy Days, when an encounter with her God apparently led to a temporary thaw in Millie's frozen heart.

He bounds up the wooden staircase in the Dickensian building, taking two stairs at a time and creating puffs of ancient timber dust as he lands on each second step. He pushes open the door to the clerks' room.

'Good morning,' he announces, but no one hears him.

The large room is its usual clatter of noise. Four desks pushed together in the centre form a large rectangle. At two, the typists, Wendy and Margaret, are typing with furious concentration while at the same time giggling. Jennie, the junior clerk, is making four mugs of tea in the corner, and Jeremy, her counterpart, is doing nothing but holding a bottle of milk for her. Clive, the spotty office boy — sixteen, deficient in experience and over-endowed with confidence — is completing a story that has all the others laughing. Even Barbara, Chambers' senior and very serious clerk, is smiling. For once the laughter doesn't die away as Charles enters the room; another good sign, signifying that, for once, it's not about him. He scans his pigeon hole — disappointingly empty of cheques — and turns to go up to his room.

'Good morning, sir,' says Barbara, shouting over the noise. 'Do you have a moment?'

'Sure.'

'Okay, that's enough,' she calls to the other clerks. 'Let's try to get some work done.'

Barbara collects a sheaf of papers from her desk. 'Follow me,' she says.

Charles frowns but does as instructed. With a swish of her tweed skirts and a waft of Scottish Fine Soap, Barbara leads the way up the stairs to Charles's floor on the opposite corridor of Chambers. She enters the first room she finds. It's unoccupied and, as she closes the door, she slides the "Conference" sign across so they won't be disturbed.

'Why all the secrecy?' asks Charles, puzzled, as Barbara takes a seat at a desk.

'We've had a rather odd approach to Chambers, or rather, to you. Do you remember anyone called Maynard? Julian Maynard?'

Charles looks up in thought. The name rings no immediate bells. 'I used to know a Maynard once, in the RAF. I can't remember his first name.' He shrugs.

'Well, it might be the same chap as there's definitely an RAF connection. Over the last couple of days, a woman called Jean Maynard has been phoning repeatedly, demanding to speak to you. She says you knew her husband during the war. At first she refused to say what it was about, although she was obviously very distressed. When I insisted that I wouldn't put her through to you without knowing a bit more, she said her husband had been murdered and she needed your help.'

'Murdered?' says Charles, a wry eyebrow raised.

'That's what she said.'

'Okay. Where does she live?'

'Bedfordshire.'

'Well, we know solicitors on the Midlands and Oxford Circuit. Can we give her a couple of names and numbers?'

'I tried that. She's not interested. It has to be you.'

'Why me?'

'She says you're the only person she could trust. Her husband used to talk about you a bit, whenever you were in the press. Said you were okay.'

Charles reaches back in his memory, trying to place Julian Maynard. A thin fair-haired man in oil-stained overalls bearing a Senior Aircraftman's badge comes to mind, but nothing more.

A member of ground crew when I was flying Spitfires?

One thing is certain: if ever he knew a Julian Maynard, they were not close.

'That's very nice of her, but —'

'There's more. She says there's been a cover-up. She and her small baby are being evicted from their RAF married quarters, and she's facing a stone wall whenever she tries to get anything done. But she has documents which she says prove that her husband was murdered. And, here's the rub...' She pauses, waiting to land the punchline.

'Come on then; what is it?'

'She's looking for representation in the coroner's court. And she can't pay.'

'Oh Jesus!' Charles sighs. 'Is she bonkers, do you think?'

Barbara shrugs. 'It has occurred to me. She alternates between being very distressed, almost hysterical, over the phone and very calm. It does seem as if she's reading from some documents when giving me information, but the

Bedfordshire police say this was a common or garden motorcycle accident. There's no suggestion of foul play at all.'

'When's the inquest?'

'At the end of the month.'

'Am I free?'

'If it starts as predicted on the Monday, and it runs for no more than two days, yes. On the Wednesday of that week you're starting at Middlesex Assizes, prosecuting that pornography trial.'

Charles pulls out chair out from behind another desk and sits heavily.

It's almost certain that these allegations are groundless: a grieving wife struggling to come to terms with the accidental death of her husband. On the other hand, the inquest will be an ordeal for her, especially if he declines.

In Charles's opinion, one of the scandals of the justice system is the absence of legal aid available for coroners' inquests. One can be charged with a minor traffic infraction or non-payment of one's rates and, subject to means, legal aid will usually be available for appropriate representation. In coroners' courts, whose function is to decide the infinitely more important issue of "how, when and where" someone died, there is no legal aid. Shocked and bereaved family members with no legal training find themselves dragged into court to face medical, technical and other experts called by the coroner, and they are somehow supposed to be able to marshal the evidence and the law so as to cross-examine those experts successfully. Invariably the "other side" — big insurance companies for potentially guilty drivers, hospital boards, police forces and possibly, in this case, the RAF — will have pockets deep enough to pay for their own experts, barristers and solicitors. The bereaved family is at a complete disadvantage and usually can play no meaningful part in the process. They are bystanders, victims too, and all too often the inquest merely compounds their emotional damage. Unless, of course, they're rich, able to pay thousands to redress the inequality of arms.

'Where's the inquest?'

'The coroner's sitting at The Shire Hall in Bedford, in one of the magistrates' courts. If you're thinking of taking it, I'm afraid it'll mean you have to go up to Bedford to get instructions. She has a young baby and no money to travel to London.'

'Wonderful.' Charles turns it over and eventually nods. 'Fair enough. We need to start doing more pro bono work in these Chambers.'

Barbara smiles. 'I couldn't agree more. That's why I asked you. Between you and me, I'm hoping this'll be an example for some of the others.'

Charles laughs without mirth. 'Really? I wouldn't hold your breath.'

CHAPTER 6

The "Bedpan" line train is supposedly nicknamed after its termini of Bedford and St Pancras, but the unfortunate commuters forced to use it know the real provenance of its name: its odour. Charles's carriage stinks, and it's filthy. The heating doesn't work; the toilets are out of order and the service is running half an hour late. Added to that, the branch line to the little town of Ampthill, where Mrs Maynard is apparently now staying, was closed a few years ago and Charles has no choice but keep his fingers crossed that he'll find a cab when he gets out at Flitwick station.

He descends from the train at Flitwick onto the platform of a pretty country railway station largely surrounded by fields. Along the main northbound platform is a tidy garden packed with colourful flowers and the name of the station picked out in whitewashed stones. A handwritten sign attached to the station house wall proudly proclaims that the station master has, for the second year running, won the competition for the best kept station on the line.

The station courtyard is empty. No taxis; indeed no one at all. Charles finds a sign for Ampthill and embarks on the two-mile uphill walk.

Forty minutes later, sweating and grumpy, he reaches the middle of Ampthill, a small Georgian town full of pretty pastel-coloured buildings and a pump in the centre of the market square. He checks his notebook again for Mrs Maynard's temporary address, Bedford Street, and finds the building easily. It's set back from the road, a terrace of rather gloomy brick cottages owned, according to the datestone, by the Duke of Bedford. Charles opens the gate and walks down the garden path as the front door is opened to him by a young woman.

'Jean Maynard?' he asks.

'No, I'm Angie. Are you Mr Holborne?'

Charles offers his hand. 'Yes.'

'She's inside. Come in.'

Angie leads Charles through a narrow corridor into a back kitchen.

The house is dark, with small leaded windows and blood red quarry tiles on the floor. Sitting at the kitchen table is another young woman with a sleeping baby on her lap. In front of her is a sheaf of documents. Above her, hoisted by a pulley and suspended from the ceiling, is a clothes airer heavy with wet baby clothes. The room smells of soapsuds and toast, and there is a transistor radio somewhere from which Tom Jones is asserting that it's not unusual to have fun with anyone. One look at Mrs Maynard informs Charles to the contrary; Mrs Maynard is not having fun with anyone, and Angie apparently agrees because as she enters the room she silences Mr Jones with an irritated flick of a switch.

'This is Jean,' she introduces. 'The baby's Archie. Jean's asked me to stay, if that's okay. I'll put the kettle on.'

'I'm pleased to meet you, Mrs Maynard,' says Charles gravely, 'but very sorry about the circumstances.'

The young woman offers her hand from her seated position. She has lank blonde hair and tired light brown eyes rimmed in red. 'Yes. Please sit down, Mr Holborne. I can't tell you how grateful I am that you've come all this way. Jules always said you were a good bloke, and I ain't got anyone else I can ask.'

Charles sits opposite at the kitchen table. The Formica surface is slightly sticky. He opens his briefcase and places his blue counsel's notebook before him.

'To be honest, Mrs Maynard, I only have the vaguest recollection of your husband. I'm really sorry. I don't think we were ever close, and the last time I saw him would presumably have been in forty-seven or forty-eight. But, no matter. I'm here to help if I can. Now, I'm hoping to get the three-fifteen from Flitwick, so we have a lot to get through in a short time. Firstly, can you explain why you're living here?'

'Angie and her husband offered to put me up for a while till I got straight.'

'Yes, of course, but that's not what I meant. When an RAF serviceman dies in service, his family are entitled to stay in their married accommodation at least for —'

'I couldn't stay there. It don't matter what the rules say, Flight Lieutenant Holmes made it clear they wanted me out.' Tears fill her eyes.

'Flight Lieutenant Holmes?'

'He's the CO of Julian's Flight. I used to think he was all right but he was so … unpleasant. And stuff kept happening. I didn't feel safe, so we left.'

'What do you mean, "stuff kept happening"?'

Angie intervenes from beside the sink. 'Well, there was another murder, for starters.'

'Another murder?' says Charles, trying to keep disbelief out of his voice.

'I know you won't believe it. I couldn't believe it myself at first,' says Mrs Maynard. 'But something weird is happening up on that base. Two servicemen dead in the last month. Both in odd circumstances.'

'I see,' says Charles, finding it difficult to see but not wanting to start this relationship by overtly disbelieving his client.

He has encountered this before. Unexplained sudden bereavement provides fertile ground for conspiracy theories, particularly when a large organisation, whose internal processes seem calculated to obfuscate, is involved.

He unscrews the top of his fountain pen. 'Why don't you tell me the story from the start?'

In answer Mrs Maynard slides the sheaf of papers across the table to Charles. 'Why don't you read that, and then you can ask me any questions you like?'

Charles does as instructed and Mrs Maynard lights a cigarette, vaguely waving the smoke away from her baby's head.

It's clear that the late Sergeant Maynard was a methodical man. The first document comprises several pages from a lined notebook, full of regular handwriting in blue ink. As Charles reads, he realises it's a draft statement. It tells the story of some irregularity in goods wagons about to depart RAF Cardington; how there were thirteen when there should have been twelve, and how Maynard suspected that the train driver, his mate and perhaps a storeman named McParland might have been involved in the thieving. So far, so standard.

The next document is in the form of a log, recording the steps Maynard took after letting the goods train go. By the side of some entries are what appear to be Maynard's own notes and thoughts, presumably for further investigation. There's an underlined reference to "? Snowdrop", meaning an RAF policeman, so-called after their white-topped hats. Evidently Maynard was wondering if one of his own colleagues might have been involved.

Charles turns to the log itself. At 02:25 hours that morning, Maynard contacted the RAF's Special Investigations Branch and the Bedfordshire Police to alert them to the fact that a train with an additional unaccounted wagon had left Cardington. At 03:15 hours, in a different hand, it's recorded that a telephone call was received from the British Transport Police to the effect that they were aware of the movement of the goods train, and it had been tracked to Bedford.

'Whose writing is this?' asks Charles.

'The dark blue is Julian's. I don't know who the light blue is. Probably Corporal Boyce. They worked together.'

'We might need a word with Corporal Boyce,' comments Charles.

'You'll be lucky,' comments Angie from the corner of the room.

'Stop it, Ang,' says Mrs Maynard. 'He's a lovely bloke. He and Jules were real close.'

'Yeah, maybe, but he's still avoiding you.'

'I think … I think he's just embarrassed, you know, about how we've been thrown out.'

'Or because Holmes has put pressure on him,' suggests Angie.

'Do you think he'd talk to me?' asks Charles.

Mrs Maynard shrugs. 'I don't know. Probably not. Unless…'

'What?'

'I suppose I could speak to Heather first. She and I were very good friends. I'm godmother to one of her boys. Maybe she can persuade Boycey to talk to you.'

Charles makes some further notes and resumes reading.

The next note in Maynard's log is dated the following day and records a telephone call from the British Transport Police stating that wagon thirteen had been coupled to a goods train.

As Charles reads the destination, his eyes open wide. Wagon thirteen was headed for Cricklewood.

Jean Maynard senses Charles's stillness. 'What?' she demands.

'Now that is spooky,' mutters Charles.

'What?'

Charles locks eyes with her. 'A friend of mine's a copper in the Met. He had some trouble at a goods yard a couple of weeks back. At Cricklewood.'

'More coincidence?' mutters Angie sceptically, as she places mugs of tea on the table before Mrs Maynard and Charles.

'I agree, it does seem remarkable. On the other hand … it's a huge yard, one of the busiest serving London I believe … and everyone knows that stealing off the railway's endemic. Everyone's at it. They don't have to be linked. One goods wagon full of stolen goods heading to Cricklewood, and another iffy one at Cricklewood … well … there's no necessary connection. There could be hundreds of them for all we know. But … I agree it is something to consider. Is this all there is? Any record of what happened to the goods after this, or any action taken by the British Transport Police?'

Mrs Maynard shakes her head. 'No. He didn't have time.'

'And nothing from the SIB?'

'SIB?'

'RAF Special Investigation Branch.'

'You've got everything there was.'

'Okay. Did your husband report to Flight Lieutenant Holmes?'

'Yes, but he won't help,' says Angie. 'He's a complete bastard.'

Charles looks quizzically at Mrs Maynard.

'Like I said, it was Holmes who pressurised me to leave the married quarters. He implied Julian'd been stealing and he threatened to take it to the authorities. I'd have lost the widow's pension. He said if I left quietly it would all be okay. So I left.'

'I see.' Charles makes a note. 'Okay.'

He pauses to frame his next comment carefully. 'It certainly looks as if your husband was onto something. But it's a long stretch to suggest that his investigation had anything to do with his death. If the RAF routinely murdered their NCOs every time some thieving went on, it would be at half-staff. And unless there's extremely compelling evidence, the coroner won't let us explore this at all. His job is a very narrow one. He has to identify who has died, where, when and in what circumstances. So, can we put this on the back burner for the moment and move on to what happened in the accident?'

'It weren't an accident,' insists Mrs Maynard.

'I'm sorry,' apologises Charles, 'I should be more careful with my language. I'm not prejudging it, not suggesting there wasn't something else going on. Let's call it "the road incident". What exactly happened?'

'I don't know in detail. The coroner's officer gave me a short summary of what they think happened, but they won't give me no papers. Jules was leaving the base one evening on his service motorcycle. He came off the road at a bend. They say the sidecar detached from the motorcycle which made him lose his balance, and he couldn't stop in time. He hit a wall head-on.'

'Have they shown you any engineering evidence?'

'No.'

'Anything from an accident reconstruction expert?' She shakes her head. 'Who was responsible for the investigation?'

'I'm not sure … Bedfordshire police maybe? They say they examined the bike, and decided the bolts connecting the bike and the sidecar were loose!' Her voice is full of scorn.

'You doubt it?'

'Before he joined the RAF police, Jules was a Senior Aircraftman. There was nothing he couldn't take apart and put back together again, and he was always tinkering with that bloody motorbike, improving its performance, servicing it and so on. We used to row about it. He'd never go out on the bike without checking it over. Sometimes he'd take me and the baby in the sidecar!'

Charles makes some more notes, and screws the top back on his fountain pen.

'I need to explain something to you, Mrs Maynard. There is no legal aid available for coroners' courts. Which means you have to find legal representation prepared to take the case without payment.' He puts up a hand to forestall her interrupting. 'I've already agreed that I will take this case for you, and I'll do it without being paid. Barristers occasionally do what they call pro bono work — it's short for a Latin tag that means "for the public good". But here's the thing: if we're going to suggest there was anything the investigation missed, we really need to see what the evidence is and get our own experts to look at it. Now, I can make an application to the coroner for release of any investigation undertaken. He doesn't have to grant it. The coroner himself decides what witnesses to call and what part, if any, the family of the deceased can play. To be honest, the inquest is not really for you, for the family, to find out what happened to their loved one. It's something done for the state.

'But let's assume I could make an application and persuade the coroner to release the evidence he has seen — no

53

promises, mind. The real problem is putting that evidence in front of our own independent experts. They *won't* work for free.'

'What would that cost?'

Charles considers. 'Well, it wouldn't surprise me if an engineering expert cost fifty guineas. And a road traffic expert, to deal with stopping distances, skid marks and so on, the same again.'

Mrs Maynard looks appalled. 'I ain't got that! I ain't got anything. Angie 'n' Fred're paying for everything for me and the baby.' She starts crying. The baby wakes and is soon joining in.

Charles reaches into his jacket pocket and pulls out some tissues, handing one to her. 'Now, now, it's not the end of the world. There is an alternative route, but it's not as good.'

'Which is?' sniffs Mrs Maynard.

'We keep a very low profile until the day. They'll turn up with their investigating officer expecting it all to go through on the nod. Very often family members don't bother to appear unless they're witnesses, and you're not. They'll expect you to be there on your own, if you turn up at all. And I cross-examine for all I'm worth. I'm not an engineer or a road traffic expert, but I've done enough of these cases to know what to look for, and cause trouble.'

'Is that good enough?'

Charles shrugs again. 'We'll have to keep our fingers crossed. Most coroners run their courts as if they were tribal chiefs dispensing palm-tree justice. There's almost no control over them. They decide what evidence will be called, whether or not I can ask questions on your behalf, all of that. But with a half-decent coroner, and enough suspicion, I may be able to get enough leeway to start asking real questions.'

'Let's do that, then,' she says with a trace of a smile.

'One last thing: you need to be sure you want to put yourself through this. Nothing is going to bring Jules back. The court has no power to award you damages or make any finding of criminal or civil liability. The coroner's job is just to decide who died, when and in what circumstances. This will be hard, painful, and you may well walk away no wiser.'

Charles is surprised by the firmness of the young woman's jaw and the steel in her eyes. 'Jules was the love of my life. I don't know what I'm going to do now. But I'm sure of one thing: I want everyone to hear what happened.'

'Everyone?'

'The whole world.'

Charles considers this. 'Well, a few phone calls to the local press wouldn't do any harm. They often cover inquests, particularly of service personnel. And having members of the press there, even from the local paper, might help keep the coroner on the straight and narrow.'

'Would that come better from us, Mr Holborne?' asks Angie. 'Photos of the grieving widow, an' all that?'

Charles smiles. 'Yes, it would, Angie. Definitely.'

Charles closes his notebook and puts it back in his briefcase. He looks up. 'Okay, so Corporal Boyce: where can we find him?'

'If he's not actually on duty at the camp, he'll be at Shortstown.'

'Shortstown?'

'It's just outside the base, where all the families live. It's become a sort of village now.'

Charles turns to Angie. 'Any chance you could look after the baby for a couple of hours?'

'Right now?' asks Angie.

'Why?' asks Mrs Maynard.

'Why not?' replies Charles. 'I can get a later train, I'm here now and Shortstown's, what, fifteen minutes away? I need to see where the crash occurred, so we might as well make a short detour. It's quite a schlep for me to come up from London each time and, without wanting to make a big deal of it, I'm not being paid, so every train journey comes out of my pocket.'

'I ain't got a car,' says Mrs Maynard.

'There must be a taxi company somewhere in Ampthill or Flitwick.'

'Yes,' replies Angie. 'I've got a number here. And I'll look after Andy.'

'Good, that's settled then,' says Charles, rising.

Thirty minutes later, having looked briefly at the scene of the accident — where there was nothing of interest beyond the double bend and the barn into which the motorcycle crashed — Charles and Mrs Maynard step out of a minicab in Shortstown.

The place was obviously constructed for service personnel. Neat squares and crescents of identical housing built in the same pink brick, most with bare but tidy gardens, many with children's toys, bikes and scooters in evidence.

Mrs Maynard leads Charles up a garden path and knocks on a door. The sound of a female voice shouting an instruction to children can be heard, and the door is opened by a young woman in a housecoat and hair curlers.

'Jean?' she says with some surprise.

'Sorry just to turn up like this, Heather.'

'No, no, I'm pleased you came. I've been meaning to...' She catches sight of Charles.

'This is Mr Holborne,' explains Mrs Maynard. 'Look, Heather, could we possibly come in for a moment? I need to talk to you.'

Heather hesitates for a moment and Charles sees a contest occurring in the young woman's body. It only takes a second or two for kindness to win.

'Of course you can. I'll put the kettle on.' She opens the door fully to allow Mrs Maynard to lead Charles into a modest rectangular living room.

The house is like every service home Charles has seen, all of similar design and all decorated with the same institutional pale green paint. Heather's home is tidy, allowing for the two children Charles can see playing on the swing in the back garden, but it's in need of a lick of paint. The effort to render the house more personal is evident, although undermined by the ubiquitous photograph of the Queen given pride of place above the mantelpiece.

Heather enters and clears some toys and ironing off the couch. 'Please sit down. Boycey should be back any minute.' She bustles into the kitchen but shouts through the serving hatch into the room where Mrs Maynard and Charles sit. 'Are you still at Angie and Fred's?'

'Yes,' calls back Mrs Maynard.

'I can't believe how badly you've been treated,' replies Heather. 'I keep asking Boycey to persuade Holmes to let you back, at least while you find something more permanent.'

'It's fine, Heather,' replies Mrs Maynard, 'don't worry about that. I feel better off the base anyway.'

Heather brings in a tray with a pot of tea, four mugs and a milk bottle. She places the tray on the floor, clears more space from an armchair and sits facing Mrs Maynard and Charles. 'What can I do, then?'

'Do you think Boycey would speak to Mr Holborne here? He's helping me out on the inquest, and he's got some questions which Boycey might be able to answer.'

Heather moves from the armchair suddenly and crouches on the floor next to the tray. She busies herself with stirring the tea leaves in the pot, and it's a few seconds before she answers. 'You can ask him, when he gets back,' she says, sounding doubtful.

'But he's been avoiding me, hasn't he Heather? I don't think he'll help unless, maybe, you ask him. Please? It's really important.' Mrs Maynard is almost begging.

Heather sighs and shakes her head sadly. 'Honestly, Jean, I don't know what's got into him. He's been really strange since the accident.'

The front door opens and closes with a bang. A tall man in RAF uniform appears in the lounge doorway. He sees Mrs Maynard and looks surprised. He then notes Charles's presence.

'Hello, Jean,' he says guardedly. 'What's all this?' He nods toward Charles.

Charles stands and puts out his hand. 'My name's Charles Holborne. Mrs Maynard has asked for some help in preparing for her husband's inquest.'

'You a solicitor?'

'Sort of. A lawyer.'

'I've got nothing to say to lawyers,' says Boyce, and he turns without a further word and goes directly upstairs. The bedroom door slams.

The three other occupants of the room stare after him. Heather bows her head. 'I'm so sorry, Jean.'

She looks across at her friend. Jean Maynard is sitting with her head in her hands, crying.

'Oh!' exclaims Heather, and she crosses the room swiftly and crouches before the bereaved woman, taking her hands in hers.

'Here,' says Charles, offering Heather another clean tissue from his jacket pocket. She takes it and gives it to Mrs Maynard.

'I don't know what to say,' says Heather, her own voice trembling. 'I can't imagine what you're going through. And I really don't understand why Boycey's being like this. He and Julian were so close!'

They hear noise from above them and Heather stands. 'Give me a moment,' she says, now determined, and she turns and runs up the stairs after her husband.

Charles sits again, next to his crying client. They wait patiently for a few minutes, as the voices above them get louder and more argumentative.

'I'm ashamed of you!' they hear Heather say. 'He was your best friend!'

Boyce's answer is unclear, but Charles definitely hears the word "crazy".

Heather's response is almost shouted. 'And what if she isn't crazy, and they did kill him? You're really going to hide in here and do nothing?'

Both he and Mrs Maynard hear Boyce's shouted reply clearly. 'If she isn't crazy, all the more reason to do nothing! You want the same to happen to me?'

Mrs Maynard stands. When she speaks, her voice is under control again. 'Come on, Mr Holborne. We're wasting our time here.'

She strides out of the front door, and Charles follows.

CHAPTER 7

Sean Sloane ducks down to open the bedside cupboard to make sure he's left nothing behind. Bending down still makes his face hurt, like a weight running on rails from the back of his head to his teeth, but it's bearable with the painkillers. His right eye still leaks unpredictably, and he still has a tendency to dribble when chewing solids. It's not a good look; embarrassing, particularly in front of Dr Alexandrova. He's shaved carefully today, for the first time; he hopes it might be she who returns with his discharge letter and he wants to look his best.

Dr Alexandrova attracts and disconcerts him in equal measure. He sometimes sees laughter in her eyes when he speaks to her, which makes him feel like the shy schoolboy he once was. But he'll miss the sound of her sensible shoes as she hurries about the ward and, when she has time, the flirtatious banter.

He's never met a woman quite like her. Leaving aside the exotic South African accent, she's several years older than the other trainees — by his calculation only a year or two younger than he — and very confident, with a cynical sharpness to her conversation. In Ireland you almost never meet a woman professional. The doctors, the Garda, magistrates, even the dentists — all are men. As a lad he once went out with a myopic girl in his village who nurtured the ambition to be an optician. But a woman doctor? Sloane's four sisters are all farmers' wives, responsible for running their homes, producing babies and meals for their husbands and helping with the livestock. The concept of studying at university, becoming independent professionals, would have been inconceivable to them, although they were certainly sharp enough, especially the eldest, Siobhan, on whom you could cut yourself.

So Dr Alexandrova is intriguing; scary and sexy all in one package. Nonetheless, he's glad to be leaving. He's spent ten days on the noisy ward, much longer than expected, courtesy of a late-diagnosed concussion, and he longs for the relative peace of his own bed in Mrs O'Connor's draughty boarding-house full of young Irishmen. That and a complete night's uninterrupted sleep.

He is finishing packing his holdall when he hears the curtains move. He turns, a smile fixed to his face, or at least as fixed as his broken jaw will allow, and is disappointed to see not Dr Alexandrova but his detective inspector, DI Perry. Sloane's posting is still so new, he barely knows the man.

'Afternoon, Sergeant Sloane,' says Perry.

The inspector's short for the Met — had to have been standing on tiptoe when he applied, thinks Sloane — but he has close-cropped grey hair, a thick neck and he's broad and powerful. He looks like a rugby player, and Sloane guesses he can look after himself.

'Afternoon, guv.'

'Are they discharging you?'

'Just waiting for the letter now. Any news on the section house?'

Sloane's transfer to S Division occurred so quickly that when he presented himself to the little Commander responsible for overseeing all the young unmarried officers in West Hendon, he was told he'd not been expected and no room was available. He was directed to a boarding house the police used occasionally as an overflow. He's been there ever since.

'No, but I'll chase again. What do they say about returning to work?'

'It'll be in the letter, but I've got to take it easy until they see me in outpatients in two or three weeks' time. I can manage desk duties in the meantime.'

'That won't be necessary. Take the time off.'

'I'd like to follow up on the goods wagons at Cricklewood, guv. I've done a short statement about what happened. Here.'

Sloane holds out a sheet of paper densely covered with handwriting on both sides. Perry doesn't take it. Instead, he looks at it for a moment and shakes his head. 'No need. We've got it covered. You just get better, okay?'

'What do you mean? That bastard busted my jaw in two places! I've got a good independent witness, too, a barrister. Gervaise is bang to rights.'

Perry compresses his lips in irritation. 'Sorry, Sloane, but it isn't going to happen. Like I said, we've got it covered.'

He takes a deep breath, and when he speaks again his voice is less aggressive.

'Look, Sean, I know you collected a nasty injury and if I were you, I'd want to pursue it. But you're new to the team. Don't go ruffling feathers before you've got your feet under the desk, okay? Everyone knows what happened to you in Vice, and people are sympathetic, honestly. But leave this one alone. Wheels are in motion. Got it?'

Sloane stares at him for a long time. His busy inspector has obviously come expressly to make this point. Sloane nods and shrugs. 'If you say so, guv.'

'Good. If you're about to be discharged, do you need a lift?'

'No, thanks, I'm being picked up.' At least so he hopes.

Sloane knows few people in London, fewer still with a car. He left a message at Charles's chambers asking if it would be possible to cadge a lift back to his digs, but Charles hasn't replied. In any case, he doesn't want to be in a car with Perry; he doesn't want Perry to see his lodgings; he doesn't want anything more to do with him than is unavoidable. Sloane doesn't yet know who to trust, and the last few moments have not left him optimistic about Detective Inspector Perry.

'Fair enough. Make sure the hospital sends us a copy of your letter, yeh, and don't hurry back till you're ready for full duties.'

'Understood.'

As Perry leaves the ward he is passed by Dr Alexandrova, an envelope in her hand. She approaches the bed and pulls the curtains back fully.

'Here you are. As discussed. And here's a box of painkillers.' She hands both to him.

'Thanks, doctor.'

'You need to take it easy, Mr Sloane. The face you know about, but the dizziness can last weeks, sometimes months. And it can come and go.'

'Got it.'

Sloane hesitates and so does Dr Alexandrova.

'Look...' he starts.

'Yes?'

'Well, the thing is ... I don't suppose I'll see you in outpatients, will I?' She shakes her head. 'So, in that case ... I'm not sure if this is a breach of protocol, but if I'm no longer your patient, do you think I could take you out for a drink? Maybe a meal?'

Dr Alexandrova looks up at the tall Irishman, a half-smile playing about her lips as if she were teasing him. 'You couldn't handle it,' she says.

Sloane smiles uncertainly. Is she teasing? 'That sounds like a challenge.'

'Not at all. I like steak,' she replies, 'and you can't eat steak. Yet.'

'So, you're saying no?'

She pauses for a moment. 'I'm saying let's make it a drink until your mouth works better.'

'Great. Here … let me give you my number…'

But the doctor's hand has already reached into her white coat pocket and pulled out a scrap of paper. 'That's mine. At least, it's the house where I'm staying. It's in Notting Hill. I've put the address as well.'

Sloane's smile broadens. 'I'll call soon.'

'Leave it a few days. I start a week of nights on Monday, so wait till after then. In any case, don't underestimate the injury you've sustained. Take it easy for a week or so.' She half-turns. 'But do call.'

'Doctor?'

'Yes?'

'What's your first name?'

She throws the name back over her shoulder as she departs across the squeaky linoleum: 'Irenna.'

'Irenna Alexandrova,' says Sloane quietly, rolling the words around in his mouth as if savouring Irish whiskey. 'Like a Russian spy.'

He grins, picks up his holdall, waves to the men on either side of his bed, neither of whom ever spoke to him, and leaves the ward.

As Sloane opens the main swing doors to the hospital he sees, with some relief, Charles pulling into a space in the car park in his rust-bucket Austin Healey sports car. Charles gets out and waves.

'Been waiting long?' he calls. 'Sorry I'm late. I expected to be finished by mid-morning, but we started late so the judge sat through lunch.'

'You're fine,' says Sloane, walking over.

Charles notes the slightly wider gait than usual; Sloane's still a little unsteady on his feet.

'Perfect timing,' says Sloane. 'This is very kind of you. I only asked on the off-chance. I could've got a bus.'

'It's two or three buses from here, and I bet you're not supposed to be on public transport for a while,' says Charles. 'Really, it's no problem.'

Charles opens the tiny boot, clears some space and lets Sloane drop his holdall inside.

'Sorry,' Charles says, 'the old girl smells a bit.'

He and Sloane get in and Sloane sniffs, his nose wrinkling. His ability to detect odours has been affected by the blow he received to his face — temporarily, he hopes — but even to him the car has an unpleasant wreak of burnt oil and rotten carpet.

'The soft top's been leaking all winter, and there is usually a puddle of water behind the seats,' explains Charles. 'The carpet's had it.'

'So, get it fixed. You're wealthy enough now. Or, better still, buy an appropriate vehicle. I can't imagine what your rich clients think when you turn up in this heap. It can't be good marketing.'

'I know. It's just a case of finding the time. Right, guv; where to?'

Sloane gives him an address in Kilburn and Charles moves off.

'Still no room at the section house?'

'No. But to be honest, Mrs O'Connor's is preferable to sharing living space with a load of sex- and snooker-obsessed single young policemen.'

They drive in silence for a while.

'Well?' prompts Charles impatiently.

By way of answer, Sloane brandishes the piece of paper with Dr Alexandrova's address and telephone number.

'Well done.'

'I didn't really have to ask. She had it ready for me.'

Charles grins. 'Sounds promising.'

Charles drives westwards and turns left onto the A41. Sloane is unusually silent, a deep frown creasing his brow.

'What's up?' Charles eventually asks.

Sloane sighs deeply. 'I couldn't wait to get out and start poking into that Gervaise bloke. Especially given the damage he did to my face. But my new DI came to the ward to warn me off. More or less ordered me to take some leave.' There's another long pause. 'I was so hopeful...'

'There are bad apples everywhere, Sean, but S Division isn't the same as Vice. There'll be an honest copper or two amongst them.'

'Can you let me have their names?' replies Sloane bitterly. He stares morosely out of the window.

'What're you going to do?' asks Charles.

'I haven't decided yet.'

'I need to tell you something. It may help you decide.'

'What's that?'

'I've been instructed in, on the face of it, a simple road traffic accident at the coroner's court.'

'So?'

'My client's convinced her husband was killed deliberately after discovering some hooky goods on a train. And there may be a connection with Cricklewood goods yard.'

Sloane swings round sharply to face Charles and claps his hand to his head with the pain. 'How long have you known this?' he demands, grimacing.

'A couple of days.'

'What? Jesus Christ, Charles! And you were thinking of not telling me? Your friend who's got concussion, a fractured jaw and — oh, yes! — is a detective investigating the same bloody case?'

'Calm down, Sean. I'm not sure there's any connection; I'm not sure if my client's bonkers; plus, there's the small issue of legal professional privilege. But I've been turning it over, and I've decided I must have implied instructions that if any investigation can throw further light on her husband's death, my client would want it pursued.'

'Well, that's very good of you. Where did this supposed road traffic accident occur?'

'That's a matter of public record: in Bedfordshire, specifically, close to RAF Cardington.'

'Thank you.'

'There's one other detail you should probably have.'

'Yes?' says Sloane, still cross.

'The deceased, a chap called Julian Maynard, was a sergeant in the RAF police.'

That silences Sloane for a while. 'That puts my busted jaw into perspective.'

'Indeed. So, if you're going to pursue this, you really need to watch your back, mate.'

'Who investigated Maynard's death?'

'That's all a bit fuzzy at the moment. The coroner's released no papers. Maynard's note says it was reported to SIB, but I've not seen anything to suggest they followed up. You know what it's like with overlapping jurisdictions —'

'Everyone's very busy —'

'— and hopes someone else'll pick it up —'

'— and no one does.'

'Exactly. And here there were four, Beds, RAF police, SIB and the British Transport Police. I'm hoping to learn more at the inquest.'

'Not before?'

'Probably not.'

'Is there anything to stop me going? As a civilian?'

'Other than the fact that you can barely walk, you mean?'

Sloane slumps back in his seat, nursing his aching head, and Charles decides to leave him in peace.

As they join the Finchley Road they pass a large construction site, scaffolding covering an emerging building several storeys high. As the car drives past, Charles sees Sloane craning his head painfully to watch the men working a hundred feet up.

'Miss it?' he asks.

'What, working the lump? You've got to be joking! I managed two years, and that was quite enough.'

'I can't imagine you as a labourer. How did that come about?'

Sloane scoffs. 'You've really no idea, Charles, have you? People like me had no choice. Rural Ireland in the early Fifties … it was destitution. Honestly, people starved. You'd be congratulated on being picked.'

'Picked?'

Sloane takes a deep breath. 'The village priests run the schools. They have contacts in construction gangs, previous lads who've gone over and are making a living. When they need a couple of likely boys, your priest comes into the class, points, and says: "You for Cricklewood" or "You for Birmingham" and that's it.'

'Some career choice,' comments Charles wryly.

'I hated it,' Sloane says quietly.

'The work?'

'Everything. Being away from the farm, the work, the way we were treated like cattle, the "No Irish" signs everywhere. And the constant movement from pillar to post. You could never make friends. You'd be on a job for six months and suddenly the gang would be split up, sent to all points of the compass, and you'd never see those lads again. So I gave it up, went home.'

'Why'd you come back?'

'Me older sisters persuaded me to do a couple more years while taking night classes. O levels. Then I applied for the police.'

'So that all worked out fine, then,' says Charles, grinning.

Sloane scowls, and then laughs, patting Charles's knee affectionately. 'You're a good pal, Charlie.'

A short while later, Sloane directs Charles to turn off at Brondesbury Villas. The suburban streets become quieter and wider and the houses more substantial.

'This'll do,' he says, pointing towards a large bay-fronted house reached via a neat and tidy garden. A large sign swings in the breeze informing the world that they have reached "Mrs O'Connor's boarding house for young working men". Underneath the title, the "Vacancies" sign has been prefixed by a flap of wood swinging on two hooks which says "No".

'It looks nice,' comments Charles.

'It's okay. Unlike many, the sheets are clean and Mrs O'Connor can cook.'

They climb out of the car and Charles goes to the boot to lift out Sloane's bag. Sloane holds out his hand.

'Oh, I wouldn't fink of it, guv,' says Charles in his best Cockney cabbie voice. 'Door-to-door service, this,' he says as he precedes Sloane up the steps.

Sloane joins him, fishes in his jacket pocket and is about to insert the latchkey when the door opens inwards. A ruddy-faced middle-aged woman in a housecoat faces him, long greying hair tied in a bun.

'So, Mr Sloane, is it?' she says.

'Afternoon, Mrs O'Connor,' says Sloane, making to step over the threshold.

'And where would you be going?' she asks.

'To me bed. I've been in hospital.'

'To his bed, is it? Well, Mr Sloane, you've no bed here.' Sloane frowns, puzzled. 'Your rent ran out four days ago, and I haven't heard a word. Supposed to be a week in advance, so it is, and you're eleven days behind. I even rang the station.'

'What did they say?'

'That you were living at the station house.'

Sloane claps his head in frustration. 'No! That's wrong. There wasn't a room available, which is why I'm here.'

The landlady shrugs. 'I'm sorry, sergeant. You're a clean boy, and a nice one at that, but I can't afford to leave the room empty. These other lads —' and she nods backwards into the hall from where the noise of men's voices can be heard — 'earn more'n you, and one of them needed a room for his cousin.'

'You're saying that you've re-let my room?'

'I'm saying that exactly.'

70

'Well, let me have another room, then. I'll take anything. I just need to lie down.'

Mrs O'Connor nods towards the sign at the front of the garden, and Sloane looks behind him. By the time he's turned back, Mrs O'Connor is holding out a heavy suitcase.

'I'm sorry, Mr Sloane, but there it is.'

She opens her other hand, palm up, and after a moment's hesitation Sloane places his latchkey in it. He takes his suitcase and the door closes.

'Fucking hell,' whispers Sloane to himself. 'And the day started so well.'

His shoulders slump and he retraces his steps down the garden path. Charles follows him.

'That's bloody bad luck,' says Charles cheerfully. 'But I've got nothing on this afternoon that can't be put off. We've passed dozens of boarding houses; we're sure to find something acceptable if we look.'

'I'm supposed to get clearance first. I can't just stay anywhere I please.'

'Really? Why not?'

'They have to approve it, make sure there are no undesirables living there. It can take days.'

'You haven't got days. What do you want to do?'

Sloane pauses, undecided. 'I suppose I could find somewhere and get it approved later. Are you sure you don't mind? This is turning into a lot more than a lift from hospital.'

'One of the nicer things about being at the Bar is that I'm self-employed. Unless I'm actually in court, I work when I want. Anyway, you think I'm going to leave you on the pavement, like a slightly dazed lost sheep? It's fine. Give me a moment and I'll drop the top so you can put the suitcase on the dickey seat.'

71

Charles's optimism proves unfounded. They start with the better boarding houses and gradually work downmarket. They follow various landladies' suggestions to Willesden Green, Brondesbury Park and Kensal Town, gradually heading south. Even the shoddy ones have no vacancies, and many they now pass have "No Coloured, No Irish, No Dogs" signs outside them.

After three hours of searching and with dusk falling, Charles pulls into the kerb and turns off the engine.

'Shall we keep going south? Notting Hill, maybe? Not exactly an Irish area, but it's definitely bedsit land. We're less than a mile away now.'

Sloane's eyes are closed, and for a moment he doesn't reply. A sudden thought occurs to him and the eyes are wide open again. His hand goes to his other jacket pocket, coming up with Dr Alexandrova's address. He raises his eyebrows at Charles. Charles shakes his head.

'You must be bonkers. That's a very bad idea. She's up for meeting you for a drink. That's not an invitation to turn up on her doorstep with a suitcase!'

'I'm not suggesting I move in with her, you eejit! But she might know somewhere. She's been there two or three years. She's bound to have friends or something who'd know of a vacant room.'

Charles looks doubtful. 'What sort of message does it send? Do you want her thinking you're a vagrant?'

'She knows I'm not a fucking vagrant, Charles! And apart from you, she's the only person in England who seems to give a shit about me and me welfare.'

'Why don't you come back to me for a few days? The couch is comfortable. Until you get settled?'

'No — thank you — but I've seen how tiny your place is, and that couch wouldn't sleep a child comfortably. I remember all the grousing when your dad was living with you, and he's not even five foot six. It'd be impossible. Anyway, the City's too far from the police station.' He waves the piece of paper. 'Come on, let's give it a go.'

Charles shrugs. 'On your head be it. I think she'll take one look at you and run a mile. Where're we going?'

Sloane checks the piece of paper. 'Colville Terrace.'

The character of the streets changes rapidly as they move further south. Life is lived on the streets here and the houses, once elegant homes for the nouvelle riche, have been divided and sub-divided for multiple occupation. No Irish round here; this is the heart of the north London West Indian community, and these streets saw the Notting Hill race riots. They cruise past walls daubed in white paint shouting "Blacks Go Home!" and then the offices of the White Defence League, whose wire-covered windows bear large posters: "Keep Britain White" and "The Evils of the Coloured Invasion".

'You sure this is right, Sean? Seems a strange place for a single white girl to live.'

'That's what she's written,' he replies, but he too sounds uncertain.

They arrive at the address, a four-storey terrace in bad need of a coat of paint, with half a dozen steel rubbish bins rusting at the front. Three young black men sit smoking on the steps leading to the front door, and another is leaning out of a first-floor window shouting to them over the sound of Caribbean music. Charles smells curry, and his stomach grumbles loudly. He missed lunch.

He casts a glance at Sloane. The policeman looks exhausted, and Charles isn't even sure he has the energy to climb out of the sports car. 'Stay here,' offers Charles. 'I'll make enquiries.'

As Charles gets out of the car, the three men on the steps fall silent and study him cautiously. He is acutely aware that he's still in his barristers' "uniform" of pinstriped trousers, black waistcoat and jacket, white shirt and tie. He sticks out like a sore thumb, especially as it's now early evening and the pavements are crowded with people, all black, returning from school and work. Charles finds himself the subject of some scrutiny. He waits for a small group to pass between the car and the steps and walks towards the men.

'I'm looking for a Dr Alexandrova. Does she live here?'

The faces of the three men are impassive and give nothing away. Charles hitches a thumb back towards the car. 'This is her friend. He's not well.'

Still nothing from the men. Then one of them, who'd been staring particularly hard at Charles's face, leans sideways to talk to one of his companions. He straightens up and points at Charles with his rollup.

'Me seen you.'

'You have?'

'On TV, las' year.'

'Maybe.'

'You dat brief, defen' dat queffa.'

'Possibly.'

He leans sideways again and gesticulates towards Charles even more vigorously, a smile creeping across his face. 'An' ain't you dat guy work for Neville Fylde?'

This is more surprising still. Neville Fylde is a successful Soho club owner and gang boss whom Charles encountered following Henrietta's murder. Successful enough now to be burnishing his credentials as a supporter of Caribbean good causes, he would be known to most people in the close-knit West Indian community. Charles's connection to him, on the other hand, was not widely publicised.

Charles smiles. 'He offered me a job, that's true. I didn't take it. So, Dr Alexandrova?'

The man shakes his head slowly. 'Never 'eard of her.'

Another answer comes from a second-storey window.

'Don't believe anything that kaffir tells you,' says a female voice. Charles looks up. It's the doctor.

'Don' lissen anyting dat commie Jew tell you!' retorts the man, looking up at her, and he and the others laugh uproariously.

Irenna calls down again. 'You'd better bring him up.'

CHAPTER 8

Charles carries Sloane's suitcase and follows him up the stairs. Every room they pass seems to be a bedroom crowded with several beds. The house smells of cooking, laundry, and unwashed bodies.

'Keep coming!' comes the doctor's voice from above.

They reach the second floor and a half-open door. Through the gap, Charles sees the doctor manically tidying her room.

Actually, she's not just tidying; she's hiding.

The room is a small tall-ceilinged bedsit. Two of the walls are lined with makeshift shelves constructed of wooden planks on brick piles, and they bow under the weight of files, papers and — and this intrigues Charles — law books. The doctor's in the act of tucking an envelope under her mattress.

She sees Charles looking in and kicks the door further closed. 'Keep going up, top landing.'

Sloane and Charles climb the remaining flight of steps and find themselves on a landing that leads to a box room and a loft hatch. The box room itself is inaccessible, full to bursting with unused furniture, but the space on the landing, illuminated via a grubby window overlooking the garden of the property, is equipped with a mismatched selection of dining chairs set around a threadbare rug.

Dr Alexandrova appears behind them, slightly out of breath. 'Sorry, but this is the only place to sit,' she explains. 'Every other space, except the bathroom, is a bedsit. What on earth are you doing here, Mr Sloane? I said a drink, not lifetime commitment.'

Sloane collapses onto one of the chairs. He doesn't look good.

'He's having a rough afternoon, and you were his last hope,' explains Charles. 'I told him it was a bad idea. May I ask: "Commie Jew?"'

'It's a joke,' she answers shortly, avoiding his gaze.

'Which bit, the "commie" or the "Jew"?'

Now she stares at him angrily. 'Do I know you, Mr…?'

'Holborne. Charles Holborne. We met at the hospital, remember?'

Charles sees recognition light in her eyes, but it doesn't dampen her displeasure. 'Who the fuck do you think you are? I'm not going to be cross-examined by a complete stranger.'

'He does that a lot,' says Sloane weakly, his eyes closed. 'You'll get used to it.'

'Sorry,' says Charles, appreciating his rudeness. He tries to explain. 'I was curious because the same accusation's been levelled at members of my family. At the time of my *bris*, I was "Charlie Horowitz", and several of my father's generation would've claimed Communist sympathies, even if they weren't card-carrying. They fought Mosley's Blackshirts in 1936.'

'Is that true?' she demands of Sloane, still suspicious.

'As far as I know, yes. Although what's a "bris"?'

'Circumcision,' say both Charles and the doctor in unison.

'I see.' She seems slightly mollified. 'Not that it's any of your business, but my parents were Lithuanian Jews who emigrated to South Africa in 1933. Now, what are you doing here?'

Charles explains what they've been doing for the last several hours. 'I think Sean just wondered if you might know anyone with a spare room,' he concludes. 'I've offered him the couch at mine, but it's not very comfortable.'

'And you don't know anyone else in London?' she demands of Sloane sceptically.

'No one I could ask.'

'That's difficult to believe.'

'It's another long story,' says Sloane.

'I wouldn't let you stay here even if there was room, which there isn't,' says the doctor simply. She shrugs. 'Sorry.'

Silence follows.

'I'm very sorry we've disturbed you then, doctor,' says Charles eventually. 'Come on, Sean. Fetter Lane it is.'

Sloane nods in acceptance. He takes several deep breaths as he summons the energy to stand. Dr Alexandrova intervenes. 'Hang on a second. There might be something … stay here.'

She jumps up and runs back down the stairs. They hear her light footsteps along each landing and down the following flight until they hit the concrete of the outside staircase.

'Jesus, what a fucking mess,' says Sloane. 'You think I've fucked it up completely with her?'

'One hundred percent. But, if you'll forgive me, that's the least of your problems. You look like shit, Sean. How do you feel?'

'Drunk, without any of the benefits.'

They wait ten minutes. Sloane has closed his eyes again, and his light breathing leads Charles to suspect that he's fallen asleep. Dr Alexandrova runs back up. Behind her is a young boy, about eleven years of age.

'This is Jaquan. He'll take you to another house, just round the corner, where we think there's an available room. Its usual occupant is away for a few weeks. If you can cover the rent he should be paying, the woman who runs the place may be okay with it. Her name is Kholwa. She doesn't speak much English, but Jaquan will explain to her.'

'Thank you,' says Sloane.

'It's okay. Looking at you now, I don't think you're faking; we should never have discharged you. So I'll give you the benefit of the doubt. But if this is some sort of weird stalking thing, Mr Sloane, you'll regret it, I promise.'

CHAPTER 9

The telephone rings in Charles's apartment on Fetter Lane. He's in the lounge, having arrived home seconds earlier with what was, fifteen minutes before, a hot salt beef sandwich collected from Blooms in Aldgate on the way back from court. He shrugs off his coat, reaches for the phone and, as he answers, leans round the wall into the kitchen to get a plate out of the single cupboard. He is famished, having again eaten nothing since breakfast. He jams the handset between shoulder and ear.

'Yes?' he says, retrieving a plate and one-handedly tipping the sandwich out of its paper bag onto it. 'Bugger!' he mutters, as the sandwich, over-filled as always, separates into its component parts of bread, mustard-covered beef and gherkin.

'Charles?'

'David? Sorry — just give me a second!'

Charles throws the handset down, takes the two steps required to reach the kitchen, and grabs a fork from the draining board.

He sits on the couch in the lounge, puts the plate on his lap, shovels a huge forkful of food into his mouth and picks up the phone. 'Ready,' he says indistinctly, mouth full.

'If this is your usual way of answering the phone,' laughs Charles's younger brother, 'it's no surprise you've no friends. You're disgusting!'

'Starving. Talk,' he orders.

'I'm in good health, thank you, Charles. Sonia? Yes, looking definitely pregnant now, but feeling very well indeed,' says David.

Charles swallows. 'I'm sorry. Shall I call you back?'

'No. Are you in court on Thursday eighteenth November?'

'No idea. I'd need to speak to Barbara.'

'I shall never understand how you guys allow other people to manage your diaries. I'd hate being sent to all parts of the country because some spotty teenage clerk told me to.'

'Tradition. That's how it's been done for the last four hundred years, and that's how it'll continue. If I started trying to manage my own diary, or mentioned in passing that I no longer fancied the journey to Taunton Assizes, I'd be asked to leave Chambers.'

'You're serious aren't you?'

There's a pause while Charles swallows. 'Completely. What's with eighteenth November?'

'Mum has an appointment at the hospital, and I don't think dad should drive her. He won't admit it, but he can barely see. And I'm at an audit in Manchester.'

'Can't they take the tube?'

'Yes, and I suggested it. It's a couple of stops and a bit of a walk, but dad was oddly resistant.'

Charles pauses while he bolts down the last of his sandwich. 'I'll ask Barbara tomorrow and get back to you. But Mum won't be able to get in or out of my car.'

'I've thought of that. You can borrow mine. I'm going to Manchester by train. If you can do it, I'll drop the spare keys off at Fetter Lane for you and you can collect it from outside ours. You're on the insurance.'

'Fine, I'll do it as long as I'm not already in court, but I'm sorry, David, I've got to go. I've got about twenty minutes to shower, change and get to Belgravia.'

'Oh! Is it tonight?'

'Yes.'

'Good luck.'

'Thanks. Speak soon.'

'Well, well, well! If it ain't that well-known thief, thug and barrister wanker, Charlie Horowitz!'

This is Charles's greeting from Paddy Kennedy, the landlord of *The Star Tavern* in Belgravia. To be singled out by Kennedy for abuse is a mark of respect; he swears like a sailor at all his favourite celebrity customers. It has become one of the unique characteristics of his establishment, adding to its glamour. For some years *The Star's* been frequented by members of the *haute monde*, TV and film celebrities and professional criminals. Indeed, as he entered the bar, Charles recognised Peter O'Toole drinking with two other men at a corner table. Charles knew before the police that the pub was being used for meetings between Bruce Reynolds, Gordon Goody and Buster Edwards to plan the Great Train Robbery; he'd seen them there, although at the time he'd no idea what they were plotting. Celebrities love to rub shoulders with daring men of violence, as evidenced by the success of the Krays' establishments.

Charles has chosen this venue because there's slim chance of bumping into other members of the legal profession, but it's no more than twenty minutes from the Temple. He doesn't know if Sally will come direct from her chambers, but the early hour, half past six, suggests that she will.

'You missed out war hero,' complains Charles as he approaches the bar.

'Wanker,' repeats Kennedy, with a smile, by way of punctuation. 'What'll it be?'

'I need a large whisky and a quiet table please, Paddy. Tricky meeting.'

Kennedy nods to his left. 'Take the one by the window. I'll bring your drink over.'

Charles leaves a pound note on the bar and walks to the table, draping his wet raincoat over the back of his chair.

He's deliberately arrived early, anxious not to keep Sally waiting. He wants to be calm and prepared by the time she enters, and he needs the drink to steady his nerves. Because he *is* nervous, more so than he'd admit.

Sally and Charles's relationship has been ... complex. Sally was originally the junior clerk in Charles's former chambers. She'd always liked Charles — he was, after all, an East Ender like herself and had none of the airs and graces of his colleagues — and he was charming and brilliant (not to mention gorgeous). Like everyone else in Chambers, she watched the slow disintegration of his marriage to Henrietta, the daughter of the head of chambers. Then Sally and the world's media were witness to him being accused of Henrietta's murder and his run from the police as he battled to find evidence to clear his name.

A year later, contrary all expectations, Charles and Sally's unspoken passion for one another was consummated and after a few torrid months they moved in together — which merely poured petrol on the media flames all over again.

It just isn't done for a barrister to have a relationship with a clerk, especially one in his own chambers and especially when the barrister in question is already far too prominent for all the wrong reasons, like a "colourful" East End past and an uncertain relationship with the Kray twins.

The taboo against barrister/clerk relationships is supposedly justified to keep professional jealousy within chambers to a minimum. Barristers are intensely interested in how briefs are allocated amongst them, and any suggestion of favouritism by the clerks causes resentment and conflict. Indeed, the actual or perceived favouring of a certain barrister or barristers is a frequent cause of chambers splits.

In Charles's opinion, the rule against "walking out" with one's clerk is less to do with professionalism than with snobbery. Barristers, almost exclusively privately-educated Oxbridge graduates with money, tend to treat their clerks as paid servants. The purpose of a clerk is to liaise with the source of the barristers' work, namely solicitors, book cases in the diary and deal with the grubby business of negotiating and taking fees. Many are additionally used as personal servants, collecting their guvnors' dry-cleaning, organising their social life and hiding their indiscretions. A clerk is a common functionary whose existence allows barristers to inhabit a higher plane of ivory tower intellectualism and hypocrisy; they're certainly not suitable as life partners.

Charles doesn't share the snobbery but, to his shame, he can't hand on heart say it played no part in the failure of his relationship with Sally. Constantly the odd man out in the Temple and the subject of gossip and scandal, in the back of his mind always lurked the worry that a public relationship with her would make things worse. And then there were his parents, particularly his mother. Millie Horowitz actually liked Sally, but that didn't make Sally, a non-Jewish *shiksa*, a suitable mate for the Horowitz firstborn.

So these were the factors, together with Charles's pathological inability to trust anyone, which finally combined to leave Sally with no option. She walked out. Charles protested that he still loved her — and she believed him — but it wasn't enough. The big house in Hampstead, where they lived together for just a few short months, was sold again and

Charles moved back to his bachelor flat on Fetter Lane. Neither he nor Sally was happy.

Nine months and two short-lived transitional relationships later, Sally is still at home with her mother, and finds herself increasingly susceptible to Charles's rather sweet and courtly re-wooing, conducted in correspondence. Charles insists he can change and she wants to believe him. She misses him. Tonight, for the first time since they parted, she's agreed to meet him for a drink, somewhere away from the Temple and its prying eyes.

Charles's letters have been deliberately light and jocular, and she has come to look forward to them. He tells her the highlights of his working day, the current state of his relationship with his parents, about which he can be hilarious, and interesting anecdotes from the Temple that he knows she'll appreciate. He tries hard to avoid sentimentality or the slightest suggestion of tenderness lest it frightens her off. The letters are his only way of maintaining contact with her while she refuses to see him; he hopes he's reminding her how he can make her laugh and that, once, she felt safe with him.

He has no idea if he's hit the mark. At first her agreement to meet him seemed encouraging, but then David pointed out gently that Sally's purpose might merely be to let him down, finally, face-to-face. That, Charles admits to himself, is also a perfectly plausible explanation; he knows he has to overcome both the pain he caused her and her mother's natural protectiveness. Nell Fisher liked Charles but thought him too old and too notorious for her daughter.

Every time the pub door opens Charles looks up, his heart quickening, but time slips by in interminable five-minute chunks and by five to seven he's convinced she isn't coming. The pub is filling up now. Kennedy has to date, mercifully, resisted his regulars' pressure to install a jukebox, so there's no loud music, but conversations are becoming more intrusive and Charles begins to worry that this isn't the quiet and reflective venue he'd planned.

Finally, at a minute to seven, the door opens again and Sally enters. She's still in her work clothes, a formal two piece dark suit with a shortish skirt and a cream-coloured blouse, her coat carried over one arm. The outfit accentuates her tulip figure. Although only slightly more than five feet tall and with a face younger than her years, Sally is voluptuous. Charles notices that she is wearing the pearl necklace that he gave her, and he wonders if anything can be read into that fact.

She sees Charles immediately. 'Hello, Charles,' she says cautiously, pulling out a seat. He notes the "Charles" when, at their most intimate, he was always "Charlie", but at least it's not "Mr Holborne" or, worse still, "Sir".

'Hello. Thanks for coming. What can I get you?'

'I'll have a glass of white wine, please,' she says, manoeuvring her large work bag, from which Charles can see files protruding, under the table. So, she has definitely come straight from the Temple. But she smells good and her make-up has been refreshed. Charles studies her face before standing. There is nervousness around her eyes, but the fact that she seems to have made an effort to look attractive may be a good sign.

Maybe reminding me what I'll be missing when she shuts the door for good.

He returns with her wine and another large scotch for himself. She takes a sip, puts the glass down and speaks without looking up at him.

'What do you want, Charles?'

'I want to start seeing you again.'

'To what purpose?' Now she looks up and stares him in the face, challenging. 'I'm not going back to the way we were.'

Hope flares in his chest.

But you could go forward, with something different, maybe?

'I know that. I ... I won't make you easy promises. I know I have to change. But I want to, and with your help I believe I can. I miss you so much and ... I still love you. All I'm asking is that you trust me enough to take a first step.'

Sally looks into Charles's large dark brown eyes framed by their long, almost feminine, lashes. They seem to be glistening with tears, but perhaps it's just the smoky environment. Her expression softens a little. 'Well, that's honest at least.'

'Haven't you missed me, even a little?' he asks, and notes with frustration the appeal he can't entirely keep from his voice.

'That's not really the point, is it? As I said when I left, you need to grow up. I didn't think then you could do it, and I've no reason to assume you've changed so fundamentally. In the space of a few months.'

'I've done a lot of thinking, Sal,' he replies, fiddling with his glass. 'I see that I didn't treat you well. I put you in a box to be taken out when I wanted —'

'— Even when we were living together!' she interrupts, anger colouring her voice for the first time. 'Even when you were there, you...' she shrugs, 'you weren't.'

'I know, I know! I didn't let you in, not properly. But I want to be better, and surely that's a start? And with your help...?' he tails off. 'You thought you could see a life with me, didn't you? That's why we bought the place in Hampstead. I won't pretend some Damascene conversion, but what I *will* say is I've never felt like this for anyone, I trust you in a way that I've never trusted anyone, and if anyone can help me open up and become … better … I think it's you.'

'You hurt me,' she says quietly.

Charles hangs his head. 'Yes.'

'I walked out, but the truth is *you* dumped *me*. That's how it felt. That woman…'

'Nothing happened with her while you and I were still together,' he insists.

'Nothing physical, maybe. But you were more "with her" than you were with me.'

'That's not really true, Sally. I was attracted to her, yes, but I did and said nothing to encourage her. She chased me.'

Sally waves her hand as if swatting away a fly. 'It doesn't matter now, does it? Whether you had your head turned by her or not, it wouldn't have happened if you'd been committed to me … to us … to our new home … to our future! Your absence from the relationship, that's what caused it.'

Red spots have appeared on her creamy cheeks and her eyes flash, and for the first time she looks really angry. Charles reminds himself that this is the first time she's had the opportunity to express her sense of betrayal directly to him. He can't complain; it's his duty to hear and bear it.

'Yes. I do see that. I'm ashamed of the way I behaved. I let you down.'

Sally takes several deep breaths, calming herself. 'Yes, you did,' she says finally.

She reaches down to her bag and Charles thinks for an instant that she is getting something out of it, but no, she is dragging it out and getting ready to leave. She stands, places the bag on her chair and slips on her coat. Charles remains seated.

'You're going?'

'I have to get back to mum.'

Sally's mother is an invalid and Sally is primarily responsible for her care.

'Stay and finish your drink. Please.'

She shakes her head firmly. 'No. I'm sorry but … I think this was a mistake. I'm still too angry with you.'

'Can I see you again?' he asks.

She looks down on his curls, noticing a few more stray white hairs in the black than she remembers and, despite his Mediterranean skin tone, he looks pale. He looks like a lost boy.

'I put so much hope into us, Charlie.' She shrugs. 'I don't know yet. We'll see.'

He notes the "Charlie" and a trace of the former tenderness in her voice. 'Can I call you?' he asks.

She shakes her head. 'No.' She lifts her bag and turns to leave. A pace closer to the door, she turns to him again. 'But I like the letters, so you can carry on writing. If you want.'

And with that, she slips out onto the evening street and is gone.

CHAPTER 10

Another doomed pub. Another clandestine meeting.

Two middle-aged men sit in silence in the upstairs room at *The Black Friar* in Queen Victoria Street, London. Pub noises drift up the stairs from the bar below. There is talk of the Grade II listed building, built on the site of a former Dominican monastery, being demolished when Ludgate Circus and the pub's eponymous mainline station are redeveloped. As far as DI Greene is concerned, it can't come soon enough. The place is a dump, its former glories long behind it. But this upstairs room, full of old barstools, dusty optics and upturned tables has at least provided a discreet meeting place for the last couple of years, and it may not be easy to find somewhere so convenient.

The man sitting opposite Greene is also employed by the Metropolitan Police Commissioner at C8, otherwise known as The Flying Squad or, as they are actually referred to on the streets of London, "The Sweeney". That man, Detective Superintendent Cathcart, is technically Greene's superior officer. He looks superior in every way. Tall and handsome, with dark hair and distinguished grey sideburns, Cathcart has the bearing of a leader of men, which is what he was during the war.

However, appearances can be deceptive. Over the last couple of years there has occurred a subtle shift in the relationship between the two men. In their day-to-day professional dealings, it is Cathcart who gives the orders and Greene who carries them out. Here, as they sit drinking and waiting patiently in the half-darkened room, both are aware that it is Greene who calls the shots.

The situation has long made Cathcart uncomfortable. He has tried to pinpoint how and when the power balance shifted away from him; perhaps when he allowed greed to overcome his common sense and he started accepting the odd payment, the odd very large payment, from his subordinate to look away; perhaps when he and Dot began accepting Greene's invitation to his and Vanessa's home on the Costa del Sol, all expenses paid. Then of course there was the new car. No matter; whatever marked the genesis of this change of roles, it is now established and undeniable, and this meeting will mark a significant further step on Cathcart's increasingly steep, slippery slope. The stakes have suddenly doubled, and the Superintendent has to go along with Greene and up the ante or fold, with unknowable consequences.

Cathcart closes the file he's been reading. 'It's not working, is it?'

'Doesn't look like it, no. He's been to the goods yard and the BTP at Waterloo.'

'I thought he was signed off.'

'He is. He's doing it on his own time, and against his inspector's orders.'

'Has anyone talked?'

'I don't think so.'

Cathcart sighs. 'Have you offered him money?'

'It's been tried before.'

'And?'

'He's a boy scout. That's why he was moved out of Vice.'

Cathcart pauses for thought. 'What about having a word with his Chief Super, what's his name...?'

'Ackroyd. I can try, but I wouldn't put money on it. He's not what you'd call authoritative, is he?'

'Oh, not Frank Ackroyd?'

'Yes.'

Cathcart laughs shortly. 'We used to call him Macavity: *"He always has an alibi and one or two to spare,"* he quotes. 'That man's made a career of making sure he was never there when anything happened. Let's leave that as a last resort. See if you can come up with something else. But we've got to get this Mick…'

'Sloane. Sean Sloane.'

'We've got to get him to stop.'

'You don't have to tell me.'

Silence falls. After a few further minutes, Cathcart looks at his watch. 'You confident Billy's coming?'

Greene nods. 'He'll be here.'

Barely have the words left his mouth when there's a quiet knock on the door, two taps, one tap, two taps. Greene rises, strides silently to the door and opens it a crack.

'Evening, Billy,' he says, opening the door fully.

Billy Gervaise enters the room. He wears his trademark trilby hat, which he removes, and the camelhair overcoat. He starts when he sees that Greene is not alone.

'Evening, Mr Cathcart. Didn't know you was gonna be 'ere.'

Gervaise's Cockney voice is harsh and loud; an advantage when you're Warrant Officer Gervaise of the RAF, thinks Greene.

'Like I said on the blower, Billy,' says Greene, 'things are getting out of hand. Mr Cathcart's insisted on being here. He's in charge now.' He shrugs, as if he'd like things to be different, but they're out of his hands.

'Take a seat, Mr Gervaise,' says Cathcart. 'Do you want to get a drink before we start?'

'No, I'm fine, thank you, Superintendent.' Gervaise lifts a third chair from a pile and joins the two police officers at their table.

Cathcart stares at Gervaise for a long time. 'You've been very sloppy, Billy. Very sloppy.' Gervaise makes to speak, but Cathcart interrupts him. 'All of a sudden, everyone's asking about you.'

Gervaise shakes his head and smiles confidently. 'It's all under control now, Mr Cathcart. I guarantee it.'

'Just explain to me how everything's under control. Corpses don't go unnoticed.' The superintendent picks up the Manila folder from the table, opens it, and flicks through several documents. 'The RAF, British Transport Police and now S Division — all sniffing about. I've got reports from Cardington to Cricklewood, Cricklewood to the East End. It's a total fucking shambles, Billy!'

Greene intervenes. 'You've pushed it too far, Billy. There's a limit to what we can do.'

'And you've reached it,' finishes Cathcart, throwing the file onto the table in front of Gervaise.

For the first time Gervaise's calm demeanour looks a little frayed. He looks from one police officer to the other. 'Look, gents, on me oath, it'll all be tidied away in the next couple of days. The RAF sergeant's now sorted, courtesy of my young Sprout-eater.'

'What?'

'Sprout-eater. It's what they call people up in Bedfordshire.' Gervaise shrugs. 'I guess they grow lots of sprouts up there or something. And the Bedfordshire traffic copper who investigated, well, he's squared away. He's gonna say common or garden road crash, so the inquest'll be a formality. There's only one remaining loose end, and I'm taking care of that personally.'

'It's not just one loose end,' says Cathcart. 'There are three separate investigations! How's it going to look if the Met just ignores it?'

'We can't just pull their files, Billy,' explains Greene. 'We've no jurisdiction over 'em. There must be half a dozen other people to sort. Probably more.'

Gervaise is about to answer, but then stops suddenly. He detects the glimmer of a possible solution in Greene's response. 'So it's a question of money, then?'

'Absolutely not,' says Cathcart, but there's something about the silence that follows that strengthens Gervaise's suspicion.

'Money always helps, you know that, Billy —' starts Greene apologetically.

'Out of the question,' intervenes Cathcart. 'Too many people involved, too many separate investigations.'

'You can forget the inquest,' repeats Gervaise. 'An' I've already paid off the SIB at Cardington, so their investigation's mothballed. The BTP Sergeant, Hawkins, is on the inside. He'll keep *schtum*, I guarantee it, though I don't suppose it'd hurt were you to give him a little reminder. That just leaves the Met, specifically that Irishman at West Hendon.'

'And his inspector. And his Chief Super. There's got to be at least two, maybe three people at S Division.'

Gervaise spots his opportunity. 'The money ain't an issue, gentlemen. Whatever you need. You know how much I appreciate your … discretion. And, without putting too fine a point on it, if we shut down, your regular payments'll stop.'

Greene suddenly leaps to his feet, hauls Gervaise towards him by his collar with his left hand and hits him hard around the face with his right. Gervaise and his chair go over, his head and back thudding heavily onto the bare floorboards. Greene stands over him, fists raised, snorting like a dragon. 'Is that a threat, you weasel?' he shouts. 'Are you threatening us?'

A kick lands in the region of Gervaise's left kidney followed by another to his thigh.

From the floor Gervaise studies Greene's red face, wild eyes and the spittle flying from his lips. He can't work out if this is simulated for Cathcart's benefit or if it's genuine. Using his facial expression he tries to convey that Greene should take it a bit easy, but the DI is still ranting. 'We've got enough on you to send you away for the rest of, and no parole. Fraud, blackmail, theft, conspiracy and now murder!' Another kick, this time to his buttock.

'I know! I know! I'm sorry!'

'Unless you want a ton of that crap descending on your head, you little worm, you'll keep up your end of the bargain!'

'Please stop, Mr Greene!'

'Now, now DI Greene,' placates Cathcart. 'We need cool heads here if we're to find a solution.'

Another kick lands on Gervaise's thigh, but Greene seems to have lost interest and the blow is more cursory than vicious.

'I meant no offence, gents!' says Gervaise from the floor. 'I thought I was just pointing out the obvious. What if … what if I had a name or two, to sweeten it?'

There is a moment of stillness in the room as Cathcart and Greene share a glance.

'Names?' says Cathcart. He stands and intervenes between Greene and the man on the floor, pulling Gervaise upright.

Gervaise dusts himself down, moving stiffly. 'I could give you three … no! four of the team who robbed Barclay's Bank in Tottenham. Remember, last September? In fact, now I think about it, one of them has a slaughter full of stuff you might like to … recover.'

'Where is this lock-up?' asks Cathcart.

'Limehouse. Some very tasty antique clocks, Persian rugs and so on, stolen from a house in Mayfair. Worth a fortune.'

'Well, I'm sure the owners would like their property restored…'

'Are you sure about this, boss?' asks Greene.

'If Mr Gervaise says he has the Bedford end under control, perhaps we can deal with S Division for him. A few good arrests on other jobs will divert attention.'

'But it'll cost at least twenty grand to make something like this go away,' says Greene. 'The Met don't come cheap nowadays.'

Now they're talking money, Gervaise relaxes a little.

'That's a very big further investment, sir,' continues Greene calmly. His fury has completely dissipated; now he sounds like a broker warning his client against a risky business venture.

Cathcart shrugs, as if complaining about the cost of living is a waste of time.

Gervaise takes a deep breath and forces a smile to his sore face. 'Not a problem.'

'Good. Shall we say, within a week?' says Cathcart, standing and bringing the meeting to an end.

Greene casts a sly look at Gervaise, and winks.

CHAPTER 11

Charles occupies a window table in the cafe on the corner of St Paul's Square in Bedford. In view of the poor rail service on the last occasion, he decided to take an early train. If he arrived early, he'd have time for breakfast near the courthouse.

He uses his last piece of buttered toast to mop up egg yolk and tomato sauce from his plate and sits back, happy. He has to ration his beloved fry-ups nowadays. Last year, when training for his last fight, he could have a daily plateful of eggs, bacon, mushrooms, sausages, beans and, where offered, fried bread, without a second thought. Now he has to be more careful. He continues to run and work out regularly at the sweaty little gym at Elephant and Castle and there is still little fat on him, but he's noted that he's having to release his belt-buckle a notch nowadays.

He peers through the steamy windows, keeping an eye on the steps leading to the courthouse on the far side of the square. Mick Jagger complains from the transistor radio on a shelf behind the counter that he can't get no satisfaction. Can't get *any*, Charles corrects silently. Notwithstanding the grammar, the Stones' new release is growing on him.

Barbara arranged this pre-hearing conference and it was Jean Maynard who suggested the cafe, away from the courthouse but close enough to walk in a couple of minutes, but Charles is not entirely sure he's in the right place. Mrs Maynard is now ten minutes late.

The bell above the door jangles and the front end of a pram appears through the door, followed by Mrs Maynard pushing it and, behind her, her friend Angie. Angie spots Charles away to their right and waves. She's a good friend, thinks Charles, having agreed to come and support Mrs Maynard throughout the inquest and care for the baby when Mrs Maynard's actually in court.

The two young women queue at the counter and order tea. Mrs Maynard gesticulates to Charles to ask if he would like a top-up, and he shakes his head. Angie pushes the pram along the narrow aisle between the tables, Mrs Maynard following with a mug of steaming tea in each hand.

'Hello, Mr Holborne,' says Angie, arranging the pram so it won't be in anyone's way and sitting down. She lights up immediately.

'Call me Charles,' he instructs, declining a cigarette.

'Hi,' says Mrs Maynard, and she too sits. She wears a dark suit which, Charles guesses, had its last outing at her husband's funeral.

Charles studies her face. It's taut and pale with lack of sleep and apprehension. He leans forward, trying to keep his voice down, but is forced to speak more loudly than he'd like due to the noise from the kitchen and the hiss of steam from the water boiler behind the counter.

'Any joy with the local newspaper?' he asks.

Angie shakes her head. 'I phoned several times. Their news desk said they'd get someone to call back, but no one ever did.'

'That's a shame,' says Charles. 'Well, my clerk's made enquiries and ours is the only case on the list at present. That doesn't mean something else can't be slipped in at the last minute, but I think we're pretty sure to start prompt at ten. As I explained, it's the coroner who calls the witnesses, in whatever order he likes, and he who asks them whatever questions he wants. It's the only court in the country where the judge is in charge of the investigation. He'll usually allow the family to ask questions, but he doesn't have to.'

'What if he doesn't?' asks Angie.

'That'll depend on how bad it is and what questions he blocks. In an extreme case the Divisional Court could say he's overstepped the mark, but let's not worry about that now. As long as we keep him interested, make him wonder about the answers to the questions we're asking, the more chance we have of getting a bit of leeway.'

'Go on,' Angie says to Mrs Maynard, 'show him.'

Mrs Maynard searches in her handbag and comes up with an envelope. She hands it to Charles. 'This come through the letterbox yesterday.'

Charles turns the envelope over in his hands. It's unmarked and unstamped. 'Do you know who delivered it?'

Mrs Maynard shakes her head.

Charles opens the ungummed envelope and pulls out two typed sheets of paper. He starts to read and then whistles softly. 'Wow,' he says quietly. He leans even closer to Mrs Maynard and Angie, who follow suit. 'Do you know what this is?' Mrs Maynard frowns, uncertain, but Angie nods tentatively. 'It's part of an RAF Special Investigation Branch file,' explains Charles. 'These are two pages taken from draft witness statements. Why haven't we heard about this investigation? There must be a complete file somewhere. And I can't believe SIB are unaware of the inquest.'

'Do you think someone's got at them?' asks Angie.

Charles considers the question. 'I suppose that depends on how much money's involved. Do you have any idea where this might have come from?'

'I did wonder if it was maybe Boycey. Or possibly Heather.'

Charles resumes reading. 'Look at this!' he says, pointing. 'They examined your husband's bike. "There was no evidence that any of the four principal bolts failed by sheering or deformation. The last inch of thread on each was shiny and clean…"' Charles turns over the page, but the passage ends in mid-sentence and the next page deals with something else. 'Is this all there was?'

'Yes. Is it any use, as it's only a bit of the evidence?'

'Definitely. We may not have the report's conclusion, but it's unlikely there was a mechanical failure with the sidecar breaking away from the motorcycle. The bolts were intact and had clean ends. If they'd worked loose over a period of time, they'd have been dirty from road grit, engine oil and so on. The clean ends suggest they were loosened deliberately. Let me read the rest.'

He does so.

'This is even more helpful.'

'Why?' asks Mrs Maynard.

'They examined the front brake cable. "The cable was in two parts, having been divided approximately 3 inches from the brake end. Generally the cable showed no signs of wear and was neither frayed nor corroded. I examined the cable at the point where it is divided under a microscope. Approximately half of the individual strands making up the cable were stretched and could be seen to have suffered from heat deformation. The other half of the strands however had no such signs but had been cut through. I have seen motorcycle front brake cables which have been severed in the course of an impact, but in such cases all the strands will show evidence of stress immediately before breaking. In this case, half of the sheath and the strands appeared to have been cut prior to the final braking manoeuvre. The incision into the sheath was

100

narrow and not frayed, which suggests a tool such as wire cutters or perhaps tin snips, rather than a hacksaw." Blimey, Mrs Maynard!' whispers Charles, astonished. 'I think you're right. I think someone interfered with the bike!'

Jean Maynard starts to weep. She tries to control herself, but tears sprout from her eyes and course down her cheeks. Angie digs into her handbag and finds a tissue, which she hands over. Charles reaches over and pats her hand.

'I thought…' she sobs, 'I thought … I was going mad. I knew it was all wrong, but I couldn't actually believe it.'

'Does this change anything, Charles? Tactics and so on?' asks Angie.

'No, not at all.' He pauses, lost in thought. 'It's just a shame we can't get these Xeroxed. I'd like a copy to show the coroner, and maybe the witnesses.'

Angie stands and starts fishing around inside the baby carriage. Her hand emerges with another envelope. 'Me brother-in-law's got one of them new machines at his office in Northampton. We thought them pages was so important, we didn't want to risk losing the only copies.' She hands across the other envelope. 'There's two copies of each page.' She smiles and resumes her seat.

'Angie, you'd make a bloody good solicitor's clerk!' exclaims Charles, surprised and very pleased.

She waves away the compliment, but blushes.

'Have you finished your tea?' he asks. 'You should be getting across the road.'

The Shire Hall, Bedford, a typical redbrick Victorian building with a green tiled roof, is a surprisingly imposing structure to house a small county town's magistrates' and county courts. The archivolts of the entrance are unusually detailed for a court building, lending it the appearance of a Victorian church.

He deliberately allows the two young women to precede him up the steps, struggling somewhat with the pram, and watches as they are greeted by a man with a clipboard in the entrance lobby. In common with most coroners' officers, the man's bearing marks him out unmistakably as a former police officer.

Coroners fall into two categories: those who are legally qualified, usually solicitors or barristers, and those who are medically qualified. Both tend to employ former police officers as their coroner's officer, someone with a basic understanding of the law and evidence, capable of obtaining and collating statements and other evidence at the coroner's direction.

Charles watches as the coroner's officer directs Mrs Maynard and Angie up some further stairs towards the courts. He knows Mrs Maynard will be asked if she's to be represented, and he's instructed her to say that she's taken some advice but can't afford to pay for legal representation; the truth, but not quite the whole truth.

Charles keeps watch on the entrance to the court, but over the next fifteen minutes only one other person enters, a police officer in the uniform of the Bedfordshire Constabulary. At five to ten, Charles enters the court building himself. The lobby is now deserted. The list, pinned inside a cabinet on the wood panelling, informs him that there is indeed only one case for the day, that of Julian Maynard, to be heard in Court 1. Charles opens the swing doors and slips inside.

The coroner is yet to enter. Sitting with his back to Charles is the police officer he saw enter court, a constable in uniform. A file sits on the bench before him. Mrs Maynard sits a few yards away on the same bench, to his right. Charles can't see Angie, the pram or the baby, and assumes they've been allocated a side room. The coroner's officer is at a desk between counsel's benches and the bench for the coroner, above which hangs the

Royal Coat of Arms. Otherwise, the court is entirely empty; no members of the public, no one from the local newspaper.

This case has been buried almost as quickly as the deceased.

As Charles proceeds down the aisle between the two banks of benches, the coroner's officer looks up. He stands and approaches.

'Are you in the right place?' he asks.

His expression is polite, inquiring, as if Charles had wandered into the coroner's court by accident and needed to be redirected elsewhere.

'Yes, I think so.' Charles nods towards Jean Maynard. 'Mrs Maynard asked me for some unofficial advice in relation to her husband's death, and I find myself at a loose end, so I've come along as her representative.'

'And you are?'

'Charles Holborne, of counsel.'

The introduction does not seem to faze the coroner's officer. He smiles and says: 'Your client's there, sir. Do you need time to take instructions?'

'No, thank you very much. But if you have any documents or reports you could let me see, I'd be very grateful. It will certainly save time.'

'I'll need to ask the coroner, sir, but give me a moment.' He disappears out of the court.

Charles turns and enters the bench where Mrs Maynard is sitting.

The police officer observes him carefully. He leans across. 'Are you acting for the family?'

'Yes,' replies Charles shortly.

The coroner's officer returns and approaches Charles's bench. 'Mr Cook says he's not prepared to release documents at this stage. He will call the witness and let you cross examine if necessary. But he'll keep his decision under review. Okay?'

'Just one witness?'

'Yes,' replies the coroner's officer.

He returns to the door from which he entered and left the courtroom. There's a knock on the door.

'All rise!' he calls, and the coroner enters. At the same moment there is movement behind Charles, and he turns to see two men slipping into court, both in RAF uniform.

There we are. The top brass, right on time, to make sure the RAF's reputation is untarnished.

Charles turns to face the bench. He has no experience of Mr Cook, a small slight man in his sixties wearing a grey three-piece suit and wire-rimmed spectacles. The coroner takes his seat.

'Thank you, Mr Noble,' he says to the coroner's officer. 'Would you like to announce the case and give a brief summary of the events to date?'

As Noble starts to speak, the door bangs again and Charles sees another man, a gangling youngster who looks little more than a teenager, slipping into court and taking a seat at the back. He carries a notepad.

Local press?

'This is the inquest into the death of Mr Julian Maynard, a sergeant in the RAF, based at Cardington, date of birth 27 September 1925, who met his death on ninth October this year at the junction of the A600 and Harrowden Lane, Bedfordshire,' says the coroner's officer, reading from a prepared note. 'Following identification of the body by Mrs Maynard, you opened the inquest on fifteenth October, sir, and adjourned it to today for further enquiries to be made.

'A short summary of the evidence as it appeared is that Sergeant Maynard was travelling on an RAF motorcycle and sidecar at twenty-one twenty-five hours when he approached the bend in Harrowden Lane from an easterly direction. At the site of the farm the road describes an S-bend, and at some point along that bend it appears that the motorcycle and sidecar parted company. The deceased's motorcycle continued for some distance before colliding with the stone wall of a barn. The deceased was pronounced dead at the scene by the ambulance service and the body was taken to Bedford Hospital for examination. A post-mortem examination was carried out on eleventh October, and the report of Dr Patel is before you. Toxicological analysis revealed no alcohol or drugs in the deceased's blood, and no health issues thought to be relevant. The deceased died from a broken neck received in the collision.' The coroner's officer resumes his seat.

'Thank you, Mr Noble. Right,' says Mr Cook. 'I think we have PC Malone?'

The police officer stands. 'Yes, sir.'

'Come forward and give the oath, please.'

The constable does so, taking the Bible offered to him by Mr Noble, and reading the oath from the card. He does not appear very familiar with the process of giving evidence, because he immediately sits down in the witness box without identifying himself.

'Please can you give us your name, rank and posting, constable? And then remain standing.'

PC Malone does as requested.

'Thank you,' says the coroner. 'Now, were you responsible for investigating this road traffic accident?'

'Yes sir, I was.' His voice is slightly tremulous.

Why're you so nervous, constable? First time in court? Or something else?

'And?' prompts the coroner.

'Oh, yes. I made some notes, sir. May I use them?'

'Do the notes refer to matters that you did yourself, and were fresh in your memory when you made the notes?'

Ah, good. Cook's a lawyer.

'Er, yes.'

'Well then, you may look at your notes.'

The young constable looks down and starts to read from the notes without looking up.

'I was called to the scene of the accident on ninth October this year following a telephone call made by a member of the public. After a search, I found the body of a middle-aged male in RAF uniform in the bushes growing between the road verge and the wall of the barn. His motorcycle, a BSA B40, manufactured in 1961, was lying on its side next to him. The front forks were almost destroyed, and there were bits of brick and brick dust around them, which led me to assume that the motorcycle had collided with the wall.'

'Was Sergeant Maynard wearing a helmet?'

'No, sir. During the course of the investigation I searched the area of the collision and could find no helmet, so I concluded that he was not wearing one.'

'Thank you, please continue.'

'I called for support from HQ at Goldington Road and cordoned off the road. When my colleagues arrived with lights, I was able to look for marks left on the road surface.'

'What marks did you find?'

'Well, sir, there were very few. It had been dry for twenty-four hours, so we'd expect to find skid marks left by the tyres on the tarmac, caused by emergency braking. In this case there were no such marks. There was a light scuff mark which I subsequently matched to the deceased's left boot heel. The motorcycle had severe scratching on its left side which matched scoring marks on the road surface, so I concluded that it hit the ground on that side and continued sliding towards the wall. I believe the deceased tried to slow down or regain some control by using his left foot on the road surface. But there were definitely no skid marks from tyres.'

'What conclusions did you draw from that absence?' asks the coroner.

'Well, firstly that for some reason the deceased didn't use his brakes or, if he did, they didn't operate. Secondly, that he would have hit that wall with significant force. That is corroborated by the damage to the front of the bike, which was compressed into a half its normal length.'

'Very well. Did you take the bike away for further examination?'

'Yes, sir. I conducted a full examination of both the bike and the sidecar. There are usually four principal bolts connecting them, but I could find only two. The other two bolt holes were empty and full of dirt. I reached the conclusion that the bolts had been working themselves loose for a long time, two of them had already been lost, and shortly before the accident the remaining two separated from the sidecar.'

'And the brakes? Did you examine the brakes?'

'Yes, but it was difficult to draw any conclusions because the front brake assembly was completely destroyed in the collision.'

'So your conclusions as to how this accident occurred?'

'I think the bike was poorly maintained and when Sergeant Maynard came to this bend, probably at too great a speed, the sidecar detached itself and he lost balance. He tried to brake in time before hitting the wall but was unable to do so.'

Jean Maynard gasps at this evidence and is about to speak out before Charles places his hand gently over hers. The coroner continues making notes of the evidence for a few moments. 'Yes, thank you officer. Now, it's Mr Holborne isn't it?'

Charles stands. 'Yes, sir.'

'And you're a member of counsel here on behalf of Mrs Maynard and the deceased's family?'

'Yes.'

'Are you formally instructed?'

'I am. I act pro bono but I have accepted instructions to represent the family.'

'Very well. Would you like to ask any questions of this officer?'

'If you please, sir.'

'Off you go then.'

Charles turns to address the young constable. 'I notice, PC Malone, that you are reading from your notebook. May I see it, please?'

The officer holds it out and the coroner's officer takes it to Charles.

'Thank you, Mr Noble,' says Charles. 'Now, PC Malone, did you make these notes at the time of the incident?'

'Yes.'

'I note they appear to be very clean. Pristine, in fact. I'd have expected dirt or oil marks if these had been made up, in the dark, at the roadside.'

'Er, well, I made some notes of my findings on various bits of paper, but they were a bit scruffy so I re-wrote my evidence into my pocket book.'

'So you aren't actually looking at a document created shortly after the events, are you?'

'No, I suppose not, strictly. But it contains the same information.'

'Have you got the original documents that you made as you were actually conducting your investigations?'

'No.'

'Do you have any greater recollection than is contained in this pocket book?'

'I don't know what you mean.'

'Well, if I were to ask you about other parts of the motorcycle, for example, you wouldn't be able to remember about that, and you have no contemporaneous documents that would help you.'

'Perhaps not. But I remember all of the relevant information.'

There is a note of combativeness now in Malone's voice.

'Did you check the RAF service history of the motorcycle?'

'No.'

'Why not? If one of the important findings was that, in your opinion, the retaining bolts connecting the bike with the sidecar had loosened over a prolonged period and two had been lost some time before, surely it was relevant to look at the service history?'

'I wasn't concerned with what the service records might say. They might say anything, but that wouldn't mean the work was actually done, or done well. I'm giving evidence about what I saw.'

'The reason I ask, PC Malone, is that Mrs Maynard, the lady sitting next to me, says her husband was a motorcycle fanatic. Constantly tinkering with the bike, improving its performance, making sure it was in peak condition. The amount of time he spent working on and servicing the bike actually caused disagreements between them.'

'All I can say is, the bolts must have been loose. The two I found weren't damaged in any way and yet they came apart from the sidecar. When I arrived at the scene, the bike and the sidecar were twenty yards apart.'

'Do you think it likely, PC Malone, that Sergeant Maynard would allow his wife and new-born baby to travel in the sidecar of a motorcycle that hadn't been serviced properly?'

'I can't answer that. Some people take terrible risks, with themselves and others. It never ceases to amaze me. I think Maynard was one of those, just careless.'

It is a hurtful comment to be expressed in open court before Mrs Maynard, but Malone appears either unaware or unconcerned about its effect on her. She begins weeping.

'When bolts such as this loosen over a period of time, so they're no longer within the bolt holes, dirt accumulates on the threads and inside the empty boltholes, doesn't it? They get as dirty as the rest of the frame, from oil and road grit picked up during normal driving.'

'I don't know.'

'What do you mean you don't know? Have you investigated traffic crashes in the past?'

'Yes.'

'Do you disagree with me that the exposed thread of a bolt such as this will get dirty over time?'

'No, I don't disagree.'

'Did you examine the thread of the two remaining bolts?'

'Yes. They looked the same colour as the rest of the frame. They were dirty almost throughout their length. Which suggests that they had not been fully screwed into place for a long time.'

'Are you aware of the RAF SIB investigation into this so-called accident?'

The constable's face reddens instantaneously, but it's not noticed by the coroner, who is leaning forward to address Charles. 'Are you implying that this was not an accident, Mr Holborne?'

'I can't place an affirmative case before you at the moment, sir, but I'm sure you will keep an open mind until the evidence is complete. I will make legal submissions at that time, if you will permit me.'

The answer surprises the coroner, and he pauses for a moment before half-smiling. 'You may proceed.'

'Let me repeat: are you aware of the investigation conducted by the RAF Special Investigations Branch into this event?'

'There was no such investigation. No other force was involved … as far as I know.'

Charles takes out both copies of the first page he was given earlier and holds them up. He addresses the coroner's officer. 'Please can you give one of these to the witness and the other to the coroner?'

'Now,' continues Charles, 'this is a single page from an investigation carried out by SIB. You see the footnote at the end of the page which reads "F/Sgt Maynard — SIB Investigation Report, page 3"?'

'I've never seen this before,' says Malone.

'Maybe,' says Charles. 'But do you see what it says at the foot of the page?'

'Yes, I see it.'

'This appears, on the face of it, to be a genuine document emanating from RAF SIB, does it not?'

'I don't know what such documents look like. I never seen one before. This might be genuine or it might not.'

'I will give you a moment to read that page to yourself before I ask any questions about its content.'

Charles pauses, keeping his eyes riveted to the coroner who is reading carefully, every now and then looking up at Charles.

'Now, PC Malone. Can you explain to me how it is that whoever was conducting the SIB investigation managed to examine all four bolts whereas you only saw two?'

Malone brandishes the piece of paper as if it were worthless. 'I repeat, I don't know where this has come from. For all I know you typed it out yourself.'

'That's an improper suggestion, PC Malone,' says the coroner. 'Just confine yourself to answering questions, if you please.'

'Just assume for a moment, PC Malone, that this is a genuine document, and that there was an SIB investigation which involved one of their officers examining all four bolts. Would you agree with me that their examination would be much more complete than yours? Twice as complete, to be precise.'

'Well, if there was such an examination, and you could call evidence to substantiate it, and if they saw all four bolts whereas I saw only two, then yes, that would stand to reason. I can only form an opinion based on the evidence I saw.'

'Thank you. Did you read the passage regarding the last inch of thread on each of the four bolts being clean and shiny?'

'I read it.'

'I suggest to you that the SIB description of four bolts is inconsistent with your conclusion in two ways. Firstly, it would demonstrate your finding of only two bolts — two others having worked their way out and been lost before this event — must be wrong. Do you agree?'

Malone answers rather sullenly. 'I suppose so.'

'And secondly, it would demonstrate that the two remaining bolts had not been hanging loose for a long period of time. Because "shiny and clean" implies, does it not, "until recently, in position."'

'It's possible. But, I repeat, who knows where this document's come from.'

The coroner leans forward again. 'Mr Holborne, you are allowed to put anything into a witness's hands and ask him questions about it. I'm familiar with that rule of evidence. And if he accepts the contents of the document, it then becomes part of the evidence. So far, so good. But the point made by PC Malone is still valid: where has this document come from?'

'It was posted through my client's door, anonymously. If you consider it is genuine, or it may be, it suggests that there has been a further and much more detailed investigation into the cause of Sergeant Maynard's death than you are being told about. One question I shall be asking you to consider, sir, is why you've not been told about it. May I continue for the present?'

'Yes. Please do.'

Charles takes out the second sheet of paper and waits for a copy to be placed before both the witness and the coroner. In view of the damage already done by production of the first sheet of paper, the tension in the courtroom is now palpable.

Malone looks extremely uncomfortable, fidgeting and moving his weight from one leg to the other.

Charles waits as the coroner and the witness read the second document. The coroner looks up and gives PC Malone a hard stare, waiting for him to finish reading.

'PC Malone, you told us that it was not possible to examine the front braking mechanism of the bike because it was destroyed in the accident,' starts Charles. 'This document suggests otherwise. Whoever conducted this examination was perfectly able to form a conclusion, namely that the brake cable had been cut.'

The young constable's ears redden. He opens his mouth to speak, but at first nothing emerges. 'I … I don't understand. Maybe these documents come from a completely different case!'

The coroner speaks. 'Where is the motorcycle now?'

Malone looks flustered for a moment. 'I … I think it's still in the property store at The Pines. Normally we'd wait until after the inquest and ask the family if they want it back.'

'So we could adjourn now and drive the ten minutes to police HQ and all have a look for ourselves, could we?' asks the coroner. He is already screwing the lid back on his fountain pen and closing his notebook.

'I need to ring ahead, I suppose, just to make sure it's —' starts Malone.

'No, I don't think so, thank you, constable. I'd like you to wait in open court with Mr Noble, and then we will meet at the front of the court. Mr Holborne?'

'Sir?'

'Did you travel to Bedford by car or by train?'

'By train, sir.'

'Then we shall need to arrange a lift for you. Will your client be attending police HQ with us?'

Charles takes instructions from Mrs Maynard. 'No, sir. She has a small baby with her.'

'Very well. We therefore need space for only four people. I think we'll manage fine in my car, so I shall drive. Thank you, Mr Noble. We'll assemble in five minutes, at the front of the court, please.'

'All rise!' calls Noble.

The coroner stands and sweeps out of court. Charles takes a couple of steps to intercept Noble. 'Who is Mr Cook? I assume he's a lawyer?'

'Mr Nigel Cook, QC, sir. He's been practising in crime for the last thirty years, the last ten as a judge.'

'I've never heard of him.'

'That's because he was in Hong Kong, sir. He returned last year to take up this appointment.'

CHAPTER 12

So, I seem to have a tiger by the tail. What looked like a simple pro bono traffic inquest (and a real schlep to Bedford — have you ever used the Bedpan Line? Never was a railway line more aptly named) now looks like conspiracy to murder. And this Nigel Cook — what a star! I've no idea how they do things in Hong Kong, but my God, I wish there were a few more like him on the English bench. Can you imagine any of the Bailey hacks up and adjourning in a search for the truth? Most of them wouldn't know the truth if it bit them on their fat upholstered arses. I shan't ever forget the performance of that young copper. In the witness box his face got redder and redder — you could almost see the steam issuing from his ears — but when Cook unwrapped that oilcloth in the property store to reveal all four bolts, all with nice recently unscrewed shiny ends, I thought he'd have a heart attack. Everyone turned and looked at him, but he couldn't make eye contact. Rarely have I seen anyone so blatantly caught out in a lie. And the brake cable! I'm certain it was cut but Cook gave little away; he just looked at me and handed it to his officer. He's instructing his own expert to examine them.

Anyway, the whole thing's been adjourned. My hope is it's now too big to brush under the carpet. Whatever persuaded Malone to lie (he surely can't be in this on his own?) it's all going to come out. It wouldn't surprise me if Cook pushes the police to bring charges.

So, that's my exciting day. Just a pity I wasn't paid for any of it!

Charles lifts his pen from the paper, carefully blots the page he has just completed, and pauses. He takes a second page and starts:

I hope you don't mind me sharing these little triumphs with you. It's one of the things I miss most. You understand this stuff immediately, and there's no one else I would want to share it

He stops again. Too plaintive? He scrunches up the second page, lobs it into the waste bin on the far side of his room where it joins several other balled rejections and starts a fresh sheet.

Davie asked after you and wishes you well. Sonia's glowing, and very excited. It's lovely to watch them together; they are so totally in love. I'm no expert, but she seems to be getting pretty big with three months still to go. They've not said anything, but twins maybe? I'm going to suggest "Ronnie" and "Reggie". Or too homicidal? Maybe "Cain" and "Abel"? Too fratricidal?

I am so looking forward to being an uncle or an auntie. That reminds me: how is Michelle and Frank's baby? She must be almost 2 now. It's ages since I last saw your sister; unless you think it's inappropriate, please say I was asking after her.

I told you that Sean's fallen for his doctor, didn't I? It's usually one's nurse, but then he's always been ambitious. She's a bit of a conundrum, this Irenna Alexandrova, and I'm looking forward to finding out more about her. I haven't seen Sean since I delivered him into her care in Notting Hill and I don't think there's a telephone in the building, so I'm going to drop by tonight and see how he's getting on. I'll report any additional gossip as soon as I have it.

I hope your mum's back is a bit better, and you're not working until silly o'clock every night.

I'll write again soon.

Charles's hand rises, poised, undecided, over the page. Here is his recurrent problem: how to sign off? In all his previous letters to Sally he's simply signed "Charles", with no further valediction, but this evening he feels especially close to her. This letter, recounting his day's events, reminds him keenly of their former domesticity which he values much more in retrospect than he did at the time; both returning home, he from court and she from chambers; laughing and chatting in the kitchen as they recount their respective workdays, preparing a meal together. He misses it. More than ever he's desperate to express some of the affection swelling in his chest for her.

His hand descends and he adds: *Love, Charlie.*

Before he can change his mind, he carefully folds the two sheets of paper, places them in an envelope, seals and addresses it and runs downstairs to the clerk's room to leave it in the basket for outgoing post. As always whenever passing the pigeonholes, he looks to see if there might be fees cheques awaiting him. There aren't, but there is an envelope with his name on it. He stops, reaches up and opens the envelope.

Inside is a copy of the *Bedfordshire Times* and a short note from Jean Maynard. Charles reads the front page.

RAF INQUEST — MURDER PROBE?

The inquest into the death of Sergeant Maynard was sensationally adjourned yesterday after evidence emerged at Bedford Coroner's Court suggesting foul play. Sergeant Maynard was killed on 9 October when his motorcycle ran off Harrowden Lane near its junction with the A600 and collided with a wall. The Bedfordshire Police investigation concluded the cause of the accident was poor maintenance of the vehicle, but the court heard evidence of a different investigation conducted by the RAF's own Special Investigations Branch which appeared to conclude that tampering may have occurred to the brakes of Maynard's BSA B40 motorcycle.

HM Coroner, Mr Cook QC, adjourned the inquest to permit further enquiries and for the author of the Special Investigations Branch report to be called before the court. Sources speculate that attention may now focus on personnel at RAF Cardington who would have had access to Maynard's motorcycle. The family of the deceased were represented by Mr Charles Holborne of counsel, who was not available for comment.

The report continues in its second paragraph with the background history of the RAF base at Cardington and the part it played in the war.

'Well I'll be damned!' mutters Charles to himself.

It's not raining for a change and not that cold, so Charles decides to drive with the top down. With luck the circulating air might dry the perpetually sodden carpet. He dons a warm overcoat, gloves and a scarf and sets off.

The journey from the Temple to Notting Hill takes thirty minutes, but he's in no hurry. For Charles, convertible sports cars aren't for posing or acquiring a tan. He dislikes city driving in the isolated bubble of a sealed car, far preferring to cruise open-topped through bustling communities where life is lived on the streets, feeling as if he were part of the crowd, only an arm's length from the hawkers, musicians and everyday pedestrians.

He turns onto Colville Terrace. Fifteen minutes later, and onto his third circuit of the surrounding streets, he is forced to accept that he can't remember, or can't find, the property where he left Sloane ten days before. He has tried all the roads leading off Colville Terrace, and none looks familiar.

He pulls into the kerb to decide what to do. He is reluctant to go to Dr Alexandrova's building, which he has already passed twice. He didn't exactly hit it off with her on the last occasion and he doesn't want to exacerbate matters by again turning up unannounced, especially when Sloane seems so smitten with her. On the other hand, he has no other way of finding Sloane. After a few moments' consideration, he decides to return to her address. Perhaps one of the young men who sat on the staircase will direct him.

He completes half a block and pulls up outside the house. Lights shine from various windows, but the front door is closed and the staircase vacant. Charles gives up. He will head back down to the city. More to kill time than anything else, he turns off the ignition and lights a cigarette.

'Charles?' calls a voice.

Charles looks up. Sean Sloane is hanging out of the same second-storey window as was used by Irenna Alexandrova when he was last here.

'What the hell are you doing there?' says Sloane.

'I was looking for you, actually, but was about to give up.'

'Why didn't you come in?'

Charles shrugs. 'I didn't know you were here,' he calls up. 'And I didn't like to trouble Dr Alexandrova. Not after last time.'

The doctor appears by Sloane's side in the window. There is something about their proximity which tells Charles instantly that their relationship has moved on in the last few days. She smiles and puts an arm round Sloane's shoulder.

'Don't be an idiot,' she says with a broad smile. 'Any friend of Sean's is a friend of mine. I'll come down.'

Charles gets out of the car and extinguishes his cigarette. The front door opens and the doctor holds it wide.

'Will my car be okay here?' asks Charles. 'I could put the top up, for what good it'll do.'

'I wouldn't recommend leaving a vehicle unlocked on this street,' she replies, 'but to be perfectly honest, I'm not entirely sure that pile of iron oxide on wheels actually qualifies as "a vehicle".'

Charles laughs, slams the Austin Healey's door shut and runs up the stone steps. He follows Alexandrova up to the second floor and into her bedroom.

The room has been spruced up since he was last here. The hundreds of books and files have been tidied onto the makeshift shelves, the bed is covered with a multi-coloured bedspread and several mismatched cushions, and a small card table has been erected by the window with two chairs beside it. Evidently the doctor and Sloane have just finished eating a meal as the table bears empty used plates. Charles notes a milk bottle in the centre with a few blooms in it. Someone has made an effort to make the tiny bedsit look attractive. He also notes a mug on the sideboard by the door containing two toothbrushes. He logs that for further enquiry when Sloane and he are alone.

Sloane pushes back his chair and advances towards Charles. He shakes Charles's hand warmly.

'You're looking better,' says Charles.

'Feeling much better,' says the policeman. 'I was going to call your chambers and tell you how to reach me. Also, to thank you for helping me out when I came out of hospital. I was feeling proper shite by the time you left, and I don't think I thanked you. I felt bad about that.'

Charles waves away both the apology and the gratitude. 'That's what friends do.'

'Would you like a drink, Charles?' asks the doctor.

'Yes, thank you, doctor.'

Irenna laughs. 'For God's sake, call me Irenna.'

She goes to the table and picks up a bottle of wine. As she does so, her other hand runs up Sloane's back between his shoulder blades. The gesture, so reminiscent of Sally's touch, stabs Charles's lonely heart. Sloane turns and kisses Irenna lightly on the side of her neck.

'You forgave him, then?' teases Charles. 'For landing on your doorstep?'

She turns to Charles, holding out a glass of wine for him, grinning like a Cheshire cat. 'How could I resist? The perfect blend of Irish charm and manly vulnerability.'

'Hey!' protests Sloane.

'Sit on the bed, Charles. There's nowhere else,' says Irenna.

'This is very timely,' says Sloane, 'as I've got some news.'

'So have I.'

'On the same subject?'

'Yup.' Charles looks pointedly at Irenna.

'She knows what's going on.' He sees Charles's doubtful expression. 'Look, if anyone in the whole of London can keep a secret, it's this girl.'

'I wasn't thinking about her keeping secrets; more about keeping her safe.'

Irenna laughs. 'Don't you worry about me, Charles,' she says, and there's something about her assurance that raises his curiosity a notch further.

'Okay,' concedes Charles. 'You first.'

Sloane pours himself another glass of wine, angles the chair from the little card table towards Charles and rests his elbows on his knees so their heads are at about the same height. Sloane takes a deep breath, and launches in.

'I'm still technically off work. In fact, I've not been to the station at all since Perry ordered me to take time off. But last week I thought I might wander by the office at Cricklewood goods depot.'

'And?'

'Well, there was no one willing to talk to me, but I kept making a nuisance of myself. Finally, I was given the name of a constable in the British Transport Police based at Waterloo. So, I thought, no time like the present, and I went down there. And he refused to talk to me too.'

'Wrong force?'

'Well, we wouldn't routinely share intelligence, but that wasn't the reason. He was terrified.'

'Of whom?'

'That's the sixty-four thousand dollar question, and he wouldn't say. But after I told him what happened to me, I think he decided he could trust me, at least so far, and off the record. Remember the trail seemed to go cold after wagon thirteen reached Bedford?'

'Yes.'

'Well the British Transport Police followed it to Bedford, and then to Cricklewood, where it was unloaded onto vans. The BTP told the Met, gave them the licence plates of the vehicles and even told them the goods were heading for a warehouse in the East End. Their theory was that they were to be sold in the London markets, especially Petticoat Lane.'

'That doesn't surprise me. The Lane's huge. You can get anything there and half of it's always been hooky. What did they do?'

'The BTP? Nothing more.'

'Is that usual?'

'Well, jurisdiction usually remains at the point of origin, so Beds police would deal with it. But with handling stolen goods, the goods move so the offence continues elsewhere. Normally there'd be an inter-force discussion to decide who investigates all of it.'

'But that didn't happen?'

'Apparently not. BTP told the Met and the Met said they'd take over. A while later, a detective sergeant from C8 arrived at Waterloo and started throwing his weight around. He demanded the file, told Waterloo guy to forget what he'd seen, said that people were being murdered all the way down the route from Cardington. He claimed he didn't want Waterloo guy to be the next.'

'Well, he wasn't wrong about that.'

'Now … wait … tell me your news.'

Charles gives a quick summary of events at the coroner's court. 'So,' he concludes, 'against all expectations, I think my client's suspicions are right. Her husband was murdered, either because he stumbled onto what was going on, or because he was part of the gang and they're shutting it down behind them.'

'So we have Greene —'

'— Flying Squad,' clarifies Charles for Irenna's benefit.

'— protecting Gervaise at Cricklewood, and the DS —'

'— also Flying Squad —'

'— putting the frighteners on the BTP to look the other way at the London end. It all comes back to them,' says Sloane morosely.

'And you're surprised?' asks Charles sardonically.

Sloane sighs. 'I suppose I hoped it was confined to West End Central. Yeh, naïve, right?'

'Care to wager who was behind Maynard's death at Cardington, the other end of this wagon train?' asks Charles bitterly.

Silence descends on the room.

Sloane shakes his head. 'No. Sorry, but I can't see them committing murder. The Flying Squad may be corrupt as hell, but murder…?'

'It doesn't actually have to be them. They're working with Billy Gervaise and God knows who else. They're probably just taking a cut and, as the Yanks say, running interference.'

'What are you going to do?' asks Irenna.

Sloane turns to her, shaking his head. 'Not sure. If I had some hard evidence —' and he looks directly at Charles — 'I could try taking it to my inspector. Assuming he's straight.'

'You're talking about the SIB investigation file from Cardington,' says Charles.

'Well…'

'I don't have it and I may never have it.'

'Then I need to keep digging. Maybe I'll take a trip to Cardington myself. See if I can find anyone prepared to talk. What?'

Sloane sees Charles wrestling with something. 'Well … just let me say something without you jumping down my throat, okay? You've just started a new job. You were lucky to get it after what happened in Vice. Your DI's warned you to leave it alone and he may just be looking out for you. Corruption's endemic in C8. Is now the right time to tilt at this particular windmill?'

'Windmill?'

'Sorry. It's Cervantes. Start a quixotic one-man crusade against the Flying Squad. You can't win this one, Sean.'

'That's rich, coming from you! I've seen you take on far worse odds.' He turns to Irenna. 'Don't be fooled; this guy's got some sort of Superman complex.'

'That's bollocks. I didn't choose the vendetta with Ronnie Kray; it was forced on me.'

'And that explains why you take on hopeless cases without pay? Why you're always fighting for the little guy? Why you turned down silk to do the right thing? I remember Teddy Behr, even if you don't.'

'Teddy bear?' asks Irenna, looking from one to the other.

'I'll explain later. I know you too well, Charlie. Like you, I came into this job to do some good, not turn a blind eye to a police force that's worse than the criminals they claim to fight.'

The room falls silent.

'More wine, Charles?' Irenna says with a smile.

'No, better not, thanks. So, is this where I'll find you in future?' he asks of Sloane.

Sloane takes Irenna's hand across the table. 'I don't actually live here…'

'You'll find him here most evenings, though,' finishes Irenna. 'Apart from anything else, the man can't cook to save his life. But there's a callbox in the hallway of the house where he spends the rest of his time. Here.'

She stands and takes a postcard from the wall where it was pinned. Charles makes a note of the number written on it.

'Are you looking for somewhere more permanent?' asks Charles.

'Not right now,' replies Sloane with a wide grin on his impish face.

'I'm pleased to find you so … happy. But I should go,' says Charles, standing, reminding himself that he has intruded on a romantic evening.

The others also stand. Charles sees a glance pass between the two of them and Sloane nods his assent to something.

'Before you go, Charles,' says Irenna, 'I have a favour to ask.'

'Ask away.'

'You have access to a law library, right?'

'Yes. Several.'

'Do any of them have Hansard?'

'Of course. Why?'

'I need a transcript of some questions and answers in the House of Commons. Could you get them?'

'Yes, as long as they're not too recent. We get updates every few months, I suppose. To be honest, I've never looked. May I ask why?'

Another look passes between Irenna and Sloane. 'Sit down again,' instructs Sloane. Charles does so.

'What do they call it ... Chatham House Rule?' says Irenna. 'This isn't exactly a secret, but I don't want to advertise.'

'I can't imagine any unlawful reason for wanting to read the transcripts of a parliamentary debate,' replies Charles light-heartedly, but Irenna's not smiling. He composes his expression accordingly. 'Sorry.'

'You didn't recognise my name, then?' she says.

'No, sorry.'

'South African? Jewish communist?' she prompts.

Charles frowns. 'Wait! Your parents aren't ... Yitzhak and Miriam, are they?'

She nods.

'I told you he knows more about politics than me,' says Sloane.

'But ... weren't you all arrested? With Mandela?'

'My parents were. I got out just in time. Hence, Notting Hill.'

'Jesus!' Charles turns to Sloane. 'Do you know who your girlfriend is? She's famous!' Charles stands, excited. 'It's an honour to meet you, really, I'm amazed!'

'Subside, Charles,' she says kindly. 'It's no big deal. My parents were the real activists.'

127

'"No big deal"? You and your parents make my do-goodery look like amateur hour. These guys are a really big deal in the ANC,' he says to Sloane.

'Were,' corrects Irenna. 'My father died in prison earlier this year. Republican Intelligence tortured him to death. The last I heard of my mother, she was alive, but they're withholding her drugs. I've heard nothing in almost three months.'

'Jesus! I'm so sorry,' says Charles.

'Yeh.'

Irenna disappears into her thoughts for a while. Sloane takes her hand again and holds it gently on his lap.

'Are you still working for the ANC?' asks Charles.

'Not directly; for the Anti-Apartheid Movement in London. But yesterday's declaration of UDI in Rhodesia might change that.'

'Yes, of course.'

'It's the same struggle.'

'And is that why you need to see Hansard?'

'No. That's something else.'

Sloane intervenes. 'All this —' he points at the shelves lining the room, bowing under the pressure of their books and files — 'is for the West Indian community. Did you know that, in addition to all the usual racial prejudice, they're effectively prevented from joining ordinary trade unions?'

'No, I didn't.'

'The 1962 Act has authorised outright hostility towards West Indians,' explains Irenna. She sees Charles's puzzlement. 'Not your field, I suppose. The Commonwealth Immigrants Act 1962. There's been a horrible upsurge in attacks, criminal damage ... hatred. There was no organisation in London specifically to advocate the rights of the West Indian community, and when some people found out who I was and about my experience in South Africa, they asked if I'd help. Anyway,' says Irenna, bringing the matter back to the point, 'if I give you the dates and speakers, can you find the transcripts?'

'Certainly.'

She goes to the shelves, takes down a file, leafs through it and jots down some details on a piece of paper torn from a notebook. She hands it to Charles. He looks at it, nods, and slips the note into his pocket.

'How urgent is this?' he asks.

'Not urgent. Anytime this evening will do.'

He smiles. 'The impossible I can do immediately, but miracles take a little longer.'

'As soon as you can, please.'

Charles leaves them to enjoy the rest of their romantic evening.

As he climbs into the Healey, he looks up at the lit window of Irenna's bedroom. He feels an odd mixture of emotions: slightly overawed at the identity of Sloane's new love and, embarrassingly, a little jealous of their new-found intimacy, which is so lacking in his life. Furthermore, a certain irony is not lost on him: his closest friend, a Catholic, is going out with a Jewish woman who, on Charles's arm, would be instantly welcomed in the Horowitz household, and in a manner that none of his former women friends had ever been.

God, I miss Sally!

CHAPTER 13

The telephone on Charles's desk rings, disturbing his concentration. There are half a dozen leather-bound law books before him, all open with torn strips of paper marking important passages. He is presently deep in a speech of Lord Hailsham concerning the *mens rea* required to be guilty of receiving stolen goods. He continues reading as his hand reaches out to still the intrusive noise.

'Mr Holborne?'

'Yes, Jennie?' he answers distractedly.

'I got a lady on the phone for you. I think she's a lay client.'

'Then I'm not allowed to talk to her directly. Get the solicitor — '

'There's no solicitor, sir. She's the widow in your pro bono inquest.'

'Oh,' sighs Charles, now focusing fully on his junior clerk. 'Yes. I'm allowed to talk to her. Best put her through, please.' Pause, click. 'Hello, Mrs Maynard?'

'Good afternoon Mr Holborne,' comes Jean Maynard's wavering voice. 'I've got some news.'

'Yes, what's that?'

'Heather rang me. She says another person has been killed at the base. An NCO blanket-stacker.'

Charles is familiar with the derogatory term; a "blanket-stacker" is RAF slang for someone who works in the stores.

'A young aircraftman called McParland.'

'I see,' says Charles heavily. 'Did she tell you how he died?'

'He was squashed between two goods wagons, a couple of nights ago.'

'Might it have been an accident, then?'

'Yes. But he worked in the stores that Jules was investigating. If anyone was stealing from the stores at the base, he'd either have to have been involved, or known about it. He did all the paperwork.'

'Are the police investigating?'

'I don't know. The RAF police would normally investigate all accidents where a serviceman's killed.'

'So, that would be Corporal Boyce, then?'

'I suppose so. But he's been signed off for a few weeks.'

'Why?'

'He says he's done his back in.'

'How convenient,' comments Charles cynically.

'That's what I thought. He's scared, even more so now.'

'So he's keeping his head down. Can't really blame him. Could you ask Heather to see what she can find out?'

'I don't like to. She had to call me from Bedford town centre. She and Boycey ain't talking now. I don't like to ask, if it's going to make things worse between them.'

'I understand. And if Boyce is off work anyway, he'll just say he doesn't know. Okay. Thanks for letting me know.'

There is silence on the line. Charles waits. When Mrs Maynard speaks again, her voice is tremulous. 'I'm really frightened.'

Charles pauses for a moment to consider how much to reveal of his own story.

'I know what you're going through,' he eventually says. 'You might not know, but a couple of years back my wife was murdered, and it was almost impossible to uncover the truth. The police were convinced they had the murderer and weren't interested in investigating further. So I know how lonely you feel. But you have Angie and her husband, and you have me, and as long as you continue to instruct me I promise I'll do everything I can to find out what happened to Julian and bring whoever was responsible to book. And, if this helps, I don't think you or the baby are at the slightest risk. Even if this McParland chap was killed deliberately, like Julian, it's because he also knew too much. You don't know anything. You're not a threat to whoever is doing this.'

'Are you sure? I'm so anxious. I haven't slept for weeks.'

'I am sure.'

There is another long pause. 'Okay. Thank you. I can't tell you how grateful I am for your help. What's our next step?' she asks, making a determined effort to keep her voice business-like.

'Well, I'm going to write to the coroner.'

'Write to him? What for?'

'There's no formal procedure for a third party to request that any particular witness be called at an inquest, but we can informally suggest that a coroner calls certain witnesses. I'm going to ask him to instruct an expert to examine the brakes from Julian's bike, which he seized. And to issue a witness summons to compel Flight Lieutenant Holmes to give evidence when the inquest resumes. I'll let you know how I get on.'

'May I speak to Flight Lieutenant Holmes, please?'

'Who's calling?'

'Squadron Leader Horowitz, No. 19 Squadron.'

'Hold the line please, sir.'

The line goes quiet and Charles waits, smiling quietly to himself.

Charles has a certain disdain for ex-servicemen who need to announce themselves with their wartime ranks. He's uncomfortable doing it, but he suspects that Flight Lieutenant Holmes will refuse speak to him if he gives his current name and status. He has to hold for over ten minutes before he hears Holmes's voice.

'Flight Lieutenant Holmes,' announces a voice. 'Horowitz, you say?'

'Well, yes —'

'We've just been looking you up. Are you the Squadron Leader Charles Horowitz who was at No. 19 Squadron, demobbed in 1948?'

'That's me. Although I now go under the name of Holborne. I'm a barrister.'

'Ah, now I know who you are. You were at the inquest.'

Word gets around fast. Who's he been talking to?

Charles speaks swiftly. 'I'm representing Sergeant Maynard's family. Maynard was in your flight. I really need to speak to you.'

'I can't help but feel there's some subterfuge going on here. Why present yourself with your old name?'

'I didn't think you'd take a call from Charles Holborne.'

'You're damned right.'

Charles senses that he has only seconds before Holmes hangs up. 'I'm appealing to you on behalf of the grieving widow of a man in your flight, a widow with a very young baby, who just wants some answers about how her husband died. Come on man, you were his senior officer!'

Holmes pauses before answering, but when he speaks Charles realises that his appeal to sentiment has failed. 'I'm sorry, but I can't help you.'

'Mrs Maynard's got it into her head that this wasn't a motorcycle accident, but murder. I confess I was pretty sceptical —'

'Complete nonsense.'

'I thought so too until I saw the SIB investigation.'

'I don't know anything about an SIB investigation.'

'Well, the court's seen pages from the report, and examined Maynard's motorcycle brakes. There's no doubt: they were tampered with.'

'I'm not prepared to speak to you further.'

'It'll only take a minute —'

'I've nothing further to say, save this: I've done my homework. I spoke to the Bar Council last week. Barristers are not supposed to act as private investigators, even on pro bono cases where they're not instructed by a solicitor. You're breaking your professional rules by calling me, and if you don't desist, I will report you formally to your professional association. Now that's enough.'

The line goes dead.

Less informative than Charles had hoped, but far from useless. The fact that word got back to Holmes that Charles is representing Jean Maynard, and that Holmes contacted the Bar Council to arm himself against any enquiry from Charles, speaks volumes. These are the actions of someone with something to hide.

Charles takes out a sheet of headed notepaper from his desk drawer. Time to ask the coroner to compel the flight lieutenant to give evidence.

CHAPTER 14

Charles is working late again. A bag containing his decorating clothes sits on the chair in the corner of the room, but he's beginning to realise he won't make it to Wren Street tonight. Tomorrow is Millie Horowitz's Outpatient appointment, and it's at the most inconvenient time of one-thirty, which means he'll need to be at his parents' home by noon. Nowadays it seems to take his mother ages to get ready to go out; she forgets something essential for her handbag, then her scarf, then her keys; then she starts turning the house upside down for the essential thing that she has already forgotten is now in her handbag. By the time he has collected David's car, taken his parents to the appointment at the New End Hospital, waited for Millie, got her and Harry back to the car, driven them home and dropped off the car again, the whole day will have been lost. Charles is doing what he can now to mitigate the effects by working late.

Miles Davis spins soundlessly on the record player in the corner. The first side of *Sketches of Spain* finished a few minutes earlier, but Charles doesn't want to break his concentration by rising to turn it over. Cigarette smoke drifts lazily towards the ceiling from the ashtray beside him and a glass of scotch stands by his elbow. The glass is still half-full and hasn't been replenished during the evening.

Charles decided a while back that the time had come to reduce his alcohol intake. It began to slip out of control during his short-lived relationship with Patrizia Conti, a dangerous woman who matched him shot for shot and barb for barb. For a few terrifying weeks after her disappearance, Charles's consumption was in freefall. It cost him a lost month to realise that drinking himself into insensibility wasn't making him feel any better.

And now, of course, there's Sally — or the possibility of Sally. She'd not tolerate it for any reason, less still if motivated by self-pity; most especially self-pity prompted by the departure of that strumpet. Sally would use a much earthier descriptor of the American actress, but Charles's literary bent inclines him to the Middle English: strumpet. Not to forget murderess.

So, for all these reasons, Charles's alcohol consumption is now under rigorous control. The glass by his side is less for drinking and more an ingredient of the ambience he creates and in which he works best: peaty Scotch, cigarette smoke and Miles Davis.

He finishes correcting a difficult bit of typing done by Wendy, full of complicated foreign case names and citations, and finally rises. He stubs out the cigarette, knocks back the half-inch in the glass and strides to the corner of the room to turn over the album.

Maybe another twenty minutes or so; just enough time to draft a relatively simple indictment for a conspiracy to rob.

He returns to his desk, pours another small shot of whisky and settles back to work.

At quarter past eleven Charles flicks off the desk lamp and leaves his room, pulling closed the three-inch thick oak door that shuts off his corridor. Chambers is in darkness and silence; legal professional privilege guards the empty rooms' secrets. As is often the case, he is the last to leave Chambers. He takes the corrected Advice and the draft indictment downstairs and leaves both in the wire basket marked "Urgent" next to Wendy's typewriter. He locks up the main door of Chambers, pulls his overcoat tight around him, jams his hat on his head and sets off.

The river smells are strong as he descends the stone steps of Chambers. Yellowish fog has rolled in off the Thames, as it frequently does at this time of year, and it has infiltrated the courtyards and gardens. It's so thick Charles can barely see the opposite side of the lane into Inner Temple Gardens. It curls around his legs like a jaundiced cat. The sound of traffic, only one hundred yards to his north on Fleet Street, is completely muffled; even his footsteps on the cobbles are deadened. He passes one of the gas lamps fixed to the wall of Middle Temple Lane. Condensation drips steadily off it, its yellow glow barely penetrating the miasma. London's pea-soupers are infamous, but even Charles can't recall a fog as impenetrable as this.

He reaches the top of Middle Temple Lane, the part where the pavement narrows and the chambers at the top of the Lane project at first floor level across the road, creating a tunnel. The gas lamp here is extinguished, and the last twenty paces to the twelve-foot studded doors that block the Lane from Fleet Street are in almost total darkness.

As it turns out, it is the fog and the darkness which save Charles from a serious beating. A fist suddenly flies towards his face from a doorway, appearing at the last second. Charles utters an inarticulate cry but has no time to block or duck. It strikes him with full force between his right eye and his ear and he collapses to the pavement. Seriously dazed, for a second, perhaps two, he doesn't know where he is or what's going on, but he's on his backside, half-on and half-off the pavement, so he rolls to his right, off the pavement and fully onto the cobbles.

His senses return and he regains his feet as fast as he can, crouching, but he can't see his attacker and, evidently, his attacker can't see him either. Charles remains crouching, trying to hear past the ringing in his right ear to place whoever has struck him. He hears a leather-soled shoe scrape on the cobbles almost immediately behind him and he whirls around, lashing out blindly with a fist. He connects with something soft, something clad in material, and the shock of the contact travels right up his arm to his shoulder. He knows that he's landed a good blow, so he swings again, this time with his other fist, but his arm sails harmlessly through the air. He takes half a step forward and lashes out with his foot. He connects again, and this time his attacker is definitely hurt because the blow produces a *crack!* and a cry of pain. Charles hears retreating footsteps. He's pleased to hear that they're irregular, as if the man is limping. He catches a brief glimpse of a large shape as it runs beneath one of the gas lamps before it is lost completely.

He waits until silence once again descends before striking a match and looking for his briefcase. He finds it, four or five yards away. He feels the side of his face for blood but, although tender, it feels dry — more than can be said for his backside, which is now cold and damp from the wet cobbles.

He can't believe that this was a random attack. He has plenty of enemies, both from his previous life and from the growing cohort of criminals he has successfully put away, but he suspects no one from those groups.

Being warned off the Maynard case?

'Might've been more effective if you'd bothered to tell me!' he mutters quietly after the long-departed assailant. 'As threats go, it's a bit non-specific.'

He takes a deep breath and resumes his journey.

Two hundred yards away, parked on the Embankment and almost invisible in the fog, Billy Gervaise waits patiently in his

Daimler 2.5 V8. He hears footsteps approaching and turns off the radio.

The door opens and a young man slides onto the leather passenger seat. He is breathing heavily and his woollen overcoat is sheened with tiny beads of water from the fog. He cries out and clutches his knee as it bends.

'Well?' asks Gervaise.

The man shakes his head. 'I got one good punch in, but he's tough, that brief. Got ring experience, I guess. You're gonna have to take me to the 'ospital, Billy.'

'Did you tell 'im?'

'I think he broke me knee! He's fucking kicked it and it bent the wrong way!'

'I ain't interested in that, Cyril. Did you tell 'im?'

'No! I'm trying ter explain, ain't I? How could I with a busted knee?'

'Jesus Christ. You're fucking useless. I shoulda done it meself.'

Gervaise leans back in his seat to think, ignoring Cyril's groans. 'All right. Gonna have to be a bit clever to get this geezer. But it's got to be quick; we need him out the way before the inquest resumes.'

'What about my knee?' wails Cyril.

'Oh, for fuck's sake! I'll drop you outside Tommy's.'

CHAPTER 15

Millie Horowitz is too flustered to remember to be unpleasant to Charles, for which he is silently grateful.

He arrived at his parents' suburban semi-detached in north London just after noon. His diminutive father, Harry, opened the door to him, gave him a hug and led him to the living room where he resumed his seat, wearing his scarf and overcoat, hat held loosely in his hand. Harry had, as dictated by his wife, been ready to leave by 11:30. The knowledge that if they did indeed leave by 11:30 they would arrive at the hospital almost two hours early, he kept to himself. After almost forty-three years of marriage, Harry has learned how to negotiate his way to a quiet life.

Charles has not seen his parents' living room during the hours of daylight for some time. For a long period he was unwelcome here; he was not sufficiently Jewish; he was not sufficiently attentive to his mother's needs (which meant living the way she would have Charles live, rather than the way he would prefer to live); and he was not sufficiently married. When Charles "married out" — to the non-Jewish Hon. Henrietta Lloyd-Williams — his parents disowned him and sat *shiva* — seven days of mourning — and then refused to have his name spoken in their home. In many ways, Charles's period of excommunication was a relief. For once he could get on with his life without his mother haranguing him that he was living the wrong life.

A reconciliation of sorts was brought about after Henrietta's murder, but it was superficial at best and broke down frequently. The present state of armed neutrality means that

Charles is usually only invited to the house for Friday Shabbat evening meals.

So, seeing the living room in daylight is novel and rather disconcerting. Millie Horowitz is clean and tidy to the point of obsession. Charles has a recollection of sitting with spotless clothes and scrubbed face and knees on the couch in their East End lounge before the war. David, aged about three, was sitting next to him. Both were on best behaviour, allowed to sit silently while Millie and Harry greeted some guests. The female invitee was smoking, using an ashtray on an occasional table by her side. Barely had she stubbed out her cigarette when Millie moved smoothly across the room and, with a deft flick of the wrist, covered the soiled ashtray with a clean one, inverted the pair and left the clean ashtray. Charles still remembers the awkward hiatus in the conversation that followed.

He is therefore surprised to find that the room is dusty and he can see, reflected in the glass covering the sideboard, circular sticky marks left by a bottle. He looks about him. This is not just a missed patch; even by his laxer standards, the room needs to be dusted and the carpet vacuumed. In fact, there is a dark stain on the carpet near the door which he has not noticed before. In times past, Millie would have scrubbed it out of existence within moments of discovering it.

'Is Mum struggling with the housework?' he asks Harry.

'Not at all,' Harry replies, and he looks away, out of the window.

Charles nods.

He attributes his father's defensiveness to his failing eyesight. He and David have spoken about it several times over the past months. Harry has cataracts forming in both eyes. He insists he doesn't need surgery and that he can still see well enough to drive, but his sons have noticed a distinct reluctance to do so, particularly during the winter months when it gets light late and dark early. Perhaps that explains Harry's failure to see the deteriorating state of cleanliness in the house, and his refusal to use the underground to accompany Millie to the hospital. But it would not explain the decline in Millie's rigorous standards. Perhaps she's becoming more relaxed in her old age, wonders Charles, which might be no bad thing.

The door opens and Millie enters, at last dressed to go out.

'Hello son,' she says. 'Would you like a cup of tea?'

Though pleased and somewhat surprised at his mother's hospitality, Charles is puzzled. After all these minutes waiting, with Millie finally ready to leave, it's odd for her to offer tea.

Charles stands. 'I think we should get going, Mum. It may be difficult to park and it's very hilly at New End, so you and Dad will have to take it slowly. And I don't know exactly where we're going in the hospital.'

Millie has to present herself at the reception at Outpatients and then be directed to X-ray.

'Okay,' she says equably.

Charles precedes them out of the door to check the street. He's aware that he's on high alert following the attack in the Temple and he might be imagining it, but on the drive from Fetter Lane to his brother's house he wondered if he was being followed. He deliberately drove off his route once, looping back on himself through the backstreets of Swiss Cottage to see if the car behind him followed, and he lost it only for it to reappear behind him further north, on the Hendon Way.

However, his parents' street is completely deserted of both pedestrians and, as far as he can detect, people sitting in cars, and he loads his parents into David's Volvo and drives back south towards Hampstead without incident.

The journey takes twenty-five minutes, and Charles's prediction about finding a parking space proves frustratingly accurate. He eventually finds somewhere at the far end of East Heath Road which will involve a twenty-minute walk back uphill for his parents. They decline his offer to turn round and drop them at the entrance and meet them after parking the car.

'By the time you've dropped us off, the space'll have gone,' points out Harry.

So he parks and they walk back up, Harry and Millie arm in arm. It's a fine day, skies bright and blue, but it's cold, the wind whistling down the street into their faces.

Charles guides his parents to Outpatients reception and then to the X-ray department where Millie is to have her arthritic hip x-rayed. Once she is changed into her gown, they leave her in the charge of a nurse and find a café.

Charles and his father sit opposite one another across a small table, nursing brown drinks that might, at a stretch, be described as coffee. Charles scans the room for anything suspicious.

'Are you going to tell me?' asks Harry.

'Tell you what?'

'What's making you nervous.' Harry points to Charles's face. 'And how you acquired that.'

Charles feels his tender cheekbone where the blow landed the night before. 'It's nothing,' he smiles.

'But you're not training at the moment, are you?'

'I am, but I'm not sparring. No. You'll laugh, but I bashed it on a cupboard door in my kitchen.'

'Really?' replies Harry, sceptical. 'You've never done that before.'

'Not the kitchen at Fetter Lane. At Wren Street. I'm not used to the layout yet, and I was carrying tools,' he lies.

Harry Horowitz is a quiet man who says little and misses nothing. He's aware of Ronnie Kray's animus towards Charles and knows there are still scores to settle. It's a permanent source of worry for the little furrier, which he is careful not to share with Millie. Harry knew the twins' father, Charles Kray, before the war, and even tried to use that faded connection to square things with the twins, without success. Whenever Charles turns up with unexplained bruises his heart misses a beat, worried that Charles has, yet again, escaped Ronnie's violence by the skin of his teeth.

'And before you ask, no, all is quiet with the Krays. Ronnie still thinks he'll be able to make use of me at some point and is keeping me up his sleeve.'

'Will he? Be able to use you?'

'He has stuff on me, arising out of the trouble with Izzy. If he were to send it to the police or the Bar Council things might get … uncomfortable. But I doubt he will. He hopes to manipulate me into doing something really dodgy at some point, probably with some evidence or something like that. He can be irrational, especially when his mental health dips, but when he's well he's a calculating man, and I understand him. He wants the pleasure of forcing me to do something illegal for him.'

'Which would represent a greater triumph than simply reporting you.'

'Exactly.'

'What will you do if he asks?'

Charles sighs. 'That'll depend on what he wants. Don't worry, Dad, I know what I'm doing and I can out-think Ronnie on my worst day. I'll find a way out of it, should push comes to shove,' he says with a smile and much more confidence than he feels.

The two men chat inconsequentially, about Sonia's pregnancy, Harry's hopes for his future grandson or granddaughter and other family matters. Time ticks by as the unsatisfactory drinks cool on the table before them.

After about forty-five minutes Charles looks at his watch. 'She should be finished by now. Why don't you wait here in the warm while I go and find her? I expect she'll want a cup of tea anyway before we get in the car.'

'Yes, okay,' says Harry and Charles rises.

He retraces his steps through the old hospital and arrives at the X-ray department. The reception desk is unattended, but he can hear talking behind the doors bearing a notice saying "No Entry While Red Light Is Illuminated — X-Rays" so he sits on the bench to wait. A few minutes later the doors open and a trolley is wheeled out carrying a woman in a hospital gown. Charles stands, but is surprised to find that the woman is not his mother.

'Sorry,' he says to the attendant. 'I'm looking for Mrs Millie Horowitz.'

The attendant, a young man, looks at the clipboard hanging at the back of the trolley. 'This isn't Mrs Horowitz.'

'Yes, I know that. Do you know where she is?'

A woman in uniform who Charles takes to be a radiographer comes out of the x-ray room. 'We finished with Mrs Horowitz twenty minutes ago. She was just getting dressed. Have you come to collect her?'

'Yes.'

The radiographer walks further up the corridor to another door, which is ajar. She taps on it. There's no answer and she looks inside. Then she re-emerges with Millie's overcoat and blouse in her hand. 'Are these hers?'

Charles examines them. They are indeed his mother's. The rest of Millie's clothes, her underwear and shoes, are still on the bench.

A wave of anxiety washes over Charles. 'Yes. Where on earth is she?'

The woman suddenly looks a little flustered. 'I saw her go into the room and I heard the door lock. Then I took in the next patient.' She gestures with her hand to the woman on the trolley. 'I assumed Mrs Horowitz would get dressed and leave the Department.'

Charles thrusts his mother's coat and blouse into the woman's hands and sets off towards the far end of the corridor.

'That's a dead end,' she calls. 'Go back the way you came.'

'Can you put a call out, please?'

Would someone harm her to get at me?

The possibility, now identified, raises his anxiety and heartbeat further. 'She must have wandered off,' he says, praying that's all it is.

'You think she may be wandering around the hospital, just wearing a gown? Does she have memory problems … confusion?'

'She's never done anything like this before. Which is why this is so odd.'

The radiographer hurries back into the x-ray room. Charles hears a phone being lifted. She speaks for a moment and then returns.

'We don't have security as such, but I've asked the people on the main reception to look out for her, and one of the porters is having a look round. Do you want to do the same?'

'Yes. If I find her, I'll bring her back here to get changed. Can we leave her clothes in that room for the moment?'

'Yes, that's fine. There's an hour before the next patient, so it won't be used. If we find her, I'll have a discreet announcement made over the tannoy. What's your name and relationship to Mrs Horowitz?'

'Charles Holborne ... no, sorry, Charles Horowitz. I'm her son.'

Charles sets off, walking swiftly down corridors, putting his head into rooms to the surprise of secretaries, doctors and other hospital staff. After fifteen minutes of fruitless searching he is becoming frantic, and the idea of calling the police seems increasingly sensible.

As he is running through the Endocrinology Department, he sees a pair of bare knees protruding around a corner. He turns and retraces his steps. Millie is sitting on a bench in a waiting area together with several other patients, all of whom are fully clothed.

'Mum?' he says, crouching before her, breathing heavily. 'What on earth are you doing here?'

'Hello, Davie,' she says.

'It's Charlie, Mum.'

'Yes, of course it is. That's what I said.'

'What are you doing here? You left your clothes back in the changing room.'

'I was waiting for you. Didn't you tell me to wait for you?'

'Yes, I did. But not here.'

'Oh, well, take me to where we're supposed to go, then.'

Charles helps her up. The hospital gown is designed to be tied with ribbons at the back, and as she stands Charles realises with a shock that Millie's is undone. He takes off his coat hurriedly. 'Put this on, Mum. You'll be cold.' She obeys meekly. 'Come on then. Let's go and find your clothes.'

Charles escorts her back to the changing room in the X-ray department.

'You found her,' says the radiologist with some relief.

'Yes. You can call off the search.'

Charles waits in the corridor. It takes Millie a few minutes, but when she emerges she looks as immaculate as always and as if nothing untoward has occurred.

'Where's your father? I for one could murder a cup of tea,' she says conversationally.

CHAPTER 16

It's the following morning and Charles is at his desk in Chambers. He has a plea at Middlesex Sessions at two o'clock and his desk is loaded with outstanding paperwork, but he is unable to focus on work. He awaits two urgent telephone calls, the first from his brother. Charles returned David's car the night before, but David and Sonia were not at home, so he posted the keys through the letterbox with a note requesting that David phone him urgently.

The second call he awaits is from Sean Sloane. Awaiting Charles's arrival in his pigeonhole that morning was a Manila envelope identical to the one delivered anonymously to Jean Maynard. Its contents are no less eye-popping, and he needs to share them with Sloane.

Charles stares out of the window to the River Thames. Seagulls dart and wheel over the water, which today is a beguiling white-flecked blue. Charles knows, from painful experience, that the waterway's apparent beauty is only surface-deep. It's still the most poisoned river in Europe — "biologically dead" was the Natural History Museum's verdict in 1957, so lacking in oxygen that nothing could live in it — and little had been done since to improve it. When he worked as a lighterman on the Thames during the war, stomach-pumping was mandatory for anyone who fell in.

He is suddenly struck by the parallel — the beautiful surface hiding effluence beneath — with the British Establishment. Since Charles's call to the Bar he has had to stomach a daily diet of corruption by the criminal gangs ruling London and the large sections of the Metropolitan police residing in their pockets.

His reverie is broken by the telephone ringing, and he starts forward to lift the receiver on his desk.

'Yes?'

'There's a Detective Sergeant Sloane here to see you, sir, if you're available,' says Jeremy. 'He knows he's turned up on spec, and if you're too busy he says he'll phone later.'

'No, that's fine, send him up. And you couldn't scare up a couple of cups of tea, could you?'

'Yes, sure.'

Five minutes later, there's a knock on Charles's door and Jeremy enters bearing a tray of tea and, Charles notes with approval and surprise, a small plate of biscuits. He is followed into the room by Sean Sloane.

'DS Sloane for you, sir. Shall I leave these on the desk?'

'Yes, thanks, Jeremy. Much appreciated.'

All the other barristers in Chambers expect the junior clerks to drop more important tasks to keep them regularly supplied with drinks, and Charles doesn't like to do it. So, for him to ask one of the staff to make him tea is exceptional and, as a result, the clerks are happy to oblige when they can. Charles is respected by them for his restraint; hence the biscuits.

'Thank you. Pull up a chair, Sean,' says Charles.

The door closes and Charles hears the "Conference" sign sliding across.

'I know I said I'd ring, but I'm heading for the East End anyway so…'

'It's absolutely fine, probably better anyway. Still signed off?'

'Till tomorrow.'

'Good. Look at this. It arrived this morning, addressed to me.'

150

Charles hands the envelope to Sloane and waits while he takes out four sheets of paper.

'Don't bother,' he says as Sloane feels around the inside of the envelope. 'There's nothing. No covering note, no name. We appear to have an anonymous mole at Cardington. The document in your hand is an RAF goods inwards receipt for the base, listing all sorts of equipment, boots, uniforms, blankets, enamel mugs, and —' Sloane's eyebrows shoot up and he brandishes the sheet and points to an item listed at the bottom — 'yes. Sidearms.' Sloane whistles and Charles continues. 'It's dated thirteen days before Maynard's death. And the next one, in your left hand, I'm not a hundred per cent sure of. But if I had to guess, I'd say it's an inventory check from the stores. It's dated four days later.'

'It's less than half the length,' points out Sloane. 'The goods inwards receipt has got at least a dozen categories of goods which don't show up on the inventory.'

'Exactly. I think that whoever sent this is trying to show us what was going missing from the stores.'

Sloane leafs through to the third and fourth sheets. 'Same pattern.'

'Yes. They're from the previous month.'

'So, if half the stores received were disappearing on outgoing wagons every month…'

'It was costing the RAF a fortune. There are no values, just lists of goods, but this must come to hundreds of thousands over a year,' concludes Charles.

'So, who's doing this?' Sloane brandishes the papers. 'Not the thieving; who's supplying you with this information?'

Charles shrugs. 'I've no idea. My client thinks it might be Corporal Boyce, Maynard's sidekick before his death, but having met the bloke, I think that's unlikely. He's doing everything he can to keep his head down, even faking an injury to stay off base. I don't think he's part of the conspiracy or even turning a blind eye to it. I think he's scared. And with good reason.' Sloane frowns. 'That's the other piece of news. Another body's turned up on the base. An NCO working in the stores. Squashed between goods wagons, apparently.'

'Is anyone investigating that?'

'I've no idea. SIB should be, but their report into Maynard's death was suppressed so, who knows?'

Sloane drinks some of his tea. 'Have you got copying facilities here?'

'No. I'm told that one of those new Xerox machines is going to be installed soon.'

'I'm going to have to take these, Charles. They're important evidence.'

'I need them back in time for the resumed inquest. They go a long way to establishing a motive for silencing Maynard. Can you let me have copies?'

Charles's telephone rings again. He picks it up. 'Yes, hang on just a second.' He puts his hand over the mouthpiece. 'I've got to take this, I'm afraid.'

Sloane rises and knocks back the last of his lukewarm tea. 'That's fine. I've got to go anyway. Can you pop round to Irenna's this evening? I'll get these copied in the meantime.'

'Yes. And I've got those pages for her. How is she?' asks Charles, smiling knowingly.

'Ah, she's grand!' replies Sloane, face lighting up with his trademark cheeky grin. He slips out of the room and closes the door softly behind him.

'Yes, sorry about that, please put him through,' says Charles, resuming his seat. 'David.'

'Morning, Charles. Thanks for dropping the car back. How did it go?'

'Has it ever occurred to you that Mum might be suffering from dementia?'

'No. Why?'

Charles tells David what occurred the previous afternoon. There is a long silence at the end of the line.

'I know she's getting slightly forgetful, but she's not as young as she was,' says David.

'She's sixty-three. And this wasn't forgetfulness.'

'She seemed perfectly okay when I saw her recently.'

'But you mostly see her in her home environment, don't you? Or at *shul*, where she has all the familiar props and people around her. Yesterday she was somewhere unfamiliar. I'm telling you, Davie, forgetfulness can't explain what I saw. Wandering round a hospital without her clothes? Mistaking me for you? It's not as if we look alike.'

David has to concede that that's true. He is taller, half Charles's girth and has fair hair and blue eyes.

'I think we need to have it checked out. It's young for dementia,' says Charles.

'What, you mean take her to a psychiatrist?'

'Aren't they the speciality that deals with dementia?'

'She'll never go. How do we present it? "Sorry, Mum, but we think you're losing your marbles, so can we get a doctor to confirm it?" She'll go completely bonkers, if you get what I mean. Did you speak to Dad about it?'

'No. There was no opportunity without Mum being there, and I wanted time to consider what I'd seen. But, honestly David, her behaviour really worried me.'

'Is it possible she'd taken some drugs before leaving home? Too many painkillers, for example? Her hip's been very painful.'

Charles considers the suggestion. 'Yes, I suppose that's possible.'

'Don't do or say anything yet, okay? Let's keep an eye on her for a while. If we're agreed that she needs to see someone, we must speak to Dad first. Apart from anything else, without his help we'll never persuade her to go.'

'Fair enough. In the meantime, I'll do some research on what can be done about early dementia. I'm not even sure there's any treatment.'

'Well, if that's so, what's the point taking her to a psychiatrist? She'll just be distressed for no reason. And furious at whoever suggested it.'

'I'm ahead of you. She'll accuse me of wanting to put her in a home!'

'Probably. Which is why, if anyone has to say anything, it had better not be you,' says David.

CHAPTER 17

Detective Inspector Greene pushes open the door to West Hendon Police Station. The foyer is crowded. An elderly couple sit on the bench just inside the door. It looks as if the man has been assaulted, because his wife is helping him hold a bloody handkerchief to his forehead. At the counter is a woman trying, in very fractured English, to report a crime to a uniformed sergeant with dark hair and a bushy moustache. The patient sergeant, finding it almost impossible to understand the complaint, asks her yet again to slow down and start from the beginning. Greene flashes his warrant card at the sergeant and speaks loudly over the distressed woman.

'Is DS Sloane on duty?'

'Excuse me, madam,' says the sergeant, holding up his hand in a vain attempt to halt her flow. When she doesn't stop, the sergeant shouts over her shoulder.

'He's not in, guv. He's been off duty for the last few weeks. Got a head injury making an arrest.'

'Do you know when he's back?'

''Fraid not. DI Perry'll know. He's in the duty office.' The sergeant hitches a thumb over his shoulder indicating a room behind him and at the same time lifts the flap in the counter to let Greene through.

Greene knocks on the door of the duty office and enters without waiting. DI Perry sits at a desk. He looks up.

'DI Greene,' he says sardonically. 'What brings you to leafy West Hendon?'

'Looking for one of your sergeants. DS Sloane.'

'Yes? Why's that?'

'I need a word with him.'

'What about?'

'Look, don't make life difficult. We want a word with him about some thieving at Cricklewood goods yard.'

'Where he was assaulted by one of your narks.'

'Well, that's Sloane's story, certainly.'

'Is there another?'

'I want to know what Sloane was doing there, that's all, and the nature of his dealings with Gervaise. I think there's more to this than meets the eye.'

Perry throws his pencil onto the table. 'Don't give me that. He's had no "dealings" with Gervaise, and you bloody well know it. Unless you count concussion and a fractured jaw.'

'Balls.'

'I can show you the letter from his consultant.'

Greene waves that away. 'If that's true, he probably deserved it. You might not be in possession of all the facts, inspector.'

'He didn't even know who Gervaise was,' says Perry. 'He's only been here a few weeks.'

'You know Sloane left Vice under a bit of a cloud, don't you? That Paddy has some questions to answer.'

Perry stands. 'I know exactly what happened in Vice. I know half of those officers only too well, and you and I both know they set Sloane up. It's not the first time they've tried it.'

Now Greene raises his voice. 'I'm following a perfectly reasonable line of enquiry, inspector, and I want to interview your sergeant. Now are you going to assist me, or do I need to speak to your Chief Superintendent?'

'Sloane's still signed off as sick.'

'Then give me the address of his section house.'

Perry shakes his head. 'He's not at the section house. There was no room. Stay here, and I'll see if anyone knows where his digs are.'

DI Greene, now accompanied by a detective constable, stands on the threshold of Mrs O'Connor's boarding house for young working men. A frustrating morning is getting worse.

'All right, when did he move out?' demands Greene.

'I couldn't tell ye,' replies Mrs O'Connor, a bucket of dirty water in one hand and a dripping mop in the other. 'Three weeks or so ago.'

'Where did he go?'

'I've no idea. He left.'

She makes to shut the door, but Greene inserts his foot in the gap. 'Where are you sending his post?'

'I'm not. He didn't get any post while he was here. And if anything arrives, I can't forward it to him, *because I don't know where he is!*'

Greene points a threatening finger at the landlady, his colour rising. 'Don't you shout at me, you old bag, or I'll arrest you for obstructing a police officer in the execution of his duty!'

'Well I'm sure I don't know how to make you understand. The lad left; I don't know where he is! And before you ask, all of my present lodgers are new. The boys working the building sites move on all the time. So there's no point you hassling them.'

Greene pauses, stymied. 'Right.'

'Is it alright if I finish washing my floor now?'

Greene turns and descends the stone steps to the pavement followed by the young constable. The door closes behind them.

'Fuck,' says Greene.

Charles changes out of his three-piece suit and tunic shirt into sweatpants, lightweight running shoes and "Kennington Institute" club shirt. It's a Wednesday night, his usual night for training, but what with burning the midnight oil in Chambers and late-night working at Wren Street, he's missed it for the last two weeks. He needs a good workout, and he's looking forward to seeing his boxing friends.

He packs his towel and some clean underwear into his ex-serviceman's rucksack, slips it on and leaves the flat. It's a fifteen-minute run to the gym at the Elephant and Castle, and it's a good warmup. He enjoys running along the Embankment and over Blackfriars Bridge, especially at dusk, when the gas lights lining the Embankment have been lit.

Charles has been training at the Kennington Institute since he was thirteen. The rundown club, now part-owned by the Krays who also trained there as boys, is a second home to him. Duke, the aging fighter who was "encouraged" to sell a fifty-five percent stake in the club to the twins, is a good friend.

Charles arrives at the end of the service road out of breath, and checks his watch. The run has taken him eighteen minutes, between three and four minutes longer than it should.

'Bollocks,' he swears softly, annoyed at himself for having allowed his fitness to decline over the last months.

He pushes open the gym's doors to be greeted by the familiar smells of mould, liniment and stale sweat, and heads to the changing rooms. He throws his rucksack onto the sweat-stained wooden benches and, following his invariable superstition, winks at the black and white photograph of himself on the wall, taken when he was fourteen, the winner of the 1939 London Schoolboy Championships.

Changed into his boots and pulling on his gloves, he walks down the corridor to the gym itself. As he approaches the swing doors, he notices the absence of all the usual sounds: no grunts of men as they thrash the heavy punchbag; no scuffed footsteps of boxers dancing around the ring; and, most surprising of all, no Duke shouting expletive-laden commands to the youngsters. He pushes open the doors.

Three men wearing identical vests and shorts sit in a line along the back wall of the club. Charles doesn't recognise them or the club colours they wear.

'Hello,' he says.

One of the men, the smallest, stands. 'Do you know where Duke is?' he asks.

'No,' answers Charles. 'He should be here by now. How did you get in?'

One of the others answers. 'The door was open. Our club captain arranged with Duke for us to train here tonight. Our club's been flooded.'

'Burst main,' offers the third, a giant of man with the characteristic flattened nose and scarred eyebrows of a man who's spent his life boxing.

'Oh, I see,' says Charles. 'Welcome, then.' He approaches the three men, still fiddling with the laces on his gloves. 'What club is that?'

'The New Ring,' says the giant. 'It's new.'

'You don't say,' says Charles.

'We're all warmed up. Do you mind if we use the ring to spar?' asks the small man.

'I don't mind, but I've no idea what plans Duke has for any of the other boxers this evening.'

Charles looks round.

Where's the old man got to?

He shrugs. 'Seeing's no one else is here yet, I can't see why not.'

'Thanks,' says the middle of the three.

'You don't fancy sparring with Tommy here, do you?' says the smallest, pointing to the giant, who is pulling on his gloves. 'He's a bit big for us,' he laughs, and looking at the speaker's physique, Charles can't disagree. He doubts this man could punch his way out of a paper bag.

'Well, I'm a bit out of shape so I was going to do some rope work for a while,' replies Charles, 'but I suppose I can give you ten minutes.'

The giant lumbers towards the ring and climbs in. Charles follows, looking him over. The man's enormous, six inches taller and as much as four stones heavier than Charles. He looks a bit flabby round the belly, but Charles imagines that if he were to land a serious punch, it would do considerable damage. Charles is not unduly concerned; he's fairly confident he can keep out of the giant's way and, in any case, sparring partners are supposed to punch at no more than fifty percent or so.

The other two men each take one of the corners of the ring, and for a split-second Charles has a sixth sense that something isn't right, but before he has the chance to do anything about it the giant is throwing punches. Charles dances away, keeping his feet moving, and the giant plods slowly after him. The man throws a great right-handed haymaker which Charles easily ducks, but as he skips backwards he trips over an outstretched boot protruding through the ropes. Suddenly Charles is falling backwards onto the canvas. Before he can get to his feet, the two others are in the ring too and leap to grab an arm each, pinning him down. Charles wriggles furiously, thrashing his legs, but is rendered incapable of further resistance when the giant lands an almighty kick between his legs. There is a second's delay before agonising pain hits him, travelling deep into his abdomen.

'Listen, Holborne,' says one of the others, but Charles is incapable of listening. He's in a world of pain, waves and waves of it, every cell in his body screaming.

'You're gonna give up the inquest, d'you hear me?' shouts the voice in his right ear.

Charles cannot respond. A blow lands on his ribcage followed by another to his solar plexus. The air in his chest is forcefully expelled and he gasps like a drowning fish, fighting to re-inflate his lungs, but nothing comes. He hears what sounds like a donkey braying, and realises that it's he who's making the noise.

'Or Mr Gervaise will have you killed,' continues the voice softly, right into Charles's ear. The speaker must be lying on the canvas next to him as he can feel the man's breath on his face, like a lover's. 'Do you understand?'

Charles manages to nod, still incapable of drawing in a lungful of air.

'Good. Goodnight!' And with that, another colossal blow lands on Charles's head. He sees a shower of stars, manages the thought that he's been a right mug, and thinks no more.

CHAPTER 18

'Mr Holborne! Charles!'

Someone is calling him, and something is wailing, but he doesn't want to wake up from his deep dreamless sleep. He allows the noises to wash over him and drifts back into unconsciousness. One tiny niggle as he descends into the black is that he can't work out why he's on a train, because he must be on a train, as there's a rattling and the surface beneath him is bumping up and down. But it's unimportant, so he pushes the concern away and allows himself to continue falling.

He stirs again, maybe immediately or maybe after a more prolonged delay, he can't tell. The rattling and wailing are still there, and he racks the part of his brain that's working in an effort to remember where he was going before he fell asleep. Then he becomes aware of discomfort around his nose and mouth.

Something's fallen on top of me!

It's a strange pressure, as if a mug's being pressed into his face, and he reaches up and tries to swat it away.

'Easy, easy!' says a voice. 'Stay still. It's an oxygen mask.'

'Don't be fucking ridiculous,' he says, or tries to say, as his tongue doesn't seem to be working and whatever's over his face makes the words indecipherable.

He opens his eyes. He is flat on his back staring up at a white roof. He's not in a train carriage, he's in a vehicle, and the wailing resolves itself into the noise of a siren.

'He's coming round,' someone says.

'Mr Holborne? Mr Holborne, can you hear me?'

Charles tries to sit up and finds hands pressing his shoulders back down to the shaking bed. He reaches up to take whatever it is off his face, but someone else grips his hand and pulls it gently but firmly back to his side.

'Please try to stay still, Mr Holborne. That's an oxygen mask. You've had a nasty concussion, and your heart stopped for a while. We're taking you to hospital.'

Charles is still completely confused but then a wave of nausea hits him, and a roil of pain emanating from his groin sweeps over him. And he remembers.

'Sick,' he declares, and manages to roll slightly to his side and tear the oxygen mask to one side before he vomits.

DS Sean Sloane pushes open the door to the Collator's Office at West Hendon Police Station. He's not been here before — indeed he barely knows the layout of the station, so soon after his new posting was he injured.

A uniformed police constable sits at a desk completely covered by postcard-sized cards with holes punched along one edge. He looks up. His hair and moustache are grey, and there are deep folds in his face descending from the corners of his nose down to his mouth. The thought passes through Sloane's head that the man should have been drawing his pension years ago.

'It's DS Sloane, isn't it?' says the old constable.

'Yes,' replies Sloane. 'And you're PC Winkworth, our collator?'

'That's me,' says the older man, standing with a smile and shaking Sloane's hand. 'Ray Winkworth. Pleased to meet you. I gather you've had an interesting start to life at West Hendon.'

'You could say that. Have you got a few minutes?' says Sloane, gesturing at the confetti of cards on Winkworth's desk.

'Oh, don't worry about that. It's like painting the Forth Bridge. Most of these should have been thrown out years ago; dead men, dead connections and forgotten crimes. I try to do a few minutes every day and slim the files.' He points to an entire wall of grey metal cabinets made up of postcard-sized drawers. 'What can I do for you?' he asks, gesturing at the seat facing him.

'I assume you have something on Billy Gervaise?' asks Sloane, taking the seat.

'Do I ever,' says Winkworth. 'There's probably half a drawer's worth. I've been recording Billy's activities since he was a tearaway running errands for Jack Spot. You could say we grew up together. What do you want to know?'

'Known associates, hangouts, where he lives, properties he owns … everything you have.'

'That's a lot. Do you mind telling me the nature of the enquiry? It'll save time.'

'I think he's involved with a ring stealing RAF kit from a base in Bedfordshire. Large quantities, moved on freight wagons on a disused branch line down to London. I stumbled over him checking the goods once they'd reached Cricklewood. That's where he assaulted me. Last night he, or some of his associates, beat a barrister friend of mine unconscious. He almost died.'

'A barrister?'

'He's representing the family of an RAF policeman called Maynard who poked his nose into the wrong goods wagon at Cardington. Maynard turned up dead, officially in a bike accident, but the barrister started unpicking that at the inquest. He's acting pro bono, and I think Gervaise is warning him off.'

'A barrister working without a fee? That'll teach him.'

Sloane laughs. 'I doubt it. Gervaise doesn't know the barrister concerned — a dog with a bone.'

Winkworth stands and goes to the bank of files. He pulls out a couple of drawers, each eighteen inches in length, rejects them, and tries a couple of others.

'Here we are. The cards on William Arnold Gervaise go back from here over six inches, cataloguing almost thirty years of criminality.'

'Before we dive in, you might be able to resolve a straightforward question that's been bothering me,' says Sloane. 'This looks like a complex operation, detailed planning, people bought or recruited all the way down the line from Bedford to London, storage in various warehouse properties somewhere in London and then transport to the markets. Is Gervaise capable of organising all that, or would he be a minor player? Based on what you know of him?'

'Oh, he's quite capable of all that. Don't be fooled by appearances. He may look like a middle-aged Clark Kent, but he's cunning and, when the need arises, capable of extreme violence. He got an eight-stretch for a robbery at Lloyds Bank, very well-planned, using an inside man and kidnap of the bank manager's wife. He's been arrested twice for murder, not charged on either occasion due to witnesses disappearing. And he was a Warrant Officer in the RAF stores during the war, so he'd know the system inside and out. Purchasing, stores, distribution throughout the estate, all of it. He's got perfect qualifications for what you're describing.'

Winkworth takes a spare card from his desk, turns it on end and inserts it in the drawer he has just opened to act as a flag. Then he lifts out two fistfuls of cards.

'Drag that chair across,' he says, pointing to an unoccupied desk in the corner of the room, and placing the cards in its centre. 'You can sit there while you go through them. It's going to take you a couple of hours. Try to keep them in order, please.'

Sloane does as suggested, draws a chair up to the desk, slips his jacket over the back of it, and settles down to work.

Fifteen minutes later, Winkworth interrupts him. 'You said "various properties"?'

'Yes. We're talking about a lot of stuff. He'd need warehousing or similar.'

'Have you heard of a bloke called Arnold Cooper?' asks Winkworth.

'No.'

'He's some sort of accountant, and he works for Ronnie and Reggie Kray. Not exclusively, but increasingly so. A year or so ago, a company he controls bought some warehouses down by the docks. He and the Krays are off this patch, so not normally my brief, but I made a record of it because Gervaise's name was mentioned in the context of those buildings. I don't know if there's a connection or not, but it might be worth exploring. In fact, you might like to have a word with a chap called DI Read.'

'Who's he?'

'Nipper Read. Made DI a short while ago and posted to City Road. Word is, he's tasked with getting the Krays. Has the reputation of being incredibly meticulous. Secretive too, which is probably as well after the last investigation into the twins.'

Sloane nods. He knows all about that scandal, in which the Metropolitan Police Commissioner had his arm twisted by both the Conservative Home Secretary and the Labour opposition into denying the existence of an investigation into the Krays; an investigation that had inconveniently revealed the identities of the Establishment figures, household names, who

166

took part in Ronnie's gay sex parties; an investigation that was subsequently buried. Charles represented one of the abused boys and Sloane had done his best to get the lad moved out of range, to protect him until trial.

'Read may not talk to you,' continues Winkworth, 'but it's worth a try. The warehouses will be within his area, and he's bound to look into them, if he hasn't done so already. You might be able to help each other.'

'Yes, sounds like a good idea. Thanks Ray.'

'My pleasure.'

CHAPTER 19

'Charles?'

Charles opens his eyes, trying to locate who has spoken. He was half-asleep. The ward is noisy throughout the night and he's slept very little since he was admitted but, even allowing for that, he feels more fatigued than he can ever remember, an aching tiredness deep in his bones which makes it hard even to lift his limbs. A consequence of concussion, he's been told.

'My God, Charles, you look dreadful!'

Charles locates the plummy voice in the habitus of an enormously fat man standing by the side of his bed.

'Hello, Percy,' he says weakly. 'How nice to see you.'

'I think you look worse than you did after your last fight.'

'Yeh, well, then I was only fighting one bloke, not three.'

Percy looks down on him, a bunch of flowers gripped in his pudgy hands, his old-fashioned wing collar splayed almost flat against his chest by his multiple chins.

Percy Farrow, ex-copper and lifelong gourmand, has the reputation as the best crime journalist in Fleet Street. He has sources and connections everywhere, but most importantly within the Metropolitan Police's supposedly incorruptible intelligence branch, C11. The two men first met when Charles was just out of pupillage and reading for libel. Junior barristers can supplement their income, up to five guineas per night, by reading the forthcoming daily newspapers to make sure no one is being libelled therein. Then, a couple of years later, Farrow covered one of Charles's early trials, and a friendship began.

'How did you track me down?' asks Charles hoarsely.

'Your delightful clerk. Someone should snap that woman up.'

'She's too tall for you.'

'Not me, you dolt!' replies Farrow, alarmed. 'I'm far too settled in my ways for a further bout of matrimony.' He pulls up a plastic chair and sits next to Charles's bedside. 'How are you, my dear fellow?'

'I have concussion, apparently my heart stopped for a while but there seems nothing wrong with it now, and I received a thunderous kick in the balls. I'm told that my nether regions are interesting shades of purple and black, but I haven't had the nerve, or a mirror, to check for myself.'

'No permanent damage, I hope?'

'Who knows? The idea of anyone touching me in that area, even the nurses, is currently unthinkable.'

'I'm very sorry to hear it, Charles. Although the womenfolk of London might have a different perspective. I'd been meaning to get in touch with you before you got yourself beaten up.'

'Was I about to receive another invitation to one of London's finest restaurants?'

'I'm sure that could be arranged but, you know, there's now a more pressing matter. Is your current state anything to do with a certain William Gervaise, by any chance?'

Charles's attention is now all on his journalist friend. 'Yes. Or rather, three men employed by him. One giant and one weasel. I didn't get much chance to look at the third.'

'For future reference, the weasel was probably Bertie Gervaise, Billy's younger brother. He's a lockman. They both were, actually, until Gervaise graduated to more complex crime. Why is Gervaise having you beaten up?'

'I think he killed someone, or had someone killed, at the Bedfordshire end of a massive conspiracy to steal from the RAF. I'm representing the deceased's family at the inquest. I've been asking difficult questions, and he'd like me to desist. What's your angle?'

'I've been on Gervaise's trail for the last couple of years. He's becoming as big an operator as your friends the Krays, but he's much cleverer in the sense that he stays under the radar. Then I saw this.'

Farrow holds up a newspaper which Charles recognises: the *Bedfordshire Times*.

'Which is why you're here,' says Charles.

'My dear fellow, I'm here because you're my friend. But I saw this article, and put two and two together. I think you've been unravelling one end of the conspiracy, while I've been investigating the other end in London.'

'What do you know about this, then?' asks Charles.

'I know that hundreds of thousands of pounds-worth of army surplus have been moved through the London markets, particularly Petticoat Lane, and that Gervaise is the prime mover. I didn't know the extent of his involvement, the source of the surplus or how he was doing it.'

'It's not "surplus"; it's nicked.'

'And you've discovered the source.'

'Not definitively. I've seen evidence supporting that conclusion, and I hoped I could get more at the resumed inquest. But obviously I'm not going to be well enough.'

'When is it?'

'Day after tomorrow. I can't walk yet, and even standing up sets the world spinning.'

'Pity. Will your clerk be able to find someone to take your place, do you think?'

'I've asked, but I doubt it. It means traipsing all the way to Bedford without pay. My colleagues in Chambers are not much given to pro bono work. But surely you've enough to run with a story now?'

'Yes, probably, but Gervaise is not my primary target. My editor and I think there are bigger fish, out of sight at the bottom of the pond.'

Farrow built his reputation on stories of corruption in high places and abuse of power. It was he who got the *Sunday Mirror*'s scoop involving Ronnie's gay sex parties and the participation of elder statesmen such as Lord Boothby.

'You mean the Flying Squad?' asks Charles.

'Oh, you know about that too, do you?'

'Specifically, Detective Inspector Greene.'

'Him, yes, but it goes much higher, believe me.'

'There's someone you might want to talk to, then,' says Charles. 'Although he might not speak to you on the record. Now, Percy, he's a friend of mine, so I'll need your word you won't use his name unless he says you can.'

'Who is he?'

'A DS currently posted to S Division. He was hounded out of Vice because, unlike the rest of his team, he wouldn't take backhanders from Humphreys and Silver.'

Farrow nods. Like everyone in London with one foot in the underworld, he knows all about the two pornographer kings.

'Are you talking about the young Irish copper who investigated your murder charge? What was his name, Sean something ... Sloane, was it?'

Charles is not surprised that the journalist remembers Sloane's name. Farrow is possessed of a very sharp intelligence and a phenomenal memory for names and faces.

'Promise me, Percy.'

'I promise. Are we talking about Sloane?'

'Yes. He moved to the Met and is presently based at West Hendon, but he's been off sick since he had his jaw broken by Gervaise — in person. He's more or less living with a trainee doctor. I can give you her address. Have an off the record conversation with him. You may be able to help each other out. And tell him he owes me a bunch of grapes. The very least he can do is sit where you are now, and eat them for me. Now, leave me alone, old chap; I need my beauty sleep.'

CHAPTER 20

'I'll buzz you in,' says Charles. 'Fourth floor.'

He hangs up the intercom, leaves the door to the communal hall ajar, and moves gingerly back to the couch. The constant pain in his groin and abdomen has now gone, but he still moves cautiously. Today is the first day the swelling has permitted him to wear normal trousers — as against pyjamas — since he was discharged from hospital three days earlier. The tiny dining table on the living room wall, which would not seat more than two people, is piled over a foot high with all the briefs and supplemental papers delivered to the flat by the clerks. He has made no attempt to start on them yet.

'Hello?'

'Come in, Sean.'

Irenna enters the apartment, followed by Sloane. They have to shuffle around the internal lobby while getting their coats off and shutting the front door. Charles can hear Sloane wrestling with coat hangers.

'I can see now why Sean thought sharing with you might be a bit claustrophobic,' says Irenna as she enters the living room. She crosses the room and places a kiss on Charles's cheek. 'How are you?' she asks, crouching in front of him, not wanting to displace him by sitting on the couch with him.

'The head's better; no fractures, I'm pleased to say. The ECG's were all fine apparently, and my blood had none of the enzymes supposedly probative of a heart attack. The consultant's best guess was the intense struggle while fighting off three people led to an overload of adrenaline and a brief cardiac arrest.'

'I'm no cardiologist, but that's what we're all taught. They'll probably monitor you, but you may escape without long-term problems. And what about…' She points downwards.

'Still tender and a worrying shade of black.'

'Do you want me to take a look?'

'No, thank you, Dr Alexandrova,' replies Charles, grinning.

'I'm sure everyone here is grateful,' comments Sloane as he comes in.

'Can I offer you anything? Tea?' asks Charles, pushing himself upright.

'Stay put, Charles,' says Irenna. 'I'd love a cup of tea, but I'll do it. In there?' she says, pointing towards the kitchen.

Sloane grabs one of the dining chairs and turns it to face Charles. 'You okay?'

'Yes. Physically I'll be fine. But … it's a bit odd … but taking such a beating has left me … shaky. Emotionally.'

'I'm not surprised. Your size and your ability with those —' he points at Charles's enormous fists — 'have always been enough. Superman complex, remember? Being beaten up, especially being kicked in the knackers … your manhood … well, bound to make you feel vulnerable.'

'Samson with his hair shorn, you mean?'

Sloane shrugs. 'If your vanity likes the Old Testament comparison, perhaps.'

'That's surprisingly perceptive for a thick Mick,' calls Irenna from the kitchen.

After a few moments, she returns with a tray bearing a teapot, milk and three mugs. She places it on the floor and begins to pour.

'So,' says Charles. 'Bring me up to speed. Did you make it to the inquest? Did Chambers find anyone else to take over the case?'

Sloane shakes his head while lifting a mug and blowing on his tea. 'There was no one there from your chambers.'

Charles shakes his head sadly. 'Bastards,' he says softly. 'I phoned several of my colleagues personally, almost begged them to step in. I knew it was a forlorn hope, but ... I still hoped. Did the coroner call Flight Lieutenant Holmes?'

'He did, and Holmes turned up, lawyered up to the gills. There must've been three of them at least, but God knows why, 'cos Holmes refused to answer any questions.'

'On the grounds that the answers might incriminate him?'

'Exactly. So that was a waste of time. You haven't heard the worst. Someone waltzed into the coroner's office and lifted the brake assembly and bolts from his filing cabinet.'

'What?' exclaims Charles.

'Apparently the coroner pays for an office at the county council buildings.'

'Yes, that's usual. The council contributes to his costs.'

'Well, someone blarneyed his way into the building, broke into the office and stole the parts.'

'Wasn't the office locked?'

'Yes, it was, but that didn't seem to prove an obstacle.'

'And the inquisition?'

'The what?'

'The verdict.'

'Still waiting. He said he'd hand it down in writing.'

'So Gervaise's won. He managed to shut it down. I need to write to Mrs Maynard. Got any good news? Can you tell me the state of your investigations?'

'I probably shouldn't, but I shall. I now know the entire route and who's involved at each stage. It ends in some warehouses owned by a company, the secretary of which is a chap called Cooper. There may be no connection, but he's reputed to be the Krays' financial wizard. I took the whole lot to my inspector. At first I didn't think he'd be prepared to go up against DI Greene, but I was wrong. He went into bat for me with Chief Superintendent Ackroyd. Laid out all the evidence.'

'And?'

Sloane shakes his head. 'I don't know. Ackroyd listened, asked all the right questions, but he didn't seem keen. Perry told me afterwards that Frank Ackroyd's a nice man and honest, but he's weak, and only a year from retirement. Perry doubts he'll put his pension at risk by going out on a limb. And if Gervaise is being protected by Greene, probably more senior officers too … well, Perry warned me not to hold my breath.'

'Now what? Are you going to drop it?'

'Not on your life. This is now doubly personal. I just got a busted jaw, but they almost killed you. The Bedford end might be hopeless, but I'm making ground here in London. I've been advised privately, by more than one source, that the more noise I make, the less easy it'll be for Ackroyd to continue looking the other way.'

'Who told you that?'

'Perry, and an inspector in the East End, a guy called Leonard Read. He's been really helpful too, but he has to stay in the background for the moment. So I've decided to start making some arrests, not of Gervaise but of some of the others in the team. I'm going to make a lot of noise, shake the tree as hard as I can and see who falls out. Your mate Percy Farrow's on board, too.'

'He got in touch with you, then?'

'He certainly did.'

'Good.'

'That's a very useful contact you have there, Charlie.'

'He's one of the good guys. He's got an old-fashioned sense of morality.'

'Like you?' chimes in Irenna.

Charles's head swivels to her sharply, unsure if she's being sarcastic, but her face is open and innocent. 'Yes, like me. Oh, Irenna, I might have something for you.' Charles struggles to his feet.

'Hey! I can do it!' says Sloane.

'I'm not supposed to sit for long periods,' says Charles. He crosses to the table and the pile of documents from Chambers.

'How long're you going to be walking like John Wayne?' asks Sloane.

'I might be able to walk normally now, but I thought I'd be cautious for another day. I'm going to go into Chambers tomorrow. Now … let's have a look…'

Charles flicks through the envelopes, Instructions to Counsel and miscellaneous documents until he finds an envelope with no stamp on it and his name on the front written in manuscript.

'This might be it. I asked Jennie to put those sections from Hansard into an envelope for me … yes! Here they are.' He hands the envelope to Irenna. 'Do you mind telling me why you need them?'

Irenna sits cross-legged on the floor and takes out a sheaf of papers stapled at the top corner. 'Let me read you something, Charles,' she says. She takes a moment to find a particular passage, folds the top sheets over, and starts to read. *"If I send the Minister evidence that there are people who would like to return home but have not the fare, would he look at it? Is he not aware that the overwhelming number of English people would like to see these immigrants return to their own countries if they so wish; that the bulk of our people would like to see no more of them come to this country, and that, particularly, they want to know why he and his colleagues voted 100 times during the passing of the Commonwealth Immigrants Bill against any control of immigration? Let us have an answer to that.'"*

'Sounds a delightful bloke. Who is he?'

'That was Sir Cyril Osborne, Conservative MP for Louth, on ninth February. He's rabidly anti-homosexual and anti-immigrant. Your government encouraged West Indians to come here and help rebuild the British economy after the war, and now they've done it Osborne wants to repatriate them whether they like it or not. Regardless of the fact that some of them have been here almost twenty years, have married and produced children who have known no other country.' Her eyes flash and her cheeks colour as she speaks. 'This is the thin end of the wedge. If he can get the government to pledge funds for repatriation grants, believe me, they'll be offered no choice.'

'What are you going to do with it?'

She smiles and puts a gentle hand on Sloane's knee. 'Like my boyfriend here, I'm going to make as much noise as I possibly can.'

CHAPTER 21

Detective Inspector Sidney Greene sits at the kitchen table in his untidy semi-detached in Camberwell, studying a hard-backed notebook full of neat figures. His tie is loosened and his suit jacket hangs over the back of his seat. The kitchen still smells of the steak and kidney pie Vanessa made them for their evening meal, and she didn't finish the washing up before she left.

He hears the front door open and close.

'I'm back,' calls Vanessa from the hallway. She clip-clops in her high-heeled shoes into the kitchen and clears a space on the kitchen counter for her handbag. 'You're not still doing that, are you?' she asks.

'Almost done.'

She lifts the kettle and goes to the tap. 'Tea?'

'Yes, please,' he says distractedly.

She puts the kettle on to boil and approaches him from behind, placing her hands on his shoulders and massaging gently, as she watches his stubby fingers move up and down the row of pencilled figures.

'Should I be worried?' she asks.

Greene sighs. His hand reaches up to hold one of hers. 'No, I don't think so. I've got a plan, but if everything goes tits up, we should be okay.' He pauses and twists his neck to look up at her. 'You've not said anything, have you? To your bingo pals?'

'Don't be daft.'

He nods. 'Good.'

'Should I be making plans? I'd need to tell Mum if you intend moving us suddenly.'

'Your passport's up-to-date, isn't it?'

'Of course.'

'Then, no. Don't do anything out of the ordinary.' He pauses. 'You've left clothes and so on in Spain, haven't you?'

'Yes, but only summer things.'

'That's all you'll ever need.'

'What are you going to do about Maisie?'

He swivels in his chair to examine her face above him.

Vanessa has known about the girl for years. Greene thinks she's more or less come to terms with it, even feels protective of Maisie in a way. They couldn't have children — God knows they tried for long enough, and the years of failure changed that side of their marriage — but sometimes Greene thinks that Maisie might have been the daughter Vanessa never had. No, that's not quite right, he corrects himself. Vanessa hopes that if Maisie had been her daughter, someone would have looked out for her in the way he had — Vanessa too, in a fashion, by accepting the situation. Between them they'd saved Maisie's life, and they both knew it.

For her part Vanessa has no illusions as to the sort of man her husband is. Nonetheless, mixed in with the sludge, the dodginess and the tendency to use fists and boots when clear thinking would've been better, she still finds tiny diamonds of kindness.

'She's well set, come what may,' he answers.

There's silence in the kitchen for a while as the kettle boils.

He stands. 'Shall we give tea a miss? Let's go to bed.'

The two young black men sitting on the steps of 14 Colville Terrace, Notting Hill, eye the two white police officers approaching them with outright hostility, but don't actually impede their progress up the steps. The front door is again wide open, and DI Greene enters the hall, checks a scrap of paper in his hand and starts climbing the stairs towards the second floor. The young detective constable following him carries a bundle under his arm.

They pass no one else on their way to Irenna's bedsit door. Greene inclines his ear to the door, holds his breath and listens carefully. No sound emanates from behind the door. He stands back and knocks. No reply, and more silence. He knocks again and waits. He stands back and nods to the young police officer, who steps back half a pace, takes a deep breath, raises his right foot and kicks at the door lock with as much force as he can command.

The door bursts open inwards, crashing against the adjoining wall. The bedsit is unoccupied. Strewn about every surface, including the bed and the floor, are magazines, newspapers, textbooks and other documents. The two men enter, trampling on everything under foot. They search the place, swiftly and efficiently.

To the right of the window is a small rail on which hang clothes.

'Are you sure we've got the right bedsit, guv?' asks the constable. 'These are all women's clothes.'

Greene walks across. He leafs quickly through the clothes on their hangers. 'Except these,' he says, finding a pair of man's trousers and a couple of shirts.

He scans the room again, this time focusing more on signs of the occupant's sex. On the bedside table is a tooth mug with two brushes in it and, on a small dressing table with a spotted mirror, he sees a dry shaving brush and some shaving cream.

'No, I think we've got the right place. He's got some bird in tow, that's all. Go into the corridor, close the door behind you, and don't let anybody in.'

DI Greene and his colleague have to wait until after nine o'clock in the dark room before Sloane and Irenna return. The DS had travelled to north Finchley to meet Irenna after her shift, and they ended up going out for a few drinks with some of her hospital colleagues. Had they returned earlier, the other occupants of the house would have warned them as to what awaited them, but the two young men who were smoking on the steps earlier that evening have both gone out and so Sloane and Irenna are unprepared.

They climb the steps to her bedsit, talking and laughing. It is Sloane who notices the damaged door and broken lock. He puts a finger to his lips and pushes the door open gently, only for the room to be flooded with light. Greene is standing by the window, having watched the couple approach the street steps. His colleague, sitting on one of the two plastic chairs, is by the light switch.

'Detective Sergeant Sloane?' asks Greene.

'Yes?'

'And you are?' Greene directs the question at Irenna.

'Dr Irenna Alexandrova.'

'I'm Detective Inspector Greene of the Flying Squad, and this is Detective Constable Lincoln. Is this your flat?' asks Greene of Sloane.

'It's mine,' says Irenna.

Sloane spots the look of surprise passing between the other two men; not the answer they expected.

'Are these yours?' asks Greene, and he lifts off the clothes rail two waterproof jackets bearing RAF insignia.

'Who are you asking?' asks Irenna.

'Either of you.'

'I've never seen them before,' replies Irenna.

'Nor have I,' says Sloane.

'These are stolen goods, and I'm arresting you both on suspicion of receiving them. You don't have to say anything unless you wish to do so, but anything you say will be taken down and given in evidence.'

'Got a minute, boss?' asks Greene, his head round Cathcart's door.

Cathcart is in the process of putting on his coat. 'Not really. I was due home two hours ago.'

'I've arrested that paddy, Sloane.'

'Fine.'

'Thing is, it turns out that we were given the wrong address. Or, rather, it's the right address, but it's not his bedsit.'

'Whose is it, then?'

'Some South African doctor with a Russian name. She works up at Finchley Memorial Hospital.'

'Anything known?'

'No. No criminal record, at least not here.'

'How on earth are you going to make receiving stolen goods stick against Sloane, then? If it's not his bedsit?'

'That's what I was thinking. But I probably can make it stick against the doctor.'

'What good's that?' demands Cathcart impatiently, trying to head towards the door. Greene remains in his way.

'Well, that's the point. She's his girlfriend, and I think we could get her deported if we can make the charges stick. She's some sort of political activist, judging from the crap in her room, working with the blacks. That's an even better lever against Sloane. He's on a crusade anyway, so suspending him on an iffy receiving charge probably wouldn't have stopped him. But she's a different kettle of fish. So, unless you think it's a bad idea, I propose charging her and letting Sloane go. But not without making absolutely clear to him what he has to do, if he wants the charges dropped.'

'Fine, whatever you think's best. Now, I really must go. My wife will already have thrown my dinner in the bin — or the dog, depending on her mood.'

'I'm going to keep them both in overnight!' calls Greene to the departing back of his superior officer.

Cathcart simply lifts his arm in acknowledgment as he strides away down the corridor.

CHAPTER 22

'How are you feeling, sir?'

Charles has just walked through the door of Chambers into the clerks' room for the first time in over a week. He is, at last, walking normally. The tenderness has more or less resolved, although the black and purple bruising would still be visible to anyone intimate enough with Charles to get a look. In other words, no one.

'Much better, thanks, Barbara.'

'We're all very pleased to see you in one piece. I've been feeling rather guilty about persuading you to take Mrs Maynard's case.'

'Don't be daft; it's certainly not your fault.'

'Everyone's talking about it in the Temple.'

Charles's heart sinks. 'What? Really?'

'Not because it's you specifically. I've heard only sympathy, especially as you were acting pro bono. I think what's happened has alerted the Bar generally to the risks counsel faces, particularly in circumstances when he's essentially litigating "blind" without a solicitor investigating first. In dock briefs, for example.'

'Not just "he"; "she" too, nowadays.'

'Good point. Thank you for correcting me. A woman in those circumstances would be even more vulnerable. You'll find a lot of "Get Well" cards on your desk. Oh, and that journalist friend of yours called. He'd like a call back at the *Mirror*.'

'Can you get him for me, please? I'll take it upstairs.'

Charles walks, gently, up to the first floor and his room. The phone rings as he's dropping his briefcase onto his desk. Barbara puts the call through.

'Good morning, Percy.'

'Morning. I've got a bit of news for you.'

'Oh yes?'

'Your coroner handed down his verdict yesterday afternoon.'

Charles sighs. 'I heard about the debacle at court. Very disappointing.'

'Wait till you hear this. Tommy Benson, that youngster from *Bedfordshire Times* and I are working together on this now, and he read it to me over the phone last night. The coroner has found homicide by person or persons unknown! He's referred the case to the DPP.'

'I don't believe it. How could he, with the bike parts missing?'

'He's given a narrative verdict. I've never seen it before when there's no jury. He says that having examined the bike parts himself, on the basis of his mechanical knowledge he has no doubt that they were deliberately interfered with, with the intent of causing the bike to crash. Did you know that he was a tank commander in the war?'

'No.'

'Well, I guess he's fixed enough tanks in his time to know.'

'This is good news, and very unexpected. Thanks for letting me know.'

'I'm sure it's an oversight, but I don't suppose you've got a copy of today's *Mirror*, have you?' asks Farrow.

'No, sorry, Percy. I meant to pop into…'

'Stop lying to me; I don't expect you to read my rag. But you might see something of interest if you make an exception this morning.'

'You've broken the story! I didn't think you had enough.'

'Buy a copy, and you'll see,' says Farrow with a chuckle.

As soon as he hangs up, Charles heads to the newsagent on the Strand. He buys a copy of the *Mirror* and takes it back up to his room to read. Taking up half of the front page is the headline: ***MURDER ENQUIRY LINKED TO RAF SWINDLE*** *by Percy Farrow and Thomas Benson*. The article continues:

A hitherto suppressed RAF Special Investigations Branch investigation has been leaked to this newspaper indicating that two members of RAF personnel have been murdered by London gangsters. It is alleged that Sergeant Maynard and Aircraftman McParland, both based at RAF Cardington in Bedfordshire, were killed to suppress evidence relating to a long-running fraud against the RAF.

At yesterday's inquest into the death of Sgt Maynard, HM Coroner for Bedford, Mr Nigel Cook QC, found homicide by person or persons unknown, and referred the case to the Director of Public Prosecutions.

The fraud involves the theft of £100,000s of equipment from RAF stores which have made their way into the markets of London where innocent members of the public have been duped into buying the stolen goods.

Well-placed sources indicate that Detective Inspector Greene of the Metropolitan Police's Flying Squad is leading the enquiry and that arrests are imminent.

The article continues on an inside page with information about Mr Cook QC, HM Coroner, and the London markets where the goods were found, together with a photograph of a grinning market trader holding up a blue serge RAF jacket, presumably taken before the police impounded it as evidence. Farrow's final flourish is a photograph of Greene himself being doorstepped by dozens of journalists outside Scotland Yard, a bristle of cameras and microphones pointing at him. The Detective Inspector looks decidedly uncomfortable.

Naming him as leading the investigation has got to force his hand.

Charles laughs out loud. 'You wily old fox! Thank God for the Fourth Estate!'

Farrow's article is not the subject of celebration elsewhere in London.

'I'm not prepared to argue any longer about it!' shouts Detective Superintendent Cathcart. 'Either arrest Gervaise — and I mean by tomorrow — or I'll get someone who will!'

'But, boss —'

'That's enough, Detective Inspector Greene! I'm giving you a direct order. Your bright idea of arresting Sloane and that doctor was a waste of time, and now this! The whole thing's slipped out of your grasp, and we've got to get control of it again. I've been called to see the DPP and the Commissioner at noon tomorrow, and I need to be able to tell them that Gervaise is in custody. Have I made myself clear?'

'Yes, sir. I'll get onto it immediately.'

'Thank you.'

'One last thing, sir?'

'Well?'

'What do you want me to do about Dr Alexandrova?'

Cathcart pauses and considers. 'She's been charged, hasn't she?'

'Yes. She's downstairs in the cells.'

'Will it stick?'

'It will. I'll make sure it does.'

'I'm not going to shed any tears over some black-loving Communist activist. Let justice take its course.'

'Yes, sir.'

CHAPTER 23

It's a cold, damp morning and sunrise is not for another hour and a half. DI Greene and two of his Flying Squad colleagues clambered out of their warm, cigarette-smoke filled squad car a few minutes before, still yawning. Insofar as possible, they have scouted around the perimeter of the property and have been unable to find any exit other than the grand front entrance; the grounds appear entirely surrounded by ten-foot high walls topped with railings and CCTV cameras.

'Who has fucking cameras?' Greene complained miserably.

'We do,' pointed out one of the constables.

'Yeh, Scotland Yard maybe, but what fucker has them on a private house?'

'Well … he does,' said the other, perhaps unwisely. 'Look at it,' he added, pointing at the house. 'I'd want cameras too.'

They are in the richest part of suburban London, an area named Hampstead Garden Suburb, and this road, The Bishop's Avenue, is the richest of all. It's known to estate agents and local residents as "Millionaire's Row". The property next to Gervaise's is the mansion of King Constantine of Greece; the two buildings are equally opulent.

Although DI Greene was aware that Gervaise lived in this area, this is the first time he's actually seen the gangster's house, and the more he looks at it, the less ambivalent he becomes about the arrest he's about to make. It makes his little house in Camberwell look like a hovel. Time to take Gervaise down a notch or two. Or ten.

Greene looks up and down the road, gauging the angles of the cameras.

'Go back to the car,' he finally decides. 'If he sees all of you, he's more likely to bolt. Once I'm let in, see if you can slip in after me.'

Once satisfied that his colleagues are out of camera range, Greene presses the button on the intercom.

'Yes?' says a female, perhaps foreign, voice.

'This is Sidney Greene to see Mr Gervaise.'

'Please wait.'

After a short delay there's a buzz and the gates swing open. As Greene strides across the gravelled drive towards the columned porch, the front door opens. Gervaise appears in a dressing gown, a cocktail glass in his hand. Greene sees immediately that, despite the hour, Gervaise is drunk. *Early start or late finish?* wonders the policeman.

'Good morning, Mr Greene,' he calls cheerfully from the front step. 'This is a surprise.'

'Hello, Billy.'

'Wanna come in f'r a drink?'

'No, thanks. I just need a quick word.'

Gervaise's eyes flick towards the gates which are still closing slowly. Both of Greene's colleague have made it inside and are approaching. His friendly expression fades away.

Greene arrives before him and halts. 'William Gervaise, I am arresting you on suspicion of conspiracy to commit murder. You do not have to say anything unless you wish to do so, but anything you say will be taken down and given in evidence against you.'

Gervaise is so stunned that he's incapable of any reply.

'Record "No reply",' Greene directs the others.

Gervaise reflexively pats his pockets again for his cigarettes, only to remember, yet again, that he has none. DI Greene allowed him to get dressed before putting him in the police car, but he grabbed whatever was to hand and that included no cigarettes. In any case, what few personal possessions he had on arrival were taken from him.

He estimates that he's been in the cell at West End Central Police Station for at least two hours and has seen no one since he was locked in.

He is still confident and reasonably cheerful. He doesn't believe Greene will actually charge him; he knows too much, can point a finger too accurately at members of the Flying Squad. Greene's been stirred into action by the newspaper reports, and this is all for show. Most importantly, Greene has no evidence to link him with either of the deaths at Cardington.

He stands, goes to the door and starts kicking it repeatedly. The noise reverberates around the cell area. He continues kicking. There's no official response but the man in the cell opposite starts shouting, bleating about having been woken up. All to the good, thinks Gervaise; the more noise the better. He redoubles his efforts.

It takes several minutes, but eventually he hears footsteps. The wicket opens.

'What?' demands an angry desk sergeant.

'I'm entitled to a meal now, and a call to my lawyer.'

The wicket slams closed without a word. Gervaise resumes kicking.

He continues making a din for several minutes, now singing "Jerusalem" at the top of his voice, kicking in time to the beat. Gervaise never listens to music, but he remembers the hymn from his Sunday school days and what he lacks in musicality he makes up in enthusiasm. To his surprise and pleasure, the prisoner opposite joins in with those snatches of lyrics he remembers. He starts enjoying himself.

Gervaise doesn't hear the approaching footsteps over the noise this time but, finally, keys jangle and one is inserted into the lock. The door opens. DI Greene stands in the corridor with the sergeant.

'Interview room one, inspector,' says the desk sergeant. 'Come on, vicar,' he says to Gervaise.

Gervaise is conducted to an interview room on the ground floor. Greene sits in front of him, and his young colleague silently takes a seat at the end of the table with a notebook and pen.

'I want my lawyer.'

'All in good time. For the moment I'm declining your request on the grounds that allowing you contact with anyone outside the police station will put witnesses at risk. Mr William Gervaise, my name is Detective Inspector Greene and this is Detective Constable Lincoln. You are still under caution.' Greene pauses to consult some documents. 'Where were you on eighth October nineteen sixty-five?'

Gervaise shrugs. 'No comment.'

'Do you know an aircraftman named Freddie McParland? He was based at RAF Cardington.'

'No comment.'

And that is the format of the interview for the next forty minutes. Greene consults his papers and puts questions, Gervaise answers with no comment and DC Lincoln records it all. Finally, Greene and Lincoln share a glance and Greene puts his file down.

'Billy, make no mistake that whatever you say or don't say, by this afternoon you will be charged with conspiracy to murder Maynard and McParland.' Greene leans forward and drops his voice. When he next speaks, he cannot quite keep the excitement from his expression. 'That lad made a full confession before you killed him.'

It's Greene's excitement, not his words, that penetrates Gervaise's nonchalance. For the first time, there's a flicker of doubt on the bland, bookkeeper-like face.

'Yes,' continues Greene, 'he wrote to his mum. You terrified him, see? He mightn't have been the sharpest tool in the box, but he knew his life weren't worth tuppence once he'd done as asked and fixed Maynard's motorbike for you. So he told his old mum everything. And when the Bedford police didn't take it seriously, she sent the letter to the coroner. And now we have a copy.'

For a second Greene thinks that Gervaise is about to answer with something other than "No comment," but he is disappointed.

'No comment.'

Greene shrugs. 'And we've got the whole of the SIB report now. There's no doubt that Maynard's motorbike was tampered with. Which corroborates McParland's account.'

'No comment.'

'Fine.' Greene stands. 'You can go back to the cell and mull it over. Up you get.'

But Gervaise doesn't get up.

'Well?' asks Greene.

'Can we have a private word?' asks Gervaise, nodding towards Lincoln.

Greene hesitates for a moment and then inclines his head to the door. 'Give us a minute, lad,' he says to Lincoln. The DC stands and leaves the room.

'Okay. Now what?'

'What if I give you names?' asks Gervaise.

Greene shakes his head. 'We're way past that.'

'No. I mean real names.'

'What're you getting at?'

'What if I could give you the names of everyone involved in the Heathrow bullion robbery? And the Southend post office, where that old lady was shot. Enough detail and evidence for convictions. Watertight.' Greene studies the other's face. Gervaise continues. 'What if I could give you the names of everyone in the RAF conspiracy, the NCOs on base, the railwaymen, the guys who moved the stuff, the warehouses the goods was stored in, and the stalls flogging it; everyone?'

'I told you, names won't cut it.'

'Not just names. What if I agree to turn Queen's Evidence?'

Greene resumes his seat. 'You'd grass them all? You'd have to give first-hand, admissible evidence, Billy. Not just tittle-tattle.'

'I can do that.'

'What would you want in return?'

'Immunity. Total immunity. And a new identity. If we do this deal, my life won't be worth shit. There'll be contracts out on me within the hour. And I want my solicitor to sit in from now on, to handle the negotiations.'

Gervaise watches Greene's greedy eyes as the corrupt policeman savours the prospect of being the officer who solved some of London's biggest crimes of recent years.

'And of course there's the rewards,' adds Gervaise, as if in afterthought.

'Rewards?'

'The rewards on the banks and post office jobs. I'll be entitled to them if I give evidence leading to convictions. There's thirty grand on those alone. I'll give you two thirds.

You can share with Detective Superintendent Cathcart. One third each.'

'I can't make a deal like this…'

'Shame. You'd get chief inspector on the back of it, no problem.'

'What I mean is, it can't be done on my say-so. It's way beyond my pay grade.'

Gervaise sits back in his seat, confident again. 'Then pop me back in the cell with some breakfast, and speak to whoever you have to.'

CHAPTER 24

Charles has no time to take his coat off before the telephone on his desk rings. Jeremy speaks.

'Detective Sergeant Sloane for you, sir.'

'Morning, Sean,' says Charles cheerfully. 'Did you see yesterday's *Mirror*? Percy's done for DI Greene —'

'Charles, I need your help, and I need it right now!' interrupts Sloane. His voice is frantic.

'What's happened?'

'I've just spent the night in the cells at West End Central. Greene arrested Irenna and me. He was waiting at her bedsit yesterday evening for us to return.'

'On what charge?'

'You won't believe it. Receiving goods stolen from RAF Cardington. I think his plan was to plant the stuff on me — he thought it was my flat — but this is even better for him. I think they're going to deport her.'

'Has she got bail?'

'Greene refused police bail on the grounds that she'd abscond back to South Africa. Which is obvious nonsense.'

'So they'll have to produce her to a magistrate.'

'But I don't even know where they've got her! Greene released me without charge an hour ago. I waited outside, expecting Irenna to appear. Then I saw her being driven away in a police van!'

'All right, Sean, calm down and let me think.'

Sloane stops talking, but Charles can still hear the panic in his friend's breathing. Charles sits slowly at his desk, thinking furiously.

When Sloane speaks again, his voice is calmer. 'She's the one, Charlie. I love her … I can't let this happen. And if she goes back to South Africa, God knows what they'll do to her.'

'Meaning?'

'She'll be arrested, certainly. She might never get out of prison alive; look what's happened to her parents!'

'Does Greene have a price? He always has a price.'

'Yes. Backpedal on the Gervaise investigation and he'll let her go. But the press coverage means it's out of my hands now. I couldn't stop it even if I tried!' Sloane hears scuffling and thumps from the other end of the line. 'What the hell are you doing, Charles?' he demands angrily.

'I'm trying to … hang on! I'm trying to get down … Halsbury's Statutes…' Sloane hears more grunts and then a final 'Got it! They're on the top shelf. I don't use them much. Okay, just give me a moment. Or shall I call you back? This isn't my usual area of law so it might take a few minutes.'

'I'll wait.'

Sloane hears a heavy book landing on Charles's desk and pages being flicked. 'Here we are … Commonwealth Immigrants Act 1962.' Charles reads the first section. *"The provisions of this Part of this Act shall have effect for controlling the immigration into the United Kingdom of Commonwealth citizens…"* blah, blah … here we go! Section 6, *"Deportation"*… Just let me read for a moment…'

Sloane hears further pages being turned.

'How long has Irenna been in the country?' asks Charles suddenly.

'Since January 1960. Why?'

'Continuously?'

'Yes. Er … no! She arrived just before South Africa was suspended from the Commonwealth, but then two years later she went to Ontario. She was going to settle in Canada but it was too cold, so she came back here after a year.'

'Okay, so not five years continuously. Well, it looks as if she can be deported ... if she's convicted of an offence punishable with imprisonment. Which includes receiving.'

'Jesus Christ! What can I do, Charles?'

'Firstly, don't panic. The evidence against her is completely crap. Even if Greene were to be believed about finding RAF kit in her bedsit, that wouldn't mean she had the requisite knowledge to make her guilty of receiving. If you buy something, entirely honestly from a market stall, you're not guilty of anything. You have to know or believe it's stolen.'

'Yes, Charles, I know all this. I'm a fucking detective sergeant, remember?'

'Of course you know all this. But you sound really anxious, so I'm just reminding you; it's highly unlikely Irenna would be convicted. I think the first thing is to get her a good solicitor.'

'You can't do this alone?'

'No. I can't take direct instructions. And the solicitor will have to be paid.'

'What about you?'

Charles hesitates before replying. 'I'm offended that you even ask, my friend,' he says gently.

'Thank you. Thank you. But what will a solicitor cost?'

'Well ... we could try to apply for legal aid. I'm afraid I don't know if someone in Irenna's position would be eligible. I can look it up but, failing that, we have to find the money to pay privately. They'll need to take instructions at the prison or deportation centre, prepare a witness statement, attend the committal and the trial ... around three hundred and fifty pounds?'

'I haven't got that sort of money! Do you know what I'm paid? And Irenna's even worse; she lives hand to mouth.'

'How about your parents? Would they lend you the money?'

'They're dirt-poor tenant farmers. They'd do it if they could, if I told them how much she means to me, but I can't ask them.'

Charles stops to consider this new problem. 'How long has she worked for her West Indian union organisation?'

'I don't know exactly. A couple of years?'

'Maybe her employers could help?'

'I doubt it. They're run on a shoestring.'

'All right, let's shelve that for the moment. I need to find a good solicitor who'll act for Irenna, at least for the purposes of applying for legal aid, and/or defer payment. I've a couple of ideas on that subject. Leave it with me and I'll call you back before close of play. Now, practicalities. If and when they charge her, they'll have to give her a phone call and access to a lawyer. You've got no phone, have you, so who will she call?'

There's a pause on the line while Sloane considers the question. 'I doubt she'd waste it calling me at the nick, as I'm not always here. You, maybe?'

'Okay, I'll let the clerks know to put her through or take details if I'm not in. In the meantime … Sean? Are you listening?'

'Yes.'

'Don't worry. We'll sort this out. I promise.'

CHAPTER 25

Charles climbs the steps of 3 King's Bench Walk and scans the board listing the barristers practising from the chambers. Finding the name he seeks, he steps inside and pushes open the door to the clerks' room.

'Afternoon, sir,' says a fresh-faced young man.

'Good afternoon. Is Mr Sowande in chambers today?'

The clerk opens the diary and runs his finger down until he finds the relevant initials.

'He's not in court, so possibly. Who shall I say…'

'Charles Holborne, of counsel.'

The clerk dials an internal number. 'Sorry to disturb you, sir, but there's a Mr Charles Holborne of counsel here to see you, if you've a moment. Yes … yes … okay.'

He hangs up. 'Would you like to go up, sir? Second floor, on the right. Mr Sowande will meet you on the landing.'

Charles thanks the clerk and climbs to the second floor.

A very dark-skinned African man with a round face and a big smile awaits Charles. 'Charles! My dear friend,' he exclaims. He speaks with a Nigerian accent softened by years spent in England. 'What brings you over the road?'

'Hi, Tunji. I'm sorry to disturb you, but I have a problem which you might be able to solve.'

'What, a legal problem? You were always better at those than me!'

This isn't true. Tunji Sowande was ranked higher than Charles in the results for their Bar Finals. Sowande, with degrees in pharmacy and law, a baritone voice good enough for a professional career, and a multi-instrumentalist who plays

201

both classical music and jazz with greats such as Ronnie Scott and Johnny Dankworth, is a true polymath, and someone of whom Charles has always been slightly in awe. Sowande came to the Bar late, almost as an afterthought, and is a decade or more older than Charles. However, as the only black man and the only Jew to study for the Bar that year, they formed an alliance against the daily sneers and sniping they both faced, which soon became a friendship. Their paths continue to cross regularly as both practise in crime and are often sent to the same courts. Charles makes the effort to go to Sowande's jazz gigs whenever he can.

'Come in and tell me about it,' says Sowande, putting an arm round Charles's shoulder.

Sat before Sowande's desk, Charles briefly relates the events leading to Irenna's arrest.

'So,' summarises Sowande, leaning back and rubbing his hand through his short hair as he thinks, 'you need a cunning, sympathetic solicitor with big balls, prepared to work for nothing.'

Charles laughs grimly. 'That's about the size of it. Easy, right?'

'Why come to me?'

'You know everyone in the black community, African and West Indian. And Irenna Alexandrova is a bit of a heroine in both. I thought maybe that might help us find someone…'

'Sympathetic?'

'Exactly.'

Sowande's chair creaks as he leans even further back and considers the problem. 'There may be someone,' he says. 'Do you know Hansie Fischer?' Charles shakes his head. 'He has a law firm called Churchills in south London. An Afrikaner, but a good man, a member of the Zimbabwean National

Democratic Party. Very clever. He escaped here a few years ago after two years of house arrest. Your doctor will know of him, certainly. Give him a call and use my name.'

'I shall. But … what about fees?'

Sowande's face creases into a big grin. 'My guess is that he's plugged into some of the same organisations as your doctor, so he might be able to solve that problem for you too. Good luck, my friend,' he says, standing. 'Now, I have an urgent Advice to finish.'

The phone rings on Greene's desk. 'Greene,' he announces.

'Can you come up?' says Cathcart. 'I've news.'

'On my way.'

Greene runs up the stairs to his boss's office, knocks, enters and shuts the door carefully behind him. Cathcart's been in difficult meetings since seven that morning, but he still looks perfectly groomed; he reminds Greene of Robert Taylor, the American film star — one of the reasons Greene took such pleasure in corrupting his too-handsome Chief Superintendent.

'The DPP and Deputy Commissioner won't go for immunity,' says Cathcart. 'Just not possible. He'll have to agree to plead to something, and he'll have to serve some time.'

'He'll never plead to the murders. What would be the point? He might as well have his day in court.'

'They're not fixated on the murders. The letter from McParland probably isn't admissible, and without that we've got nothing. But otherwise, in principle, there's a deal to be had. Assuming he comes good.'

Greene's eyes shine with excitement. 'Righto, boss.'

'Get his lawyer in for later today if possible.'

'He's here already. Billy's wife called him, and he's been waiting downstairs since this morning.'

'Good. I want the outline agreed tonight. Then we can see what he's actually got to offer.'

An hour later, still in the cells, Gervaise is sensing a change in the wind. He's not seen Greene or Cathcart again, but he's been allowed to change into the more appropriate clothes brought by Betty from home, and the late lunch he's just finished came direct from the station canteen, still hot and not at all bad.

Keys rattle again, the door opens and a different sergeant escorts him up to an interview room. Waiting for him is his solicitor, a Bombay Jew named Cohen who represents most of the major criminals in London and whom Gervaise has used when required for over twenty years. The sergeant closes the door and leaves them alone.

'All right?' asks Cohen.

'Not bad, all considered,' says Gervaise, sitting.

'They've been discussing with me this deal you've offered them. Are you sure, Billy? You know what it means.'

'They reckon they've got me on murder —' Cohen starts to interrupt, but Gervaise holds up a hand to stop him — 'and even if they ain't, they've definitely got evidence to stick me as the ringleader of the gang knocking off the RAF gear. And what would I get for conspiracy to steal three quarters of a million or so from the RAF, with my record?'

'Ten to twelve on a plea.'

'Exactly. Whereas if I can get immunity and then a new identity, with no risk on the murder, it makes sense. I don't care about those fuckers,' he finishes, referring to his colleagues in crime.

Cohen believes him. Billy Gervaise is a different breed from most of his big-league criminal clients. Gervaise didn't grow up in the East End; he doesn't like socialising with or feuding against other villains; and he keeps his family well away from his business affairs. He and his wife like their bridge and their French language classes, and his two daughters attend a good school and are occupied with their studies, their chess clubs and their hockey matches. So the concept of honour amongst thieves, and keeping *schtum* at all costs — even at the cost of doing time — is not one to which Gervaise subscribes.

'I've thought it through,' he concludes.

'They won't give you immunity,' says Cohen simply.

Gervaise sighs but is not deflated. That was his first offer, and he didn't expect it to be accepted. At least not initially. 'What'll they agree?'

'Well, they want a plea to a minor part in the conspiracy, say moving the goods off the train to the warehouses, and a plea to assaulting the DS in that goods yard.'

Now Gervaise does look surprised. 'Why're they bothering with that? It was nothing. Nah, I ain't having that one.'

'Sure? Seems innocuous to me.'

'I'm sure. How long, then?'

'Six.'

'Fuck off!' says Gervaise, outraged. 'That's taking the piss, that is! Four years, max.'

Cohen shakes his head. 'They won't have it.'

Gervaise pauses, thinking hard. 'What if I offer them Ronnie and Reggie?'

'On the murder?'

'Don't be silly. That'd never stick. But on the warehousing and finance of the RAF thieving.'

'I can ask.'

Cohen stands and knocks on the door. It's unlocked from outside and Greene is there in the corridor, waiting. Cohen pulls the door closed behind him and speaks softly to the inspector.

'He won't agree to six, or to that copper at Cricklewood. He says four max, but … he can offer you the Krays.'

'Which ones?' asks Greene.

'The twins.'

'What, for murder?' asks Greene quickly, suddenly excited by the prospect of potting the twins for life, something no one has been able to do.

'No. For the London end of the RAF thing.'

'Hmm. Pity. I'm not sure, but I'll take it upstairs.'

The deal is eventually done. Four years, provisional, as Cathcart keeps repeating, on the quality of the goods Gervaise has to offer.

Within the hour Gervaise is moved to Pitsea police station in Essex, away from the prying eyes and ears of London, and he starts squealing: names, dates, associates, the location of stolen goods, cars and, in one case, a body. Twenty-four hours later, DC Lincoln's wrist is aching so much from the scores of pages he's taken down from Gervaise, he has to be replaced by a different scribe. Another twenty-four hours, and Greene, Cathcart and their superiors have enough good information from Gervaise to arrest thirty other criminals, and the buzz through the police station is palpable; everyone is excited. Some of these cases went cold months, even years, before. Everyone involved has an eye on career advancement.

Gervaise is moved to a different cell, one with a TV and a fold-out bed, and starts receiving meals and drinks, including wine, from a local Italian restaurant.

Nonetheless, despite the move to Essex, as always, word gets out and now Greene has to field calls from other forces and Met Divisions who also want to mine his rich seam of information. All requests are declined; he and Cathcart jealously keep Gervaise to themselves.

Later, on the third day, a secret bail application is held before the local magistrates who, somewhat over-awed by having a Detective Chief Superintendent and a letter from the Metropolitan Deputy Commissioner before them, do as they're told and order Gervaise to be kept at Pitsea so he can keep talking.

On the afternoon of Day 4, after another twelve pages of confessions and details, Gervaise asks to see Greene in his cell. Greene is asleep just down the corridor in one of the other cells — he's not been home for six days — but he gets up nonetheless, rubs the bleariness from his eyes and presents himself at Gervaise's cell door. At this critical juncture, before the grass has pleaded guilty, received his sentence and started to give Queen's Evidence, the Flying Squad will do almost anything to ensure the Gervaise goose continues to lay golden eggs.

'Yes, Billy?'

Gervaise is watching his television. He's in the largest cell offered by the police station, but it's still crowded. In addition to his bed, the armchair in which he presently reclines and the television, there is now a drinks cabinet and a small dressing table.

'I ain't seen Betty for five days.' He leaves the sentence hanging, and both men know what has been omitted.

Greene pretends he doesn't. 'Yes. But it can't be helped. It's too risky for you to go home.'

'Then bring her here.'

'She's not going to want to come to Pitsea police station to see you, surely?'

'She is. And I want her to stay over.'

'What are you saying? You want a conjugal?'

Billy grins and has the good grace to blush slightly. 'I don't see why not. I got bail, but on condition I stayed here. But if I was out on bail in any other circumstances and about to go inside, I'd certainly be getting me oats. I'd be at it like a bleedin' rabbit, wouldn't I? Stocking up for a long gap.'

'You can't be serious.'

'I'm totally serious. You want me happy, doncha? You don't want me all cross and frustrated … not to mention forgetful.'

Greene sighs and shakes his head in disbelief. 'I'll ask.'

Charles is working in Chambers, late. Again. Barbara puts her head around the door. She's wearing her raincoat and scarf and has her voluminous handbag over one forearm.

'I've locked up the other side and downstairs,' she says. 'You're the last one in.'

'Thank you.'

There's a noise as the outer door opens and hesitant footsteps approach down the corridor. Barbara turns and addresses someone. 'Can I help you?'

'I'm looking for Charles Holborne,' says a man's voice with a strong Jamaican accent.

'Who are you?'

'My name is Joseph Campbell.'

Barbara turns to Charles. 'There's a Mr Campbell here for you, sir. Do you want to see him?'

Charles rises from his desk. 'Sure.' He sees uncertainty on Barbara's face. 'It's fine, Barbara, you can go. I can deal with whatever Mr Campbell wants.'

'Are you sure? I'm happy to wait.'

'No, you get off. Why don't you ask Mr Campbell to come in?'

Barbara hesitates. 'You do know that I'm most unhappy about personal approaches from potential clients, don't you, sir? We've had this discussion before.'

Much as Barbara is delighted that Charles is a rain-maker and frequently receives new referrals direct from satisfied lay clients, she finds his informal approach and his tendency to bypass the clerks infuriating.

'I'm well aware of that, but I don't believe Mr Campbell is a potential client.' Charles approaches the door and opens it fully to find a short middle-aged Jamaican man a few steps away in the corridor, nervously twiddling his hat. 'Are you a potential client, Mr Campbell?'

'No, sir, not at all, sir. I've come to … with a message about Dr Alex's case.'

Charles turns to Barbara. 'There you are.'

Barbara remains by the door, still looking concerned. 'Very well. Goodnight, then. Don't forget, ten-thirty con at Pentonville.'

She turns, smiles perfunctorily at Mr Campbell and departs.

'Would you like to come in?' Charles asks the little Jamaican, standing back to let him enter. 'Take a seat.'

'No, that won't be necessary. I've just come to tell you something which I hope will help.'

'If you are a witness, Mr Campbell, I'm not allowed to speak to you —'

'No, no,' says Campbell hurriedly, 'it's nothing like that! I work with Dr Alex. I just came to tell you that there's been a collection for her defence. Everyone's outraged at her arrest.'

'It's a complete fabrication, you know that, don't you?' says Charles, suddenly anxious for Irenna's reputation.

'Of course it is. It's a joke, that's what it is. We've all enough experience of the police in London to know what they're like.

Anyway, the message is this: this afternoon a cheque for just over two hundred pounds has been delivered to Mr Hansie Fischer's offices. Do you think that will be enough?'

'That's wonderful,' exclaims Charles with warmth. 'I know she'll be very grateful, as am I. As to whether it'll be enough, we'll see, but it's certainly enough for the moment. Please pass my thanks to everyone who contributed.'

'I will do that.'

Campbell leaves and Charles returns to his papers, very relieved.

The previous week he went to see Fischer, to whom he warmed. A tall, heavy-set man with a shaved head and a very fast, no-nonsense way of speaking, Fischer was sympathetic to Irenna's plight, having represented scores of clients framed by the Met over the years, and he knew of her work. But, somewhat to Charles's surprise, he wasn't prepared to represent her without being paid. With what seemed to be genuine regret, he showed Charles the door, saying he'd be happy to reconsider if some arrangement could be made regarding funding.

Charles made numerous other enquiries, seeking a solicitor with deep pockets and a social conscience, with no success. Mr Campbell's news will make all the difference.

It is almost eleven o'clock before Charles leaves Chambers. He's exhausted, but determined to maintain progress on the house at Wren Street, so he drives there, changes into his overalls, and continues sanding the kitchen floorboards. He finishes shortly after midnight. He's not seen or heard any neighbours, to either side, but he's worried that if there are any, he may be disturbing them.

By the time he reaches Fetter Lane it is almost twelve-thirty. He almost goes directly upstairs without looking to see if there's any post for him, but changes his mind and pauses by Dennis's desk. There's an unstamped letter addressed to him in manuscript, obviously hand-delivered. He takes it upstairs with him.

Once in the flat and with a nightcap in his hand, he opens the envelope. It's signed merely "P", but Charles recognises the almost illegible handwriting of the journalist, Percy Farrow.

I thought you might like to know that my sources in C11 indicate that BG has turned grass. He's being entertained somewhere outside London (Essex, it's thought) and has named 30 or more people. There are to be co-ordinated arrests across London tomorrow morning, with the accused men taken to a variety of police stations. And of particular relevance to you, a Sergeant Hawkins of the British Transport Police and a train driver named Carragher are included. In return for a lenient sentence, BG is grassing on the members of his own team like there's no tomorrow. My sources also indicate that there are at least two contracts out on the life of Gervaise, one of them underwritten by the twins. How they're involved, time will reveal. I'll keep you informed of developments, and I'd be grateful for a quid pro quo insofar as your client confidentiality allows it.

P

CHAPTER 26

Despite the fact that Hansie Fischer was put in funds a week earlier, Charles has received no instructions and has been unable to make a bail application on behalf of Irenna. She remains at HM Prison Holloway, along with several hundred other women prisoners, some on remand but most already serving time. Sean Sloane has been anxiously phoning Charles on a daily basis for news on the legal front. Charles has tried to calm him, pointing out that Irenna has spent much longer periods in much worse prisons than this, and Sloane has himself reported that she's befriended some black prisoners apparently willing to defend her should the need arise, which it hasn't. Charles is sure it will only be a matter of days.

Finally, a brief arrives in his pigeonhole from Fischer and Co. Charles rips off the pink ribbon as he runs upstairs to his room.

THE QUEEN

- and -

IRENNA ALEXANDROVA

BRIEF TO COUNSEL

Enclosures:

1. Full bundle of prosecution depositions

2. Copy charge sheet

3. Copy custody record

Counsel is instructed on behalf of Dr Irenna Alexandrova, who is charged with receiving stolen goods contrary to section 33 of the Larceny Act

1916. The subject of the charge is a pair of waxed jackets allegedly stolen from the RAF stores in Cardington, Bedfordshire. An indictment has yet to be received, but Instructing Solicitors enclose as Item 2 herewith a copy of the charge sheet from West End Central police station.

The client remains in custody at HM Prison Holloway and no application for bail has yet been made. The officer in charge of the case, Detective Inspector Greene, has indicated informally that any such application will be opposed on the grounds of the accused's lack of connection with the United Kingdom, the fact that she has relatives in Canada and a home in South Africa to which she could easily return.

It will be recalled that when counsel spoke to those instructing about the case, the question was raised as to how the Crown would prove that the jackets were in fact stolen, because the case against the accused was that she acquired them from a market stall at Petticoat Lane. That apparent defect in the Crown's case has now been remedied as Counsel will see from the enclosed depositions, by a witness named William Gervaise.

'What?' cries Charles, skimming ahead for more detail of this worrying development. What on earth has Gervaise got to do with this? Finding nothing immediately, he returns to his Instructions.

Counsel may be aware from the press reports that Gervaise is being referred to in the press as a "Supergrass" and it appears that he has given evidence against many of his former colleagues, including those involved in this case. Unfortunately, that appears to include our client.

Your Instructing Solicitors are in the process of arranging a conference at HM Prison Holloway later this week at which Mr Fischer will attend. Also in attendance will be DS Sloane of West Hendon Police Station, who is, we understand, known to Counsel and who has a particular interest in the case. It is an odd and very helpful circumstance that, for once, the Defence have a serving police officer on their "team". The purpose of the conference will be to discuss tactics, bail application, and to consider further investigations to be undertaken. The prosecution depositions have been sent to the client for her comments, which will be forwarded to Counsel as soon as they are received.

Counsel is instructed to advise in conference at the prison and thereafter to conduct the accused's bail application, the committal proceedings and in due course her defence at trial.

Fischer & Co.

Charles returns to his search for the deposition from Gervaise.

Deposition of William Arnold Gervaise
Occupation: Lorry driver
Address: Care of [ ] Police Station
Magistrates Court Rules 1952: This deposition of William Arnold Gervaise, care of [ ] police station, is sworn before me, Harrison Fitzwilliam QC, Justice of the Peace, on [insert date] in the presence of the accused, Irenna Alexandrova, at Marlborough Street Magistrates Court.
Signed:
Signature of deponent:

William Arnold Gervaise WILL SAY AS FOLLOWS:
I am a lorry driver by original profession. In the summer of 1963, I became involved with a group of criminals who planned to steal goods from the RAF base at Cardington, Bedfordshire. I was asked to drive a lorry and take the goods from wagons at Cricklewood goods yard to one of three warehouses in the East End of London. I had no other involvement in the crime, although I can name the others involved and have already given evidence to the police concerning them. I have pleaded guilty to my part in the conspiracy and I wish to give Queen's Evidence for the Crown in its

214

prosecutions against various other members of the gang.

In the course of moving the goods I came to know a young woman by the name of Irenna Alexandrova who was working part-time on a market stall at Petticoat Lane. I cannot remember the dates on which I spoke to her, but it was several times during the autumn of 1965. I understood that she worked at a hospital and, although we did not discuss it, I assumed she was a trainee nurse who was supplementing her income by working the occasional day at the market. Miss Alexandrova was joking that she wished she had some of the warm winter clothing that she was selling to other people. She told me she came from South Africa and was unused to the cold winters in the UK, but she did not have a heavy coat or, so she said, the money to buy one. Eventually, one very cold day while I was delivering further stock to the stall, she mentioned it again and I saw that she was shivering and not appropriately dressed for the conditions. It is very cold standing all day in an outdoor market. I therefore said she could take one of the coats. I asked her if she wanted also to take one for her boyfriend. I didn't know if she had a boyfriend or, if so, who that person might be, but I hoped to learn whether or not she had a boyfriend, because she was very pretty. I thought maybe I could ask her out. She said she didn't have a boyfriend. I remember very clearly that she looked at me cautiously and asked if the coats were "hooky". That is a slang expression used in the markets to mean stolen. I answered to the effect that "Of course they are, love. You've seen me bringing them in, and you've seen their prices." She shrugged and said something like "Who'll ever know?"

Detective Inspector Greene of the Metropolitan Police has shown me two jackets with RAF insignia stitched on them, and I confirm that one of them is the jacket I gave to Miss Alexandrova. I am sure of this because it is an unusual size, size 34 inch chest, which is the smallest the RAF do. Very few of that size are delivered to the RAF stores because most men are larger than that. I gave this one to her because I thought it had the best chance of fitting her.

Although it is possible to buy other army surplus from various market stalls in London, none are of the current design like these were. I would like to add that, although I agreed to let Miss Alexandrova keep one at the end of her shift, it looks as if she stole a second one from the stall, because I certainly didn't give her permission to take two.

Signed:

Signature of deponent: William Arnold Gervaise

Charles makes some notes when he finishes reading, goes back to the start, and runs through the statement again more carefully. He shakes his head at the last sentence, an unnecessary kick in the ribs as Gervaise passes. Leaving aside the legal question of whether someone can steal stolen goods from the thief who himself has stolen them from a third party, she is only charged with receiving, so this last comment is designed simply to throw mud.

There are two further statements included, one by DI Greene and one by DC Lincoln. Charles addresses Greene's first.

Deposition of Sidney Lancelot Greene

Occupation: Detective Inspector

Address: West End Central Police Station, 27 Savile Row, London, W1

Magistrates Court Rules 1952: This deposition of Sidney Lancelot Greene of West End Central Police Station, 27 Savile Row, London W1, is sworn before me, Harrison Fitzwilliam QC, Justice of the Peace, on [insert date] in the presence of the accused, Irenna Alexandrova, at Marlborough Street Magistrates Court.

Signed:

Signature of deponent: Sidney Lancelot Greene

Sidney Lancelot Greene WILL SAY AS FOLLOWS:

I am a Detective Inspector working in Department C8 of the Metropolitan Police, and I am based at West End Central Police Station. During the course of enquiries into a different matter I had cause to go to 14 Clifton Terrace, Notting Hill, London N4 in company with Detective Constable Lincoln on 26 November 1965. We arrived at 21:15 hours. The main front door of the property was open and we entered. As we were climbing the stairs to a flat on the top floor, we passed a doorway on the second floor which was half-open, and I noticed that the timber around the lock was splintered. Suspicious that a burglary had occurred, I looked into the room. It appeared from the state of the room, which had papers and books strewn all over the bed and floors, that there had indeed been a burglary. While taking stock of the situation I saw two jackets hanging on a rail in the corner of the room which drew my attention. They were RAF jackets, with appropriate insignia, and I knew them to be the most recent design and colour. I did not know how a member of the public might be the possessor of such clothing, but it occurred to me that the occupant of the bedsit might be a member of the armed forces. As DC Lincoln and I were preparing to leave the room, two people arrived, one of whom identified herself as Dr Irenna Alexandrova, the occupant of the room. I informed Dr Alexandrova that it appeared that her room had been burgled and that I would call the local police station to send a detective to take statements and to conduct a forensic examination. She appeared to me to be extremely nervous, and her eyes flicked to the jackets on the rail behind where I was standing. I was suspicious that she had come by the jackets unlawfully, so I asked her about them. She refused to answer any questions concerning the jackets, raising my suspicions further. Accordingly, I arrested her on suspicion of receiving stolen goods and took her to West End Central. I took possession of the two jackets which are now produced and shown to me marked SLG 1.

While DC Lincoln drove us back to the police station I took the opportunity to ask Miss Alexandrova more questions, and she admitted to knowing that the jackets had been stolen. I made notes of the questions and Miss Alexandrova's answers in the car in my pocket book, a typewritten transcript of which is now produced and shown to me marked SLG 2.

Signed: Signature of Deponent: Sidney Lancelot Greene

Charles has not seen Irenna since she was arrested, and of course she's had no time to give instructions on the prosecution statements, but he is one hundred percent certain she did not make the confession alleged against her. For over a decade the Flying Squad's tendency to fabricate confessions has been so ubiquitous that it has acquired its own term of art: a "verbal". Irenna has, without a doubt, been verballed.

He turns to the statement of DC Lincoln, but finds it almost word for word the same as that of the DI. He too produces a typescript of the interview which he heard and which was recorded in the inspector's pocket book. The thing that most strikes Charles, however, is that neither statement mentions Sean Sloane. If both were arrested together, and only one car used to transport them to the police station, Sloane would have heard the alleged confession. How is Greene going to explain that?

Charles turns to the typewritten notes of the alleged confession.

[Caution administered]

Q: Look, Dr Alexandrova, we both know there's no honest way you could have got hold of those jackets.

A: I don't have to answer your questions.

Q: But if you acquired the jackets honestly, why won't you tell me? You'll save us all a load of bother and you can get back to your flat and start tidying up.

218

A: I'm not answering any questions until I've spoken to a lawyer.

Q: Now, you see, that's an interesting answer. Have you got a lawyer? It'd be a strange thing for a student doctor to have, don't you think? Unless of course they've been in trouble with the police before.

A: [No answer]

Q: Well? Why would someone like you have a lawyer? Maybe your political activism's got you into trouble in the past? Yes, I saw all the documents scattered around the room. You're a communist, right?

A: [No answer]

Q: Suit yourself. But I guess you've been quite a handful, back in South Africa. Is that why you've got a lawyer? Come on, Irenna, don't be daft. You're escalating all of this when answering a couple of simple questions could bring it all to an end.

A: I got the jackets from Petticoat Lane. They were on a stall with a load of other army surplus.

Q: There you go. That wasn't difficult, was it? Perfectly reasonable explanation, if one believes it. Why were you so worried about the jackets when you came into your room?

A: I wasn't worried.

Q: Yes, you were. Your eyes kept going back to them and you looked really nervous. Honestly, Irenna, I've been doing this job for decades and I recognise things like that. Yours wasn't at all the sort of response I'd have expected from a burglary victim.

A: I don't know what you mean. I was just shocked at coming back to find the flat broken into, and two strange men in it. I didn't know you were policemen.

Q: Yes, you did. I introduced us as you walked into the room.

A: I was just frightened, okay?

Q: Let's get back to these jackets, shall we? You say you got them from Petticoat Lane?

A: Yes.

Q: Do you know the market well?

A: Quite well.

Q: How many times would you say you've been in the past?

A: A dozen or so.

Q: And you would agree with me that it's pretty rough there? Lots of wideboys and spivs selling all sorts.

A: Maybe.

Q: You've got to be careful, look out for yourself.

A: I suppose.

Q: And you have to be careful what you buy, because a lot of it is obviously too cheap, isn't it?

A: I don't know.

Q: Well, that's why people like going to these markets, isn't it? They can find bargains.

A: Yes.

Q: And it's common sense that when stuff is sold for much cheaper than it should be, you have to be careful because it might be stolen. Do you agree?

A: Yes.

Q: And did you ask yourself when you saw these jackets, is there anything about them that worries me?

A: Not really. They were just on a stall with a load of other similar things.

Q: How much did you pay for the jackets?

A: I don't remember exactly. Ten shillings maybe.

Q: Ten shillings for each of these? Surely that would have alerted you to the fact that they were stolen?

A: Not really.

Q: But this sort of wax jacket would usually cost a tenner at least. Ten pounds, not ten shillings. Come on now, Irenna, do yourself a favour and tell us the truth. You're only going to make things worse for yourself by lying. If you've got no previous convictions in this country, you'll probably get off with a small fine. But if you take it to trial and put us to a lot of inconvenience and cost, you could even go inside.

A: All right then.

Q: What do you mean "All right then"? Are you saying that you knew they were probably nicked?

A: Yes. I thought they were too cheap, and that they were probably stolen. But I didn't have any winter clothes, and it was freezing. Trainee doctors earn next to nothing, you know.

Charles grimaces. He's certain that Greene's framed Irenna to put pressure on Sloane. However, as far as false confessions go, this one reads well. It contains a lot of unnecessary detail which gives it the ring of normal conversation. But then, after years of experience of writing fiction, Greene ought to be good at it.

On paper this is a simple and impregnable case. The Crown can prove through Gervaise that the goods were stolen and that Irenna was aware of it; Greene supplies the all-important confession. Job done.

Greene and Cathcart are heroes, and Detective Inspector Sidney Greene is milking it for all its worth. When he returned to West End Central earlier that day, he earned rounds of spontaneous applause both in the CID office and in the canteen, and a "Well done" from his immediate boss, a snooty chief inspector who usually has no time at all for him. To think that only a few days ago he was thinking he and Vanessa might have to do a runner!

The icing on the cake is his discovery of a new income stream. Over the last forty-eight hours, ten of the fringe players arrested have brought applications for bail, which Greene offered not to oppose on condition that a small contribution be made towards his "Costa del Sol fund". All readily agreed; eight paid £50, one £75 and the last, whose involvement was more serious than the others and who would never have secured bail had Greene raised the slightest of objections, offered £125. Greene now has £600 in the shoebox under his bed, which he has no intention of sharing with Cathcart. It's enough to buy a new car, but Vanessa insists that she wants instead to rip out the old swimming pool in Spain and install one of those new ones, with a bar in the middle. Greene's been in such a good mood, he's decided not to argue.

Charles finishes work for the day, relatively early, just before eight o'clock. He has completed his preparation for the conference with Irenna at HM Prison Holloway and knows from previous experience that the best way to clear his mind is to do something completely different; ideally something practical. Decorating a near-derelict house close to King's Cross fits the bill perfectly, and the plumbers have been working there for the last few days and have (allegedly) finished installing the central heating; he can take the opportunity to check.

The second his foot lands on the cobbles of Middle Temple Lane, Charles realises he will not be making it to Wren Street tonight or, if he does, he will be delayed. Parked incongruously in the narrow street formed of leaning Dickensian buildings is a large American car with sharp fins and a great deal of polished chrome. Charles doesn't need to look inside to know who wants a word with him. One of the Kray twins' most enduring businesses is located on the pavement close to the Regal Billiard Hall, just off Mile End Road. Here they maintain a small stock of expensive American luxury cars, partly for sale and partly to transport the twins to their more celebrated social events.

The front passenger door opens, effectively blocking the pavement and Charles's route, although he has already come to a halt by the rear doors. An enormous man extricates himself with a grunt from the passenger seat. He is a six-foot, twenty-stone oval of Glaswegian fat and aggression, his trousers suspended over a waist that forms the widest part of his spherical shape.

'Evening, Pat,' says Charles.

The last time Charles spoke to Big Pat Connolly, the Glaswegian was pointing a gun at him, a split-second away from shooting him and Charles's lighterman cousin, Izzy. That evening ended with them all taking an impromptu swim in the Thames as the tug on which they were travelling capsized, which is how Charles managed to escape. It is also how Izzy met his death. Charles wonders whether, one day, Connolly will try to complete that evening's work. He also wonders if life will ever present him with an opportunity to exact his revenge on Connolly and his employers for having murdered his cousin and best friend.

'Ronnie and Reggie'd like a word,' replies Connolly, without apparent rancour.

Charles ducks his head down and looks inside the car. Ronnie and Reggie Kray sit side-by-side on the back seat, both immaculately dressed in sober suits, double-cuffed white shirts, sleeves pinned by sparkling cufflinks and silk ties. In the driving seat, on the left-hand side of the vehicle, is a fourth man, younger than the others, whom Charles does not know.

'Get in,' says Reggie, pointing to the front passenger seat.

Charles does as instructed and Connolly, remaining on the pavement, closes the door behind him. The big man leans against the wall and lights a cigarette.

Charles's heart pounds. The manner of his interception and the relaxed poses of the twins is reassuring, and on balance he doesn't think he's about to be driven away and disposed of, as might have happened in the past; indeed, might still happen in the future. His immediate thought is that the Krays have come to call in their debt, and he's about to be told to do something that will end his career and, probably, his freedom. Maybe even his life.

'Hello Ronnie, Reggie,' he says. 'I hope you're well.'

'We're well, and you're still too fuckin' smooth by 'alf,' replies Ronnie.

Again, there is no real violence in the words. Ronnie looks alert. The sleepy droopiness around his eyes, usually a sign of resurgent mental illness, is absent. Charles's anxiety reduces by a further notch.

'Have you heard about Billy Gervaise?' asks Reggie, always the more business-like of the two.

'Heard what?' asks Charles, keeping his face as bland as possible.

'He's squealing. Named dozens of people, both for stuff they've done and for stuff they ain't.'

'And all the time while living the life of Riley in some police station in Essex,' adds Ronnie. 'Even forced that cunt Greene to give him a conjugal, which is just a joke! I bet he ain't fucked Betty in a decade!'

'There was a raft of arrests, all based on his evidence,' says Reggie. His eyes narrow, sensing something. 'Didn't you read about it?'

'I read about the arrests, but not about Gervaise's part in it. In any case, what can I do for you?'

'He's named us, too.'

'Ah, I see.'

'We was arrested yesterday and got bail this morning,' explains Ronnie.

Charles's eyebrows shoot up. 'You got bail?'

'It cost us five grand, paid to Greene. What he calls his Costa del Sol fund. We had to surrender our passports, pay ten grand into court and we've gotta sign on every night,' says Reggie.

'I'm still surprised, with your records.'

'Yeh, well,' says Ronnie, 'prosecuting counsel banged on about the risk to witnesses, but Greene agreed that the main witness was in police protection somewhere secret, so that argument had no legs. Anyway...'

'Yeh, anyway, we've got something we need you to do,' intervenes Reggie.

'What's that, then?'

'We're going to ask Sampsons to instruct you to defend us.'

'Me?' exclaims Charles.

'As junior, you understand. We'll use Blackburne as our silk as normal, but we want you on the team.'

'Okay...' Charles says slowly, hoping for an explanation.

'We're not sure how it's going to develop, but we might need you to offer a bit ... extra,' explains Ronnie.

Charles considers this. If he were to be instructed by the Krays on his own, it would undoubtedly stir up the rumour mill in the Temple again, all the hugely exaggerated stuff about his former criminal past and about him being part of the Firm. On the other hand, if he's to be led by Blackburne, it might not be too bad. Leading counsel often choose their juniors; in which case, according to the cab rank rule, it's against Charles's professional rules to decline, which might let him off the hook. But the potential for him to be asked to pay off his debt to the twins by doing something illegal still exists.

'Would we be quits, after this?'

The twins turn to one another. Charles can detect no change in the expressions of either man and certainly nothing is said, but some form of communication does occur. The Krays' formidable reputation in London rests partly on this supposed ability to read one another's mind and although Charles doesn't believe it, more than once he has watched them communicate in a manner undetected by those around them.

A twins thing, maybe?

'Maybe,' answers Reggie. 'We'll see how it goes. Sampson'll send papers and you'll be invited to a conference at Blackburne's chambers. Probably tomorrow afternoon. We'll tell you all about it then.'

'I'm surprised you're not using Ralph Cohen. Isn't he your usual go-to solicitor?'

'Yeh, but Gervaise's got him. Cohen reckons he's conflicted. Fuckin' nonsense if you ask me.'

Ronnie makes a sign and Charles's door opens. The interview is over. He climbs back out on to Middle Temple Lane and Connolly resumes his place. The American car executes a tyre-squealing circle around Essex Court and heads back down the lane towards the Embankment.

CHAPTER 27

The three men step out of Holloway Prison on to Pentonville Road, catcalls still ringing in their ears. Charles has often wondered, on his infrequent visits to the women's prison, what causes some of its inmates to metamorphose into shrieking sexual viragos once incarcerated. On their short walk from the gates to the interview rooms, Charles was flashed once, had his backside pinched twice by passing female prisoners, and all of them were subjected to a ribald running commentary that would have made seasoned sailors proud. It's not sex, concludes Charles; it's an expression of power. Their confinement renders them safe from men, and anonymity within the female herd gives them a temporary freedom to repay the male sex in kind for generations of objectification, by taunting those passing through the prison.

Hansie Fischer rushes off to another appointment, leaving Charles and Sloane on the busy pavement.

'Well?' asks Sloane.

'To be honest, I'm not sure we know anything more now than we did an hour and a half ago. We didn't need Irenna to tell us that the jackets were planted or that she'd been verballed.'

'Waste of time, then?'

'Not completely. I've got useful stuff for the bail app. And Greene's made a mistake by not charging you as well.'

'He'd never have made it stick. It wasn't my flat.'

'Agreed. Believing you lived there and planting the jackets without making sure has left him with a problem. Charging you was likely to fail, whatever false confession he concocted for you, but leaving you out of the story has created an even bigger problem for him.'

'So, you're confident?'

Charles notes the anxiety on his friend's twisted face. He puts a hand on Sloane's arm. 'I am. Did you hear that the people Gervaise has fingered include the Kray twins?'

'Yes. There can't be anyone in the Met who hasn't. Greene's the hero of the hour,' he says sourly.

'What you've probably not heard, is that I've been instructed to act for them, as junior counsel.'

Sloane regards Charles for a long moment. 'Shit, Charlie, that's going to make things … complicated.'

'Potentially, yes. But equally it gives rise to some interesting opportunities.'

'Meaning?'

'Leave it with me for a couple of days. I'm seeing the Krays in conference this afternoon with Maurice Blackburne. I'll let you know how it goes.'

'You'd have thought, now that Gervaise has done his deal and Greene is riding so high, they'd leave Irenna alone,' says Sloane sadly. 'If he started this just to pressurise me into backing off, what's to be gained now, when the whole story's about to be told in any case?'

'I agree, but Gervaise seems to have taken against you, or maybe Irenna. God knows why. Maybe he just hates honest coppers —'

'— Or women,' adds Sloane.

'Or Micks,' says Charles, pointing at Sloane.

'Or Yids,' replies Sloane, pointing at Charles.

'Or any combination thereof,' concludes Charles.

They both laugh grimly.

'Anyway, the prosecution now has a life of its own whatever you, Gervaise or Greene might do. I'll call you this evening.'

'Not tonight. I'm on early turn tomorrow, so I'll be getting an early night. Call me at the station in the morning if you've anything to report.'

Charles has never actually spoken to Maurice Blackburne QC other than a very few words when they were involved in the same case some years back. Blackburne's practice is enviable by anyone's standards. He rose through the ranks of juniors on the backs of several high-profile criminal trials and was appointed silk, or QC, at the relatively early age of forty. Since then he has been the "go-to" silk for the gangsters of London and is often instructed by Ralph Cohen to act for defendants such as the Nash gang, Freddie Foreman and, in particular, the Krays.

It is generally assumed within the profession that Blackburne is bent for that fact alone but, while similar rumours have acted as a constant brake on Charles's career, they seem to have done nothing to impede Blackburne's steady rise. But then Blackburne was educated at Eton and Oxford and his father was a well-respected Conservative politician, whereas Charles was schooled in the East End, was a scholarship boy at university, and his father was a furrier. In addition, Blackburne didn't have the further handicap of being Jewish. Until Henrietta's murder, being the son-in-law of Viscount Brandreth provided Charles with a measure of camouflage; thereafter all pretence was over.

Blackburne's room is twice the size of Charles's and is better appointed, with newer chairs and rugs and more expensively constructed book cases. An occasional table by the window carries a tray with cut glass decanters, one of whisky and another of port. It is also evident that the room is not shared with anyone else.

Blackburne sits behind his wide desk facing a semicircle of chairs occupied by Charles, their mutual instructing solicitor Arnold Sampson, a junior from Sampson's offices to take notes, and the Kray twins, looking as smart as always.

Charles has never seen the Krays in these circumstances. He's surprised to find that they are extremely deferential towards Blackburne and address him as "Mr Blackburne, sir". Charles even detects an effort by them to moderate their language.

Charles's principal task in this conference is to listen to the pearls of wisdom as they drop from his leader's lips. Some silks don't like their juniors to ask questions at all; some will permit an intervention. Charles is interested to see to what extent he is allowed actively to contribute to the discussion.

Blackburne runs through the evidence against the twins in his Lancashire accent, softened by many years of working in the south. The case consists almost exclusively of Gervaise's evidence and a short statement regarding Alan Cooper, the Krays' alleged money man, whose warehouses were used to store the goods. Interestingly, Greene has not verballed the twins. Charles supposes that he knew better than to try; the Krays have never once responded to questions in interview in the past and are not the sort of men to be intimidated, even by DI Greene.

'My first questions to you, Ronnie, Reggie, concern the evidence about Mr Alan Cooper. The police have done a Companies House check, and it does appear that Mr Cooper, through several intermediary companies, is the leaseholder of these three warehouses. He is a director of all the companies concerned, and secretary of two. Gervaise says that Cooper is your "money man", and he gives a number of examples of dealing with you through Mr Cooper. Now, we can't get round the records held by Companies House. It's almost certain that the Crown will prove Cooper's connection to the warehouses. But what is his connection with you?'

Reggie answers. 'Alan Cooper's a business associate of ours, but you couldn't describe him as our "money man". He's acted for us in getting finance and properties sometimes. But he does that for dozens of clients. The fact that he's connected with the warehouses doesn't make us connected with them.'

'You should go down there,' adds Ronnie. 'There's stuff coming in and going out round the clock, owned by dozens of different people. He lets the space by the square yard. Some people have loads of stuff in there, stored for long periods; others have just a few items there for just a few days.'

Sampson and his clerk start writing, and Charles sees over the former's shoulder that he has begun a "to do" list, headed by sending an investigator to the warehouses.

Blackburne also makes some notes, and nods in satisfaction. 'Okay, that's good. Now I have some questions about the most important evidence concerning the conspiracy to steal. In summary, Gervaise paints the picture of you two as the brains and the money behind it. Acting on your instructions, he arranged the acquisition of two lorries, loaded goods when ordered to do so, and took them to the warehouses. Additionally, he transported goods on a couple of occasions from the warehouses to the markets. Essentially, his case is that he was just a driver or deliveryman, and the Crown have accepted that.'

Blackburne pauses to make sure the import of what he's saying has sunk in.

'Gervaise will be sentenced before any of the other trials start, and his sentence will reflect his involvement merely as a driver acting under your orders. Now, on the face of it, his allegations against you are not too serious — serious enough — but there's no explicit evidence implicating you in the murders at Cardington. But you can see how it might develop. If you two were the brains, it would be difficult to avoid the conclusion that you ordered the murders.' He looks at the Krays, Ronnie then Reggie. It's Ronnie who answers.

'None of it's true, Mr Blackburne, sir. We had no involvement with this at all.'

'Did you know about it?'

'Of course. Most of the villains in the East End heard something about it. It's been going on a couple of years, and we've got eyes and ears everywhere.' Ronnie is unable to keep the pride out of his voice. It flatters his vanity to be seen as the ringmaster of a circle of spies and informers.

'Why has Gervaise chosen to point the finger at you? What's his motive if you had no involvement in it at all?' asks Blackburne.

'We've been thinking about that,' says Reggie. 'There's an old grudge.'

Ronnie continues. 'He thinks we stole some of his emeralds. His younger brother, Bertie, is a twirler who got his hands on some stolen emeralds in Amsterdam.'

'Twirler?' asks Blackburne.

'Lock-picker or, sometimes, safecracker,' explains Charles, wishing immediately he hadn't. Blackburne is bound to assume his knowledge is born of personal experience, but in fact the older man smiles at him.

'Thank you, Charles,' he says.

Ronnie continues. 'Apparently the Filth was watching the brother, so he needed someone to bring the gems back. Billy asked us and we provided a courier, a clean young lad with no form. He got back to Heathrow, no problem. Then he put the duty-free bag with the emeralds down for a second at passport control and, when he looked for it, the bag'd gone. It was unfortunate, but Gervaise never believed it was an accident. He was sure we nicked them but just couldn't prove it, so he let it go. He's had a grudge ever since.'

Charles turns to study the Krays, a half-smile on his lips, but they look innocent and aggrieved. Still, Charles has little doubt that the loss of the emeralds was never some unfortunate mischance.

The room is full of the sound of scratching pens for a few moments and then Blackburne looks up. 'I see. There is of course a difficulty about this explanation. You would have to go into the witness box to give it. Our case will be that Gervaise is lying, in other words we're attacking his credibility and character. As you know, normally the jury can't hear about the previous convictions of the accused; it's too prejudicial. But if you attack the honesty of a Crown witness, the jury's entitled to know the character of the person making the attack. So they get to hear your previous convictions when you're cross-examined.'

The twins look at one another, their expressions not changing.

'Now,' continues Blackburne, 'of course you already have pretty bad reputations, and there can't be anyone in London who's not read press reports about you, but were the Crown to run through all of your convictions since you were boys, well, it would be pretty devastating.'

Charles makes a note in his blue counsel's notebook and places a large asterisk beside it. He has an idea which he will ventilate when Blackburne has finished taking instructions.

'As you possibly know, it's called "throwing away your shield", your shield against the jury hearing about your past. But in this case, you wouldn't just be throwing away your shield; if we're to run that explanation of why he's fingered you two — because he holds a grudge against you — we're forced to tell the jury about your involvement in the emerald job. It would almost certainly lead to further charges against you.'

'What of?' asks Ronnie.

'Conspiracy to steal or perhaps conspiracy to handle stolen goods depending on the exact allegations. Do you agree, Charles?'

'I do.'

'Almost as bad as the charges you already face,' says Blackburne.

'Do we have to mention it, then?' asks Reggie.

Blackburne shrugs. 'It's not essential. If we don't, we can attack Gervaise on his past dishonesty to throw doubt on what he's now saying, and like in the last case you and I did together, we don't call you to give evidence. So the Crown can't attack you in return. But that leaves us unable to explain to the jury what Gervaise's motive would be, in lying about your involvement.'

'Professional jealousy?' suggests Sampson. 'It wouldn't be the first time one gangster has tried to get others put away so he can take over their territory.'

Blackburne smiles. 'With great respect, Mr Sampson, that's not much of an improvement on the other explanation.'

'May I make a suggestion?' asks Charles tentatively.

'Certainly,' says Blackburne.

All heads in the room turn towards Charles.

'You're probably not aware of this, but I am also instructed on behalf of a young trainee doctor who has inadvertently got caught up in all this. Gervaise planted a couple of the stolen RAF jackets in her room and DI Greene verballed her, so she now faces a charge of receiving.'

'Why?' asks Reggie.

'Her boyfriend is that rare thing, an honest copper in the Met. He was after Gervaise but couldn't get any of his superiors to listen. He wouldn't let it go. Our theory is that Greene, who's been protecting Gervaise for years, came up with the idea to pressurise the copper to back off.'

'How might this be relevant to our clients here?' asks Blackburne.

'Well, it looks as if the doctor's committal proceedings will be next week. It started before Gervaise decided to turn Supergrass, so her case will be heard first. The case against her is the weakest of all of them. It relies entirely on the very unlikely scenario of the trainee doctor working part-time at Petticoat Lane and DI Greene just happening to discover a burglary at her bedsit, which let him into her room to find the stolen jackets. It's very weak. But here's the point: alone of all the defendants brought in as a result of Gervaise's grassing, she has no criminal record, at least not in this country.'

'What about elsewhere?' asks Blackburne perceptively.

'No formal convictions, but she was involved in political activism in South Africa until she and her parents fell foul of the South African Security Service. Her parents were both arrested and imprisoned, and I don't believe any trial has occurred. She escaped to England.'

'What's her name?' asks Blackburne.

'Irenna Alexandrova.'

'She's the daughter of Yitzhak and Miriam.'

'Exactly. I was thinking that I could go in, all guns blazing, against Gervaise, put all of his previous criminal record before the jury, without any risk. Whatever one thinks of her politics, Irenna Alexandrova is honest and has no criminal convictions to be thrown back at her. Compare that to counsel for all the other defendants, including us as we defend Ronnie and Reggie, all of whom have as bad records as Gervaise himself. It'll become a mud-slinging match as to who is the most dishonest and untrustworthy. That won't happen with Irenna. I'll get a clear run at destroying Gervaise's credibility.'

Blackburne tips his chair back and stares at the ceiling as he considers Charles's proposal. 'Yes, that could work,' he concludes.

'And if we can destroy Gervaise's credibility during Irenna's trial, make him look like a total liar whose evidence can't be trusted, well —' he turns to face Ronnie and Reggie directly — 'you may never have to go to court on yours at all.'

'That's quite right,' agrees Blackburne. 'Gervaise is essential to the success of the Crown's case on almost all the other trials. If we can destroy him in the very first trial, they'll pull the plug on any other cases which rely exclusively on him. Which includes the cases against you two.' He turns to Charles. 'Thank you, Charles. This might work. Well done.'

'Would it be sensible for you to be led by Mr Blackburne in that case?' asks Sampson.

Charles pauses while considering how to answer. He doesn't want Blackburne leading him on Irenna's case. It would send the wrong message to the Crown and the jury. It would suggest that Irenna has some connection with professional criminals, especially the Krays, because those are the people who usually turn to Blackburne to defend them. Furthermore, Charles trusts his own skills more than anyone else's. Finally, he knows he will give everything for this client, above and beyond the call of duty, which no other barrister would.

He is still trying carefully to frame his response when Blackburne intervenes.

'No, I think that would be tactically unwise. You don't want a heavyweight silk representing someone on their very first charge, especially of receiving two stolen jackets. It sends exactly the wrong message and would raise questions in the minds of the jury. Far better for Charles to do it. Indeed, Charles, some would say that you're too senior yourself, but I think we need to strike a balance between that factor and excellence as an advocate.'

'Kind of you to say so,' replies Charles.

'I mean every word of it. Your reputation precedes you, and why you're not in silk is a complete mystery to many of us. Although … perhaps it's no great mystery when one considers the prejudice at the Bar. As a rough and ready Lancastrian, with an accent as thick as a farm doorpost, I know something about that.'

Charles smiles. It's nice of Blackburne to say it, but Charles doesn't think that prejudice against a Northern accent is equivalent in any way to the obstacles he has faced.

'That just leaves the question of listing,' says Blackburne. 'It becomes all-important that the Alexandrova trial is held first.'

'Well, it ought to be, as it's very simple and much closer to trial, but my clerks can keep an eye on it, and someone can have a word with the relevant listing officer in due course,' says Charles.

'I don't suppose you know where it'll be committed to, for trial?' asks Sampson.

'Not yet. But it's being put forward by the Crown as one of this group of "Supergrass trials" so I'd expect the Old Bailey.'

'Good,' says Blackburne. 'This has been very useful. Do you have anything further?' he asks of the solicitor.

'No, thank you,' says Sampson, closing his notebook.

'Right. It might be sensible for my clerk to keep in touch with yours, Charles, so we know the state of play regarding the Alexandrova trial. Do you agree?'

'Yes, I'll have a word with Barbara.'

Blackburne rises and the others follow suit. 'Thank you very much, everyone,' he says, bringing the meeting to a close.

CHAPTER 28

Charles allows Eileen out of the front door at Wren Street, pulls the door closed and locks it behind him. He glances at his watch, tuts in irritation, and jogs swiftly across the pavement to the Austin Healey. He didn't want to come to the chilly house this evening — he hasn't quite finished preparing for Irenna's bail application and committal tomorrow morning — but Eileen, the soft furnishings lady, couldn't make any other time, so he worked until the second she arrived, threw his pen down, hurried downstairs and into the damp Austin Healey, and drove her the five minutes to Wren Street where he paced while she measured the windows.

He drops her off at Chancery Lane station and returns to the Temple just before seven.

One of the factors that makes Charles successful is the fact that his clients know that he will always give everything to their cases. Whether he believes them or not, they get the most intensive preparation, the most meticulous study of the evidence and the law and the most committed advocacy of which he is capable. Barristers are always being asked at parties how they can represent someone they don't believe to be innocent, and his answer is always the same.

'I'm a mouthpiece, that's all. I put their account in the most attractive and articulate way possible. Then it's up to the jury.'

Nonetheless, it is fair to say that for Irenna's case he is giving everything, and then some more. Firstly, he likes her and respects her work. Secondly, and more importantly, Sean Sloane has fallen desperately and completely in love with her, and he couldn't bear to see his friend suffering were he to be separated from her. That's one of the reasons barristers are often hesitant to represent friends or family; it's too close, too personal. If the case is lost, it invariably affects the relationship, even when the losing litigant and their loved ones acknowledge that the barrister did everything possible.

Finally, however, and most importantly, he knows that were Irenna to be returned to the tender mercies of the South African Secret Service, it could well prove a death sentence.

So he returns to his notes. He has almost finished when he hears a distant telephone bell from the clerks' room. He ignores it, but the caller is unusually persistent, because they hang on the line until the call trips to one of the upstairs rooms on his corridor. Most people would know that Chambers closes for the evening at six o'clock, and any that don't would by now have left a message when invited to at the end of Barbara's recording. This person has obviously accepted the invitation to dial an additional number if they know the extension of the person to whom they wish to speak.

After a while, the telephone next door ceases to ring. A few seconds later the phone starts ringing again in the clerk's room and, when it is still not answered, it comes through to the telephone on Peter Bateman's desk on the opposite side of Charles's room. Charles tries to keep working, but the noise is insistent and eventually he shoves his chair back and crosses to the other side of the room. He picks up the receiver angrily, about to give the caller a piece of his mind, when he hears his brother's voice.

'Can I speak to Charles Holborne, please?'

'Davie, it's me. What on earth's the matter?'

'I've been trying to reach you. I called the flat, and the gym. You've no phone at Wren Street, so this was my last hope. I tried on the off chance that you were still in.'

'I am. What's so urgent?'

'Now, don't panic, but Dad passed out this afternoon.'

'His heart again?'

'No. His GP has been out and says he could find nothing wrong. However, Mum called me and I went round while we were waiting for the doctor to arrive. I saw the doctor examine him. Have you seen Dad without his shirt on recently?'

'No. How would I?'

'He's painfully thin. Thinner than I have seen him … well, ever.'

'Cancer?'

'Unlikely. He had some routine blood tests done only a few weeks ago and it would've shown up. But I'm still worried and the doctor is puzzled. Dad stayed with you before the High Holy Days, only a couple of months ago, so I'd be interested to know if you think there's been a significant change since then.'

'Okay. When?'

'Tonight? I'm still here, and I could wait for you.'

Charles looks at his watch. It's quarter to eight, and with the rush-hour traffic now cleared he could probably be there within thirty minutes. He looks at the papers on his desk. He has pretty much finished his prep, and anything outstanding can be done in the morning.

'All right.'

'Thank you. I'll see you soon.'

Charles leaves his desk as it is, ready to pick up where he left off. He throws on his jacket and raincoat and within five minutes is driving up Chancery Lane.

He enjoys one of those rare and wonderful journeys across London where every traffic light turns green at his approach and, twenty-two minutes later, he is pulling up outside his parents' semi-detached house.

He receives a hug from his younger brother and is taken into the lounge where he greets his father.

His mother shouts from the kitchen. 'Hello, son. This is a nice surprise. Will you stay to eat with us? I can't remember the last time just the four of us sat down together.'

As in the last time Charles saw his mother, at the hospital, her tone is kinder than normal.

'Hello, Mum. Yes, that would be lovely. I'll just go and wash up. I've been shaking hands with criminals all day.'

Charles returns downstairs and joins his brother and father in the lounge. They chat for ten minutes. The ten minutes turns into twenty, and then thirty. Harry rises and goes into the kitchen to see if he can help. Millie shoos him out.

'I'll never get anything done with you standing over me,' she says, but her good humour persists.

David turns to his father. 'Please don't be offended, Dad, but I was very surprised when I saw you without your shirt and vest. You looked a little thin to my eye.'

'I'm fine, Davie.'

'I'm sure you are, but would you mind taking off your shirt and showing Charles?'

'What? So you're a doctor, already? I'm not undressing for you.'

'Please, Dad?' asks Charles. 'David's not one to worry unnecessarily. And I understand the doctor was a little concerned, too.'

'I've told you: no.'

The two brothers continue to pester him, but Harry is adamant. After a while, to get them off his back, he announces he's going to the kitchen to see if he can help Millie, but he is soon back in the lounge.

'Not long now,' she calls.

Another twenty minutes elapse, and Charles realises that there's no smell of cooking emanating from the kitchen.

'What are we eating?' he asks Harry.

'Lamb, I think. She asked me to pick some up from the butcher this morning.'

'You usually eat earlier than this, don't you?'

'Well, we had a late lunch,' his father replies, and Charles notes that Harry avoids making eye contact with him.

Millie re-enters. She takes a seat next to Harry. She sits placidly for a moment or two as if she had nothing to do. 'Would anyone like a cup of tea?' she asks.

David and Charles look at one another, puzzled. Harry answers. 'No, thank you, darling, I think we'll wait until after we've eaten. Can I do anything to help?'

Millie looks lost for a moment, but then she stands. 'No, everything's fine. I'll only be another minute or two.' She returns to the kitchen.

It takes another ten minutes before Millie calls from the kitchen, 'Ready! Go and sit down.'

The three men go into the dining room. Millie follows them in with what looks like a platter of sandwiches. She doles them out, one sandwich on the plate of each of her menfolk. Charles looks at his. His mother has never in his life served sandwiches for a meal. Harry is a meat and two veg man, and that's what he's got, every night of his married life.

'Sandwiches, Mum?'

Millie frowns and pauses, still standing with the platter in her hands, for several seconds. 'Yes,' she says. 'I thought maybe a change…'

Charles examines what's been put on his plate. There are two rough-cut doorsteps of *challa* bread, but nothing between them.

'There's nothing inside them. Did you forget to fill them?' asks David.

'No,' replies Millie, offended, 'of course not.'

She opens up the remaining sandwich on the platter and her face changes. It sort of caves in. After a moment, she turns on her heel and retraces her steps to the kitchen. Harry glares at his two sons, one after the other, and follows her, leaving Charles and David looking at one another. They hear soothing muttering from their father but cannot make out the words. Then there are footsteps as Millie walks swiftly past the dining room door and heads upstairs. A bedroom door closes.

After a short while, Harry returns and resumes his seat at the head of the table.

'You had no right to interfere,' he says quietly, staring at the table cloth.

'But we're worried about you,' replies David.

There's a long silence. 'What's going on, Dad?' asks Charles. Another long silence. 'Dad?'

Harry sighs and, when he looks up, his opaque eyes are full of tears. 'Your mother's forgotten how to cook,' he says simply.

'Why didn't you tell us?'

'It's not all the time. Some days she's fine or, at least, better. And I didn't want anyone to know. She's a proud woman.'

'We understand that,' says David, 'but you won't protect her dignity by starving to death.'

'Don't be ridiculous,' retorts Harry angrily. 'No one's starving to death.'

'But you have lost a lot of weight, haven't you?' says Charles.

'A couple of pounds, maybe,' says Harry defensively.

'And Mum?'

'I don't know. I've not asked.'

'But you can cook, can't you?' says David.

'Before my eyes got so bad, yes. But she's cooked all our meals for forty-two years. Even if I could see properly, if I took over what would it do to her self-respect? It says "You're failing".'

'I'm sorry to point out the obvious,' says Charles, 'but she *is* failing, isn't she?'

Harry offers no answer. He takes out his handkerchief, wipes his eyes and blows his nose noisily.

'Dad,' says Charles softly, 'pretending the problem isn't there is no solution. You'll both get ill. And it's not just a case of not putting food on the table; what if she gives you something that's gone off?'

'That won't happen. I've been checking the fridge and throwing stuff out without telling her.'

'With your eyes? Look, we can find a solution to this. Maybe the *shul* will know someone who can help.'

'No! I don't want anyone from the synagogue here.'

David intervenes. 'I'm pretty sure the Jewish Welfare Board could find someone to come in and help Mum.'

'What, and take over her role in the kitchen?' says Harry. 'It'd kill her.'

'Not if we present it properly. She's in her sixties; she's entitled to slow down a bit, put her feet up.'

'Will you let us make enquiries?' asks Charles. 'What harm is there?'

After a prolonged pause, eventually, Harry nods.

'And ... Dad ... she'll need to be seen by someone.'

'What do you mean?'

'If her memory is this bad, and she's getting confused now and then, it might be the start of something else.'

'What are you saying?'

Charles puts his hand over that of his father. Harry's hand is veiny and shows early signs of mottling. 'She might have early Alzheimer's,' he says gently. 'Or maybe she's had a small stroke. Either way, you want to make sure it doesn't get worse, don't you?'

He stares at the carpet but eventually nods. 'Of course.'

'And the first step is to find out what's going on.'

Harry nods again.

'Right,' says David, standing up. 'I'll see what I can knock up for us in the kitchen.'

'I'll lend a hand,' says Charles.

'No, you stay with Dad.'

CHAPTER 29

Charles pushes through the crowds thronging Marlborough Street Magistrates' Court foyer. It's been raining heavily since he woke, and the marble floor is slick with water, sodden cigarette ends and other rubbish. It's also very cold, and there's a thick fug of exhaled condensation and smoke. It seems that every person in the foyer has a cigarette in their hands.

He excuses his way to the door leading to the cells and rings the bell. The wicket in the steel door slides open almost instantly.

'Charles Holborne of counsel to see Irenna Alexandrova,' he says.

The wicket closes with a clang, keys can be heard in the lock, and the door swings heavily inwards to admit Charles.

As the uniformed dock officer leads Charles downwards, he speaks over his shoulder. 'You might have to wait a few minutes to see her. The police surgeon's with her now.'

'Why?' asks Charles, immediately concerned.

'Looks like she's been in a fight.'

'Is she badly injured?'

'No idea, sir,' replies the officer, uninterested. 'Ask the surgeon.'

Charles signs in and is pointed towards an empty cell with its door open. As he passes the other cells en route he looks inside those with their wickets open, but cannot see Irenna. He also hoped to catch a glimpse of Gervaise, who has to be extricated from his life of luxury to swear his evidence before the magistrate, but he is unsuccessful. He enters the empty cell and sits on the wooden bench built into the wall, waiting.

As always, the place stinks of faeces and fear. There is no smell like that found in the cells of the old central London Victorian courthouses. Generations of terrified prisoners have stood, sat or paced about these cells awaiting their fates. Many have been dragged off the streets after a chase or a fight; many are drunk or drugged; many have no idea what they're charged with or the evidence they face. Unlike in the cells in the higher courts or even the prisons, they have yet to see a lawyer, to receive reassurance that their case is winnable or, at least, that there's someone on their team. They are the quarry at bay, and over the decades their fear has seeped into the soft pink brickwork.

He hears a door open and voices from back up the corridor. He steps out of the cell to investigate. A man in a grey suit carrying a doctor's bag is standing next to a cell door a little further up. He calls for the gaoler, who appears at the foot of the stairs.

'I'm finished. She is fit to plead, and I've patched her up as best I can, but she's going to need stitches.'

'Immediately, or will it wait until after the hearing?'

'She might bleed a bit on the dock but, no, it can wait an hour or two.'

The police surgeon senses Charles behind him and turns to look over his shoulder. He appraises Charles swiftly. 'Your client?'

'If you mean Dr Alexandrova, yes.'

'She's got to be a medical doctor, right? Too knowledgeable.' Without a further word the surgeon heads for the staircase.

'May I go in?' calls Charles.

'Yup,' replies the officer, squeezing past the surgeon. 'I'll need to lock you in.'

Charles enters the cell. Irenna sits on the bench, a hand pressed to a recently-applied dressing on her cheek. There is a small cut above one eye which is shadowed with a dark ring. She's going to have a real shiner, thinks Charles. Dried blood has left a red streak outlining her jaw, and her blouse is dirty and spattered with red spots.

'Jesus, Irenna, what happened?'

'I'm almost too embarrassed to tell you, it's such a cliché. I was attacked in the showers.'

Charles goes to sit next to her. 'Who by?'

'A couple of white *naaiers*.' She sees Charles's puzzled expression and clarifies. 'It's Afrikaans. Means whores, or fuckers.'

'Got it. Was any particular reason given?'

'Oh, yes. They were very specific. Because I am, quote, "A wog-loving, Jewish commie". You can't fault the accuracy.'

Charles sighs heavily. 'I'm so sorry, Irenna.'

'Yes, well … I have at least the consolation that they're a lot less efficient than the SASS. The beatings my father took left him with internal bleeding, damaged kidneys, broken ribs … you name it. From some of the Afrikaner prisoners and the guards.'

'Well, I'm afraid nothing's changed since we last spoke. Getting you bail is going to be nigh-on impossible.'

She nods. 'I know.'

'But I'll do my best.'

'I know that too.'

Charles reaches out and takes Irenna's free hand, squeezing it gently. Her chest shudders with a sudden sob and her eyes water with tears.

'You going to be okay?'

'Yeah. It's the kindness that gets to me, not the beatings. Give me a second.' She releases Charles's hand, stands and walks a couple of paces from him, facing the cell door. It takes only a few seconds to compose herself. She turns to face Charles. The anxiety and fear in her expression has not disappeared, but it's been controlled. 'Okay. All good. Do you need anything further from me?'

Charles smiles with admiration. He is not entirely sure about her political aims or the steps she might endorse to achieve them, but Irenna Alexandrova certainly has grit. 'No, nothing. If you're okay, I'll leave you and go upstairs. I want to make the clerk aware of your condition so we can get on first.'

Charles knocks on the door and is let out of the cell. He goes back to the foyer and pushes his way through to Court 1. It is already busy with advocates jostling to see the clerk, who hasn't yet appeared. Charles knows a few of them. He takes the bold step of going to the well of the court, turning to face the crowd of chattering lawyers, and calls them to attention.

'Excuse me, gentlemen … and lady! Sorry to take centre stage like this, but I've just been down to the cells and my client has taken a serious beating in Holloway. The police surgeon says she's fit for the hearing, but she needs to get to hospital urgently. Would anyone object to my case going on first?'

'What is it?' calls a young male barrister.

Charles can't blame him for being cautious. The last thing you want is to be stuck behind a half-day committal when your case would take ten minutes.

'It's a committal, two witnesses, no contest. And a bail application. Being as honest as I can, I'd say no more than an hour, forty-five minutes at a pinch if we get our skates on. But my client is a young doctor with no convictions who's been the subject of some serious framing by the Flying Squad. She is deserving of your sympathy.'

There is some ironic chuckling at the last, but Charles sees a number of heads turning in private consultation.

'Fine by me,' says someone.

'And me,' says the female advocate immediately.

'Oh, go on then,' says a resigned voice from the back. And then another.

'May I take it that there is general acquiescence, if not happiness, at my proposal?' asks Charles. He receives a reluctant chorus of approval.

'Thank you. I promise to return the favour at the first opportunity.' Charles turns to see a smiling court clerk behind him. 'Aah,' he says, 'the very person.'

'Mr Holborne, if I remember correctly? I heard all that. I'll ask Mr St John Harmsworth.'

'Thank you,' smiles Charles, although his heart sinks a little.

Mr St John Harmsworth is one of the stipendiary magistrates sitting at the court. A trained lawyer, he is noted for his strict interpretation of the law but also his humanity. Unfortunately, he also has a reputation for being unpredictably bonkers. He often takes the prostitutes' cases first, the girls who've been arrested overnight, so they can get some sleep before going out again to earn enough to pay their fines. Charles once heard him refuse bail to a man on New Year's Eve, whose response was "Up your fucking ring, squire!" to which Harmsworth calmly replied, "And a happy New Year to you too."

'Morning, Charles,' says a voice behind him.

Charles turns to see Sebastian Campbell-Smythe, a tall and dark-haired barrister from Charles's former chambers. He's a decade older than Charles, but he remains a good-looking man with little grey in his dark hair. Charles and Sebastian were never friends, but of the anti-Semitic, racist and class-prejudiced barristers in those chambers, he was the least objectionable.

'Hello, Sebastian.'

'I think we're agin one another.'

'You're prosecuting DI Greene's pack of lies, then?'

Campbell-Smythe smiles but doesn't rise to the bait. 'I am acting for the Crown in the case of Alexandrova, yes.'

'Well, I've managed to get us on first, assuming Harmsworth agrees. My client's been beaten up, this morning, at Holloway. The police surgeon says she needs to get to hospital ASAP.'

'I'm sorry to hear that. As to the timing, that'll depend on you. I'm happy to have the witnesses read their depositions and sign them as true, unless you have objections or questions for them.'

'No, I'll keep my powder dry for the trial.'

'Thought as much.'

It's extremely rare for the defence to make a contest at the magistrates' court. The Crown only has to demonstrate that a jury, instructed in the law, could properly convict on the evidence, and the case will be sent to the higher court for trial. On paper the prosecution case is watertight, and any questions Charles might ask of the witnesses here will only alert Greene to the nature of the defence and give him time to remedy any defects in his case before trial.

'What about bail?' asks Charles.

'I'd like to help, old boy, but I have clear instructions. She has very little connection with this country and a home in South Africa.'

'That's nonsense, Sebastian, and you know it. She fled South Africa in fear of her life. She is hardly going to return there.'

'As far as the Crown is concerned, South Africa is a stable democracy, part of the Commonwealth, where the rule of law still applies.'

'That may be the party line, but we both know it's a load of bollocks. Her life would genuinely be in danger were she to return there. Surely you can see that?'

Campbell-Smythe raises his hands to indicate that he can do nothing.

'Very well,' concludes Charles.

The two men take their places on the front bench and get their papers out. A few of the other advocates remain in the benches behind to hear what's going on, but the majority leave court for hot drinks, cigarettes and gossip.

The clerk returns to court and approaches the barristers' bench. 'Mr Harmsworth is prepared to take your case first, gentlemen, as there are no short matters.'

'Thank you,' say Charles and Campbell-Smythe in unison.

The clerk disappears again for a moment behind a panelled door which doesn't close fully. He raps on the door twice and re-enters.

'Silence in court!'

Everyone remaining in court rises as Mr St John Harmsworth enters.

There is something military about him, thinks Charles, with his upright bearing, military tie and carnation buttonhole. Harmsworth bows to the Bar, who return the compliment, and he takes his seat.

'The case of the police versus Alexandrova, sir,' calls the clerk.

A shout is heard from the stairs leading to the dock. 'Alexandrova!'

Bangs and clanking may be heard and Irenna climbs the stairs directly into the dock, manacled to a woman prison officer. Harmsworth looks up at Irenna, frail and petite, but despite the dressing and bruising, still attractive. Blood has seeped through the dressing applied to her cheek, and she holds a tissue against it to prevent it dribbling down her face.

Charles stands. 'Good morning, sir. I appear on behalf of the defence in this case and my learned friend Mr Campbell-Smythe appears for the prosecution. Firstly, may I thank you for calling our case first? As you will see, my client has recently suffered a beating at the hands of other prisoners while in prison and the police surgeon, who has seen her, says she's fit for the hearing but needs to be in hospital as soon as possible. For that reason, may she sit?'

'Thank you, Mr Holborne. I have been apprised of the circumstances and your client may indeed sit. Tell me, are we to hear contested evidence this morning?'

'No, sir. Both sides seek a jury trial rather than trial at the magistrates' court, and I have indicated to my learned friend that we're happy for him to call each witness and have their statements read, sworn and signed. The only live dispute between us relates to bail.'

'Thank you. Then let's proceed.'

Campbell-Smythe starts with Detective Inspector Greene, who struts self-importantly into the court, takes the Bible and recites the oath without looking at the card on which it is printed. Charles listens with half his attention as the clerk reads Greene's evidence, the corrupt inspector is asked to confirm its truth, to which he swears that it is, and both he and the magistrate sign the deposition.

Then Billy Gervaise is called. Irenna is moved out of the dock to allow Gervaise to be brought up from the cells and taken, also manacled, across the well of the court into the witness box with a male officer as his guard. Charles watches Irenna scrutinising the Supergrass as he passes her. It's the first time she has seen the man prepared to lie on oath by making up a completely fictional story that could result in her death.

There is nothing about Gervaise's expression or demeanour that suggests he's concerned in the least at the possible outcome of his perjury. He's been moved twice since he finished squealing to the prosecutors, and there have been multiple leaks to the newspapers from Pitsea police station, prompting lurid stories of the five-star treatment he received. It shows; he looks well-fed and well-groomed.

As with DI Greene, Charles keeps his head down and simply allows the false evidence to be recited and signed as true.

As the lawyers outside have realised that this is the first of the Supergrass trials to reach committal, they have drifted back into court and the legal and journalists' benches are now full.

'That leaves the question of bail, Mr Holborne,' says Harmsworth pleasantly. 'Would you like to proceed with your application?'

'Thank you, sir. As my learned friend and DI Greene will confirm, Dr Alexandrova is a professional woman of a good family who has no previous convictions. As you probably know from the newspapers, she was a campaigner for black rights in South Africa, and her parents along with a large number of other political activists including the leaders of the ANC have been imprisoned, many without trial, or with show trials on trumped up charges. The only reason Dr Alexandrova is in this country is because it's unsafe for her to return to South Africa. Her father has already died in prison and she has heard nothing from her mother for nearly four months.

'There is clearly no risk of her interfering with witnesses as they are, respectively, a police officer and someone in police custody. I anticipate my learned friend's principal objection to bail will be that my client will flee to South Africa where she has a home. In truth, that is the last place on earth she would go. I also anticipate that he will say that she could go to Canada where she does, indeed, have some relatives; a first cousin and his wife, I'm instructed. Dr Alexandrova did spend a few months there two years ago but returned to this country. The flaw in the argument that she might return to Canada is that she has absolutely no funds at all. Trainee doctors are paid very little, as you know, and she has no other means. The suggestion that she ever worked at Petticoat Lane or anywhere else outside the Finchley Memorial Hospital for that matter will be disputed at trial. Leaving all else aside, the hours required of a junior doctor, day and night, would make such work completely impossible.

'It is her lack of funds which means she is unable to offer the court a financial security; it is her lack of friends or relatives in this country which prevents her from offering anyone as surety. But she is content to hand in her passport and to comply with any reporting conditions you impose, ideally at a police station near the hospital where she works. She has a steady and important job which she is likely to lose if deprived of her liberty for much longer. Finally, I ask you to bear in mind the fact of her public prominence in certain circles, and the likelihood that she will suffer further physical attacks while on remand. The evidence of that, you can see with your own eyes.

'In all the circumstances, sir, I invite you to the view that she is a very low flight risk with appropriate conditions applied, and accordingly to grant her bail.'

Charles resumes his seat and Campbell-Smythe rises.

'In my respectful submission, sir, despite all that my learned friend has said, the risk of Dr Alexandrova leaving England were she to be granted bail is simply too great for the court to take the chance. There is absolutely nothing to hold her here. She has qualifications which would allow her to work in any English-speaking country, certainly any of the Commonwealth countries, where she could also continue her political activities. She lives in a one-bedroom bedsit where she pays rent week to week and, according to Detective Inspector Greene, she owns very little except her books and papers. One could genuinely say that she is not "living" in this country but "perching" here. If convicted, she faces deportation under the Commonwealth Immigrants Act 1962, which gives her an even greater motive for leaving now, under her own steam, and to a destination of her choice, rather than risking being forcibly returned to South Africa. Indeed, the very matters Mr Holborne puts before you as reasons why his client would not disappear, I pray in aid for the opposite conclusion. It is that very risk of conviction and return to South Africa, and the risk that she would indeed suffer at the hands of the South African authorities, that makes it so likely she will run now rather than take the chance.

'Whatever view one takes of the justice of their case, the ANC is a banned political organisation. It undoubtedly has the means to provide Dr Alexandrova with a false passport, so handing in her passport to the court would be a very modest reduction in flight risk. The Crown's position is that, despite its apparent simplicity, this will be an extremely important trial, resting as it does on the evidence of Mr Gervaise, and it is essential for the administration of justice that it proceeds.

'In short, the Crown's submission is that the court cannot be confident that this accused will remain for the trial if given bail. Unless I can assist further...?'

Harmsworth shakes his head and Campbell-Smythe sits down.

'Stand up please, Dr Alexandrova. Much as I have sympathy for your situation, and I appreciate the danger you may be in while you remain in custody, I'm afraid I cannot grant you bail on the evidence I have heard today. Therefore, I commit you to stand trial at the Central Criminal Court on a date to be advised, and you will remain in custody until that time. Please take her down.'

He turns to Charles and Campbell-Smythe.

'Thank you, gentlemen, for the efficient way in which this case has been dealt with. I gather, Mr Holborne, that you estimated forty-five minutes, and you have beaten your estimate by two minutes and thirty seconds. Congratulations. That is the first time I have ever known counsel to come in under the wire. Next case!'

CHAPTER 30

Senior court staff at the Old Bailey tend not to use the public canteen for their refreshments; instead, they use the Bar Mess. Of the senior court staff at the Old Bailey, the senior listing officer is the most senior. Everyone wants the ear of the senior listing officer, and very few get it.

Fortunately for Irenna Alexandrova, the senior listing officer is Hattie Dodds, and the Dodds family lived next door to the Horowitz family on British Street, Mile End, for twenty years, until the day Hitler decided that both households might like to relocate, and dropped a bomb on their homes to give them a nudge in the right direction.

Although Hattie is a few years older than Charles, it is a reasonable summary to say they grew up together, certainly until the Blitz intervened — Hattie even babysat for Millie and Harry on the rare occasion when they had to go out without the boys at the last minute — and for the last sixteen years they've been bumping into each other professionally every now and then since Hattie joined the Lord Chancellor's Department and Charles qualified as a barrister.

So Hattie and Charles go way back, and if there is any barrister in the world for whom Hattie would do a favour, it's little Charlie Horowitz, now known as Charles Holborne, to the continuing mirth of his erstwhile neighbour.

'Biscuits?' mouths Charlie, pointing at them as he lifts the tray.

Hattie, at a circular table in the middle of the room, makes vigorous affirmative motions and Charles adds a handful of chocolate biscuits to his tray and brings it across. He hands Hattie her coffee.

'This is nice. I ain't seen you in yonks,' she says to him as he sits.

'You occupy such an elevated position nowadays, it's difficult to get an audience.'

'Balls,' says Hattie, consuming her first biscuit, and Charles once again feels comfort and familiarity wash over him. He can mimic the accent and the mannerisms of an upper-class gentleman, a member of the Honourable Society of the Middle Temple, and he's obliged to do so when in court. It's second nature to him now, but it is a relief to be with someone he's known all his life and with whom he doesn't have to pretend.

They chat amiably over the course of their coffees, and Hattie works her way through the biscuits while at the same time cross-examining Charles for family news. Charles avoids mentioning his mother's recent condition and focuses more on the imminent arrival of David and Sonia's first baby. He in turn asks after her mum and dad, both apparently in rude health and now living with Hattie in Southgate. Hattie, statuesque, bespectacled and possessing a "loud" personality, never married and seems perfectly happy with her choice.

'Now, Charlie,' she says after fifteen minutes, 'I've gotta get back to work, and you ain't come here just to catch up on old times. What do you want?'

Charles leans forward. 'Have you heard of the Irenna Alexandrova case?'

'I ain't been living in a cave. Course I have. It was committed here a couple of days ago.'

'Yes. It's the first up of the Supergrass trials involving Billy Gervaise. None of the big cases have been committed to the Central Criminal Court yet, and I doubt any will in the course of the next few weeks. They're all much more complex than Alexandrova. But I wondered if it'd be possible to get that listed ASAP so we can get it done and dusted.'

'How in God's name did that woman get involved with Billy Gervaise?' asks Hattie. Then she holds up a chubby hand. 'No, you probably shouldn't tell me.'

'She didn't. She was being used as leverage to get a certain honest copper to back off the Gervaise conspiracy. She's never met Gervaise, never had anything to do with him, and I promise you, Hattie, has never committed theft or receiving in her entire life. She's an innocent victim in all this; she's good people.'

'Whereas Billy Gervaise is very bad people.'

'You can say that again. Gervaise's plea has been listed for Monday. Can we get the Alexandrova case on as soon as possible after that? She's in custody and having a pretty tough time of it.'

Charles advised Hansie Fischer to have another go at obtaining bail for Irenna from the High Court judge, but Fischer pointed out that the funds were already tight, and he wouldn't agree to spending any more on what he was sure was a lost cause. In his heart Charles knew Fischer was right but he wasn't prepared to give up, so he went ahead anyway, drafting and filing the necessary documents and appearing alone before the High Court judge. He paid the issue fee out of his pocket and charged nothing for his time or attendance.

As Fischer predicted, he failed. Irenna has now been at Holloway for a further ten days since the committal.

'All right, cocker, I'll see what I can do,' says Hattie. 'To be honest, she'd've been in and out the sausage machine long before the other trials start, but I'll make sure there are no upsets.'

'You are princess among women,' says Charles fondly.

'You know it, and I know it, but the rest of the world…'

Charlie pats her hand as he stands. 'Thanks, Hattie. God bless you.'

'You behave, Charlie!' she shouts at his departing back.

'Always do,' he says, still walking.

CHAPTER 31

The office of the Recorder of London, the senior judge at the Central Criminal Court, has existed since 1298. That office is presently occupied by His Honour Judge Pullman, QC. Pullman is the forensic mirror-image of Mr St John Harmsworth, namely, sane, brilliant and an utter bastard. A career at the Bar that consisted almost exclusively of prosecuting an endless stream of evil, mendacious and violent men has over the years added a layer of unyielding cynicism to what was already an unforgiving personality. It has become his opinion that, expressed in legal terms, there's a rebuttable presumption that anyone appearing before him is guilty and will be going to prison for a long stretch. It is a predisposition which makes life difficult for defence barristers.

Furthermore, having completely forgotten what it was like to start at the Bar and learn one's trade, he is impatient to a fault with all advocates appearing in his court. God help the young barrister who stands before him ill-prepared or who asks irrelevant or repetitive questions. Pullman's putdowns are legend. As a result, the Recorder is both respected and loathed by all the advocates contesting cases in his court, but particularly by the defence.

Due to the high-profile nature of the Supergrass cases and their importance to the public, not to mention the Met, the Recorder has been assigned all of them. He will hear the trials one after the other over a period estimated to be nine months to a year, and the first up is Gervaise's own case followed, later that day, by that of Irenna Alexandrova.

Charles sits in Court 1 of the Central Criminal Court, the Old Bailey, in the last bench reserved for counsel, the one furthest away from the Recorder's bench and closest to the dock. He is robed, but for this part of the proceedings he is merely an observer. He's told Hansie Fisher not to arrive before half past eleven; Irenna's case is listed "Not before noon."

Although keyed up, Charles feels good. To Barbara's puzzlement, he negotiated hard to clear his diary for a couple of days before this trial. Most barristers like a clear run-up to their biggest cases; it gives them time to prepare properly rather than burning the midnight oil in preparation the night before, a daily occurrence on less significant matters. While conceding that this is the first of the Supergrass cases, Barbara pointed out that it involves only one minor charge and two prosecution witnesses; a pupil could do it, with a couple of hours' prep. Nonetheless, Charles persuaded her that it was of particular importance to him personally and, making allowances for his friendship with Sean Sloane, she relented and returned a couple of the cases in his diary to more junior members of Chambers.

Charles has been able to do all the preparation he wanted during normal office hours, spend several hours each evening at Wren Street on relatively mindless building activities, and still retire each evening at a reasonable hour. He is rested and ready.

In the front bench, chatting to DI Greene and another police officer, stands prosecuting counsel, Marcus Stafford QC.

Charles knows Stafford well. The last time they fought a case against each other, two or three years earlier, was when Stafford prosecuted the gangland lawyer, Harry Robeson, whom Charles defended. Stafford was not yet in silk then and although Charles acknowledges that he is an outstanding advocate, he finds it difficult not to resent the fact that Stafford's career has progressed smoothly with the addition of "QC" to his name in the last April list, while Charles's has not.

Defending Gervaise is a QC named Ensley. As Charles was changing into his robes in the robing room he heard Ensley chatting to his junior, but beyond detecting a strong Northern Ireland accent, Charles knows nothing of the man.

The courtroom gradually fills up with journalists and, in the gallery above, with members of the public. The press coverage led by the young reporter from Bedford and Percy Farrow has ensured that the Supergrass cases have rarely been out of the news since the Maynard inquest verdict and, on entering court, Charles had to push through the queues of dripping spectators snaking all the way around the Old Bailey hoping for a gallery seat to watch the trial. It's only a week before Christmas, and although the weather is quite warm, it seems to Charles to have been raining for most of the month.

Marcus Stafford QC is a cold fish, not given to much chitchat with his opponents, but the events surrounding the Robeson case were so astonishing that Charles managed to get under his armour. Although still not what Charles would call "friendly", he and Stafford have been on much more congenial terms ever since. Stafford catches sight of Charles in the back row and nods towards him before resuming his conversation. He's lost some weight, thinks Charles. He is still huge, but Stafford used to be immensely and unhealthily fat, with multiple chins splaying his wing collar flat against his almost horizontal chest. He used to struggle even when walking the half mile from the Temple; his puffing and wheezing like an old steam engine has earned him the nickname "Chugger".

There is a loud knock on the panelled door behind the Recorder's bench. The usher cries 'All rise!' and Charles hurriedly jams his wig on top of his curls as the Recorder, resplendent in his red and black robes, enters court.

The court fills with the sound of over one hundred people shuffling to their feet, like distant thunder. The Bench and Bar exchange reciprocal bows and the court settles again. It takes the Recorder a moment to arrange his red notebook and pen. He looks up.

'Are we ready, gentlemen?' he asks.

Stafford half-rises to answer. 'We are, my Lord.'

'Very well. Let's proceed to arraignment.'

The uniformed man in the dock shouts down the stone stairs beside him. 'Bring him up!'

There follows the usual metal clanking, and after a moment Billy Gervaise appears in the dock, handcuffed to a prison officer. The clerk of the court rises from his position below that of the Recorder.

'Are you William Arnold Gervaise?'

Gervaise answers from across the court. 'Yes.'

The clerk proceeds. 'You are charged on an indictment containing a single count of conspiracy to steal. The particulars of the offence are that you, together with Frederick McParland, Malcolm Carragher, Derek Hawkins, Ronald Kray, Reginald Kray and other persons unknown did, between the first day of January nineteen sixty-three and the first day of November nineteen sixty-five, conspire to steal divers goods from the Royal Air Force base at Cardington, Bedfordshire. How do you plead?'

'Guilty,' says Gervaise.

A sound gathers in the courtroom, a whispering and rustling, as if an autumn breeze was disturbing crisp leaves. Everyone present knows that Gervaise was supposed to plead guilty, that he *had* to plead guilty if he was to turn Queens Evidence against his former conspirators and other criminal colleagues. But the fact that he has now done so is nonetheless remarkable, momentous. There has been much speculation in the press that the advent of the Supergrass might at last deliver to the police a powerful tool, one capable of bringing down the gangs ruling London.

'You may sit,' says the Recorder. 'Yes, Mr Stafford?'

Stafford rises slowly and ponderously to his feet. 'My Lord, I appear on behalf of the Crown in this case, and Mr Ensley appears on behalf of the defendant. I hope my Lord has had an opportunity to read the letter to the court written by the Metropolitan Police Commissioner which sets out some of the unusual background to this case.'

'I have.'

'Thank you, my Lord. Mr Gervaise's involvement in this conspiracy was that of a minor functionary, a driver. He was recruited by Ronald Kray to collect goods stolen from RAF Cardington and transport them from Cricklewood goods yard to one of three warehouses in the East End of London. He did that on three occasions. On two or three occasions he was also asked to take a smaller vehicle full of goods from one of the warehouses and deliver them to Petticoat Lane market.

'Having investigated, the Crown is satisfied that this represents the extent of Mr Gervaise's involvement. He was not one of the organisers of the conspiracy, and was brought in relatively late. He was not responsible for the thefts themselves, nor the violence that seems to have accompanied the gradual uncovering of the conspiracy. As your Lordship may know, two men have died in suspicious circumstances at the Cardington base, and that is the subject of continuing investigations. Whether or not the relevant offenders will be identified remains to be seen. However, there is no suggestion that this defendant was involved in any way with those deaths. Mr Gervaise was paid less than one hundred pounds in all for his involvement as a driver.

'As you will see from the Commissioner's letter, Mr Gervaise has been of quite exceptional value to the prosecuting authorities in identifying the other men named in the indictment.'

The earlier rustling turns into muttering, and one or two people from the public gallery begin to shout.

'Scum!' screams a woman's voice.

'You're dead, Squealer!' shouts a male voice, and others join in.

'Silence!' says the Recorder, but his intervention seems only to make matters worse. Several people from the public gallery have jumped to their feet, many pointing and gesticulating as they utter threats.

'I will have silence, or I will clear the court!' bellows the Recorder.

This produces a response and the noise gradually dies away.

'If there is any repetition of this disturbance, I repeat, I will have the court cleared and we will conduct the rest of this hearing in camera. I hope I have made myself clear.' He pauses, staring at the faces above him in the gallery, daring any to challenge him. 'You may continue, Mr Stafford.'

'Thank you, my Lord. As I was saying, of the thirty men arrested, only one has been released without charge. All the others face indictments to be heard in this court by your Lordship in the coming weeks and months.'

'Are we proceeding to an immediate trial of the other men named on this indictment?' asks the Recorder.

'No, my Lord. Additional evidence was served on the representatives of those defendants earlier this week and there remain some further witnesses to be contacted. It is expected that the prosecution will be ready to proceed in approximately four weeks' time. With your Lordship's leave, I will call Detective Inspector Greene to tell you what's known of this defendant.'

'Very well. Yes, call Detective Inspector Greene.'

DI Greene gets up from the bench behind junior prosecuting counsel and walks across the well of the court.

This is the high point of Greene's career, his stepping stone, he hopes, to Detective Chief Inspector, and in celebration his wife has bought him a new suit and a new tie. The jacket looks slightly tight, and two attempts to do up the middle button over his protuberant belly as he walks are unsuccessful. He gives up the attempt and steps into the witness box.

Greene gives the oath and is taken by Stafford through Gervaise's previous criminal convictions. Stafford resumes his seat and Ensley rises.

'Do you agree with me, detective inspector, that without Mr Gervaise's evidence, arrests of the others involved in the conspiracy might have proved very difficult?'

'Yes.'

'Furthermore, Mr Gervaise's evidence has permitted the arrest of no fewer than thirty men involved in other serious crimes, including murder and armed robbery?'

'Yes, that's right.'

This answer produces another outburst from the gallery, and one of the men who was shouting threats before actually runs to the rail and starts gesticulating again.

'You're a fucking liar, Gervaise,' he screams, spittle flying from his lips, 'and you'll never live to see the outside of a prison cell!'

'Master at Arms!' calls the Recorder, pointing up at the man. 'Arrest that man!'

The Master at Arms has already predicted such a command, as he appears instantly at the back of the gallery. He starts pushing along the front row of spectators from one end while two of his colleagues approach the shouting man from the other. The man turns and forces his way over the back of the seats, kicking a woman's hat off in the process. He climbs to the next row above him and then, seeing his opportunity, runs along that row, trampling on toes and handbags, up the aisle and out of the door with the Master at Arms and his colleagues in hot pursuit. The occupants of the court listen as the banging of doors and shouting gradually fade to silence. The last few seconds were so like a "Carry On" film that Charles has to suppress a smile.

'What that man did, ladies and gentlemen,' says the Recorder, and all heads in the court turn to him again, 'constitutes a serious contempt of court. I hope he's brought his toothbrush with him because when he comes back before me, I'm very likely to send him to prison. As I shall anyone else who interrupts the proceedings of this court any further.' He turns back to Ensley.

'Do you have any other questions for the detective inspector?'

'I don't think it would be appropriate, my Lord, to ventilate further detail. It is in any event contained in the Commissioner's letter, together with other matters which should not be mentioned in open court.'

Charles sees a few puzzled expressions in the public gallery, but he knows the code. It is not within the Metropolitan Police Commissioner's gift to vouchsafe Gervaise any particular sentence, but Charles is certain that the letter will set out in broad terms the deal agreed with the Supergrass and the sentence the Crown have agreed would be appropriate. The actual decision remains with the Recorder.

'Thank you, Detective Inspector Greene. You may stand down.'

Ensley starts his speech in mitigation, but it amounts to nothing more than a couple of further sentences. There is little more that can be said. Telling the Recorder that his client has a good solid job or that he's a family man will cut no ice in these circumstances. All that sensibly can be said on Gervaise's behalf has already been said. He's a villain, a villain's villain, who has turned Queen's Evidence but whose actual worth remains to be seen.

In striking his deal with Greene and Cathcart, Gervaise is taking an enormous risk. It could still unravel before a judge, by which time he will have made admissions to offences for which he is personally responsible, and there will be no way back. On the other hand, the police are taking a huge gamble too. Gervaise will receive a sentence commensurate with the assistance he says he's going to give in court. Whatever statement he might sign about other offenders, it will do the Crown no good if it isn't repeated, and believed, in court.

'Thank you, Mr Ensley. I shall rise for a few minutes to consider sentence.'

'Court rise!'

Some amateurs in the gallery leave their seats, but those who have the inside track stay where they are. They know that sentence has already been decided. This short adjournment is probably only to allow the Recorder, an incessant smoker, time for a quick one. Sure enough, four minutes later, another knock sounds on the panelled door and the Recorder resumes his seat, betrayed by a faint wisp of smoke around his shoulders.

He waits for the court to settle before saying: 'Stand up, Gervaise.'

Gervaise does so.

'You have an appalling record of both violence and dishonesty, and in any other circumstances your involvement with such a well-planned and well-executed conspiracy to steal, leading to the loss of hundreds of thousands of pounds-worth of goods, would have meant a very long prison sentence. People like you forget that when stealing from organisations such as the RAF, they are stealing from all of us. It is our taxes which pay for our armed forces and all the materiel they require. Nonetheless, your involvement was minor, you have pleaded guilty at the first opportunity, you have named your co-conspirators, and I accept that you have given substantial assistance, and promise to give much more still, to the authorities in bringing to book numerous other criminals.

'In those circumstances, and in those circumstances alone, I feel I am entitled to pass an exceptional sentence on you. You will go to prison for a period of four years.'

CHAPTER 32

Charles sits in the converted cell in the bowels of the Old Bailey, waiting for Irenna Alexandrova to be produced. He is already robed but for his ancient horsehair wig, which lies on the bench next to him. The wig is hot and scratchy, and he never dons it until the last possible moment, a fact that has seen him berated by several judges who have entered court unexpectedly.

He listens to the familiar echoes of toilets being flushed, prison doors opening and closing, and prisoners laughing and complaining as they are moved about. Those still in the cells have just been given their lunch and the smell of cooking, predominantly toast and fried bacon, drifts down the cell area towards Charles. It's always mealtime in the cells of the Old Bailey. Hattie's description of the sausage machine was completely accurate; prisoners being delivered and collected constantly, fed in from remand prisons across London and, following conviction, transported out to start their sentences.

There's a long delay before Irenna is produced, but Charles is unconcerned. He has plenty of time. It's only quarter past one and the Recorder won't return to court until just after two. Charles's blue counsel's notebook and the slim sheaf of papers making up his brief lie on the tiny table in the middle of the room which, as always, is screwed to the floor to prevent its use as a weapon. This conference is formally to take further instructions but, in reality, he has nothing further to say to Irenna except words of encouragement. He is as ready for the trial as he ever will be. He left Sean Sloane waiting outside the main cell door, pacing nervously and hoping that Charles would be able to persuade the gaolers to let him down. Strictly, he's a witness for the Defence and would not be entitled to access for a "legal", but he's a copper and Charles is optimistic he can get the rules to bend slightly.

The door swings inwards and Irenna appears, handcuffed to a woman prison officer. Charles stands as the handcuffs are removed. Irenna looks determined, but she's pale and looks strained. The black eye she received a few days before is fading to greeny-yellow and the swelling on her cheek has largely gone. The blood-saturated dressing has been replaced by a smaller and cleaner one. As a prisoner on remand she's entitled to wear her own clothes, and today she sports a plain blue skirt to the knee and a white blouse. Her hair is pulled back in a simple fashion and she wears no make-up. She looks little different from the prison guard.

They are left alone and she sits, staring at the table.

'How do you feel?' asks Charles.

It takes a moment for Irenna to answer. 'It feels like a dream, to be honest, a bit Kafkaesque. Arrested and put on trial for something about which I know absolutely nothing, just to manipulate a situation that doesn't involve me; a pawn in someone else's game. Believe me, I love Sean —' she looks up at Charles for the first time — 'he's a wonderful man, and I've never felt like this for anyone before, but I find myself wishing I'd never laid eyes on him.'

'I understand.'

'No, you don't. You've never been in this situation.'

Charles's eyebrows rise slightly.

Maybe he hasn't told her.

'It's not a story for now, but you're wrong there. I've been in a situation very like yours, also framed, and pursued by a corrupt police officer.'

She pauses, eyes widening. 'You have? I didn't know. Well, maybe if you get me out of this, we can compare notes sometime. Is there anything you need from me?'

'No. Just to remind you to remain calm, answer the questions as simply and shortly as you can — don't offer extraneous detail, if I need it, I'll ask more questions — and keep your voice up. I'll be watching the judge's pen and if I see him struggling to keep up, I'll put up a hand to slow you down, okay? It's not important, but if you want to address him, it's "My Lord". If you can remember this, give your answers to him rather than to me, but again, it's not important.'

She nods. 'That's fine. I'll probably forget half of it when I get into the witness box.'

'Most witnesses are very nervous, but once you've started you realise how easy it is — you're just answering questions, after all — and, if anything, you relax too much and become careless or over-confident. So, be on your guard. Prosecuting counsel's job is to trip you up and make you look like a liar.'

She nods again. 'Got it.'

'Any questions for me?'

'No, I don't think so. Will I get a chance to talk to you again before the end?'

'Yes, but not once you've started giving evidence. Then you're in seclusion and no one can talk to you about the case until you finish. Now, Sean's waiting upstairs. I'm going to try to persuade them to let him down to speak to you ... pretend it's part of the legal visit. No guarantees, but would you like to see him if possible?'

Her face lights up and he's struck again by how pretty she is.

I could really fancy this woman if I wasn't in love with Sally. And if Irenna wasn't totally besotted with my best friend.

As that passes through his head, Charles pauses to reflect. The thought that he's in love with Sally came to him so easily, unaccompanied by the slightest "but".

Because I can't have her? Or is this real?

'That would be wonderful, if you can manage it. Yes, please!' she says with intensity.

Charles stands and knocks on the door. It takes the prison officer a minute but eventually the door is opened and Charles is allowed out. Irenna is locked in again.

Charles walks to the desk at the end of the corridor which is now occupied by a different custody officer to the one who signed him in.

'Afternoon, Gilbert,' he says.

The officer looks up. 'It's Mr Holborne, isn't it?'

'Yes.'

'Signing out?' says Gilbert.

'Yes, but I have a favour to ask. There's a copper upstairs who needs to see one of your prisoners, Irenna Alexandrova? Can he come down?'

'I don't see why not. If you sign out, I'll let him in as I let you out.'

Easier than expected.

Charles does as instructed and the custody officer leads him to the main outside door. He unlocks it. Sloane is still there, pacing. He whirls round as he hears the door open.

'DS Sloane; your turn,' says Charles. 'I'll see you in the Great Hall.'

Charles sees gratitude flash briefly across his friend's face before he steps inside the door and it closes again.

Charles walks to the Great Hall, his footsteps echoing on the black and white marble. The Hall is almost completely empty; lawyers, police officers and witnesses have rushed out to grab a quick sandwich during the short adjournment. He takes a seat on one of the benches underneath the plaster figures decorating the ceiling. The light through the dome shines directly on the painting opposite him, which depicts the state of the building on 11th May 1941, the morning after the air raid which almost destroyed it. Harry Horowitz, on one of his business trips to London during the Blitz, was among the scores of fire wardens who helped dowse the flames and carry out the injured and dead that night.

Ten minutes later Charles hears Sloane's footsteps approaching. He sits on the bench next to Charles.

'Thanks for doing that, Charlie. I'm very grateful.'

'My pleasure. You okay?'

The Irishman nods. 'Yes. It's odd having someone you love on the other side of the fence. You develop a sort of cynicism, you know? Dealing with criminals all the time, it's easy to forget that the people in the cells, guilty or not, are humans too.'

Charles nods but does not reply. Then he says: 'We've time for a cuppa, if you want. Fischer's meeting me in the public canteen soon, if he's not already waiting.'

Charles leads them to the public canteen. Hansie Fischer is indeed already there with his clerk. The four men chat for a few minutes, mostly about the controversy sparked by Kenneth Tynan's first use of the word "fuck" on television the previous month.

At ten minutes to two the men climb the elegant staircase to Court 1.

Charles enters court to find it almost completely full. He sidles into the bench reserved for junior counsel. Marcus Stafford QC has already taken his place in the foremost bench and is standing before his lectern, arranging his notes.

'There you are, Holborne,' he says. 'Ready?'

'Yes, thank you, Stafford. We can go straight to arraignment.'

'Very well. I'll ask the usher to pass that along.' He squeezes out from the bench in search of the usher.

Stafford returns to his bench a minute or two later, and at the same moment there is a knock on the door.

'All rise!'

The Recorder of London enters, bows are exchanged and he addresses Charles.

'I'm told that both sides are ready, Mr Holborne. Can we proceed?'

'We can, thank you, my Lord.'

A shout goes downstairs to bring up Irenna. She and the woman custody officer must have been waiting at the top of the steps because she steps directly into the dock. As her handcuffs are being removed, she looks around her. The number of spectators and the jammed reporters' benches seem to surprise her, and for a moment Charles fears that she's going to faint, but he watches her take a deep breath to calm herself. She makes eye contact with Charles, and he smiles reassuringly. Irenna looks up sharply as the clerk of the court addresses her.

'Are you Dr Irenna Alexandrova?' she asks.

'Yes?'

'Dr Alexandrova, you are charged with a single count of receiving stolen goods contrary to section thirty-three, subsection one, of the Larceny Act, 1916. The particulars of the offence are that or about the nineteenth day of November nineteen sixty-five, you received two jackets, the property of the Royal Air Force, knowing the same to have been stolen. How do you plead?'

Irenna takes a deep, slightly shaky breath, and stares directly at the judge. 'Not guilty,' she says in a firm voice.

'Jury then, please,' directs the Recorder, not even looking at Irenna.

The usher goes to a door set in the panelling behind three banks of empty benches and knocks on it. Eighteen men and women file into court and fill up spaces on the benches. A few appraise the layout of the court and the people surrounding them, but most keep their heads down and concentrate on doing as they are told.

Charles is pleased with what he sees; the jury in waiting, from whom twelve men and women will be chosen, includes some women, one dark-skinned, perhaps Asian, and three black men. These are the jurors Charles wants on his jury.

The clerk of the court stands again and addresses those who have just entered.

'Members of the jury in waiting, please answer to your names and step into the jury box as you are called.'

She turns to Irenna and gives her the usual form of words, explaining that she may object to a juror as they come to the book to be sworn. Charles has warned Irenna of this and she merely nods to indicate that she has understood.

On behalf of his client, Charles can challenge any of the proposed jury members if he has cause, such as evidence of collusion with the police, and up to seven for no cause at all. After discussion with Irenna and Sloane, it's been agreed that he will challenge off as many as possible whom he suspects of right-wing views or who may be racist. The jury's decision is going to depend on who they trust: a lifelong criminal and an experienced policeman on one side, or a foreign, radical, possibly communist, Jewess on the other. It's not an easy call, and if they start from a position of dislike for Irenna's sex, politics or religion, she'll be fighting an uphill battle.

It is, of course, an impossible task to be certain of anything by merely looking at someone, but over the years Charles has developed several rules of thumb, and two are relevant today. Insofar as he has the numbers to do it, he'll vote off anyone clutching a right-wing newspaper or who he thinks might be ill-educated and thus, potentially, racist. He'll keep women, anyone of non-English heritage and, if there are any, clergymen because, despite the strictures of the eighth commandment, he expects them to be fair in their consideration of the evidence.

Charles studies each person as their name is called. The first six are all unexceptional, both to him and the Crown: four reasonably well-dressed white men, none of whom seems too confident (and thus, Charles speculates, potentially arrogant) and two women. One of the men, on closer inspection, might be Greek or perhaps of other Middle Eastern extraction. He looks like a retired businessman, and Charles is pleased at his inclusion. All six give the oath as requested.

There follow two challenges by Marcus Stafford QC, both men, for reasons which Charles cannot fathom. The next man called is one of the black men, and Stafford's challenge is out of his mouth before the poor chap can even rise to start the oath.

So that's how it is.

The next is a man Charles identified as he walked into court as someone to whom he would object: upright bearing, heading into his seventies, a neatly-folded *Telegraph* under his arm and an umbrella in his hand. He looks military, impatient and sour. Charles challenges him off, and the man glares at Charles as if he'd been whipped before taking his seat again.

The Asian woman is called next and Charles sees Stafford hesitate but, after a moment, decides against challenging.

That's revealing.

At the outset there were only six spare jurors and, between them, counsel have already challenged off four. Once the jury panel is exhausted, a fresh panel will be required, and it can be difficult to find further potential jurors at a busy court centre like the Old Bailey in the afternoon, after all the other trials have dipped deeply into the pool. That would require an adjournment. Charles imagined that he would be much less in favour of an adjournment than Stafford — he has a client in custody after all, and his tactic is to get Irenna's case decided before the other Supergrass cases are ready — but, perhaps because of problems with evidence or witnesses in the following cases, or perhaps for no more reason than a clash in his own diary, Stafford seems reluctant to countenance a delay.

The jury box now has seven people in it, and five more must be found from the group of seven who wait.

The next juror in waiting to be called is a woman, and neither side objects to her. Four to be chosen out of six. The next is an elderly man who Charles challenges off. He is sorry, because the gent looked benign, but he does it to make Stafford's task more difficult still: four must be found out of five. The next potential juror called is another man and Charles challenges again. That leaves four out of four. If Charles is right, Stafford will now have no choice but accept whoever is left.

Cheering silently to himself, Charles watches as the next four names to be called are all installed in the jury box without challenge. The jury, as finally constituted, is formed of seven men, two of them black, and five women, one Asian.

Not too bad.

Charles only has to persuade one of them of a reasonable doubt, and the hung jury will secure a draw, followed either by the Crown throwing its hand in or a retrial. That, however, is the lower limit of his ambitions; he needs an outright acquittal.

The jury bailiff leads the challenged jurors out of the court and the Recorder nods to Stafford that he may start.

'Ladies and gentlemen of the jury, I appear on behalf of the Crown in this case, and my learned friend Mr Holborne, who sits nearest to you, appears on behalf of the accused. My task presently is just to give you an outline of the evidence you will hear so you may place it in context as it is given. Of course, nothing I say is actually evidence; only what you hear from the witness box or any agreed evidence which is read to you by the court clerk is evidence, and you will decide the case on the basis of that and my Lord's direction to you as to the law.

'The woman in the dock is Dr Irenna Alexandrova. She's a qualified doctor, but her qualification is South African, so she's had to do some further training to be able to practise here. She works at Finchley Memorial Hospital. You will hear that she is a lady of good character, in other words she has no previous criminal convictions in this country. That is to her credit, but you will realise that everyone who is convicted of a crime must at one time have had a good character. It does not mean therefore that she cannot be guilty. The learned judge will explain to you how you should address this factor in due course.

'In order to earn a little extra money, Dr Alexandrova was working at a market stall on a casual basis in Petticoat Lane, where she was selling clothing. The Crown's case is that she needed a winter jacket, no doubt because she came from South Africa and did not have appropriate winter clothing. Mr Gervaise was involved in transporting the goods to the market stall where she worked, and he met Dr Alexandrova on a couple of occasions. She said to him that she wished she could have a jacket like one of those, and he offered her one. She asked him if they were "hooky", a slang expression for stolen, and he told her that they were. Notwithstanding that, she accepted one of the jackets, a small one with a thirty-four inch chest, knowing it was stolen.

'It was, in the end, only coincidence that Dr Alexandrova's crime came to be discovered. You will hear from Detective Inspector Greene and Detective Constable Lincoln that they were investigating a completely different offence which caused them to go to fourteen Colville Terrace, Notting Hill. That address is divided into several bedsits, and they were heading to a bedsit on the top floor. They passed the door of Dr Alexandrova's room on a lower floor, and saw that the lock had been kicked in, and the timber frame damaged. So they went in to see if they could find the burglar and found instead two jackets, the small one and another one, hanging on a rail in the doctor's room. We say that she was given permission to keep the one she wore during her shift, but she also took it upon herself to take another. That is why she is charged with receiving two stolen jackets. DI Greene found her explanations to be suspicious, and he arrested her. He questioned her on the way back to the police station, and she confessed.

'That is the shape of the case, and you will see that it's extremely simple. I should say one more thing about the evidence. As I explained, it is the evidence of William Gervaise, the man who had the conversation with the accused at Petticoat Lane, which establishes that the accused knew the jackets were "hooky". Now, you may be aware of certain press reports in which the papers name Mr Gervaise as the "Supergrass". In other words, he has admitted his part in the stealing of these jackets, along with very large quantities of other goods from the RAF, and has been sentenced for that offence already. He will be giving evidence for the Crown in this case and in several others, against his co-conspirators and other alleged criminals. It is not suggested that Dr Alexandrova was in any way involved with the conspiracy to steal; she just took the jackets, knowing they were stolen. So whatever you may have read about Mr Gervaise in the press as a "Supergrass", that is really nothing to do with this case. Here he comes before you simply as an ordinary witness who informed the accused that she was about to accept stolen goods.

'If you have any doubt that the goods were stolen; if you have any doubt that Dr Alexandrova knew that they were stolen; if you have any doubt that they were found in the possession of Dr Alexandrova; in any of these cases, you are obliged to acquit her. The Crown must satisfy you so that you are sure beyond reasonable doubt of these components. I say on behalf of the prosecution that by the end of the evidence you will be satisfied of all three, and that you should convict. With my Lordship's leave, I shall call the first witness, Mr William Gervaise.'

'You may proceed.'

'Call William Gervaise.'

A shout goes up from the dock and, as in the committal, Irenna has to stand to one side as Gervaise is brought up, handcuffed to a male guard. As a convicted prisoner Gervaise would usually wear prison uniform, but it looks as if he's been kept in the cells in his own clothes since his plea earlier that morning as they're creased and Charles sees a food stain on the breast of his jacket. The bridge of his heavy-rimmed spectacles has somehow been broken and a piece of Sellotape holds the parts together. He looks even more like a cowed, timid bank clerk.

If this presentation's calculated, it's being done well. I'll have some work to do here.

Gervaise tries to catch Irenna's eyes as he sidles past, still handcuffed, and steps down from the dock, but Irenna backs away as far as her restraints will permit. Gervaise and his escort walk across the well of the court and climb the steps into the witness box. The court clerk awaits him, Bible in one hand and printed card in the other.

Charles looks around at the packed and expectant courtroom and notices, for the first time, Ronnie and Reggie Kray sitting next to one another in the front row of the public gallery.

Of course. They want to see how Gervaise performs.

'Please take the Bible in your right hand and read the words off the card,' says the clerk.

Gervaise does so, and hands both Bible and card back to her. He remains standing, the prison guard slightly behind him but still attached.

Charles notices the double doors behind him opening, and three men file into the back of the court. One wears a uniform he's never seen before, but he understands instantly the significance of it. The proliferation of "scrambled egg" on the peak of his hat, now being removed and tucked under an arm, and his epaulettes reveal him as the Deputy Metropolitan Police Commissioner. On one side of the Deputy Commissioner is a tall handsome Detective Chief Superintendent in uniform and, on the other, a much smaller man in a conservative suit. Charles doubts that the third man is a police officer — something about his bearing and small stature, perhaps — but if forced to guess from his company and his presence at that moment in court, Charles would say that he's probably a civil servant; Home Office perhaps, or Lord Chancellor's department.

The three men cast about for seats but, finding none, sidle to one side and remain standing, their backs to the wood panelling.

So, here's the Establishment, all present and correct to watch Gervaise's performance.

Charles switches his attention back to the man in the witness box.

'Is your name William Arnold Gervaise?' asks Stafford.

'Yeah,' replies Gervaise, but he is paying little attention. His eyes scan the public gallery and the journalists' benches.

Just enjoying being the centre of attention?

Gervaise's eyes land on the Krays and he freezes for a moment.

No. He's looking for the people who've taken out contracts on him.

Charles transfers his gaze to the Krays. They stare at Gervaise, but there is nothing in their expressions to give away their thoughts. Gervaise finally focuses his attention on Stafford.

'Earlier today, you were sentenced to four years' imprisonment for your part in a conspiracy to steal goods from an RAF base in Bedfordshire called Cardington, is that right?'

Gervaise pauses before answering. His eyes land for the first time on the three men at the back of the court, and he jumps like an NCO called to attention by his commanding officer. His shoulders go back, he lifts his chin and he answers loudly. 'Yes, sir, that's correct.'

'Did your part in that crime involve transporting goods?'
'Yes.'

'From where and to where?'

'From a warehouse off the Commercial Road to Petticoat Lane market.'

'And what goods did you move?'

'All sorts. Anything that could be nicked from the RAF stores.'

'Did that include any RAF jackets?'

'Yeah, every now and then.'

'Do you know the accused?'

'I know her.'

'How?'

'She worked on the stall at Petticoat Lane. At least she did on the couple of times I saw her there.'

'Did you ever speak to her?'

'Yeah. Why not?'

'Did you ever speak to her about any RAF jackets?'

'Yeah.'

'When was that?'

'I dunno exactly. A few weeks back. During that cold snap.'

'How did the conversation begin?'

'I was just delivering as usual and she complained of being cold. She looked cold.'

'And?'

'And nothing. She said she was cold. Next time I saw her, she said she wished she had one of them jackets, so I told her she could put one on, and keep it.'

Again, Gervaise's eyes flick briefly towards the back of the court, as if seeking approval for his evidence.

'Why did you do that?'

Gervaise smiles and looks momentarily embarrassed, but something about it is hammy and Charles is sure it's an act. 'Well ... see ... don't tell the missus, but I fancied her. I thought if I gave her a jacket, she might give me something in return.' He leers at Irenna.

Isolated laughter comes from sections of the public gallery, and Gervaise turns his head to look at the press box to see if the journalists noted his answer. Charles, on the other hand, keeps his focus on the jury; they didn't find the comment funny.

'When you gave her the jacket, was anything said about whether or not it was stolen?'

'She asked me if the jackets was 'ooky, to which I said they was.'

'"'Ooky"?'

'Yeah, 'ooky. Nicked. Bent. Pinched. Fallen off a wagon. You know … stolen.'

'Thank you. And what did you reply to that enquiry?'

'I said of course they were. She'd seen me bringing them in, hadn't she? And the prices was obviously too low.'

'Did you see her put on the jacket?'

'Yeah. She was standing right next to me. I didn't see her leave with it, though. And I didn't give her permission to take two, neither. So she's nicked it, that second one.'

'Thank you. Please stay there.'

Stafford sits, the bench groaning slightly under the assault, and Charles stands.

'I wish to make it clear to you, Mr Gervaise,' he begins, 'both in fairness to you and so the jury understands the position perfectly, that Dr Alexandrova denies every word you have said about her. She denies that she's ever met you; she denies she's ever worked at Petticoat Lane or at any other market; she denies ever speaking to you; she denies asking for or accepting these jackets; she denies ever bringing them into her bedsit. In fairness to you, I make it clear right at the beginning of my cross-examination, that we say you're a liar, and you've made up this story from beginning to end.'

'I ain't the liar,' says Gervaise firmly, and he lifts his free hand, points dramatically at Irenna in the dock. 'She is.'

'I also wish to make it clear to you that you have corruptly and maliciously implicated an innocent woman in a crime she never committed.'

'That ain't true! Why would I want to frame a completely innocent woman?'

'We'll come onto your motive in a moment. For the moment, let us explore who is the one most likely to be lying.'

Charles reaches for a document on the desk before him, a list of Gervaise's previous convictions extricated from the prosecution.

'You were born in nineteen thirteen, were you not?' asks Charles.

'July nineteen thirteen, yes.'

'Your first conviction, at the age of fourteen, was for stealing money from a sweet shop till.'

Gervaise snorts. 'That was almost forty years ago. I was just a kid.'

'You went to court for it, didn't you?'

'I don't remember. Probably.'

'Did you plead guilty or did the magistrates find you guilty?'

'I really don't remember. It was just a few shillings.'

'I may be able to help you remember, Mr Gervaise. You pleaded not guilty, didn't you?'

Gervaise shrugs, unconcerned. 'Maybe.' He points to the sheets of paper in Charles's hand. 'If you've got the record, you know better'n me. What's it say?'

'It says you pleaded not guilty, and after a trial the magistrates disbelieved your evidence.'

'Whatever.'

'Your next conviction was three years after that, in nineteen thirty. You were sent to Borstal for burglaries of six houses in the Southwark and Lambeth areas. Do you remember that?'

'Yes.'

'This makes seven offences of dishonesty so far. Do you remember whether you pleaded guilty or were found guilty after a trial?'

'I think I remember a trial ... what's that say?'

'You remember correctly. It says you pleaded not guilty, which means you gave your evidence on oath, but the Quarter Sessions jury didn't believe you.'

'I admit I committed some of them burglaries, but not all,' says Gervaise, still calm, but his voice rising slightly. 'They just wanted to clear up their records.'

'That's not what twelve men and women, good and true, found though, is it?'

Gervaise makes a snorting sound, as if the opinions of twelve jurors are worthless, an unwise attitude to take, in Charles's opinion. Charles looks round at the jury. They are focusing intently on Gervaise, and Charles is pleased to note that at least two of them are making notes of the convictions as he runs through them.

'When you came out of Borstal, it only took you six months to get caught for another offence of dishonesty. By then, you'd graduated to using violence in order to steal. February nineteen thirty-three: robbery of a sub-post office in Highgate in which six pounds four shillings and eight pence was stolen. You coshed an unarmed postmaster over the head; cracked his skull and gave him concussion.'

Charles glances at the jury. Any initial impression that Gervaise might have been mild-mannered and harmless has been dispelled. Gervaise is receiving a full hard stare from most of the jurors.

'That weren't me.'

'So you say. Is that what you said at the time?'

'I've always said it. I'm telling you now, ain't I? It weren't me. I was set up by … the police.'

'So if you said it throughout, I assume that means you disputed the offences when you came to trial at Middlesex Assizes?'

'Bloody right, I did.'

'But, again, the jury didn't believe you, did they?'

'That's not my fault! I'm telling you, I was set up by a bent copper. He even offered to get the charges dropped if I gave him a pony.' Gervaise sees the puzzled expression on the faces of some of the jurors. 'Twenty-five pounds.'

'So you fought that case at trial, you gave evidence on oath, and the jury nonetheless convicted you.'

Gervaise is getting worked up now and his face reddens. He shakes his head but he doesn't answer.

'You stood in the witness box, you swore an oath on the Bible to tell the truth, the whole truth and nothing but the truth, the jury heard you cross-examined, and they convicted you. They were satisfied beyond reasonable doubt that you were lying to them.'

'It was a fuckin' miscarriage of justice, that's what it was.'

The Recorder intervenes. 'Gervaise, you will mind your language or there will be consequences.'

Gervaise takes a deep breath and mutters, 'Sorry, my Lord.'

'You were sentenced to three years and six months, weren't you? Although you only served just over two years.'

'Yes. Two years for something I never did.'

'There is then quite a long gap in your record. Was that because you didn't get caught or because you obtained honest employment?'

'What are the dates?'

There is some laughter at that answer, but Charles ignores it. 'From nineteen thirty-six to nineteen forty-six.'

'Well, I was called up. I was in the RAF for most of that.'

'Yes. And within a year of you being demobbed, you were caught stealing again: two trucks of goods full of machine parts from a factory. You got two years.'

'Suspended. On account of me war record.'

'And, presumably, because you'd not been before the courts for a decade. Did you plead guilty or were you found guilty?'

'I copped a plea.'

'Agreed. You admitted yet another offence of dishonesty, stealing. And, according to this —' Charles brandishes the document — 'you asked for a further four offences to be taken into consideration when you were sentenced.'

'I don't remember.'

'When a man's being sentenced for an offence, he may ask for other crimes to be taken into consideration, so they don't come back to bite him in the future. It's a way of clearing the police books and giving the offender a chance of a fresh start. Isn't that right?'

'I don't know what the purpose is. You presumably know better'n me.'

'The offences you asked to be taken into consideration were also offences of dishonesty — minor, I agree — but dishonesty all the same. And one of ABH, assault occasioning actual bodily harm.'

'That was nothing. Just a pub fight. He was me best mate!'

'Now we're at nineteen fifty-one, when you were convicted of robbery with a group of others, stealing gold bullion en route from the airport to a bank in central London. You got eight years for that, didn't you?'

'Yes.'

'And you carried a gun.'

The Recorder intervenes. 'Are you really going to go on at this length, Mr Holborne? The jury has the point, I'm sure.'

'I have no idea whether the jury has the point or not, my Lord, and with great respect, no one in this court does. They will keep their own counsel till they deliver their verdict.'

'Mr Holborne, this is a straightforward case and it doesn't require you to cross-examine until Christmas to make a very simple point. We've all got it: Mr Gervaise has a serious record for offences of dishonesty. Now move on.'

'With respect to your Lordship, I cannot just "move on". This case will turn on which of the witnesses the jury believes, and I'm entitled to put each and every one of this witness's previous offences to him to demonstrate the length and depth of his dishonesty. If My Lord rules otherwise, I will have no alternative but to retire from this case, because you will have prevented me doing my duty to my client.'

A shocked silence follows. Charles is entirely confident that he's right in his submission, but very few barristers stand up to the Recorder in this way, and it's a complete bluff; the last thing he wants is to be released from representing Irenna. The Recorder is looking down at his notes, and at first Charles believes him to be recording Charles's submission, but then it's apparent from the movement of his hand that he's merely doodling as he thinks.

The Recorder looks up. 'Very well, you may proceed, but make it swift.'

'Thank you, my Lord. Mr Gervaise. You carried a gun, didn't you?'

'Yes.'

'And were sentenced to eight years' imprisonment, serving six, longer than one would expect. Caused, I guess, by your bad behaviour while in prison?'

'That weren't my fault. That screw hated me, pissing in my drinks, constantly making me scrub the kharsy. He deserved it.'

'So, in summary, that's fifteen offences of dishonesty, most of which you denied but where your evidence given on oath was disbelieved. The only one I've missed out is the offence of conspiracy to steal, to which you pleaded guilty this morning. Now, Mr Gervaise, bearing in mind all the judges, juries and magistrates who have found you to be lying on your oath over the years, please turn towards this jury and explain to them why they should be any more credulous than the others.'

'Credulous?'

'Yes. Why should this jury believe your evidence on oath when so many others haven't?'

Gervaise shrugs, opens his palms as if to demonstrate to the jury that he is hiding nothing, and says: ''Cos I'm telling the truth, that's all. I ain't got no reason to lie to get her into trouble.' He nods towards Irenna in the dock. 'I've got my sentence already. Whatever I say or don't say, it's no skin off my back if she's convicted or if she ain't.'

'Well, that's not quite true, is it?' points out Charles. 'Before you decided to turn Queen's Evidence, you had to negotiate a deal with the prosecutors, didn't you?'

'I don't know what you mean,' says Gervaise swiftly, but his eyes flick away from Charles's.

'You agreed to give evidence against your co-conspirators involved in stealing from RAF Cardington, and against others involved in different crimes, in return for a reduced sentence, didn't you?' Gervaise's brow creases and he looks as if he's thinking furiously. 'Come on now, Mr Gervaise, all the newspapers are calling you "the Supergrass". That's someone who gives evidence against their former colleagues in return for a lighter sentence. There's no secret to that, is there?'

Gervaise suddenly looks up, as if an idea has illuminated his brain. 'I decided to turn over a new leaf,' he says brightly, prompting scattered laughter from the public gallery and the people sitting behind Charles. The phrase is trotted out as if rehearsed, and only just recalled. 'Seriously, I know I've done wrong and I want to set the record straight. If the judge thinks that's worth a reduced sentence, that's up to him.'

'So you *did* have a motive to implicate others, didn't you? If you agreed, you were opening up the possibility of a reduced sentence.'

'Maybe, but that doesn't mean I ain't telling the truth. I'm not gonna get much off for grassing *her*, am I? Two jackets? Don't make me laugh.'

'Now, seeing as you brought us to it, let me ask you some questions about your motive to lie in Dr Alexandrova's case. Do you know a police officer named Detective Sergeant Sloane?'

The question seems to take Gervaise by surprise. His mouth opens to answer, but then he changes his mind and shuts it again. 'I know lots of police officers,' he finally says.

'With your record, I don't doubt it,' replies Charles, producing the loudest laughter so far.

'Mr Holborne! This is not a music hall! Confine yourself to asking questions rather than making impertinent comments.'

'My Lord is right … as always. I suggest you know Detective Sergeant Sloane particularly, because on the twenty-first of October this year you assaulted him at the Cricklewood goods yard when he tried to arrest you.'

He sees uncertainty in Gervaise's expression.

He's weighing up which will look worse: admitting he hit a police officer or Charles calling Sloane to prove him a liar?

'There was a … scuffle at Cricklewood … with a copper. But Hawkins let me scarper.'

'By "Hawkins" are you referring to a Detective Sergeant Hawkins of the British Transport Police?'

'That's right.'

'The same DS Hawkins who is presently suspended?'

'Yes.'

'The same DS Hawkins who is one of the men charged with you, for stealing from RAF Cardington?'

'That's right.'

'So, you're admitting that there was a scuffle between you and DS Sloane at Cricklewood goods yard, and one of your corrupt co-conspirators, himself a police officer, let you go rather than have charges pressed against you? Is that right?'

'That's about the size of it.'

'DS Sloane didn't like being punched, did he?'

Gervaise barks a laugh. 'You'd have to ask him, but I guess not.'

'And he started investigating you, didn't he?'

'I don't know. Did he?'

'Yes, Mr Gervaise, he did. He started making a complete nuisance of himself.'

'Like I said, I don't know. He never interviewed me or nothing.'

'I suggest you know very well. I suggest that you know that DS Sloane's superior officers told him to stop investigating but, when he refused, you and DI Greene had to do something about it.'

'No, that's not true. Or, at least, if he was investigating, I knew nothing about it.'

'I suggest you and DI Greene hatched a plan to put pressure on DS Sloane to back off, and that involved you making up this fairy-tale about RAF jackets.'

'Mr Holborne,' intervenes the Recorder. 'I'm sorry to interrupt your flow…'

Of course you are. Buying time for the witness to make up more lies is completely incidental.

'But explain to us all how planting a stolen jacket in Dr Alexandrova's bedsit could possibly implicate or put pressure on this sergeant…'

'Sloane, My Lord.'

'Yes, Sergeant Sloane.' The Recorder distorts his face into something which might have been the muscle-memory of a smile.

'Because,' replies Charles, 'DI Greene believed the bedsit to be Sloane's. It wasn't. He'd been staying there —' Charles turns to the jury as he delivers his punchline — 'because Dr Alexandrova is his girlfriend.'

With satisfaction he sees several jurors nod with understanding.

'It's all a lie, my Lord,' says Gervaise. 'I never hatched no plan with DI Greene. He's a member of the Flying Squad. I don't like coppers, and I don't "hatch plans" with them.'

'Except this one,' interjects Charles swiftly.

'What?'

'Well, you certainly hatched a plan with DI Greene to give evidence against your former criminal colleagues in return for a lighter sentence, didn't you?'

'Greene's not got the power to do that. He's only a DI.'

'No, of course not, but he set it all up, didn't he? It was DI Greene who arrested you for the conspiracy to steal, wasn't it?'

'Yes.'

'It was DI Greene who interviewed you for that offence?'

'Yes.'

'And it was during those interviews that discussions began about you becoming a Supergrass, and that culminated in you pleading guilty this morning. How is that not hatching a plan with him?'

Gervaise doesn't answer, and Charles suddenly changes tack.

'Do you have any proof that Dr Alexandrova was employed by anyone at Petticoat Lane?'

'No. She never worked for me, and in any case they all work cash in hand.'

'Can you be specific on the days you say you saw her there?'

'No. I told you, in the autumn, when it got cold.'

'Of course, Mr Gervaise, if you could remember the days, we could cross-reference them with the shifts she worked at the hospital, couldn't we? We could prove you to be lying. So your failure of memory is very ... convenient for you.'

'That's comment, Mr Holborne, not a question. Leave your comments for your jury speech,' says the Recorder.

'I'm sure my Lord is right,' replies Charles. 'Now, Mr Gervaise, so as to put it to you fair and square: I suggest that DI Greene approached you and asked for two things: firstly, a couple of jackets so he could plant them in what he thought was Sergeant Sloane's bedsit; and secondly, a statement from you falsely stating that you'd had a conversation with her in which you told her the jackets were stolen.'

'None of that is true.'

'Thank you, Mr Gervaise.'

Charles resumes his seat and turns to look at the jury. All twelve of them are still staring at Gervaise in the witness box as if he were a piece of roadkill. Charles turns towards the doors of the court, but the senior policemen and their associate have disappeared.

CHAPTER 33

'Call Detective Inspector Greene!'

Greene struts into court in his new too-tight suit. Even now, the centre of attention, he somehow manages to look anonymous.

If you closed your eyes for a moment, you'd have difficulty describing anything more than the suit.

He steps into the witness box. He takes the Bible, declines the card with the oath printed on it, lifts the Bible to above head-height and recites the oath in a loud voice from memory. He returns the Bible to the usher and turns to the Recorder.

'I'm Detective Inspector Sidney Greene of C8, commonly known as the Flying Squad, based at West End Central Police Station, my Lord.'

The Recorder beams at Greene as if he were greeting a fond godson. 'Yes, thank you very much, Inspector.'

'Inspector,' says Stafford. 'I'm going to be asking you about events that occurred on the twenty-sixth of November nineteen sixty-five. Will you need to refresh your memory of those events?'

Greene addresses the Recorder. 'I would like to refresh my memory, yes please, my Lord. I made the notes in my pocket book contemporaneously with the events, on the journey back to West End Central in the squad car. DC Lincoln was driving and I was in the back with Dr Alexandrova.'

'Any objections, Mr Holborne?'

'No thank you, my Lord.'

In fact, plenty, but let's hit him when he least expects it.

'Very well, you may refer to your notes, officer.'

Stafford continues. 'Where were you during the evening of that date?'

Greene ostentatiously takes out his pocketbook, flips it open and scrolls through several pages to find the relevant entry. 'On that evening at approximately twenty-one fifteen hours I went to fourteen Clifton Terrace, Notting Hill, London N4 in company with Detective Constable Lincoln.'

'What was your purpose in going to that address?'

'We had received a tipoff about drugs being sold from those premises, in fact a bedsit on the top floor.'

And because it's a tipoff, it can't be disproved.

'What did you find?' asks Stafford.

'The main front door leading from the street was open, so we walked in. We went up to the second floor, and as I was passing a door to my left, I noticed that the lock had been broken and the door splintered.'

'What did you think happened?'

'It looked to me as if someone had kicked in the lock, and I was concerned that a burglary might be in progress. It's a rough area there, with a lot of unemployed black youths hanging about, so it wouldn't have been surprising if a bedsit had been broken into.'

'What did you do?'

'I paused, called out, and receiving no answer I pushed the door open gently. I was concerned that the burglar might still be inside.'

'What did you find?'

'It looked as if there had been a burglary, as there were papers and books strewn everywhere, over the floors, the bed, on the little table by the window. Lots of political pamphlets and communist newspapers.'

You couldn't resist that little dig, could you?

'Did anything in particular attract your attention?'

'Yes. There was a small clothes rail at the foot of the bed and on it I saw two RAF jackets. I recognised them as the most recent design and colour, with appropriate insignia.'

'What did you do?'

'Well, it occurred to me that the resident of the bedsit might be a member of the RAF, so I wasn't immediately suspicious. DC Lincoln and I were about to leave and continue with our drugs enquiry when footsteps came up the stairs and the accused came in with a man.'

'Did you speak to her?'

'Yes. I told her that it looked as if her room had been burgled and I'd call the local police station to send a detective out. But she appeared very nervous, and I saw her looking several times to the jackets on the rail, so I began to suspect something more was going on.'

'What did you do?'

'I asked questions about the jackets. She refused to answer, which made me even more suspicious. So I arrested her on suspicion of receiving stolen goods, and took her downstairs.'

'Did you take possession of the two jackets?'

'Yes, my Lord, I did.'

Stafford's junior hands him two jackets on a single hanger, an exhibit label attached to them.

'Have a look at these please, officer.'

Everyone waits as the jackets are walked by the usher from counsel's benches to the witness box. Greene takes the jackets and makes a show of scrutinising them very carefully. 'Yes, these are the ones I took from Dr Alexandrova's room.'

'Exhibit one, my Lord?'

'Yes. Mark them as exhibit one.'

'What happened then, officer?'

'We put the accused in the squad car and drove back to West End Central.'

'Did the accused say anything to you on the journey?'

'Yes. I cautioned her and started repeating some of my questions.'

'Do you have a record of those questions and answers in your pocket book?'

'Yes, I do.'

'Please read the conversation to us, exactly as it occurred.'

Greene reads the questions and answers exactly as they appear in the typewritten notes in Charles's Instructions.

'Thank you, detective inspector. What happened to Dr Alexandrova after that?'

'I gave her into the custody of the officer who deals with charging suspects, and I returned to Colville Terrace to complete my original enquiries.'

'Thank you very much. Please wait there.'

Charles rises. 'Were you responsible for investigating this conspiracy?'

'Along with other officers, yes.'

'Who was the officer in charge of the case?'

'Detective Chief Superintendent Cathcart was formally overseeing it, my Lord, but I had day to day charge of it.' Greene's chest swells, and the pride in his voice is unmistakeable.

'So you were involved in all aspects of it? From the source of the goods at RAF Cardington to their eventual destination at Petticoat Lane?'

'That is right, my Lord.'

'Starting at the Cardington end then, you were presumably aware that Her Majesty's Coroner for Bedford held an inquest into the death of a man called Sergeant Julian Maynard of the RAF Police?'

'I have been made aware of that, my Lord.'

'It is right, is it not, that another RAF man, named McParland, admitted killing Sergeant Maynard?'

Greene looks at the ceiling as if ransacking his memory. 'I'm not aware of that, my Lord.'

'Did you not see a letter written by young Mr McParland, to his mother, in which he made the admission?'

'No, my Lord, I didn't. I can't see why I would have, if the death occurred outside the Metropolitan area. It would've been dealt with by the local police or maybe by the RAF.'

'The allegation was that McParland killed Maynard because Maynard discovered the Bedford end of the conspiracy. Does that not ring any bells?'

'Sorry, my Lord, but no.'

'Let me try to refresh your memory further, then. McParland was coerced into tampering with Maynard's motorcycle to prevent him pursuing his investigation. The man who coerced him was Mr William Gervaise.'

Greene shrugs helplessly. 'I'm afraid I can't help with this, my Lord. I know nothing about it.'

'Please have a look at this,' says Charles, holding out a piece of paper full of handwriting.

The usher takes the document and puts it on the witness box. Before Greene can speak, the Recorder intervenes.

'Mr Holborne, you are trying my patience again. What one person may have written to his mother about another is not evidence.'

'I agree, my Lord, to a point. I am permitted to put any document into a witness's hand, and ask him if he agrees with the contents. If he does, it becomes part of the evidence in this case. If he does not, I accept that I can pursue it no further, as it's a collateral issue.'

'Mr Stafford?' asks the Recorder. 'Do you have a view on this?'

Stafford rises to his feet. 'It's a matter for your Lordship, but my learned friend's statement of the law is correct.'

Thank you, Marcus! Not the support Pullman was expecting.

His Honour Judge Pullman's saturnine face darkens further.

'Mr Greene, do you accept any of the contents of that document?' asks the Recorder.

'No, my Lord. How could I? I know nothing of a McParland or the man he is supposed to have killed … sergeant…'

'Maynard,' assists Charles.

'Hand the document back to Mr Holborne, if you please, and let's move on,' orders the Recorder.

'But for one matter, if you please, my Lord,' says Charles.

'Well?'

'Whether DI Greene was aware of it or not, if that letter contains a confession to murder, a murder ordered by Mr William Gervaise to cover up this very conspiracy, the jury might like to know if DI Greene proposes to investigate it further.'

'That has nothing to do with this case, Mr Holborne. I have made my ruling: move on.'

'It has everything to do with this case! The Crown puts forward Mr Gervaise as someone who had only minor involvement in the conspiracy, a man of truth on whom the jury can rely. I submit they'd never have taken that stance if they'd thought Gervaise guilty of murder; even more so a murder to hide this very conspiracy! It goes to whether or not Gervaise's evidence can be trusted. It's directly relevant.'

'My Lord…' says Greene hesitantly, pretending to re-read the letter. 'The police will of course investigate this, now it's been brought to our attention,' he concludes with gravity.

'Thank you, inspector,' says Charles.

'Although, even if he was implicated,' adds Greene, 'it doesn't mean that he's not telling the truth when he gives Queen's Evidence.'

'You'd feel comfortable, would you,' asks Charles, 'calling a witness for the Crown who's murdered an RAF policeman?'

'No, of course not, my Lord. But that's the nature of the beast. Grasses are rarely nice people. It's because they've spent their lives associating with others like them that makes them so valuable to the police and the prosecution, if we can turn them.'

'But the deal he did with the Crown was that he'd be sentenced for a minor part in the conspiracy. There's a world of difference between driving a van a few times for a hundred quid, and murder, isn't there?'

'Of course.'

'Had you thought he was a murderer, would you have recommended a sentence of four years for him?'

'It wouldn't have been my recommendation. Well above my pay grade.'

'Mr Holborne,' interrupts the Recorder again, 'I have told you twice now to move on. If you persist in this, I shall have you committed for contempt and reported to your Inn.'

Charles stares at the Recorder for a long time. He decides to drop it; he's made his point. 'Yes, my Lord.' He addresses Greene. 'Shall we move to the other end of the chain then, Petticoat Lane?'

A smug smile sits on Greene's face. 'Certainly.'

'You investigated that end too, I take it?'

'Of course.'

'Mr Gervaise's evidence is that he saw Dr Alexandrova working on the stall at the market, where he spoke to her more than once and gave her a stolen jacket.'

'Yes.'

'Did you interview anyone at the market?'

'I didn't, but one of the team would have done so, my Lord.'

'Did any police officer identify any witness who said they'd seen Dr Alexandrova working there?'

'I don't know the answer to that.'

'Well, if such a witness had been found, the Crown would have served a statement to that effect. And no such statement has been served. Is there one?'

Charles looks across at Marcus Stafford QC. The prosecutor shakes his head slightly.

'Your counsel seems to think there isn't any such statement.'

'Maybe not,' replies Greene, shrugging slightly.

'So the Crown's case that she worked there relies solely on the evidence of Mr Gervaise, is that right?'

'It is.'

'A man with numerous convictions for offences of dishonesty.'

'As I've explained, that's usually the case with ex-criminals giving evidence for the Crown.'

'A man who has repeatedly lied to judges and juries when he thought it expedient?'

'Yes.'

'A man with a very powerful motive to lie on this occasion, namely, to secure himself a light sentence.'

'That's comment, not a question,' intervenes the Recorder again. 'Members of the jury, you will ignore that last exchange.'

Charles turns to the jury box. Several of the jurors are frowning; two are shaking their heads slightly.

They're not ignoring it.

'I'll rephrase the question, then. Do you agree with me, detective inspector, that Gervaise has a very particular motive for lying on this occasion: to play down his involvement as much as possible, point the finger at others, and secure a light sentence?'

'He enters into a deal: he coughs for his part and helps the police with their enquiries, and he gets a lighter sentence in recognition of his assistance. That's how it works.'

'So, the answer to my question is "Yes".'

'I suppose so.'

'Thank you. Now, I turn to the alleged confession the accused made on the way to the police station.'

'It's not an "alleged confession". That interview occurred exactly as I have written it down.'

'You say you wrote it down as you were talking to her, in the squad car?'

'Yes, my Lord, that's right. That's how I'm so certain I recorded it correctly.'

'So, just to make sure I have the picture, there's DC Lincoln in the driving seat, with you and Dr Alexandrova in the back?'

'Yes, my Lord.'

'No one else in the car, no one in the front passenger seat?'

'Correct.'

'So when, as you claim, Dr Alexandrova made her confession, the only people within earshot would have been you and Detective Constable Lincoln.'

'Also correct, my Lord.'

'And you recorded the conversation directly into your pocketbook?'

'Yes.'

Charles extends his hand. 'May I see it please?'

There is a fractional hesitation, but Greene hands it to the usher. 'There are other unrelated matters recorded there too, my Lord,' he says.

'I shan't look at anything other than the notes you made of the conversation,' assures Charles.

Charles takes the pocketbook. The conversation goes over numerous pages. He counts them; pages and pages of small, neat handwriting, question, answer, question, answer. Seventeen pages of very neat handwriting.

Too neat handwriting.

'How far is it between Colville Terrace and West End Central police station, please, inspector?' asks Charles.

Greene looks surprised at the question. 'I've never measured it, my Lord,' he says. 'Three or four miles, I suppose.'

'Would you agree with me that it's three point two miles, officer?'

'Something like that. I said between three or four, so that could well be right.'

'And how long would it take you to drive that distance in the squad car?' asks Charles.

'That would depend on the time of day, the traffic, and whether we had the siren and blue lights on.'

'When you returned to the police station with Dr Alexandrova in custody, do you remember if you had the sirens and lights on?'

Greene looks baffled. 'I've no idea. Probably not, as it wasn't an emergency.'

'So how long did the journey take?'

'I can't be sure, my Lord, but perhaps about twenty minutes.'

'Mr Holborne, have you noticed the time?' asks the Recorder.

Charles looks up at the clock. It's ten minutes past four. 'No, my Lord, I am very sorry. Is that a convenient moment to —'

'Inspector Greene, you are in the middle of your evidence. You may not speak to anyone about it overnight. Members of the jury, you must not speak to anyone outside your number about the case until it's over. Your friends and family will ask questions and, once you start talking, they may say something that will affect your mind. It's essential that the decision in this case is of you twelve alone. Understood? No bail application, Mr Holborne?'

'No —'

'Good. Ten thirty tomorrow, then.'

Almost before the usher can call 'All rise!' the Recorder has swept his notebook and pens off his bench and is disappearing through the door in the panelling behind his bench. Charles catches a glimpse of red gown and leather heel, and the judge has gone.

'There's a man in need of nicotine,' says Charles to himself.

He leans towards Stafford, who is also gathering his papers together. 'Would you be able to get Greene's pocketbook copied overnight?'

Stafford pauses. 'The Defence aren't usually entitled to copies of a police officer's notebook.'

'They are if their case is that the notes have been concocted.'

'And that's your case?'

'Unless I have a chance to look at the notes properly, how can I tell?'

Stafford hesitates some more. Then he reaches to one of his files and skims through. He finds what he wants and takes it out, handing it to Charles: a copy of the handwritten notes.

'Ahead of me, eh?' says Charles with a smile.

'Just covering the bases, old chap.' He smiles at Charles, the first smile Charles can remember receiving from the other barrister.

'Thank you, Marcus.'

CHAPTER 34

'How's it looking, Charles?' asks Irenna.

Charles and Hansie Fischer sit on the wooden bench in one of the conference rooms in the bowels of the Old Bailey. Irenna is at the table, which today has only one chair. Sean Slone is also in the tiny room, his back to the steel door.

'It's difficult to tell when you're on your feet, but my impression is that the jury won't trust Gervaise without some corroboration.'

'I think it's worse than that,' says Fischer in his flat Zimbabwean accent. 'I think he's a busted flush. They'll never trust him.'

Charles shakes his head. 'No, we're not there yet. The point Greene makes is true: most informers, certainly all the big ones, are guilty of crimes. They've all got records, usually for dishonesty in one form or another. But if I can put it this way, he's wobbling. If we can do serious damage to Greene tomorrow, I think we might be there.'

The room falls silent. 'Is there anything we can do for you right now?' asks Fischer of Irenna eventually.

She shakes her head. 'No … no, nothing. Tomorrow, then.'

As Charles and Fischer stand, there's a knock on the door and it swings inward immediately. Sloane is pushed out of its way and finds himself in a clinch with Irenna. He smiles, and is lowering his head to kiss her, when all the occupants realise who's on the threshold next to the gaoler: Detective Inspector Greene. Sloane and Irenna disengage.

'Touching,' says Greene sarcastically.

Charles notes that another man stands behind the corrupt inspector. Greene sees his glance.

'That's Mr Yelland, from the Home Office,' explains Greene.

'What do you want?' demands Charles. 'You're in the middle of giving evidence; you shouldn't be down here.'

'Don't you worry, *Mister* Holborne,' answers Greene, with a nasty inflection on the "mister". 'I won't be talking about the case … per se. Here,' he adds and thrusts a document at Irenna.

'What's that?' asks Fischer.

'Deportation papers. Your client is officially served.'

'You can't do that,' protests Charles. 'She can't be deported unless and until she's convicted.'

'Take it up with the Home Office,' Greene replies dismissively. 'Best of luck with that.'

He turns to leave, but a thought occurs to him and he takes a half-step into the room. He jabs his forefinger into Sloane's chest. 'And, as for you, sunshine, you're finished!'

There is a split-second's silence until Sloane launches himself at Greene, grabbing his lapels. He looks as if he's about to deliver a headbutt but Charles intervenes, hauling him off. Sloane resists, desperate to get at Greene, but Charles, though shorter, is much stronger and he bundles his friend into the corner.

'No, Sean!' he hisses. 'It's what he wants!'

After a moment Sloane relaxes and he subsides. Greene's footsteps can be heard receding up the corridor. He is whistling happily.

'She won't be going back to Holloway tonight,' says the gaoler as he starts to close the door.

'Where, then?' asks Charles.

The gaoler shrugs. 'No idea. Some detention centre, I guess.' The door closes with a clang.

The converted cell rings with the echoes of the door and the silence of its occupants.

'Charles?' says Sloane. 'Can they do that?'

'No, but they have. Can I see that, please?'

Irenna hands the document over and sinks to her seat. Her face is grey.

Charles resumes his place on the bench, reading swiftly. 'I've never seen one of these before, but it looks in order on its face. Except for the glaring error, in that it assumes a conviction's already occurred.'

'Can they just deport me?' asks Irenna. 'Without anything more?'

'Not legally,' replies Charles. 'There should be a hearing before a magistrate. And that won't be listed tomorrow or the day after. We'll have the case finished by then. All we have to do is show the magistrate you've been acquitted, and this —' and he brandishes the deportation order — 'becomes worthless.'

Irenna doesn't look much comforted. 'You said "should" be a hearing. Are you saying they could just take me to an airport?'

Fischer intervenes. 'It's happened to some of my clients. The courts aren't always nimble enough to prevent the Home Office taking the law into its own hands. Then you'd have to apply to re-enter.'

'Fat chance,' says Irenna, 'from inside a South African police cell.' She looks distraught. 'Why's he doing this?' she asks. 'I'm no one to him.'

Fischer answers. 'Because he's a *bliksem.*'

'A what?' asks Sloane.

314

Irenna translates the Afrikaans. 'Bastard.'

'Can we do anything tonight?' asks Sloane.

Fischer shakes his head. 'No. But I doubt even the Home Office is quick enough to deport you tonight. If we get a verdict in the next twenty-four hours, you'll still be here.'

'How confident are you about that?' asks Irenna.

The big Zimbabwean shrugs. He doesn't know.

There is silence in the room for a long time.

'If we've finished the legal stuff, do you mind if I have a few moments with Irenna?' asks Sloane.

'No problem,' says Charles. 'We can't do anything more this evening anyway.'

Charles and Fischer make their way out and part company. Charles climbs the stairs to go to the robing room. Half a flight up, he hears his name shouted.

'Mr H, sir! Mr Holborne!'

Charles looks back. Clive, Chambers' spotty and cheerful office junior is waving a scrap of paper at him. Charles retraces his steps.

'Message for you, sir. Barbara says it's urgent.' He hands over the message and departs.

Charles continues to the robing room, reading as he goes: *Your brother rang. He says it's not an emergency and everyone is well, but he'd like you to go to your parents' home this evening before 8, if it's convenient. If not, please call him at his home after 10.*

David opens his parents' door to Charles at just before eight o'clock.

'So? What's up?' asks Charles.

'Come in. I followed up your suggestion and we have a woman coming this evening to be "interviewed".'

'Does Mum know?'

David nods grimly. 'Oh, yes. She's been making Dad's life a misery since he told her yesterday. The woman comes highly recommended … but…'

They enter the kitchen. Millie and Harry sit at the kitchen table, drinking tea, not speaking. Harry stands.

'Hello, son.' He kisses Charles's cheek.

Charles skirts the table and kisses his mother. She grunts. 'There's tea in the pot, Charles,' she says without looking up, but her tone is not unfriendly.

Charles helps himself to tea and goes to the fridge.

There was never a time in Charles's life when the Horowitz larder and, in later years, the fridge, wasn't always crammed with the foods of his childhood: chicken soup, pickles, chopped herring, smoked salmon and, when Millie had the time, baked cheesecake. She wasn't a natural cook, but what she could do, she did well. As he helps himself to a slice of cake, he wonders which member of the community baked it if, as Harry says, Millie's forgotten how.

He takes it to the table. The family chats for a few minutes until, at five past eight, the doorbell rings again.

'I'll go,' says David.

A minute later he shows a Jewish woman into the room. She is in her early forties, bespectacled, with a round, pleasant face. She appears to be wearing a *shaytl*, a wig, to hide her own hair as very orthodox women do, and a heavy overcoat. She also sports a remarkable hat covered with dusty false flowers which, in Charles's judgement, must date from some time in the early 1950s.

'Mum,' starts David, 'this is Mrs —'

'Becky? What on earth are you doing here?' exclaims Millie, standing, almost running around the table and pulling the astonished woman into a warm embrace.

'No … Mum, this is Mrs Weinstein —' tries Charles.

'— What are you talking about? You think I don't know my own cousin?' says Millie, not releasing the woman.

'No, no,' tries Harry gently, standing and flushing with embarrassment. 'This isn't Becky. Becky lives in Canada.'

'But here she is! Are you *meshuge* too? This is my little Becky! I've known her since she was born.'

Mrs Weinstein manages to extricate herself from Millie's embrace. She takes the older woman by the hands. The men in the room all hold their breath but, after a momentary hesitation, Mrs Weinstein kisses the older woman once on each cheek.

'It's so lovely to see you again, Millie,' she says warmly. 'It's been such a long time.'

'There! See?' says Millie. She focuses on Mrs Weinstein, all concerned hostess. 'Have you had anything to eat, *bubbeleh*?'

'I ate, but I'll take some lemon tea, if you're making. Tell you what: let the boys make it. We can sit in the lounge and catch up.'

'Good idea. You've not been to the new house, have you? Let me show you around.'

Mrs Weinstein takes Millie's offered hand and allows herself to be guided out of the kitchen. As she disappears through the door, she turns briefly and winks at the astonished Horowitz menfolk.

It's Charles who recovers first. 'Well,' he says. 'That's the most successful interview I've ever seen.'

'But —' starts Harry.

'What's it matter, Dad? So, Mum thinks it's her cousin from Toronto. Who cares, as long as Mum's taken to her?'

'Hang on, Charles. She's not always like that,' points out David. 'Tomorrow morning she mightn't make the same mistake. Then what?'

'Docs Mrs Weinstein cook?' asks Charles.

'According to the references, like a dream,' says David.

'Is she available?'

'She was widowed eighteen months ago,' says Harry. 'No children. The rabbi says she's desperate to find some purpose to her life again.'

'The contact came through the synagogue?' asks Charles.

'Indirectly. The rabbi heard we were making enquiries and got in touch. Mrs Weinstein's late husband was his cousin. Heart attack, God rest his soul.'

Charles shrugs, hands held wide. 'I rest my case, as they say in the US.'

'Be sensible,' says Harry. 'Once your mother realises the woman's not Becky —'

'She'll be familiar with her. Look, what do we have to lose?'

The other two men look at each other. Gradually a smile spreads across David's features and after a while Harry laughs.

'God moves in mysterious ways,' he says.

It is almost half past ten by the time Charles parks the Austin Healey in Essex Court in the Temple and heads to the flat. Mrs Weinstein stayed at his parents' house for the duration of two further glasses of lemon tea, during which time she managed diplomatically to work out where everything lived in the kitchen and to take brief notes of Millie and Harry's daily schedule. On her way out she whispered softly to David that she would be happy to help the family, starting the following week with a couple of hours' cleaning and cooking. She would come on Friday so that a Sabbath meal would be ready. Once Millie was used to her, she could come two or three times every week. She seemed less concerned about payment than the brothers were, but even that was worked out smoothly.

As Charles crosses Fleet Street and walks the few paces up Fetter Lane, he recognises a familiar diminutive shape. 'Sally?'

She whirls around. Even in the poor light from the sodium streetlamps, Charles can see that his former girlfriend is distressed. 'Oh, it's you.'

'What are you doing here?'

'Here,' she says curtly, thrusting out her hand. 'I was going to post it through the door, but you've saved me the trouble. Go on, take it!'

Charles takes a letter from her hand but before he has time to say anything further, she is already moving off, northwards, towards High Holborn. 'Sally! Wait!'

She ignores him and he jogs after her, grabbing the sleeve of her coat to slow her down. She whirls round, her little face defiant, tears glittering in her eyes. 'Take your hands off me!' Charles does so immediately. 'Just leave me alone! I've explained in that letter. I don't want to hear from you again, okay? No more letters, no more calls, nothing. We're over, get it? Finished. Just leave me alone.'

'But I don't understand. What's happened?'

'I don't want to talk about it. Read the letter.'

'Please, Sally, I beg you! I've no idea what's going on. You said I could write to you, so I have done.'

'Yes, and hedging your bets. Wooing me by post, and at the same time carrying on a new relationship with someone else!'

'What?' says Charles, completely bemused.

'Don't pretend to me, Charles. At least do me the courtesy of being honest. You've been found out, so plead guilty and take your sentence.'

'Honestly, Sally, I haven't a clue what you're talking about.'

'I saw you, right? Rushing out of Chambers with that woman. It reminded me of us, sprinting off to have sex in your sordid little flat.'

Charles gapes, unable to understand what Sally is saying.

'So, I've been watching you. I know you've not been in Chambers working late, so don't try that one. Every time I went round, the lights were off. And you've not been at the flat either. But it's so exciting isn't it, a new relationship? Taking her to all your usual seduction haunts, yeah? Theatres, concerts, all those wonderful candlelit dinners?' she says with acid sarcasm.

Light begins to dawn, and so relieved is Charles that he actually laughs out loud as he slaps his forehead.

'Yes, laugh why don't you? It must be really funny, making a fool of your little Cockney ex-clerk! Well you've been caught out, and it's over.'

She begins to turn and stride away but, to her astonishment, Charles drops to one knee on the pavement and extends a hand in supplication. 'I swear on my mother's life that you've misinterpreted the facts. I can explain it all to you. I beg you, Sally, give me ten minutes and you'll understand.'

She looks around, alarmed that any passer-by might witness Charles's ludicrous performance. 'Get up. You're wasting your time and making a fool of yourself.'

'Ten minutes, Sally? If for no other reason than old times' sake? Give me ten more minutes of your life, just ten little minutes, and if you don't believe me then … walk away.'

She takes another step away from him.

'Please, Sal. Trust me one last time.'

'I have no reason to trust you,' she says, still facing away.

'I know that. Nonetheless, I'm asking you for ten minutes.'

Her shoulders slump and the tension leaves her body. She draws several deep breaths and turns to face him. Tears run down her face and she wipes them away with the back of her hand. 'I'll give you ten minutes.'

Out of the corner of his eye Charles sees a cab with its "For Hire" sign illuminated as it trundles slowly westwards from Ludgate Circus, seeking a fare. Still kneeling, he raises an arm and shouts with all the power of his projected courtroom voice. 'Taxi!'

The driver slows, having heard the shout, but unable to detect its source. Charles jumps up, grabs Sally by the hand and drags her the few steps back to Fleet Street. He leans into the cabbie's window, clinging onto her lest she should change her mind and escape.

'Wren Street, please, and I'll double the fare if you can do it in four minutes!'

Charles jumps into the taxi, forced to release Sally as he does so. He turns and holds out a hand to her. Still she hesitates, chewing her lip. Finally, she steps in without touching him.

'Nine minutes,' she says, settling onto the seat as far from him as possible.

The journey of just over one mile takes exactly four minutes.

Charles hands a note through the cabbie's window. 'Keep the change,' he says.

The taxi's light illuminates again and it executes a neat turn, heading back towards Gray's Inn Road.

'What are we doing here?' asks Sally, staring around at the dark street.

Instead of answering, Charles reaches into his jacket pocket and pulls out a key. 'Follow me.'

He opens the door to his half-renovated house and, praying silently that none of the contractors has disconnected the power, flicks the switch in the hallway.

'Whose house is this?'

'Come in,' says Charles. 'Please.'

Reluctant or, perhaps, frightened, Sally steps slowly over the threshold. Charles leads her down into the new basement kitchen.

He's had the wall between the front room and what was the rear parlour knocked down to create a large airy space with windows at front and rear. The room has been extended out at this level into the garden and the ceiling there is fully glazed. Stars may be seen through it and an aeroplane slides silently across the night sky above them.

Between the contractors and Charles good progress has been made, and the kitchen is almost ready for use. Everything is very dusty, but the new work surfaces, sink and cupboards have been installed, the old oak floorboards have been repaired, stripped and waxed, and a new table and chairs, still wrapped, are piled to one side.

'I thought this would make a good living area. I've never much liked formal dinner parties, so I thought it'd be nice to have everything together in the kitchen area. It means whoever's cooking can still chat to everyone. It's too dark to see the garden, but it has lots of potential. Smaller than Hampstead, but much cosier.'

'This is your house?'

He smiles. 'Yes.'

'Why? Why've you bought it? You've only just sold the house in Hampstead!'

'I want a proper home, somewhere to settle down. Follow me.' He walks out of the double doors into the hallway and up the staircase to the raised ground floor. It takes a few moments for Sally's tentative footsteps to be heard following him.

He goes first to a large room opening off the hallway. It's completely empty, bare floorboards still to be addressed and not a stick of furniture. The room smells strongly of wallpaper paste. Charles enters, and Sally stands at the threshold.

'This is going to be the lounge or, as my parents would call it, the "best room". Don't examine the wallpapering too closely. I'm not as good as you.'

'You did this yourself?' asks Sally, disbelieving.

'Like I said, don't look too closely.'

He brushes past her and goes to the next room. 'Dining room, or perhaps a bedroom,' he announces. 'And this,' he opens the door to a room towards the back of the house, 'family bathroom. At least shower room and loo.'

This room is clearly unfinished. New copper pipes emerge at various points along the skirting, and the plumber has left his tool bag there overnight.

'The master bedroom and ensuite bathroom are going in upstairs.'

'Family bathroom?'

Charles smiles at her. 'Come and look at the top floor.'

He doesn't wait for her but heads up the final flight of stairs. Here is the largest bedroom in the house. A new door has evidently been installed between it and an adjoining room which is already fitted with a new shower, sink and toilet. The floor is half-tiled. He hears Sally's tread behind him but doesn't look round.

'And I thought this would make a great master bedroom. It's got terrific views up here over the park and it's surprisingly quiet.' He points to a foldable bed in the corner. 'I've spent a couple of nights here when I've been working on it really late. And one night I accidentally tiled myself into a corner when doing the hallway, so I had no choice. That's why you've not found me in Chambers or at the flat. Whenever I've had any spare time, I've been here.'

Charles ventures a look at Sally's face to see how all this information is being received. Her anger seems to have dissipated, but her brow is still contracted into a frown and she looks confused, undecided.

'Who was that woman I saw you with? You were leaving Chambers in a hurry, about a three weeks ago. Blonde, in her thirties. Pretty.'

'Yes, her. I have her card downstairs in a kitchen drawer. Her name's Eileen Cotton, and she was measuring up for curtains. Come on, I'll show you.'

Charles flicks off the light switch and leads Sally downstairs.

As they reach the first floor, Sally calls. 'What's this room going to be?' she says, pausing and turning on the light. Charles returns to her and looks inside a small box room overlooking the garden. 'Your study?'

'I've made a decision about that. I'm no longer going to work when I'm at home. I can run to Chambers from here in under fifteen minutes; in fact, I can cycle it in six! From now on, when I leave work, I want to leave work. I'm trying to change, Sal. So I thought I'd keep this as a bedroom.'

'It's too small for a bedroom. You'd only get a cot in here.'

Charles turns his face to hers. She is just inside the room and he is leaning on the door jamb, half-in and half-out. At this second, they are physically closer to one another than at any time since they ceased being a couple. 'Yes,' he says. He speaks so softly, it's almost a whisper. 'That's what I thought.'

A sob escapes her chest and, inexplicably to Charles, anger reappears on her lovely face. 'Why?' she demands. 'Why now? We had a home together in Hampstead, but you didn't seem to want it. Or, maybe you wanted a home, just not with me?'

Charles reaches forward to wipe a tear from her face, but she brushes his hand aside. 'I always was a slow learner,' he says. 'But I get there eventually.'

'Slow learner?'

'In matters of the heart … yes, certainly. Glacial.'

He reaches up again, and this time she doesn't push him away. One big hand cradles her face and with the other he gently wipes away the tears. Her mascara has run and her creamy cheeks are blotched with red, but he has never loved anyone as much as he loves Sally at that moment.

Her head leans into his caress and her hand touches his hip. For an instant Charles thinks she's going to kiss him, but then she pulls away.

'No,' she says to herself. 'No!' she repeats, louder, and now suddenly she's leaving, clattering down the remaining flight of stairs, across the newly-laid hall tiles and out of the front door.

Charles follows at a run but belatedly realises he's left the keys somewhere, and the few seconds it takes him to locate them on the kitchen counter and to lock up is enough for Sally to have run up Wren Street to its junction with Gray's Inn Road.

'Sally, wait!'

He's too late. He watches a cab slowing to a halt at the junction and within another two seconds Sally has jumped in, slammed the door after her and the taxi is carrying her away.

CHAPTER 35

Despite their elevated status, counsel are not permitted to bring food or drink into the courtrooms. Charles is onto his third coffee of the morning and loiters by the swing doors of Court 1, fully robed, hoping he'll have time to finish his present cup before entering. At the same time, he is keeping an eye open for Stafford. Having spent half an hour looking at Greene's pocketbook and a map of London, he has formulated his tactics and needs time to get copies for the jury.

Charles reaches into his waistcoat pocket and pulls out two aspirins, which he swallows with a mouthful of lukewarm coffee. His head is pounding. He slept little, replaying over and again every word spoken, every nuance of Sally's posture and expression, wondering how he could have managed it better.

It's not that he doesn't understand Sally's response; he just doesn't know what to do with it. He hoped that showing her the house would demonstrate that he is now, finally, ready to commit to her; that he is even thinking seriously about a family. He didn't imagine her falling instantly into his arms, but he did hope for, well, some hope. Of course, her anger isn't going to be assuaged immediately — he's well aware how much he hurt her, and still groans inwardly every time he ruminates on how he treated her in those few disastrous months — but he counted on her at least acknowledging his sincerity.

Maybe it was that which confused her.

Chugger's imminent approach is heralded by puffing and wheezing from around the corner.

'Morning, Charles,' says the QC arriving at the doors, and Charles notes with interest the continued thaw which now has the prosecution barrister addressing him by his first name.

'Marcus,' replies Charles.

'Got something for you,' says Stafford, and he holds out his hand and gestures impatiently to his junior.

The young barrister is unknown to Charles, but his headgear exemplifies the disparaging "white-wig" jibe. A "white-wig" is a barrister so green that his wig is still pristine. Some pupils are seen dragging their new headgear in the dust of Chancery Lane to give their wearers the semblance of experience, something this junior evidently abjured; his white wig is extremely white.

The flustered young man thrusts a sheaf of papers towards Charles: copies of DI Greene's pocketbook notes.

'There are eight copies there, just in case you need some for the judge and jury,' explains Stafford. 'We've spares if required.'

'That's very helpful, thank you,' says Charles.

'You'd only have asked for an adjournment to find Xeroxing facilities, so…'

'Much obliged.'

Stafford and his entourage enter court.

Charles finishes his coffee, places the cup and saucer, borrowed from the Bar Mess, on a nearby windowsill and pushes open the door to court. He is the last to enter. The clerk is already halfway up the aisle looking for him.

'There you are,' she says, not quite able to keep the irritation from her voice at having to go in search of counsel. 'We're ready. Are you?'

'Yes, sorry,' apologises Charles.

Within two minutes the judge has entered and sits at his Bench, his pen poised, and Greene has resumed his place in the witness box.

'You're still on oath, inspector,' says the Recorder. 'You may proceed, Mr Holborne.'

'Thank you, my Lord. Officer, please can you tell us what time you departed the address in Notting Hill to return to West End Central police station?'

Greene looks through his pocketbook. 'I'm afraid I didn't make a note of the exact time of departure, my Lord, but we were at the property for no longer than twenty minutes or so, so I'd estimate slightly after nine-thirty in the evening. Maybe quarter to ten.'

'Quarter to ten on a cold November night; not much traffic, I expect?'

'No. It's usually getting quiet by that time.'

'Remember the route you took?' asks Charles, as if it were a matter of passing interest.

'We almost certainly went via Bayswater Road, along the north of Hyde Park, as it's a straight line.'

'So, south down Kennington Park Road, left onto Bayswater Road and then due east to Marble Arch. Turn right down Park Lane at Speaker's Corner and left past Grosvenor Square towards Savile Row?'

'You ought to be a cabbie, Mr Holborne,' says DI Greene, to general laughter.

'Is that the likely route?' persists Charles.

'Yes, probably.'

'So, very few shops and any there were, likely to have been closed.'

'Yes, my Lord.'

'I suggest to you, detective inspector, that at that time of night, in a police car, whether or not the lights and sirens were on, you would have travelled that journey of just over three miles in less than twenty minutes.'

'It's possible, I suppose. It might have been fifteen.'

The Recorder makes his first intervention of the morning. 'Would you mind explaining to us, Mr Holborne, why this is so important?'

'I have some copies of DI Greene's pocketbook here, my Lord, and I seek your permission to put them in front of the jury before I ask my next series of questions. I have a copy here for your Lordship.'

The Recorder turns to Stafford. 'Any objections, Mr Stafford?'

'No, my Lord.'

'Very well.'

'I have six here for the jurors,' explains Charles. 'I'm sorry, ladies and gentlemen, but one copy between two, please.'

Charles waits for the documents to be distributed. Stafford has had each separate page of the pocketbook copied onto a single sheet of A4, and Charles watches several members of the jury flicking over the stapled sheets and showing surprise at the length of the interview. More importantly, he notices with interest and surprise that two pairs of jurors are whispering while pointing closely to Greene's handwriting on the pages before them.

Have they already got the point?

'Now, officer, you say these notes were written in the back of the car on the way back to the police station.'

'That's right, my Lord.'

'You have remarkably neat handwriting.'

'Thank you.'

'And I couldn't help noticing that there is not a single word out of place. Not one word had to be rewritten because the car suddenly turned a corner; not one word had to be scribbled out for its illegibility; not one word strays above or below the lines.' Charles pauses long enough to watch all six pairs of jurors bending to focus on the written words. 'Every one of the seventeen pages of your pocketbook recording this alleged conversation is perfect. How do you explain that?'

Greene shrugs nonchalantly as if the question were unimportant. 'Practice, my Lord. I'm used to writing up my notes in such circumstances, and it gets easier over the years.'

'Detective Constable Lincoln must be an exceptionally smooth driver, bearing in mind traffic lights … pedestrian crossings … people running across the road unexpectedly … cars cutting in and out of the London traffic, and so on.'

Charles knows that this is more a comment than a question, but for once His Honour Judge Pullman leaves him alone. He lets the comment hang for several seconds before finishing it off: 'Well? Is he?'

For the first time Detective Inspector Greene looks a little less sure of himself. 'I suppose he is, my Lord. He's received additional police training.'

'I suggest to you, Inspector Greene, that no matter how good a driver he may be, he still has to go around corners, stop for traffic lights and react to the rest of us less skilled drivers on the roads. I further suggest to you that it is not possible for this note to have been written up during that journey.'

'It was possible, my Lord. That's what happened. I don't see how I can be criticised for having good handwriting.'

'Let me put one further thing to you, please, officer. Your notebook is quite small isn't it, the pages I mean?'

'Yes, my Lord. That's why it's called a "pocketbook".'

'And because the pages are so small, you had to use up sixteen and a half of them to record this interview. Because you can't get many words per page.'

'Yes.'

'I suggest it is not possible to have written all seventeen pages during the course of a journey that was fifteen or even twenty minutes in length.'

'You can suggest what you like, but that's what happened, my Lord.'

'I suggest that you made this up; this entire conversation. Dr Alexandrova will say that she remained silent all the way to the police station. She refused to say anything until a lawyer attended, and because you denied her access to a lawyer, she never spoke to you at all.'

'That is completely untrue, my Lord.'

Greene rocks on his heels in the time-honoured manner of a policeman on the beat, and looks around the court, at the public gallery, the barristers' benches, the press gallery and, finally, the jury box. There his confident gaze falters as he notes several of the jurors, perhaps as many as eight, looking from him back to the copied notes, and then up again.

They don't believe it!

'Do you have any further questions, Mr Holborne?' asks the Recorder.

'There's one further matter I would like to put to this officer, please, my Lord.'

Charles reaches behind him for a folder with the words "Sunday Mirror" typed discreetly at the top. He opens it and takes out a sheaf of black and white photographs. He takes the topmost photograph and offers it to the usher.

'Please can you give this to the witness.' Charles waits. 'Now, Detective Inspector Greene, do you recognise the property shown in that photograph?' Greene frowns and begins to shake his head until Charles adds: 'If it helps you, I can produce the property transaction records from Spain.'

'Yes, my Lord, I do recognise it,' he now replies smartly. 'This is my holiday home in Spain, on the Costa del Sol.'

'I have further copies of that photograph for the jury,' says Charles. Again Charles waits for the photographs to be distributed. 'It has, I believe, six bedrooms, is that right?'

'Property is much cheaper over there.'

'With respect, officer, that's an evasive answer. Does your holiday home have six bedrooms or does it not?'

'It does, my Lord.'

'And three bathrooms, a swimming pool and a roof terrace which, if I'm not mistaken, has a bar and a pool table.' Charles watches the jurors bending to peer at the photographs.

'Yes, my Lord. I've saved all my life for that property.'

'May I show you this photograph, please, officer?' Charles hands copies to the usher and indicates that they should be given to the jurors and the judge.

'This is a close-up of the last photograph, and shows the garage at your holiday home. Would you please tell the jury the make of the two cars we can see through the open doors?'

'They're not mine,' insists Greene, hurriedly, now looking definitely flustered. 'They're in my wife's name.'

'Your wife hasn't had a job since the day you married, has she?'

'So?'

'Detective Inspector, you are here to answer questions,' says the Recorder, Greene's answers revealing, for the first time, a frayed edge to the judge's temper.

The detective inspector blushes, the tips of his ears turning pink. 'Sorry, my Lord. No, my wife has not had a job. She is a full-time housewife.'

'So, I repeat, please tell us the make of those two cars.'

'One is a Rover and the other a Bentley. The Bentley's very old, though.'

'The Home Office's official figures suggest that the pay band for a detective inspector in the Metropolitan Police, as from September this year, increased to two thousand one hundred and five pounds. Per annum. Let's assume that you are near the top of the band and earn a few hundred a year more than that. Would you like to explain to us how a police officer of your rank has been able to acquire sufficient wealth to purchase, mortgage-free, a six-bedroom, three-bathroom property in the Costa del Sol, complete with two luxury cars?'

'My wife's very good with the housekeeping,' says Greene, and the entire court erupts with laughter.

The Recorder has to shout for several seconds before the amusement dies away and order is restored.

Charles had planned a couple of further questions about the value of the Spanish property but Greene's answer to the last question is so priceless, he doesn't think he can improve upon it. 'Thank you, detective inspector,' he says, resuming his seat.

And thank you, Percy.

For it had been Percy Farrow and his colleagues at the *Sunday Mirror* who handed over to Charles the dossier they kept on Greene and had been unable to use until now.

'I have no re-examination for the inspector,' says Stafford. 'Does my Lord have any questions?'

'No, thank you.'

'In that case, my Lord, I call Detective Constable Lincoln.'

Lincoln is called into court. He is younger, slimmer, and better-dressed than his superior officer. Something about his bearing and the way in which he moves reminds Charles of a panther.

The detective constable takes the oath, and like Greene, asks to rely on the notes made in his pocketbook. His story is that he heard the entire conversation in the car and, on reaching the police station, checked Greene's notes against his recollection, decided they were accurate, and copied them into his own pocket book. Within five minutes Charles is again on his feet preparing to cross-examine.

'Detective Constable Lincoln. Following her arrest, you drove Dr Alexandrova to West End Central police station in the squad car, is that right?'

'That's right, my Lord.'

'Do you remember if you turned on the siren and flashing lights?'

Lincoln thinks for a moment. Charles is not sure if he is genuinely trying to remember or if is trying to work out what his guvnor would have said in answer to the same question.

'It's difficult to remember, my Lord, because I'm constantly out in the squad car with DI Greene and various suspects. It happens so often. But I think we would have treated the journey as an emergency. So, yes, probably.'

'Why is that?' asks the Recorder.

'Well, my Lord, we were in a hurry. Arresting Dr Alexandrova had interrupted the enquiry we were supposed to be making. And DI Greene is ... well, let's say he's not the most patient of men. He often tells me to put on the lights and siren, even when it isn't strictly an emergency, because we're always so busy.'

The Recorder painstakingly records Lincoln's answer and then looks to Charles. There's nothing unusual in that; judges often signal that their notes have caught up with the evidence by looking up at the barrister asking the questions, indicating that they may continue, but Charles thinks he detects something more in the Recorder's glance. There is a short-lived meeting of eyes and Charles realises that the Recorder at least has understood the significance of the last answer.

Time to nail it down.

'DI Greene and I have agreed that the distance between Colville Terrace and Savile Row, where the police station is located, is somewhere between three and four miles. How long do you think it would have taken the squad car to travel that distance with the siren on and the blue lights flashing?'

Lincoln looks at the ceiling while calculating. 'You can't go that fast, even as an emergency, in central London traffic. But I'd estimate about five or six minutes.'

Charles turns to look at the jury as he repeats the answer. 'Five or six minutes. To write sixteen and a half pages of questions and answers?'

'Yes, my Lord.'

'Without a single error or correction?'

'I'd need to see Inspector Greene's original notes but if there are no mistakes in it, then … yes, my Lord.'

Half the jury members look at Lincoln and then, tellingly, back to Charles, making pointed eye contact with him.

Got them!

'Officer, I am obliged to put to you Dr Alexandrova's case, as I have done to your inspector, which is this: I suggest to you that she did not give any answers during the course of that journey. Detective Inspector Greene certainly asked questions, but she refused to answer any of them.'

'No, my Lord, that's not right.'

'I suggest to you that either on his own or with you, Detective Inspector Greene has made up these questions and answers, and you have simply copied them into your pocketbook.'

'No, my Lord, that is untrue.'

'Thank you, detective constable,' says Charles, but as he is lowering himself to his seat, he straightens up again as if belatedly remembering something. 'Oh, one last issue if I may.'

'Yes?'

'What did you do with DS Sloane?'

'Sorry?'

'Well, Detective Sergeant Sloane of West Hendon Police Station was at the bedsit with Dr Alexandrova when she was arrested. And you arrested him, too, didn't you?'

Lincoln looks like a cow that's just been stunned prior to slaughter. Charles actually wonders if his knees might buckle from under him, because his face turns pale and his eyes stare. He looks to the back of the court where his inspector sits, as if asking for guidance, but of course no guidance can be forthcoming.

'I ... I ... I don't remember.'

'What don't you remember? The fact that DS Sloane was there or whether or not he was arrested?'

Lincoln grasps like a drowning fish. 'You see ... my Lord ... we arrest so many people ... if they're not eventually charged ... well ... you tend to forget them.'

'You'd forget arresting a superior officer, a sergeant in the Met, is that what you're saying?' asks Charles.

'No, that's not what I'm saying.'

'Then are you saying it's possible that DS Sloane was there, and that he was arrested, but you've just forgotten?'

There is a very long pause before Lincoln answers. This time he doesn't look to his inspector for assistance but keeps his eyes firmly on the floor of the witness box. The silence lengthens.

'I'm sorry, my Lord, I have no recollection if there was anyone there other than Dr Alexandrova.'

'So DS Sloane might have been?'

'Maybe. I just don't remember.'

'Thank you, my Lord, I have no further questions.'

Charles sits and looks across to the jury.

They're with me; I'm certain of it! But they still want to hear what we have to say.

Charles is, indeed, as certain as he can be that the jury won't convict, can't convict, on the evidence of Gervaise and Greene. He's a skilled barrister and he often has days when things go well but never like this, when the turn of almost every card produces a winner.

Indeed, he toys briefly with and the rejects the tactic of making a submission of no case to answer and bringing the case to an end prematurely. With many judges he'd be optimistic, but not with this one. His Honour Judge Pullman QC, the Recorder of London, is a dyed-in-the-wool prosecutor, a man so full of hardened cynicism you could carve it like black pudding. Charles doesn't believe he'd get a fair hearing.

Then there is another, more subtle, factor. Of course, the burden of proving innocence never lies on the Defence, and if the prosecution's case is so weak that no jury, properly directed, could reasonably convict, it's the judge's duty to direct them to throw it out without the accused saying a word. Charles frequently finds himself making jury speeches which start by emphasising that very fact; explaining to the twelve voiceless men and women opposite him why they haven't heard from his client because, essentially, the prosecution case is so flimsy.

But he knows that whatever direction in law they are given; no matter how critically damaged the prosecution witnesses may seem, juries always like to hear from the other side. Until this point, they've had to gather the defence case from the questions put by the accused's barrister, but there's something about human nature that makes it so much more satisfactory when they hear it from the accused him or herself. It completes the circle. When the jury hears, from the mouth of the accused, the very facts they've already tentatively concluded must be true, you can see the moment of catharsis. They sit back, tension gone, with smiles and satisfied nods as if to say: "Yes. That's exactly what we thought. Thank you for confirming it."

Accordingly, he intends to call Irenna and, perhaps, Sean Sloane. Any concerns about how Irenna might stand up to cross-examination have dissipated over the last weeks. She's proved herself to be tough, resolute and self-reliant. Even Marcus Stafford QC, an extremely skilled cross-examiner, will not dent her certainty.

'That is the Crown's case,' Stafford is saying.

'Thank you, Mr Stafford. Yes, Mr Holborne.'

'I call the accused, Dr Irenna Alexandrova.'

The door in the dock is opened and Irenna is led by the wrist into the witness box. There the female prison officer unlocks the handcuffs and stands back a pace, ready to intervene should Irenna try to run for it.

Charles stops shuffling his papers while Irenna takes the oath and looks up at her. Then, casting aside all his plans and strategies, he places his notes face down on the bench before him, put his hands behind his back and smiles at his client.

'Please give the court your name, address and profession.'

'I am Irenna Alexandrova and, before my arrest, I lived in a bedsit at fourteen Colville Terrace, Notting Hill. In South Africa I am a fully qualified doctor, but I have to take further exams before I can practise here. I'm presently training at Finchley Memorial Hospital.'

Charles had not intended to deal with any of the Irenna's background. It would be risky to highlight her political campaigning, not least because some of the jury are bound to disagree with her views. But at the last moment he decided that he needed the jury to get to know her, to like her; to move past her obviously "foreign" accent and the very different life she led in South Africa, and see the strong woman of unshakeable integrity underneath.

'Did you have a specialism before you left South Africa?'

'Yes, I was a paediatric respiratory physician. I specialised in treating small children suffering from severe asthma. My hospital was in one of the townships outside Johannesburg.'

'A poor hospital, then?'

'Very poor. Under-staffed and under-funded.'

'Could you have worked in a more prestigious hospital, for example in Johannesburg or Capetown?'

'Of course. There are asthma sufferers everywhere.'

'Why didn't you? More money, more career opportunities?'

She smiles gently. 'I was needed more in the township.'

'Thank you. Now, how did you come to be in this country?'

'I ran for my life. The South African Security Services arrested my parents and I just got away.'

'Why did they do that?'

'My parents have been involved in the struggle against apartheid. They are lawyers, and members of the ANC, although they do not believe in violence. Nonetheless, they were arrested with Nelson Mandela and many of the other leaders. Lawyers, clergymen and so on. They have never been charged with any offence.'

'Are your parents still in prison in South Africa?'

'My mother is … that is … I think she is. I've not heard from her for some months. My father died in prison. He was beaten to death.'

Charles pauses to allow the import of that evidence sink in. 'How many hours per week did you work at Finchley Memorial Hospital prior to your arrest?'

'I would say between seventy and eighty, some of which was on call.'

'Is that normal?'

'Very. All junior doctors work those sorts of hours.'

'It's been suggested by the prosecution that you were moonlighting at Petticoat Lane market.'

'That's nonsense. I worked full-time at the hospital. I had neither time nor energy to work in a market. And, frankly, had I wanted to, there are numerous markets in the north of London, one actually in Finchley, where I might have worked without travelling for hours to the East End of London.'

'Mr Gervaise says that he saw you working at the market and actually spoke to you on a couple of occasions.'

'Mr Gervaise is a liar,' Irenna answers simply.

'Mr Gervaise says he gave you a stolen RAF jacket.'

'Like I said, Mr Gervaise is a liar. I had never laid eyes on that man until the committal at the magistrates' court.'

'Mr Greene says he found two such jackets in your bedsit at Colville Terrace.'

'Mr Greene is a bigger liar than Mr Gervaise,' says Irenna, and a wave of laughter rolls around the courtroom.

'Mr Greene says that when he arrested you, you confessed to knowing that the two jackets he found in your room were stolen.'

'I've never worked at a market stall, I'd never seen those jackets before Mr Greene produced them and I didn't take them to my bedsit. And I did not make any confession to Mr Greene. I refused to speak to him on the journey in the car. When he wouldn't let me see a lawyer, I refused to speak to anyone at the police station.'

'Do you know why these two men are lying to get you into trouble?'

'Of course,' replies Irenna, looking surprised at the question. 'My boyfriend is Detective Sergeant Sloane, an honest policeman. He was onto them both, and they needed to shut him up.'

'Dr Alexandrova,' says the Recorder, but in a much gentler tone than any of his interventions to date. 'While that may be your belief, you cannot give evidence about it. You don't know what either of those men might have been thinking when they acted in the way they did.'

Irenna turns to the judge. 'I'm sorry, my Lord.'

'Very well. Any further questions, Mr Holborne?'

'No, thank you, my Lord.'

Stafford rises to cross-examine. He puts the evidence of Gervaise and then that of Greene to Irenna in minute and, eventually, tedious detail. For forty minutes Irenna sticks to her story, answering the questions, repeatedly, with denials. She never once raises her voice or evades a question. By the time Stafford has exhausted himself and sits down again, Charles sees the hoped-for catharsis on the faces of the jurors and he declines the Recorder's invitation to re-examine; there is nothing he needs to correct or improve upon in Irenna's evidence.

'Detective Sergeant Sloane, please,' says Charles.

In truth Charles doesn't believe there is much need to call Sloane. He would stake his career on the prediction that the case is already won. This, however, is the coup de grâce.

Sloane strides into court, handsome, upright and determined. Charles takes him through his oath and identification.

'What is your relationship with the accused?' he asks.

'She's my girlfriend.'

'At the time of her arrest, where were you living?'

'I had a room round the corner from hers,' he says in his soft brogue, 'but it was small and not terribly comfortable, so when we weren't out together or working our shifts, we spent most of our time in her room.'

'Did you keep any clothing or other personal effects there?'

'Yes.'

'If anyone had made enquiries as to your address at that time, would they have concluded you lived at Colville Terrace or elsewhere?'

'Probably at Colville Terrace.'

'When did you first meet Billy Gervaise?'

'A few weeks before these events. I was off duty in Cricklewood when I saw someone interfering with a wagon in the railway goods yard. I went to investigate and he attacked me with a knuckleduster. I received a concussion and a broken jaw in two places which kept me in hospital for about ten days.'

'Following that event, did you investigate his connection with the goods yard any further?'

'I tried to, but I was warned off by other officers.'

'What do you mean by "warned off"?'

'I was told that Gervaise was one of "Greene's Grasses" — that he was an informer for Inspector Greene — and he couldn't be touched.'

'Did you heed those orders?'

'No. I wasn't the only man he attacked that night. He put an elderly watchman in hospital too. I didn't think he should be allowed to get away with something like that. So I continued investigating.'

'What did you discover?'

'I discovered that two men were killed at the RAF base in Cardington, and the evidence I obtained suggested to me that they'd been killed by Gervaise, or by people acting on his orders.'

'Detective Inspector Greene said he was unaware of any allegation of murder against Mr Gervaise, until I put a letter in his hand yesterday in the course of this trial.'

'I don't believe that to be true. I told my detective inspector what I had learned, and we took it together to our Detective Chief Superintendent, the officer in charge at West Hendon. The Chief Super had a visit from several members of the Flying Squad shortly thereafter, including DI Greene, and we were again told to lay off.'

'Do you know anything about these two jackets found at Dr Alexandrova's bedsit?'

'I was there when they were allegedly "found".'

'Tell us what happened.'

'Irenna and I came in at about half past nine. We'd met for a drink after our shifts ended. DI Greene and DC Lincoln were in her bedroom, the door of which had been kicked in. They pointed out the two jackets on a rack of clothing. I can say with absolute certainty that the jackets weren't there when we went out.'

'What happened then?'

'DI Greene arrested us on suspicion of receiving stolen goods, and took us in the squad car to West End Central police station.'

'"Us"?'

'Yes, Irenna and me.'

'You were arrested?'

'Yes.'

'And you were in the squad car?'

'Yes.'

'Did Dr Alexandrova speak to DI Greene on the journey back to the police station?'

'He asked us both lots of questions, but we didn't reply.'

'Not at all?'

'Not at all.'

'What happened at the police station?'

'Eventually they released me and charged Irenna.'

'Do you know why they released you?'

Sloane hesitates. 'I don't know, but I have a very strong suspicion.'

'We're not interested in suspicions, thank you, Sergeant,' says the Recorder.

'Thank you, Sergeant. Please remain there.'

Stafford rises to cross-examine. He pauses for a long while before asking his first question, and Charles can almost see the cogs whirring inside that very capable brain.

He's not sure how to go about this. And I can't blame him.

It's an extremely unusual circumstance for one serving police officer to be giving evidence against another. By and large, unless there is compelling evidence to the contrary, juries believe police officers. Greene has already been significantly wounded by Charles's cross-examination, and here is a young, nice-looking and obviously plain-speaking police officer from outside the Flying Squad to whom the jury is warming. He's also suffered severe injuries at the hands of Greene's alleged co-conspirator.

Charles can identify two potential points of attack available to Stafford and, sure enough, the large man goes for the first.

'Sergeant Sloane, you are, and remain the accused's boyfriend?' asks Stafford in his plummy accent.

'As far as I'm aware, my Lord. She's been in custody for several weeks, but I've no reason to assume matters have changed between us.'

'You don't want her to be returned to South Africa, do you?'

'Obviously not.'

'That would bring your relationship to an end.'

'It would. More importantly, she'd be in terrible danger there.'

'Yes, I was going to come to that. The story she tells us about her parents suggests that she too might be imprisoned there, and with uncertain results.'

'That's right, my Lord.'

'And if Dr Alexandrova were to be convicted of an indictable offence, she would be deported, wouldn't she?'

'I'm not an expert in immigration law, my Lord, but I believe that to be the case.'

'So you certainly have a motive to secure her acquittal.'

Sloane smiles. 'Of course I do. I make no secret of that.'

'Securing her acquittal might even save her life, mightn't it?'

'It might.'

'I suggest you would do or say anything to secure that acquittal.'

'My Lord, I would do or say anything within the bounds of the law. But I would not commit perjury for her or run the risk of losing my job. Much as I love the accused, I have loved my job for longer.'

'That's very noble of you, sergeant,' says Stafford with icy sarcasm.

'No, my Lord, it's not noble. Mr Stafford doesn't realise the background I come from. My family are dirt poor farmers in Ireland, and he has no idea what it's cost me to get where I am today. I'd never do anything to jeopardise that. Moreover, I loathe everything that corrupt police officers stand for. That's why I wouldn't drop the investigation. For me to stand here and lie on oath, even to protect Dr Alexandrova, well … it'd make me one of them.' He jabs his finger in the direction of Greene and Lincoln sitting at the back of the court. He shakes his head and, when he speaks again, it is quietly, more to himself than to the judge and jury. 'I could never do that.'

'So you claim you were at the bedsit when the accused was arrested?' persists Stafford.

'I do. Where else would I be? Dr Alexandrova and I were close, it was the beginning of our relationship, so of course I'd want to be with her whenever I could. And it was because I was there that the jackets were planted in that bedsit. Obviously, DI Greene falsely concluded that I lived there. He was trying to plant them on me.'

The Recorder intervenes again. 'Members of the jury, you will ignore that last comment. Detective Sergeant Sloane cannot know what might have been in the mind of another person. When Mr Holborne makes his final address to you he may deal with this if he wishes, but it is for you to decide the motives of the various witnesses in this case, not for witness to speculate.'

The prosecutor launches into a long set of questions about the events surrounding Irenna's arrest. On Stafford's instructions Sloane wasn't there at all, so he probes peripheral details about the layout of the room, where everyone stood, the type of squad car they travelled in and so forth, trying to find areas where he hopes Sloane and Irenna hadn't thought to make up details. He gets nowhere. Sloane *was* there, and so can answer easily and without hesitation.

'I suggest you were not at the bedsit and you were not in the squad car on its return journey to West End Central,' he concludes.

'With respect to counsel, my Lord, that makes no sense. DI Greene was looking for leverage over me, not over a trainee doctor who had nothing to do with the investigation. Of course he arrested me. I was his target. Dr Alexandrova had nothing whatsoever to do with this. She just got caught up in it.'

'The defect in your theory,' continues Stafford, 'is that Gervaise was charged. There was no need to pressurise you into dropping your investigation, because whether by your efforts or not, it was successful. Why continue to bring false allegations against an innocent doctor in those circumstances?'

'That, my Lord, I cannot say. Malice, perhaps? Maybe DI Greene doesn't like women, or Jews, or political activists. That would be for him to answer.'

Stafford changes tack. 'You have another motive for lying, don't you, sergeant?'

'I do?'

'Well, you tell us that Billy Gervaise beat you sufficiently to leave you in hospital for several days.'

'Yes?'

347

'And it was DI Greene who protected him and prevented him from being prosecuted for that.'

'I believe that to be the case, although I'm surprised Mr Stafford agrees, my Lord.'

Stafford ignores that. 'I suggest you're making up this story not only to protect your girlfriend but also for revenge against DI Greene.'

'No, Mr Stafford. I don't want revenge. I want justice. In my mind there's an important distinction. I came into this job to catch criminals, not to let them go, whatever information they may provide to buy their way out of trouble.'

Charles cannot hide his smile. It's a perfect answer, and it seems to stump Chugger Stafford. He remains standing in his bench, evidently weighing up the hope that further questions might damage Sloane against the risk that every time the sergeant opens his mouth, he merely strengthens the Defence. Eventually Stafford decides against making matters worse, and he sits.

'Re-examination?' asks the Recorder.

'No, thank you, my Lord,' replies Charles.

The top brass lining the back of the court disappear in a flurry of activity as soon as Sloane steps down from the witness box. Charles can guess the nature of the discussions about to take place somewhere behind closed doors in the Home Department.

The barristers' speeches to the jury are something of an anti-climax. It seems to Charles that everyone in the court knows the likely verdict; they're just anxious to get to it. Never before has Charles felt that his speech was so unimportant.

Nonetheless, in a short address lasting no more than fifteen minutes, he focuses on the atrocious performances of both Gervaise and Greene as compared with the obvious sincerity and honesty of Irenna and Sloane. Now for the first time he's able to put before the jury what must have been obvious to everyone in the courtroom: that Greene framed Irenna to prevent Sloane from pursuing his investigation. He doesn't try to explain why the prosecution against Irenna persisted despite Gervaise's arrest and turning Queen's Evidence. Greene's motive is, he says, irrelevant. One might speculate, but it's what Greene did that matters, and it was the jury's duty to reach a conclusion on the evidence, whatever the motive might have been. He is heartened by seeing every single member of the jury following his words, making eye contact with him and nodding at important points in his speech.

The Recorder's summing up is likewise short and to the point. Charles enjoys watching the pro-prosecution judge's discomfiture. Judge Pullman finds himself in the novel position of being unable to take his usual course, that of forcefully commending the evidence of the police and putting the boot into the Defence, when the evidence of the police officer on whom the Crown rely is contested by another serving police officer, and one in the same force. Unable to take sides, for the first time in his judicial career his summing up is a model of even-handedness. He simply leaves it to the jury to decide which party's witnesses it prefers, and even finishes by reminding the jury yet again that unless they are sure of Irenna's guilt, they must acquit.

Forty minutes after the Recorder starts, the jury bailiff is sworn and the jury is taken out to consider its verdict.

Charles moves swiftly towards the dock where Irenna is about to be taken down to the cells.

'Are you okay?' he asks.

She nods. 'I think so. Look, whatever happens, I want to thank you. I couldn't have got through this without you … and

Sean. You did a great job, Charles; I couldn't have asked for more.'

'Teamwork,' he says. 'You did your bit, and so did the Irishman.'

She smiles. 'Maybe, but that was remarkable ... what you did. I'll never be able to repay you.'

'Let's not get ahead of ourselves,' cautions Charles. 'Juries are difficult things to predict.'

'Do you think we're going to lose?'

'I don't want to raise your expectations, just for them to be dashed. But I'm optimistic. Do you want me to come down?'

'No, I'll be fine. Maybe if they haven't come back after a couple of hours, perhaps?'

'I'd be very surprised if they took that long,' he says. 'And it looks like everyone else agrees,' he adds.

He indicates the courtroom around them. The crowds in the public gallery have thinned slightly as one or two journalists have slipped outside for cigarettes, but the courtroom is still almost full and there remains a sense of expectation. Ronnie and Reggie Kray are still in their seats. It's always difficult to judge what they are thinking — they are masters of the blank face — but as Charles looks up he makes eye contact with Reggie and sees the corners of the gangster's mouth twitch up in a fleeting smile as he winks.

Even they're confident. Could this be my "out"?

Stafford appears so certain that the jury will return swiftly that he's remained in his seat, reading a newspaper.

Charles is not disappointed. The clerk emerges after only fifteen minutes to announce that the jury have a verdict. There is a knock on the judge's door.

'All rise!'

350

The Recorder takes his seat. 'I gather we have a verdict, gentlemen. Is there anything either of you would like to say before we take it?'

Charles half-rises and shakes his head.

'No, thank you,' says Stafford.

'Very well,' says the Recorder. 'Bring them in.'

Another knock on another piece of panelling, and another concealed door opens to allow the jury to file in. Their order has been rearranged to allow one of the middle-aged white men — the one Charles pegged as a retired Greek businessman — to take the foreman's seat nearest the judge's bench.

The clerk of the court asks the foreman to stand. Despite the fact that Charles has never been more assured of the right verdict than now, his heart starts to pound.

'Mr Foreman, please answer the following question either "Yes" or "No". Have you reached a verdict on which you are all agreed?'

'Yes,' says the man with a strong and clear voice.

'On the count of receiving stolen goods, do you find the accused, Dr Irenna Alexandrova, guilty or not guilty?'

The foreman answers so quickly that he almost cuts off the last words of the clerk's question.

'Guilty.'

CHAPTER 36

There follows a heartbeat of shocked silence. Over a hundred barristers, solicitors, journalists, witnesses, court staff and members of the public are frozen in place. Then pandemonium breaks out.

The first thing Charles hears, or perhaps more accurately, sees because the noise is so great he can barely hear the words, is the clerk of the court asking the foreman to repeat the verdict. Every direction in which Charles looks there is movement and noise. DI Greene and DC Lincoln at the back of the court are being loudly congratulated by other officers. Hansie Fischer is running to the dock where it looks as if Irenna has collapsed with shock, and Sean Sloane is striding up the aisle towards the prosecution officers, fury in his eyes and fists clenched.

Charles swivels to look up at the loudest contributor to the uproar, the public gallery. Almost everyone above him is standing, shouting and gesticulating. Alone in the sea of movement sit Ronnie and Reggie. Charles notes a look of complete disbelief on their faces, together with something else which he hasn't time at that second to analyse.

The judge is trying to be heard, but his voice is completely drowned in the bedlam. Charles turns back to face him but as he does so it is another commotion, one which in all his years of experience he has never seen before, that draws his eye: the jury box. The jurors behind the foreman are outraged. Several are shouting at him and the woman sitting next to him is actually yanking the nearest part of his jacket, as if attempting to drag him back down to his seat. The faces of all of them express the same emotion, and it takes Charles a moment to name it.

They're angry! They're absolutely fucking furious! Because … because they don't agree with him!

Alone of the twelve jurors, indeed, alone of all the people thronging the courtroom, the foreman remains unnaturally calm. He has a satisfied, smug expression on his face, and Charles follows the line of his eyes up towards the gallery where he is staring directly at the Krays.

The Recorder is finally making himself heard across the melee developing in the well of the court.

'Take her down! Take her down!' He addresses counsel. 'I'm adjourning until order is restored,' he shouts, and he sweeps out of court without waiting for a response.

Several uniformed police officers enter court at a run followed by the Master at Arms, and begin separating people. The foreman of the jury, now pulled back to his seat and oblivious to the shouts of the other jurors, is still staring up at the Kray twins, with a "Now what are you going to do?" expression.

An appalling suspicion begins to form in Charles's mind. He points furiously at the twins and with his finger indicates they should come down and meet him outside. Reggie nods and the brothers stand together and push their way out of the boisterous crowd.

Charles rushes out of the barrister's bench and tugs the usher by the sleeve as she goes past him.

'How long have we got?' he demands urgently. 'Till the judge returns,' he explains angrily to the bewildered woman.

'He's gone for lunch. Certainly not before two.'

'Thank you,' replies Charles hurriedly, and starts pushing his way through the crowds to the court doors.

DI Greene has already reached the bank of public telephones. They are all occupied and there is a jostling gaggle of journalists pressing to phone their stories through. He flashes his warrant card and moves to the head of the queue. He takes the first phone to become available and dials.

'Nessa? It's me. You can unpack.' Pause. 'Yes, unanimous conviction. Makes me wish we'd pressed on against that Mick sergeant from West Hendon too, but no one'll believe a word he says now. Suspended? Fuck that! I'm gonna get him kicked off the force altogether. No, I'll be back in time for dinner. We're going out to celebrate.'

Still in his robes, Charles runs down the staircase to the Great Hall and scans the people there. Most of the other courts have yet to rise for lunch and the place is half-empty. He sees a flash of sunlight reflected off the main doors as they open and close and there, standing on the steps, he catches a glimpse of the Krays, both lighting cigarettes. He runs across the black and white marble flagstones.

Jogging down the stairs, he simply grabs each twin by an elbow as he meets them and drags them behind a stone pillar.

'What the fuck have you done?' he hisses at them, the cold air outside making his breath appear as great white clouds.

The brothers look at one another, evidently weighing up how or whether to respond. Eventually Ronnie takes a drag on his cigarette and stares across the road as he answers. 'We thought you needed a little leg up.'

'What? Tell me what you did!'

Ronnie's head swivels sharply to face Charles's. His eyes glower and his hand makes a movement towards his pocket. 'Watch it, Horowitz! You don't give us orders.'

Charles realises that he needs to control his fury.

Reggie speaks. 'We had a word with one of the jurors,' he explains more calmly.

'What?' repeats Charles stupidly. 'How?'

'Tassos.'

'Who? The foreman?'

Reggie nods. 'An old acquaintance. We recognised him the minute 'e was called. Used to be a villain, but not for twenty years or more. Since then 'e's been running a one-man accountancy practice up Seven Sisters Road. When no one challenged 'im off, we thought we'd have a word with 'im.'

'So … I don't understand! I assume he was supposed to say "*Not* guilty", right?' Neither twin answers.

There's a further prolonged pause before Ronnie speaks, teeth clenched in anger. 'Of course he fucking was!'

'Then … what happened?' insists Charles.

'He wanted money,' replies Reggie.

'Are you surprised?' says Charles, his voice rising again dangerously. 'It's a serious offence, so of course he'd want money. And you paid him, right?'

'Yeh.'

'So?'

'He wanted more. And then more again,' says Ronnie.

'And?' demands Charles in exasperation.

'And … well … negotiations were proceeding, as they say.'

Ronnie snorts with laughter but, despite his bravado, he has the grace to look sheepish at his scheme backfiring.

Charles raises his hands into the air and slams them back into his pinstriped legs in utter frustration. 'Well, they ain't proceeding now, are they? He's fucking stuffed us!' he shouts, his Cockney background slipping through the polished barristerial exterior. 'What a complete fuck-up! I had it under control! It was all going perfectly! Didn't you see how the jury was responding? I mean, you've got enough experience of this sort of thing! Didn't you see their faces? They were going to acquit!'

Charles spins away from them, hand to bowed head, eyes closed. 'Jesus fucking Christ!' he mutters.

He spins back. 'You do know what this means, don't you?' he says. 'The least-worst-case scenario means a retrial. The verdict has to be unanimous. The plan was to discredit Gervaise — and Greene for that matter — before your own trial. Now there's every chance your case'll be called on before the retrial. And that's if they don't just deport Irenna immediately.'

A prolonged silence follows.

It is nearing one o'clock and more courts are closing for the short adjournment. Police officers and witnesses leaving the court building glance towards the three men tucked away in a corner, the barrister in full court robes and the well-dressed gangsters whose faces are known to everyone in England, all clearly in the middle of an almighty row.

'Well, Charlie?' asks Reggie calmly. 'Suggestions?'

'Short of walking into the judge's chambers and telling him you bribed a juror, but you're very sorry 'cos it backfired … no!'

'Well, you ain't gonna do that, are you?' says Ronnie dangerously.

'I wouldn't recommend it,' adds Reggie.

Charles thinks furiously. 'Do you have any proof you gave him money? Any proof that doesn't connect him to you?'

The twins look at one another. Then: 'There's the bloke that handed it over, maybe…' says Ronnie.

'Not if he's a member of the Firm,' points out Charles. 'That'll lead directly back to you. And you've got a motive, haven't you? What about witnesses? Where did it happen?'

'In the *Blind Beggar*,' says Reggie. His brow creases in thought. 'We might be able to find a witness.'

'Someone who actually saw the money being handed over?'

'Well, that's what he'll say ... if that's what you want.'

Charles shakes his head and sighs. The comedy of the situation breaks through his icy fury, and he can't help laughing. 'Honestly, Reg, you two wouldn't recognise the straight and narrow even if you were corralled into it. Look, we haven't got time to mess about. I've got till two o'clock. There might just be a tiny, tiny window of opportunity to rescue this. We need a name and a body.'

'What?'

'I need the witness, here, in the next half-hour. He needs to be prepped and ready to speak to the Filth. You understand? Someone rock-solid, capable of lying bare-faced to the Recorder, in open court, if necessary. Can you do it?'

The twins look at one another for a moment. Charles shakes his head as, yet again, he observes that uncanny silent communication of which Ronnie and Reggie Kray are capable. Over the years it's won them numerous battles. Other criminals find it genuinely spooky when trying to out-guess them and, in situations where verbal intimidation has failed, without any apparent communication they can burst simultaneously into frenetic, ungoverned violence. It's a powerful edge in a world of unprincipled violent men.

'Yeah, we've got the man. He can be here in thirty minutes.'

Charles nods. 'Okay. There'll be a Detective Sergeant Sloane on these steps in half an hour, waiting.'

Charles takes a step back towards the doors but then halts. 'You do realise how this will go, don't you? The Filth will interview your Greek accountant, and he'll say it was you who bribed him.'

Ronnie shakes his head firmly. 'No, he won't.'

'How can you be so sure?' demands Charles.

''Cos we know where his ex-missus and kids live. He knows, if push comes to shove, where his bread's buttered.'

'He didn't know twenty minutes ago, though, did he? I saw his face; he was defying you.'

'Yeh,' says Reggie. 'But that was just haggling. Believe us, Charlie, 'e won't grass. He'll make something up. He knows what'll happen otherwise.'

Charles finds Sloane with Irenna in the holding pen. Irenna has not been in this part of the cells before, and she looks more frightened than ever. Sloane sits next to her on the bench, holding her hand. He has a bruise across his cheek, received, Charles supposes, while being restrained from attacking one of his superior officers. Charles comes straight to the point.

'He was bribed. That juror.'

'What, one man to persuade all the others to vote guilty? Not possible,' replies Sloane, quick on the uptake as always. 'It has to be for a hung jury and a retrial. That's the best he could've hoped for. Who did it?'

'Don't ask. In about twenty minutes, the witness who saw the money being handed over is going to be waiting for you on the steps outside the main entrance. Get a statement from him and, whatever you do, get it to me by no later than a minute to two. I'll be waiting in court.'

There's an uncomfortable silence. 'Now, Charles…' warns Sloane slowly.

Charles hates himself for doing this. Everything the Krays touch becomes corrupted: Sally's father a couple of years ago, then Charles himself, and now Detective Sergeant Sean Sloane, as honest a copper as Charles has ever met.

A good man.

His friend.

Charles looks hard at him, his eyes trying to communicate something, beseeching.

Don't ask me. Don't ask me, or I will *tell you.*

'On your honour, Charles, is that what happened? Someone bribed that juror?'

'On my honour. That's what I firmly believe occurred.'

Sloane continues to lock eyes with Charles. 'If that's what you tell me, then, I believe you. And I don't need to know how you found the witness. I deal with anonymous tipoffs all the time.'

He turns to Irenna and takes both of her hands in his. 'We'll sort this out, *a chuisle mo chroí*, my darlin' girl, I promise.'

He departs and Charles runs up to the Bar Mess. He only has a short while, but he's desperate for food. He'll need all his wits about him in the next hour, and that means carbs.

Most of the food from the buffet service has gone and he doesn't have time to order a meal from the waitress. Two lonely sausages lie cooling in an otherwise empty baking tin. He points at them.

'Can you slap those two inside some buttered bread for me?' he asks the waitress behind the counter.

'That's not a proper meal, Mr Holborne,' she chides.

'Yes, you're right. Better squirt a blob of brown sauce in there too.'

The waitress laughs and does as instructed.

Charles reaches for his pocket. 'How much?'

'We ain't got a price for sausage sandwiches, least, not up here. Go on, just take it. I won't tell no one if you don't.'

'Thanks, Sheila. I owe you one.' He points at a soggy potato mass next to the now-empty baking tray. 'Can I take a handful of those, too?'

'Really? Cold soggy chips? They were going in the bin.'

Charles scoops a few onto his plate. 'Lovely,' he explains. 'The food of princes.'

He takes his meal to the corner of the large room, avoiding the various conversations between other barristers finishing their meals. He needs time to plot.

CHAPTER 37

The wood panelling closes behind Stafford and Charles and they find themselves in the hushed and carpeted corridor behind the courts. The courtroom they've just left remains quiet, the doors still locked since the judge rose. The clerk leads them down a short flight of steps into a well-appointed corridor off which open all the judge's doors. Faint voices can be heard emanating from most of them as they pass, the trials in those courts having resumed.

'Odd coincidence, this,' comments Stafford as they follow the woman ahead of them.

'The same thought occurred to me. Although this time I think I am the bearer of answers, and not the subject of accusations.'

The barristers are referring to the last time they contested a case together, in this very building and before this very judge. Charles's reputation at the time was so poor that, when something extraordinary occurred in court, he was accused both by the prosecutor and the Recorder of manipulating the evidence. When Charles was vindicated, proven to be beyond reproach, Stafford's attitude to him changed markedly and has continued to do so since. Charles is less sure of his likely reception from the Recorder.

The woman stops and waits for the two barristers to catch up with her, her gown swishing slowly to a halt. 'Are you ready, gentlemen?'

'Yes,' they say in unison.

She knocks on a door.

'Come.'

She opens the door for the barristers. 'Counsel to see you, judge.'

'Thank you. Pull up a chair, gentlemen.'

Stafford and Charles each drag a chair from the wall and place it in front of the judge's desk as the clerk closes the door behind her. Pullman wears his robes but his wig lies upside down on the desk before him. Yet another cigarette is clamped between his nicotine-stained fingers.

'Well, I've never seen anything like that before, have you?' starts Pullman, reasonably amiably.

'No, judge,' says Stafford.

Pullman turns to Charles. 'Odd coincidence, don't you think, Holborne? We three in here again?' He raises a stained hand. 'I'm not for a moment suggesting you're behind this, but trouble does seem to follow you, doesn't it?'

'It's been said.'

'Well, you asked to see me?'

'Yes, judge. Can I show you this, please? It's handwritten, hot off the press, and at present it's the only copy. I've shown it to Stafford.'

The Recorder leans back in his creaking chair, wreathed in cigarette smoke, spits a flake of tobacco off his tongue where it lies on his desk, and squints at Sloane's pocketbook.

'Good God!' he whispers. He finishes reading. 'So, this Mr George Fellowes says he saw money being handed to the juror. Anything known of him?'

'DS Sloane has made a telephone enquiry, and the answer appears to be no. He hasn't been able to get a full CRO record yet, but it looks as if Fellowes is of good character.'

'And he just happened to be in the right place at the right time?' asks the Recorder. Charles shrugs. 'What I'd like to

362

know is how on earth the police managed to discover this since I rose just over an hour ago.'

'That I can't tell you, I'm afraid,' says Charles.

This is, strictly, true; Charles can't possibly tell the judge what happened, but it's not what he implied and is as close as he has ever come to lying to a judge's face.

'There are several possibilities though, judge,' says Stafford. 'Fellowes could have been in the public gallery and recognised the juror. More likely he already reported this to the police, but word didn't get through. I've had to complain on multiple occasions about the lack of sensible communication between the Flying Squad and the rest of the Met. It's professional jealousy; sometimes I think they deliberately hide information from one another.'

Pullman rocks back in his chair again. 'What's your suggestion, then? Mistrial and start again?'

'May I add one further matter please, judge?' asks Charles.

'Go ahead.'

'You may not have seen it as you left court, but there was complete pandemonium in the jury box following that verdict.'

'I did indeed see it,' confirms Pullman.

'Stafford and I have discussed it, and we're both convinced the rest of the jury were not expecting the foreman to say "Guilty". He was off on a frolic of his own.'

'They were incandescent,' adds Stafford. 'Shouting and gesticulating at him. I believe that without his influence they would acquit, even now.'

'As they bloody well should,' mutters the Recorder. 'Never seen a performance like that from a police officer, not in my entire career.'

'Detective Inspector Greene?' asks Stafford.

'Of course! I can tell you now that I've already sent the material produced by you, Holborne, to the Director of Public Prosecutions. Corruption in the Flying Squad's becoming a national scandal, and this time I mean to do something about it. And I've recommended interviewing Gervaise again, but this time by officers outside of the Flying Squad. Let's see what the "Supergrass" has to say about DI Greene, given the right encouragement.'

Charles raises an eyebrow and reassesses the Recorder. He has always supposed the judge's pro-prosecution bias to be impregnable, but perhaps not.

'So,' says Charles, 'focusing for the moment on this trial, and my client, I understand from the jury bailiff that the court staff were so concerned for the foreman's safety at the hands of the other jurors they put him in a separate room. So he's been sequestered throughout since he announced the verdict. If you were to ask some questions of this witness and are left suspicious that the foreman was bribed, the proper course is to discharge him, whatever the stage of the trial. But that doesn't mean that the rest of the jury is tainted. From what Stafford and I witnessed, they weren't.'

'There's no way of being sure,' comments Pullman. 'If we proceed with eleven and, after everything, they convict, you couldn't complain.'

'I accept that. I may be wrong, judge, but every instinct I have tells me that without that corrupt juror, we'd have got a different verdict. The court has an opportunity to avoid a mistrial, save three days' court time wasted here, and the time and expense of another trial. Not to mention putting Dr Alexandrova through all this stress again, which has been considerable. I'd really like to avoid that, if possible.'

The judge turns to the big prosecutor. 'What do you say, Stafford?'

'Holborne mentioned this possibility to me before we came in. We'd have to be confident the rest aren't tainted, but I also thought they were blindsided by what the foreman said.'

'We're barred from inquiring into the jury's deliberations.'

'Of course,' says Charles quickly, 'but, with respect, judge, we don't need to. You could just make a decision about possible interference with the single jury member, and discharge him if necessary. I've had a look in Archbold and, as you'd imagine, there is no precedent on this sort of event. But I can find nothing that would prevent you taking a verdict again where a jury has remained sequestered and interference with a juror, now discharged, has only been discovered at the last moment.'

'Are you quite sure about this, Holborne? If you were to apply for a mistrial, I don't see how I could resist such an application. You'd get a clean jury and another shot at it.'

'Yes, I'm sure.'

The Recorder considers the situation for a few further seconds and then launches himself forward to the desk and stubs out his cigarette where it joins a pile of others in his ashtray.

'Very well. I'd like to hear from this witness … Fellowes … first, and if his evidence looks credible, we'll have the foreman in on his own and discharge him. The police can investigate the attempt to pervert the course of justice in due course. Thank you both.'

The two barristers are escorted back along the corridor to enter court via the judge's door.

'Life's never dull around you, Charles, is it?' says Stafford, with a grin.

Fifteen minutes later, the Recorder and counsel wait in court. It is otherwise deserted.

Two uniformed police officers guarding the swing doors part to let Sloane enter, leading a small elderly man down the aisle. Charles's eyes follow the witness as he's guided to the witness box. He's in his late seventies or early eighties. He uses a stick and has a slight limp. He wears a flat cap, a raincoat and wire-rimmed glasses perched on a long nose in a thin face. Charles is reminded of an ancient whippet.

Sloane guides the man into the witness box. The usher hands him a Bible and card.

'I swear by Almighty God that the evidence I shall give will be the truth, the whole truth, and nothing but the truth,' says the man in a high-pitched nasal voice.

Stafford starts to rise, but the Recorder puts out a hand to forestall him.

'Your name is George Fellowes, is that right?' asks the Recorder.

'Yes, your honour.'

'I've read a statement contained in a police officer's notebook in which you say you were present when one of the jurors was bribed, is that right?'

'Yes, your honour.'

'Tell me again what happened, please.'

'I was in the *Blind Beggar*, after the first day, which I'd been watching. There was a chap sitting on his own about twelve feet from me, and I recognised him as one of the jurors.'

'How did you recognise him?' asks the Recorder.

'I've got a good memory for faces, and I watched him as he gave the oath. I knew him before, see? He's an accountant chap, up Seven Sisters. I used to walk past his office every day. It's closed, now.'

The Recorder turns to Stafford. 'Has the Crown any confirmation that this particular juror is indeed an accountant working in Seven Sisters?'

'Yes, my Lord. His business appears to have closed down a couple of months ago, but enquiries reveal that the premises are still there, with the juror's name on the window.'

'Thank you. Now, Mr Fellowes, what happened?'

'It *was* an odd coincidence, but the *Blind Beggar*'s a well-known pub, and it's me local, so I thought nothing of it. Then a man comes in. I noticed him 'cos there was a draught as 'e opened the door, and 'e stood there holding the door open. I was about to ask 'im to shut it when 'e saw the accountant and went straight over to sit opposite 'im. I watched 'im take a large envelope from 'is pocket and push it across the table. The accountant opened it and I saw a big wedge of cash. He flicked through it — not counting it properly but, you know flicking, like a pack of cards — put it in 'is pocket, and got up. He left straight away. Didn't even finish his drink.'

'Did you do anything with this information?'

'I reported it to the local police station.'

'Did you do anything else?'

The little man shrugs. 'No, 'cept kept coming to the trial.'

'What were you doing at the trial? Do you know anyone involved?'

'No, your honour. I come a lot. You can ask the staff up there. I'm always watching trials here. I'm surprised you don't recognise me.'

That produces a smile from the Recorder. 'Why are you always watching trials?'

'It's interesting, innit? Plus, it gets me out the 'ouse. Deirdre, that's me daughter-in-law, don't like me being under 'er feet all day.'

The Recorder draws a deep breath. 'I see. Do either of you have any questions?' he asks the barristers.

'No, thank you,' replies Charles.

'No,' says Stafford.

'Very well. Thank you, Mr Fellowes, you are free to leave. The police may need to speak to you again about this, do you understand?'

'Yes, of course.'

The little man hobbles back up the aisle and disappears through the doors.

'Well, gentlemen, I am suspicious enough not to want to take any chances. Of course, it's not impossible that the payment was some other nefarious dealing, but the coincidence in time is powerful. If I'd heard that evidence at the beginning of the trial, I'd certainly have excused the juror.' He leans over his bench to speak to the clerk sitting below him. 'Can you call the jury bailiff in, please?'

The clerk slips out of her seat and returns a moment later with a tall man also wearing a court gown.

'My Lord?' asks the man.

'Am I right in believing that the foreman of the jury has been sequestered separately since he gave the verdict?'

'Yes, my Lord. I know I'm not supposed to speak to them, but they were all talking at the same time and it was impossible not to hear. They'd all voted "Not Guilty", including the foreman, and that was what he was supposed to say. So when he said "Guilty" they were all so flabbergasted, so furious with him, I had to move him away from them. He's in the jury room for Court 2, which isn't sitting today.'

'Has someone been with him throughout?'

'Yes, one of my colleagues has either been sitting outside the door or actually inside while providing food and drink.'

'Good. Let's get the man in here.'

He looks up and gestures to someone behind Charles. Charles turns and looks behind him. The Recorder beckons to the policemen guarding the swing doors.

'Can you come and sit over here, please, officers?'

He points to the table in the well of the court in front of the QCs' bench, only a yard or so from the front jury bench. They do as instructed.

There is another short delay while the Greek ex-accountant is brought into court. He stands on his own in the foreman's position in the jury box, looking oddly vulnerable without his colleagues. The clerk hands a card up to the judge. The judge squints at it and then looks up at the juror.

'You're Mr Tassos Demetriou, is that right?'

'Yes.'

'Mr Demetriou, I have been given information which leads me to believe that you have taken a bribe to come to a particular verdict.' The Recorder put up a hand to forestall any argument from Demetriou. 'I'm not in a position to reach a conclusion on that today, and I'm not asking you to say anything. But I'm discharging you from any further involvement with this jury. Now, please go with these officers.'

The two police officers rise and approach Demetriou. He sighs heavily, shakes his head, but walks to the end of the jury box where each of the officers takes an arm. He is escorted up the aisle and out of court.

'Right,' says the Recorder. 'Usher, you can open the court now. I'll rise for a moment to let everyone assemble. Then the jury should be brought in and I'll give them a further direction.'

It takes a further quarter of an hour to allow the public gallery and court to fill up with all the relevant personnel. The court is less full than it was and some of the tension has dissipated. As far as the spectators are concerned there's been a short unexplained delay in the case restarting, but that often occurs when bail applications and other brief matters are listed directly after the luncheon adjournment. Charles notes with interest that although DC Lincoln has resumed his place at the back of the court, DI Greene has not.

The jury, one fewer than before, files into the jury box. Even this is not entirely unexpected, as juries frequently return to hear sentence passed over the people they have just convicted.

The court awaits only the arrival of the judge, but the delay lengthens.

And lengthens further.

No explanation is given. Then the dock officer appears from below and beckons the usher over to him urgently. Everyone in the courtroom cranes forward to hear the exchange. There is a whispered conversation which Charles cannot catch, but it ends with the dock officer shrugging in a way that expresses "It's not my fault."

The usher scurries over to the clerk of the court and delivers the message from the dock officer. The clerk looks across at counsel's benches, on the verge of coming across, but changes her mind. She climbs the steps behind her and disappears through the door into judge's corridor.

Stafford leans across. 'Any idea what's going on, Charles?'

'No … but I have a growing suspicion.' Charles steps quickly out of his bench and approaches the dock. The dock officer is still there and Charles calls up to him. 'Where's Dr Alexandrova?' he hisses.

The dock officer looks sheepish. 'I don't know, sir. We can't find her.'

'What the fuck do you mean you can't find her? She was in custody an hour ago! Are you saying she just walked out of the Old Bailey cells?'

'I'm sorry, sir, I can't help you. I didn't deal with her before lunch, and the officer who did has left to go to Wandsworth prison —'

He breaks off as the judge enters court without fanfare. Even before he reaches his seat, the Recorder calls across the court floor.

'Mr Holborne, Mr Stafford: I've been told that Dr Alexandrova has been removed from the premises.'

'Removed, my Lord?' asks Charles, as he skirts his way round his bench and back into his seat. 'How is that possible?'

'It seems that DI Greene together with some official from the Home Office have jumped the gun. I understand that your client is being deported.'

'That would be unlawful, my Lord,' says Charles. 'Even if convicted properly, she'd be entitled to a hearing before a magistrate before a deportation order could be made.'

'I agree. Perhaps DI Greene was unaware of that. In any case, that is where we stand.'

Stafford intervenes. 'May I suggest that we proceed immediately to re-take the verdict? That'll at least bring this trial to an end, subject, potentially, to sentencing, which can be adjourned. Your Lordship would then be in a position to issue an order halting any deportation process.'

'I doubt I have power to do that —' says Pullman, reaching for his copy of Archbold.

Charles jumps in. 'I support my learned friend's suggestion. If the rest of the jury are untainted, it's essential we proceed to a proper verdict. I think the proper course would then be for me to apply to the High Court for an injunction preventing an unlawful deportation.'

Charles sees several jury members nodding vigorously. The Recorder, usually so in command of his court, looks lost. 'Well…'

'My Lord,' says Charles, almost shouting. 'Time is of the essence!'

The Recorder, stung into action, nods. 'Yes … very well. Are you consenting to the verdict being given in the absence of your client?'

'Yes.'

Pullman turns to the jury box. 'Members of the jury, you will see that one of your number is now missing. He has been discharged.'

This is met by more nodding from the jurors, and one of the gentlemen in the back row actually exclaims, 'Hear, hear!'

'No one is permitted to enquire into your deliberations,' continues the Recorder, 'but no one who was in court can have failed to notice that the verdict given by your previous foreman met with considerable opposition from the rest of you. Now, I am not asking you to tell me any of what transpired. What I am however asking you is this: do you wish to reconsider the verdict that was given on your behalf? If so, I'm very happy for you to retire further, elect another foreman or woman, and then come back into court. Now…'

The Recorder grinds to a halt as the remaining eleven jurors begin whispering furiously amongst themselves. A consensus seems to be reached almost immediately, with a great deal of nodding and agreeing. Several of them point to the Asian woman who, by chance, now occupies the foreman's place, encouraging her to stand up. Timidly, she does so.

'Madam, do I take it from what I've just seen that the jury does not feel that it needs to retire again?' More nodding from all ten of the jurors beside and behind her. 'Very well.' He half-rises from his seat to peer over his bench at the clerk below him. 'Ask again.'

The clerk rises from her seat and picks up the indictment for a second time. She addresses the jury. 'Madam foreman?'

The Asian woman nods, although her affirmative answer is barely audible.

'Please answer the following question either "Yes" or "No". Has the jury reached a verdict on which all eleven remaining members are agreed?'

There is so much non-verbal agreement from the other jurors that Charles is reminded of a line of nodding dogs in the back window of a car.

'Yes,' says the woman.

'And on the count of receiving stolen goods, do you find Dr Alexandrova guilty or not guilty?'

'Not guilty,' says the forewoman.

The rest of the jurors actually cheer.

'Thank you,' says Pullman. 'Please follow the jury bailiff out of court. Gentlemen, I shall rise. The clerk will produce a certificate of acquittal immediately, Mr Holborne, if you wait in court. I shall remain in chambers for the next hour in case there are any further applications.'

CHAPTER 38

Charles paces impatiently at the front desk of West End Central Police Station. Sloane insisted that Charles be allowed to accompany him on his search for DI Greene, as it was Charles who held the Certificate from the Recorder of London proving Irenna's acquittal, but the sergeant on the desk wouldn't permit it and, rather than waste time arguing, Sloane went up alone.

He returns after ten minutes, puts a finger to his lips and steps out onto the street. Charles follows.

'That wasn't pleasant,' says Sloane.

'What happened?'

Sloane shakes his head. 'Cold shoulder. One told me to fuck off before he threw me out the building and another "accidentally" barged into me in the corridor. I'm persona non grata; the enemy.'

'They'll close ranks to protect him, even knowing he's being investigated?'

'They may not actively help him, but they definitely won't help me.'

'Is he there?'

'No. So, he's not at his home and his desk's been cleared. Cathcart's also unavailable; "on leave" as from this morning.'

'Someone's tipped them off about Pullman's referral to the DPP.'

'Must have. But I'm not concerned about that. I need to find Irenna. This is now formally a kidnap investigation, whether the Flying Squad helps or not. An all ports warning telex went out a few minutes ago.'

Sloane's gaze travels up and down Savile Row as if expecting Greene and Irenna to emerge from a shop doorway.

'One of those bastards in there —' he hitches a thumb towards the building they've just left — 'will have told him of the new verdict by now,' he says quietly, thinking it through to himself. 'So he must know that Irenna's been acquitted. Deportation's a non-starter.'

'It always was. If you read the Aliens Order properly, it says that a deportee can be placed on a ship, train or road vehicle about to leave the state and the master or driver is obliged to receive them, but it has to be at the instance of an immigration officer, and unless Greene's kidnapped one of those as well…'

'She's become an encumbrance,' concludes Sloane. He stares at Charles, his eyes widening. 'Oh! Jesus and Mary! He wouldn't, would he?'

'Why would he? He's nothing to gain. He'd put her somewhere, give himself some time. At best she's a bargaining chip. And it'd have to be local, right? I mean, he walks out of the Old Bailey with her in broad daylight? How far could he get with her struggling and screaming for help? Somewhere nearby … but private…' Charles's voice tails off.

'What?'

Charles isn't listening.

'What?' repeats Sloane loudly.

'There was something in Percy's file … I didn't pay it much attention at the time, 'cos I was focusing on other things. But the coincidence struck me.'

'Do I have to arrest you for withholding information, or are you going to fucking tell me?'

'Sorry … I think Greene owns a property in Soho. In Green's Court, just off Brewer Street.'

'Where's that?'

'Right in the heart of the red light district. I'll show you.'

Fifteen minutes later, they are on Brewer Street looking down Green's Court, a narrow, cobbled passageway between tall buildings.

'I think that must be it,' says Charles, nodding towards a staircase leading up from a street door about halfway down. 'There was something about it being called "Maisie's Staircase" locally.'

Sloane shakes his head. 'There might be half a dozen staircases along there. Do you know if these buildings have rear entrances?'

'I expect so. There's another little alleyway round the corner coming from Peter Street. I guess the back of the buildings form an internal courtyard.'

'How the fuck do you know all this?'

Charles shrugs and smiles. 'Scenes from my youth. This was my old hunting ground during the war. Now what?'

'We can't cover front and back. I need to call it in and get back up. And you shouldn't be here at all.'

'I'm the one with the Certificate of Acquittal,' says Charles, patting his jacket pocket.

Sloane shakes his head again. 'Sorry, mate, no civilians. He's a suspect in a felony, and I have the right to arrest him with or without your piece of paper. But...' He looks up and down Brewer Street. 'I really need to find a phone.'

'Do you want me to keep watch on the front door while you go make a call?'

Sloane looks hard at his friend. 'I would say yes, but I know your tendency to misplaced heroics. In any case, if he can be traced to the property, he's unlikely to walk out the front door in plain daylight. If he's here at all, and he had to leave, he'd be more likely to slip out the back. Come on; show me.'

Charles is right. They circle round the block to find that between a betting shop and a boarded-up clothes shop on Peter Street there's a further alley, also named Green's Court. Sloane leads the way cautiously down the alley. It opens into a small square formed by the backs of the tall buildings. It's full of refuse, some of it in the bins outside each rear door, and little light penetrates from the rectangle of grey sky above them. A woman, surrounded by bundles and bags, can be seen sleeping under a cardboard box on the back steps of a shop.

Sloane puts his hand on Charles's chest to bring him to a halt. A scraping noise can be heard from further into the courtyard, metal on stone. Sloane drags Charles back with him into the shadows. The scraping noise is followed by a further series of bangs, and they watch as the steel fire door to one of the premises is forced open in small increments of a few inches. The door doesn't look as if it's been opened in years, and it grinds on accumulated rubbish; whoever is opening it is having to push hard.

A dark head eventually pokes out. It's a young woman. Sloane and Charles back further into the recess. The woman looks out furtively, left and right, and her head disappears again. Charles thinks he can hear speaking. A few seconds elapse with no sound and then the woman's head reappears. She now wears a scarf over her hair. She slips out of the narrow gap, pushes the rubbish away with her foot to enable her to descend the few steps to the courtyard floor, and hurries in their direction. She walks briskly towards them and then past. She wears a raincoat cinched tight at the waist, high-heeled shoes and carries a shopping bag over one arm. She hesitates at the end of the alley, stops, and leans forward into

Peter Street, again checking left and right before stepping out. She disappears round the corner.

Charles looks back towards the fire door from which she emerged. Just as he does so, he sees a head being withdrawn back into the building and the metal door is pulled shut with a bang from the inside.

'I saw him!' he whispers hoarsely. 'That was Greene.'

'Yes, it was. Okay, listen to me carefully. You stay here. Keep out of sight and, for God's sake, don't do anything. I'm going to find the closest telephone, perhaps one of the shops on Brewer Street.'

'What if he moves?'

'I don't think he will. He's just sent that woman out on some errand. If we're right, Irenna's in the building with him. I'll only be gone a few moments.'

'Okay.'

'Promise me, Charles. Don't do anything! As soon as backup arrives, you must leave. Go back to Chambers.'

'I have a citizen's right of arrest where a felony —'

'For fuck's sake! I don't need a legal tutorial! Just do as you're fucking told for once!'

Charles grins sheepishly. 'Understood, Inspector.'

'Sergeant,' corrects Sloane with a smile.

'I'm not wrong. Just a little premature.'

Sloane pats him on the shoulder, looks carefully out into the alley, and slips away towards Peter Street.

Charles leans back against the door, as far into the shadows as he can get, and pats his pockets. He'd kill for a cigarette but, of course, he daren't light up even if he had any on him, which he hasn't.

Charles waits. Five minutes elapses. Then another five.

He hears footsteps approaching his position from the street. They are not the slow deliberate tread of a policeman but the fast clip-clop of heels on cobbles. He is as far back into the shadows as he can manage, but the woman approaching him will now have a much better view of his position than she did when walking in the other direction. He calculates quickly whether it's better to be seen skulking in the shadows or to be bold. He decides on the latter.

Stepping out from the recess, whistling, he walks purposefully towards the woman. As he passes her, he smiles at her and tips his hat. He has time only to notice her shocked white face and the fact that, even camouflaged with a scarf and wearing no make-up, the woman is surprisingly beautiful, before he is past and out onto Peter Street. As he rounds the corner he hears the woman's footsteps behind him falter, pause, and then start running deeper into the courtyard.

'Shit!' he curses to himself.

Sloane is nowhere to be seen. Charles is at the junction of Hopkins Street and Peter Street and now has several options. He is about to set off down Hopkins Street when he sees Sloane's tall form running towards him.

'She saw me, Sean! The woman returned and I had nowhere to hide!'

'Where'd she go?'

'She ran off, I assume back into the building.'

Sloane calculates. 'If she made you, they're going to assume you're a copper. Look at you! You don't belong here, dressed like that.'

'So Greene'll run for it?'

'Probably.'

'How long have we got till your backup arrives?'

'Not time enough. Okay. You stay here. I'm going round the front to keep watch on the staircase. If he stays put, all well and good, we'll wait for support. If he comes out the front, I'll intercept him. Maybe reason with him — at least release Irenna. He's got to realise it's hopeless. You stay here, in case he runs this way. But find somewhere different to hide here, another doorway or something.'

Sloane runs back towards Peter Street.

Charles retraces his steps, keeping his eyes fixed firmly on the rear door to Greene's property. It remains closed. He glances up. There are few windows facing into the courtyard and the top floor has dormers set back from the face of the building. Perhaps he can remain undetected.

He passes the sleeping woman and an idea seizes him. He runs to another doorway several down, almost directly opposite Greene's fire door. It too is full of detritus. Charles stuffs his hat into his raincoat pocket, clears a space on the step and is about to lie down when he sees an old bicycle pump lying in the gutter. He picks it up and hefts it. It's solid metal and so rusty that it's welded into a single short unit, rather like a truncheon.

Not really heavy enough, but better than nothing.

He lies down. The concrete beneath him is freezing and stinks of urine, but he pulls two large cardboard boxes over himself and rests his head on his arm, the pump under his armpit. A minor adjustment and he is able to cover his face but leave a gap large enough to see the foot of the metal door opposite. Realising that his shiny leather shoes are probably protruding from under the cardboard, he draws his knees up. He hopes that anyone giving a cursory glance to the bundle in the doorway will either see a mound of rubbish or another derelict.

He waits, listening to his pounding heart slowing, trying to keep his breath steady.

Around the other side of the building, Sloane is approaching Maisie's Staircase.

'Fuck, fuck, fuck!' he breathes. There is simply nowhere to hide; the alley is too narrow and the buildings on the opposite side offer nothing.

He has no choice but to continue walking. As he nears the staircase, a woman steps out. She wears a very short skirt, dark stockings and a small cardigan, the top two buttons of which are open and reveal an ample décolletage. She smiles at him.

'Looking for business, darling?'

Sloane slows slightly, smiling in reply. 'No thanks.'

Several things aren't right about the girl. Even allowing for her profession, she's inadequately dressed for the weather. She couldn't possibly stand there for more than a couple of minutes without shaking with cold. She's not wearing any make-up, which would be strange for a prostitute just coming on shift and, finally, although she holds a cigarette in a languorous fashion, Sloane notes that it's not alight. This woman is not working; she's been put in place as a last-second lookout.

Even before Sloane has passed her, the girl's professional smile has gone and she's pivoting back into the building. Sloane hears her footsteps running up the staircase. He too has been made. What a fuckup! Not for the first time, he finds himself wishing it was all as simple as portrayed in the books and films.

He runs to the far end of the passageway and out onto Brewer Street. This pavement is more crowded with last-minute Christmas shoppers, at least giving him some hope of not being spotted.

Two minutes later, the rear metal door of the building is forced open again. From his position underneath the cardboard boxes, Charles sees a man's shoes appear on the step. They halt, presumably while their owner scans the courtyard, and then emerge more fully. The door is pushed almost closed but jams on a piece of timber from a broken pallet.

He's alone!

Charles waits for the feet to step down onto the cobbles and start towards Peter Street. He leaps up from his hiding place, bicycle pump in hand. Greene, alerted by the noise, spins round. He recognises Charles immediately.

'You?' he says, puzzled. Then he sees the bicycle pump. He grins. 'Don't make me laugh. What're you going to do? Inflate me?'

Greene reaches inside his coat pocket and comes up with something that glints golden in the weak December light. It slips neatly over the knuckles of his right hand.

'Right,' he says, stepping forward. 'You're gonna wish you hadn't poked your nose in, my learned friend.'

Charles doesn't hesitate. He brings his right arm back and, spinning on the spot as if throwing a discus, he turns in a complete circle. Greene's weight is on the wrong foot. He tries to sway back out of range, but the bicycle pump comes smashing into his temple. The blow isn't enough to knock him out but he staggers sideways, dazed, and Charles steps inside and follows up with a left cross to the jaw and a second blow at short range with the pump. Greene goes down, his knees and knuckles striking the cobbles simultaneously. Charles swings his right leg and kicks hard into the policeman's chest. Greene rolls over, flat on the cobbles. As Charles stands over him, he hears running footsteps.

'No more, Charles!' shouts Sloane's voice. Other footsteps follow those of Sloane. Charles looks up to see two uniformed officers running into the courtyard behind his friend.

'We'll take it from here!'

Charles steps back as directed to let the two uniformed police officers get hold of Greene. Sloane doesn't slow up but keeps running towards the fire exit door. He hauls it fully open and disappears inside the building. Charles follows.

'Sir!' shouts one of the uniformed officers, but Charles ignores him.

Ahead of him, Sloane has reached the first landing, and is trying the handles of the doors leading off it. The first opens: an empty bedsit. He runs to the next. It opens to him just before he can reach for the handle. Another young woman wearing a dressing gown faces him. Without speaking, she points with her cigarette up the stairs towards the top of the building.

Sloane, suspicious, pushes her out of the way and looks inside. She is the only person there.

'Top floor, I said,' says the woman.

'Right,' replies Sloane.

Charles has now caught up. Sloane casts a frustrated look over his shoulder but says nothing. He grabs the banister and begins hauling himself up the next flight of stairs. They reach the top floor, a small landing with a doormat and a tall pot of dried flowers standing by a front door. It looks more like the front door of a home than a room of a knocking shop.

Sloane hammers on the door. 'Open up! Police!'

There is a momentary pause, some noise from behind the door, and then it opens a fraction.

The woman whom they saw in the courtyard hides behind the front door, only a small slice of her face visible. She has removed her scarf and coat. 'Yes?' she says.

Sloane flashes his warrant card at her. 'I'm Detective Sergeant Sloane of the Metropolitan Police. And this is…' He hesitates and turns to Charles. 'This man has a document.'

Charles laughs out loud.

Sloane continues. 'I have reason to suspect that a kidnap victim is being kept in these premises.'

There is a moment of stillness as the woman behind the door weighs her options.

'Sean!' comes Irenna's voice from the interior. 'I'm in here!'

Sloane pushes at the door and the woman behind it gives way.

He enters the flat, Charles following. Irenna sits at a small table in the centre of the room, a mug of tea in her hand.

Sloane rushes over to her. 'Are you okay?'

'I'm fine,' she says. 'This is Maisie,' she adds, pointing at the woman who has followed Charles into the room. 'She's been very kind.'

CHAPTER 39

Charles sits at his desk in Chambers. It's late afternoon, and all remaining daylight has been obscured by the heavy clouds gathering over London.

He turns on his desk lamp, takes out a couple of sheets of best quality paper from his desk drawer and places them on his blotter at the centre of the circle of light. He checks his fountain pen and starts writing. This time there are no false starts, no hesitations over what he wants to say. The words flow easily.

Half an hour later he folds the letter into an envelope, locks up and descends to the Austin Healey parked in Essex Court. He heads east, through the city of London, along the East India Dock Road, and takes the A13 towards Romford. He could, of course, post the letter, but he deems it too important to trust to the Royal Mail and, in any case, he's too impatient to wait for the post.

It's rush hour and only a few days before Christmas, and the traffic is particularly heavy. It takes him an hour and a half to reach the Fisher residence. Leaving the engine running, he posts the letter through the letterbox of the modest terraced house. There are lights on behind the closed curtains but he doesn't want to speak to Sally or her mother, so he jogs back to the car and moves off before anyone notices his presence.

My darling Sally

I promise: this is not another jokey, light-hearted account of my day. Please read on.

I don't need to tell you that I've always been too frightened to take risks where my heart's concerned — which is precisely why we're in our current situation. And I don't need to tell you why I've become like that — it was you who diagnosed it accurately, when you walked out for the last time.

But I think I can change — have changed. The indecision on your face at Wren Street convinced me that you don't yet believe it.

So, here's my last throw of the dice.

For most of my life, I've not recognised what love is. Sure, our physical passion was there from day one and, oh, my! it was glorious, but I always imagined love, when it came, would strike like a thunderbolt; I thought it would be unmistakable.

But it wasn't. My love for you crept up on me gradually, like soft summer rain, and only now do I realise that I'm drenched through. It was so new to me. I've never felt it before, not even with Henrietta, and I think I was scared to acknowledge it, terrified that if I looked at it, it would vanish.

Now, in the rear-view mirror, I do recognise it. It was love.

I love the way I could always make you laugh, how we'd spend an entire evening giggling.

I love your cheerfulness in the face of my pessimism, how you're able to glide serenely through life like a swan, making it look so simple.

I love you for how you thought of me in all those little ways, like schlepping to Harrods for my favourite olives.

I love you for your emotional honesty; there isn't a single cell of "fake" in you.

I love the way I feel safe with you to be who I really am; no masks, no pretence.

I love you for allowing me to be more vulnerable, more honest and more courageous. That's your real magic: you make me want to be a better man.

I love you for cauterising the fear that held me back.

I realise that coming home at the end of the day, having won this case or that, is valueless unless I can share it with you. The truth, I now know, is that even before our relationship began, I was doing it to make you proud of me.

I wasn't completely honest when you asked why I bought the house on Wren Street. The truth, the whole truth, is that I'm renovating this house because, in my mind's eye, you're already here with me. I don't enter a room without testing it through your eyes. I don't choose a colour, a tile, a sink or a cushion, without asking myself "Would Sally like this?"

I imagine you following a recipe in the new kitchen with that endearing expression of fierce concentration, the same look you have in that photograph taken when you were seven.

I imagine you kneeling to plant herbs in the garden.

I imagine you asleep in the big bed on the top floor.

I imagine us painting the nursery together.

I imagine bringing home our new baby.

I'm ashamed and saddened that I didn't recognise what we had, that I took your love for granted, and cast it away so cheaply. Whether you agree to give us a further chance or not, I want you to know that I will be grateful to you for the rest of my life for the months we spent together, for loving me, flaws and all.

I wish with all my defective and broken heart that I recognised our time living together for what it was but, if it's not too late, I do now.

Your Charlie

CHAPTER 40

Friday afternoon, Christmas Eve, and Charles stands at the new table in his basement kitchen at Wren Street, wrapping presents. The Beatles' "Day Tripper" is playing on the Light Programme. It's unusual for pop music to be broadcast on this frequency at this time of day, but this, apparently, will be the Christmas No 1.

He moved in the day before, although one could be forgiven for not noticing. The house is almost completely empty, the contents of the flat on Fetter Lane barely sufficient to furnish two rooms. In the New Year he will go to the barn in Putt Green where he stored the furniture from his and Henrietta's house when it was sold, and decide if anything is salvageable and will suit his new home.

He cuts a final rectangle of paper for his mother's present, the one over which he worked the hardest. It's an album of family photographs, begged and borrowed from aunts, cousins and close friends, all labelled in Charles's neat handwriting with the name of the person portrayed and, where known, the place and date. Her dementia is still quite mild, and Charles hopes this will keep her memories tethered a little longer.

The Horowitz family doesn't celebrate Christmas, but this year it overlaps perfectly with Hanukkah, so Charles plans to take presents on the following day. He and his parents are going to David and Sonia's for lunch. There will be no Christmas tree of course, nor any decorations, but it's impossible even for an Orthodox Jewish family to completely ignore the festivities when the entire country shuts down to eat too much and watch too much television.

So, like most of their Christian neighbours, they'll have a big meal — cooked this year, and for the first time, by Sonia — and watch the Queen's speech at three o'clock. That will be followed by Billy Smart's Circus, one of Millie's favourite Christmas shows. If Charles stays late enough for an evening sandwich, he might even refresh a childhood memory by watching another family favourite, Bob Hope and Bing Crosby in *Road to Bali*, which is on the BBC, again. He has no reason to rush back to Wren Street. He hasn't yet finished off the floors and some of the decorations to the upstairs rooms, but the house is now perfectly habitable and he can tackle the remaining works over the following months. In any event, he spends most of his time in the kitchen. He's looking forward to pottering around his new home, exploring the area on foot and resting after what's been a tough year.

Most of his small circle of old friends will be spending Christmas with their families; Sean Sloane is taking Irenna to meet his parents in Ireland for the first time. As for Sally, she's had his letter for some days now and he's heard nothing in response. Her silence did not precipitate another descent into whisky and self-pity, a change of which he is quietly proud. He has decided not to write again.

He will therefore have time on his hands. He's promised himself to make the effort to visit his aunt Bea at her home in Shadwell. She is special to him, having cared for him for much of the war, and Charles does feel responsible for her, but he finds it hard to visit the tall gloomy house overlooking the Thames basin. It's uncomfortably crowded with ghosts and the echoes of past laughter. But he will go.

Sloane's last call before he and Irenna left for the Liverpool ferry was to inform Charles that DI Greene is now on remand, facing charges of corruption and kidnapping. Sloane had also heard on the grapevine that the Crown are relying no further on Gervaise's evidence. Where they have sufficient evidence to prosecute without him, the trials will proceed; where success depends exclusively on his evidence, the charges are to be dropped.

Gervaise himself has started his four-year sentence. In one respect, he's gotten off lightly: his sentence can't be increased now, even though his days as a "Supergrass" ended before they even started. Nonetheless, despite being under Rule 43 — solitary confinement for his own protection — he's already received a couple of beatings in prison. In the second he was stabbed in the chest, and a punctured lung means he'll be spending Christmas in the hospital wing. The threat shouted from the gallery of the Old Bailey that he would never live to see the outside of prison is looking increasingly prescient.

Charles finishes the last present and adds it to the pile at the end of his long kitchen table — *too long if I'm only ever eating here alone* — and prepares to go out. He has one last thing to attend to before he can relax.

He pulls on his overcoat and hat, locks up, and walks south for fifteen minutes along Gray's Inn Road. At its end he descends into Chancery Lane Underground Station. He takes an eastbound Central line tube. Although it would now normally be rush hour, most Londoners have already gone home for Christmas and his carriage is half-empty.

Ten minutes later, he gets out at Mile End station and walks to the junction of Mile End Road and Eric Street. It is a cold, grey drizzly afternoon and there are few pedestrians. However, the lights are on inside the Regal Billiard Hall and two bouncers stand guard outside, blowing on their hands and shuffling from foot to foot. Charles recognises one of them.

'Merry Christmas, Chunky,' he says.

The man leans forward and squints at Charles in the failing light. 'My God,' he says, 'ain't seen you in a while, Charlie. How's tricks?'

Chunky Morgan is one of the Krays' most long-standing and reliable enforcers. Taller than Charles and as broad, he hails from Bethnal Green and is a well-known face in the East End. Charles is surprised to see him; he thought Chunky was in prison, where he'd spent most of the last decade. Although basically good-natured, he will follow whatever orders the Krays give him without a second's thought, even if it means stabbing a rival in the eye.

'Fair to middling,' replies Charles. 'Okay if I go in? Ronnie and Reggie are expecting me.'

Chunky and his colleague part to let Charles enter.

Charles pushes open the door to find the bar surprisingly full. It's so busy that the fog of cigarette smoke makes it difficult to see to the end of the long building. Most of the tables are occupied by players, but there's a score or more of other men lining the bar and a great deal of inebriated banter rings around the room.

Although the twins moved upmarket with their acquisition of the nightclub, Esmeralda's Barn, in Knightsbridge, where they hosted their celebrity and sporting friends while stealing as much as possible from them on the gambling tables, the Regal remains their spiritual home. Here they can entertain their East End friends and associates, put together a team for the next robbery or long firm fraud, store stolen goods and launch what Ronnie likes to call his "little wars" on competing gangs or large operations which refuse to pay protection money. Here Ronnie is the ringmaster responsible for entertainment, and he loves it. When he's on form, not gripped by one of his periodic depressions, he brings an electricity to the place. None of the local villains ever wants to miss a good night at the Regal.

As always, Ronnie's in his armchair at the far end of the bar from which he can see the whole room. He wears a suit, although the jacket is hanging from the back of his chair; a white shirt with sleeves held up by steel elasticated cuffs à la croupier; and a tie, slightly loosened. A bottle and a glass rest on the small coffee table before him. A dog lies at his feet, apparently asleep despite the noise.

Ronnie sees Charles hesitating at the door and beckons him over. As Charles approaches, he sees Reggie behind the bar filling some glasses with spirits from the optics. The noise levels in the bar drop as the regulars notice a stranger, but soon pick up again as Ronnie indicates a spare chair to Charles and they realise that the newcomer is welcome.

'We've been expecting you,' he says. 'Drink? Scotch, yeah, no ice, splash of water?'

'Thank you,' replies Charles, sitting down.

A drink appears over his shoulder, held out by Reggie. He takes it while the other twin also draws up a chair.

'Cheers,' says Ronnie.

'*L'chaim*,' says Charles, raising his glass.

'Yeah, I'll drink to that,' says Reggie. 'To life. Especially, not getting it.'

The three of them drink.

'I doubt it would've been life,' says Charles. 'Not unless they could've added the murders. But many years, certainly.'

'Yeah, well, either way, you done good, Charlie. 'Specially when we made things worse.'

Charles smiles. It's not often one hears either of the Kray twins apologising, but this is as close as he's ever experienced.

'Thank you. So, what now?'

'What do you mean, "What now?"?' asks Ronnie.

Charles studies the gangster's expression. There's a half-smile and Ronnie looks relaxed, but there's also a challenge.

'You always said that one day you'd ask me for a favour, and … if I … came through, we'd be quits,' explains Charles, heart already sinking.

'Yeah, that's true,' replies Reggie. 'But the way we see it, you didn't just do us a favour. We did you one an' all. You got your commie doctor off; ain't that what you wanted?'

'I don't follow you, Reg. How did you help get her off?'

'We let you take her case first, didn't we? Kept Blackburne on the leash till you had your shot.'

Charles shakes his head. 'I don't see it that way. Yes, I wanted her case to go first, but in winning it I made sure the cases against you would never proceed. Your charges have been dropped, haven't they?'

'They have,' replies Ronnie.

'Well, there you are. That's got to count for something.'

Reggie leans forward, his elbows on his knees. 'Course it does. But it ain't enough. You've caused us no end of trouble over the last coupla years. Harry Robeson's still inside, ain't he?'

'Last I heard,' says Charles.

'And I ain't forgotten that ducking you gave me in the Thames, you cunt,' says Ronnie, a spark of anger igniting in his eyes. 'Fuckin' nearly drowned!'

'And besides,' intervenes Reggie, 'now we've seen, close up, what you can do. Seems to us you're even more useful than we thought.'

Charles finishes his shot of whisky, sighs and leans back in his chair. 'What d'you want, then? Money? I'll pay you money, a lot of money, if you let me have those documents back.'

The twins both smile and shake their heads. Their expressions are so similar, it's like looking in a trick mirror.

Reggie points at Charles's nearest shoulder and then prods it, none too gently. 'Horowitz, you've gotten away with more'n anyone where we're concerned. Got to be some sort of Guinness record. So just be fuckin' grateful you're not holding up part of the Hammersmith Flyover.'

'I see,' says Charles.

'Good,' says Reggie cheerfully, leaning back again. 'Glad we got that sorted. Want another drink before you go?'

Charles shakes his head. He stands. 'Have a good Christmas, boys. Give my regards to Vi.'

Charles salutes, turns, and leaves the billiard hall.

Had to give it a try.

Charles finishes setting up his record player on a table under the windowsill in his kitchen, places the cleaned Miles Davis album on the revolving turntable, and carefully lowers the needle. *Kind of Blue* washes into the room, a gentle tide of calm coolness, and Charles wonders if the house has ever heard the virtuoso trumpeter before.

He checks the oven. The grated cheese on top of the lasagne is beginning to brown nicely. Having just acquired a new freezer, he decided to make a large dish, sufficient for several meals over the festivities. A bottle of Chianti is open on the table. He remembers that something distracted him from finishing laying the table, and he still hasn't brought down a wine glass. Space was so restricted at Fetter Lane, he only had two wineglasses there, and they're still buried somewhere upstairs in one of the unemptied boxes. He considers just using a regular tumbler or even a coffee mug.

'No. Sod it!' he declares out loud. 'Let's do it properly.'

Charles runs upstairs, past the front door, and up again into a bedroom. He finds the box marked "Glassware" and is fortunate; the wineglasses are at the top. He pulls crumpled newspaper off one and runs back downstairs again. As he passes the front door again, he notices a shadow darkening the stained glass. Imagining it to be the final postal delivery of the day, he waits for the new brass letterbox to spring open, but nothing happens. Charles remains behind the door, waiting. The shadow outside is still there.

The Krays?

He rejects the idea; he only left them a couple of hours before and relations were fine — or as "fine" as they ever will be, given the circumstances.

One of Gervaise's men?

Not impossible. Charles made the man look like a liar and a fool, but the fact that he won't have to testify against his former associates means that, theoretically, his life is less at risk than it might have been. So, unlikely.

Someone from C8?

Again unlikely; Flying Squad officers don't hesitate; they kick the door down first and ask questions later.

The shadow moves but doesn't disappear, and Charles takes the initiative. He yanks the door open, the wineglass still in his other hand.

Sally is on the threshold. She's been crying and her face is a mess.

'What is it?' he asks urgently. 'Is it your mum?'

She shakes her head, unable to speak, and brandishes a piece of paper. Charles recognises his letter.

'I was 'aving second thoughts,' she gulps. 'Actually, fourth or fifth thoughts, to be honest. Each time I do, I read it again.'

She grins through her tears sheepishly and reaches into her coat pocket for a handkerchief.

Charles looks down for the first time. To one side of Sally's feet is a suitcase; to the other, her toolbox.

His chest suddenly feels as if it might burst with hope. He indicates the suitcase. 'You coming in?'

In turn, she indicates the toolbox. 'Well, you can't hang wallpaper for toffee. So I thought…'

Charles feels tears blurring his vision. To hide them, he reaches down and grips the suitcase by the handle. 'Well, come on then. The lasagne's ready … and I know exactly where the other glass is.'

HISTORICAL NOTE

As regular readers will know, all of the books in this series are based on actual events and cases, and the criminals, coppers and lawyers I came across during my practice. *Force of Evil* is slightly different. I knew nothing of the case until a luncheon event in January 2020 where I was a speaker. As I was signing books, I was approached by a member of the audience who said he had a tale that might interest me.

I am frequently approached after speaking events by at least one person with a Krays story. Ronnie and Reggie still exercise a remarkable posthumous hold over the public's imagination, notwithstanding the passage of over half a century since their criminal careers were brought to an end by Chief Superintendent "Nipper" Read and his team (of whom more will be said in the books which follow).

Most of the Kray stories are fleeting or innocuous and once or twice, I have suspected, imagined. However, this occasion was quite different. The gentleman, a spry and dapper silver-haired man in his late 70s, had been a "Snowdrop", an RAF police officer, at RAF Cardington at the time of the events portrayed in this book, and was a first-hand witness to much of the stealing, corruption and murder that occurred there. So complete was his story that the writing of *Force of Evil* took much less time than any of the preceding books, with the exception of *The Brief*.

Permit me two brief comments about scandals.

Firstly, the event which kicks off *Force of Evil,* Charles being instructed pro bono for an inquest, still happens routinely today because, amazingly, legal aid is still unavailable for the vast majority of cases heard in coroners' courts. I find it incomprehensible that for the worst thing that can happen to any family — the sudden and unexplained death of a loved-one — successive governments have refused to provide adequate legal aid for their representation. This lack of common decency led me to establish the first pro bono lawyers' service in this country, to assist any family arriving at the local coroners' courts who needed legal help.

Secondly, as I write this, the Windrush scandal has yet to reach a conclusion. Very few of those wrongly thrown out of their jobs and homes, denied access to benefits or to NHS treatment or, in some cases deported by the Home Office, have yet received compensation. Some have died while waiting, here or in the West Indies. For someone like me, for whom the rule of law is all-important, indeed the most fundamental pillar of our democracy, it is deeply distressing. On a personal level it makes me angry and ashamed of the country I love.

Few people realise that the shameful "hostile environment policy" instituted by Theresa May in 2018 had its roots as far back as the early 1960s. The section of Hansard read by Irenna Alexandrova in the book, reporting the speech of Sir Cyril Osborne, MP, is accurate, and is an ominous presage of the attitude of some of our present parliamentarians. Even as early as the 1960s there was an attempt to throw out the West Indian workers who had, as little as twenty years earlier, been encouraged to uproot their lives and return to the "motherland" to help rebuild Britain after the war. By the early 1960s they were no longer needed. The Commonwealth Immigrants Act 1962 was passed in that atmosphere.

The character of Dr Irenna Alexandrova is entirely my creation, but readers familiar with the history of South Africa will probably see some echoes of the life and work of Joe

Slovo and Ruth First, both Communist members of the ANC. Ruth was murdered on the orders of a major in the Apartheid security police.

A NOTE TO THE READER

Dear Reader,

Thank you for taking the time to read the sixth Charles Holborne legal thriller. I am following Charles's story through the 1960s and another book is in the pipeline.

Those of you have been to my one-man show, "My Life in Crime", will know that Charles and his history are based upon me and my own family. Mine was the first generation of Michaels to be born outside the sound of Bow Bells (as you will know, the test for being a "true Cockney") since 1492, when they arrived in the Port of London as refugees from the Spanish Inquisition. Much of the series is autobiographical. Thus, Charles's love of London and the Temple are mine; at the start of my career I experienced the class and religious prejudice faced by him; the plots are based to a greater or lesser extent on cases in which I was instructed as a criminal barrister; many of the strange and wonderful characters who populate the books are based upon witnesses, clients and barristers I have known, represented and admired respectively. I try to take no liberties at all with the operation of police procedure, the criminal justice system or the human heart; the books are as true to life as I can make them. If you find any mistakes, I shall be delighted to hear from you. I always reply, and if you're right, I will make sure future editions are changed.

Nowadays, reviews by readers are essential to authors' success, so if you enjoyed the novel I shall be in your debt if you would spare the few seconds required to post a review on **Amazon** and **Goodreads**. I love hearing from readers, and you can connect with me through my **Facebook page**, via **Twitter** or through my **website**.

I hope we'll meet again in the pages of the next Charles Holborne adventure.

Simon Michael

www.simonmichael.uk

Sapere Books is an exciting new publisher of brilliant fiction and popular history.

To find out more about our latest releases and our monthly bargain books visit our website:
saperebooks.com

Printed in Great Britain
by Amazon